VEILED IN MOONLIGHT

MINISTRY OF CURIOSITIES, BOOK #8

C.J. ARCHER

C.J. ARCHER

❀ Created with Vellum

Thank you to Roshelle Perera for coming up with the title of this book.

CHAPTER 1

LONDON, SPRING 1890

*T*he problem with weddings is that everyone has an opinion, from the date of the ceremony to the length of the bridal veil. In the two months since Lincoln and I announced our engagement, I'd been inundated with advice from the Lichfield Towers household. Even Cook insisted the wedding cake be topped with an effigy of both Lincoln and me made from sugar. Apparently, all society wedding cakes sported outlandish decorations, these days. I didn't think someone with my past could be considered part of *that* society, but if Lady Vickers had her way, and half of the peerage attended, Cook may have a point.

Not that I would yield to Lady Vickers on the issue of the guest list. I would not have anyone at my wedding I'd never met in person. It was bad enough that Lord Gillingham would be there, but his presence was unavoidable since I liked his wife. As for Lady Harcourt and her two stepsons, I couldn't yet decide. Lincoln had left it up to me. When I'd called him a coward, he'd retorted that he'd prefer there be no guests at all and we be wed the following day. It was impossible to argue with him after that.

1

Seth and Gus bickered over who would walk me down the aisle, and occasionally tried to bribe me with sweets or gifts, until I put them out of their misery and asked both. The truce lasted less than a day as they took issue over who would walk in the traditional father-of-the-bride position at my left. Lincoln tried to act as a peacemaker, of sorts, by giving them quelling looks, but unfortunately neither man found him as frightening as they used to.

"They need something to do," I said to Lincoln on a cool yet sunny March day. He had suggested we take a turn in the garden to admire the daffodils bravely poking their golden heads through the cold earth. I'd readily agreed to walk with him, partly to get away from Seth and Gus and partly because I wanted to be alone with Lincoln. Despite living in the same house, we rarely saw one another privately. According to him, we shouldn't be alone until our wedding night. Even our outdoor walks were restricted to areas of the garden that could be seen from the house.

"They're irritating when they're bored," he agreed. "I'll set them a task. Their injuries have healed, and there's work to be done." He slipped his arm around my waist, drawing me to him. "Are you warm enough, Charlie?"

"No. Hold me closer."

"Liar," he murmured but tucked me tighter to his side anyway.

I tilted my face up. "Kiss me."

He kissed my forehead.

"I meant on my lips."

His gaze slid to the house. "Lady Vickers is watching."

"Nothing short of you ravishing me on the lawn will shock her. Besides, are you telling me you're afraid of Lady Vickers?"

"It's not her censure I fear but her lectures. She has a habit of droning on and on about preserving your virtue. Glaring at her doesn't make her stop, nor does threatening to evict her. She's a unique individual."

"She certainly is." I took his arm, linking my gloved hands at his elbow, and we resumed our walk along the drive. The lawn was too damp and slippery and the orchard too far from the house for Lincoln's newly developed prudishness. "But I don't think it's Lady Vickers's lectures that are stopping you from kissing me. It's your own self-imposed ban. You're afraid that kissing me on the lips will lead to intimate encounters in the bedroom."

"Not just the bedroom," he muttered.

My cheeks heated despite the chill in the air. Winter may be over but its tail had some wag left in it. I had never been fond of winter, having spent years walking in thin shoes on streets slick with ice and huddled with other children in crumbling buildings that failed to keep out the damp and cold. Spring meant the slow climb to warmth had begun. I looked forward to the first appearance of flowers because it meant that somehow they had survived another harsh winter. Like me.

This spring signaled my fourth season at Lichfield Towers. I had been here nine months, and I would remain here for the rest of my life. Sometimes I had to pinch myself for reassurance that I wasn't dreaming. I breathed in the sweet air and took in the view in front of me and the handsome view walking beside me.

Lincoln stopped watching me from beneath lowered lashes, gathered me in his arms, and kissed me passionately on the mouth.

A moment later, we parted and I looked back at the house. No one spied on us.

"She moved away from the window," he said.

"And I only get one kiss?"

"I didn't bring you out here to kiss you. I want to talk."

I narrowed my gaze at him. Lincoln wasn't much of a conversationalist. "That sounds ominous. Is it about tonight's dinner party? Because you have to be there. You can't get out of it, so don't pretend your injuries still bother you when I know they don't."

"I've long given up hope of getting out of tonight. Indeed, I don't want to. I'm looking forward to seeing you shine."

Tonight's party, my first as hostess, had been planned to the finest detail. Cook began preparations weeks ago. Mrs. Cotchin the housekeeper and Doyle the butler had employed extra staff on a temporary basis, and everything was in order for our guests' arrival in seven hours' time, from the polished doorknobs to the ice cave in the basement ready to receive Cook's ice molds. Under Lady Vickers's guidance, I'd left nothing to chance.

"So what do you want to talk about?" I pressed.

"Doors."

"Pardon?"

"Doors. More specifically, one door—Alice."

"Ah. *That* kind of door."

When Lincoln's mother had met my friend, Alice Everheart, she'd called her a door to other realms. Alice had dreams that came to life and caused havoc for those near her, but it seemed we'd been wrong about their cause. It wasn't her imagination that came to life, but real individuals from other realms who made their way here, searching for her. Somehow Alice's dreams brought them. Lincoln had been researching other worlds, portals, and traveling between realms ever since, but with little luck. I'd urged him to visit his mother to ask her what she knew, but he'd refused.

Instead, he'd gone to Frakingham House in Hertfordshire where a gentleman by the name of Jack Langley lived. Lincoln had met Langley and his wife in Paris a year ago, where he learned that the gentleman could start fires simply by thought. Lincoln added him to the ministry's files upon his return to London and had not been in contact with him since. But an inkling had sent him to the manor, which the locals called Freak House, to try to find out more about realms. He'd come home disappointed a week later. Mr. Langley had acted as if he didn't know what Lincoln spoke about. Lincoln had known he was lying. His mother's seer's abilities flowed through him, albeit in a diminished capacity, but it meant his instincts were strong.

"I had a letter from Langley yesterday," Lincoln told me.

"He's decided to tell you everything he knows?" I asked, hopeful.

"He's still refusing. That's what I wanted to talk to you about. I want your help informing Alice that we've got no answers to explain her predicament or rid her of it. You'll deliver the news better than me."

"We wouldn't have to deliver bad news at all if you agreed to see your mother and ask *her* questions instead of a stranger in Hertfordshire."

The muscles in his arm stiffened. "We don't know if Leisl will have answers either."

"Precisely. We don't *know*. We'll never know if you don't visit her." I sighed. There was no point pressing him on the issue. I'd tried countless times, to no avail.

A cold breeze swept up the drive, and I huddled into Lincoln's side. He steered me toward the house and helped me out of my coat and hat in the entrance hall. We didn't need to ask Doyle where to find Alice. The dramatic notes of a Beethoven sonata filled the house and she was the only one who could play the piano that well.

We bypassed footmen carrying silver to the dining room and found Seth lounging against the wall outside the music room, reading a folded newspaper. He could not be seen from the room nor could he see into the room. He put a finger to his lips to silence us.

"I'm not here," he whispered.

"Where are you?" I whispered back.

He rolled his eyes and made a shooing motion toward the door, ushering us inside.

Lincoln bent his head to mine. "Do you know why he's avoiding Alice?"

"He's in love with her but is afraid of being rebuffed."

"I can hear you," Seth hissed, thrusting the newspaper under his arm. "And that is not the reason I'm avoiding her. Indeed, I'm not avoiding her at all. I merely remained out here so as not to distract her from her playing."

Gus emerged from the music room, his features scrunched into a frown. "Either come in or stay out, but be quiet." He disappeared inside again.

I followed him, Lincoln behind me. Seth finally came in too and set the newspaper down on a table by the armchair. Alice glanced at me with a small smile then returned to her playing.

Seth moved to stand by the piano, his hand poised to turn the page of Alice's music book. Her fingers faltered and she hit the wrong key.

He quickly turned the page. "Sorry!"

She turned the page back. "I'm not up to there."

He looked at the book then looked at her still hands and frowned. "Then why did you make a mistake? Your playing up until now has been perfect. Better than perfect."

"There ain't no such thing as better than perfect," Gus said. "Perfect is already perfect. You distracted her, you dolt, that's why she made a mistake."

Alice turned her face away from Seth, no doubt to hide her small smile. She was enjoying his awkwardness, it seemed; perhaps even enjoying it in *that* way. It was the first sign she'd ever shown that she welcomed his attentions. Not that he'd been paying her much attention of late. He'd done more lurking outside of rooms than actually addressing her. I suspected that might be my fault. Ever since I'd urged him to be more himself in her presence and less like an eager schoolboy, he'd withdrawn when Alice came near.

"Something is afoot," Alice said, swiveling to face the room. "Or have you all suddenly developed an interest in the piano?"

"We do enjoy your playing," I told her. "But you're right. That's not why we're here."

Her pretty features tightened, as if she braced herself for bad news. "Go on."

"What is it, Charlie?" Seth said in a rush. "What's wrong?"

"Nothing terrible," I quickly reassured them. "It's just that Lincoln has reached a dead end in his research into your condition, Alice. His books are of little help, and Mr. Langley in Hertfordshire refuses to tell him what he knows. Lincoln heard from him again today after sending yet another request for information."

Alice crossed one hand over the other on her lap. "Why would he deny me knowledge about myself? It's so unfair."

"Langley claims he knows very little anyway," Lincoln assured her.

"A little is better than nothing."

Seth went to lay a hand on her shoulder but pulled back before touching her. "Who does this Langley fellow think he is? Alice has a right to know. It's not up to him to decide who the keeper of the knowledge is, even if it is insignificant."

"He doesn't want the knowledge to be in the hands of too many, which implies it's dangerous," Lincoln said. "I cannot blame him for that. I'd do the same thing, in his position."

"Did you tell him about the ministry?" Gus asked.

"Yes."

Seth folded his arms. "Did you tell him the ministry is the official organization for cataloging supernatural knowledge?"

"We're not official," Lincoln said.

"We have an emblem," Gus said, as if that made all the difference. "Told you we should have ordered a letterhead with the emblem on it. He'd have to take notice then."

"I think it'll take more than a letterhead," I told him. "If Lincoln couldn't get Mr. Langley to talk, nothing will."

"Did you threaten him?" Alice asked, her eyes huge.

"No," I told her.

"Only a little," Lincoln said at the same moment.

I frowned at him, and he shrugged, all innocence.

Alice swiveled back to the piano and began to play a tune more suited to a funeral than a sunny spring day. Seth, still standing beside her, glared at me over her head. Lincoln, too, turned to me and nodded in Alice's direction. It would seem they were relying on me to cheer her up.

I joined Alice on the piano stool. She shuffled over to give me room without breaking her rhythm. "I am sorry, Alice. We all are. We've failed you."

"It's further than I was able to get on my own," she said. "And at least I know I am not alone. I have all of you to support me if the dreams reoccur."

"Yes, you do. We're here to help you."

"We are," Seth said. "Do I need to turn the page yet?"

She laughed softly. "I'm playing from memory."

Gus snickered.

Lincoln rose and Alice suddenly stopped. "Before you go, Mr. Fitzroy," she said in a sweet voice that warned me, but not Lincoln. "Tell me, where does your mother live?"

The ticking of the mantel clock suddenly seemed too loud for a music room. Gus expelled a breath. We all looked to Lincoln. I had a strong urge to rescue him, and make excuses as to why he couldn't speak to his mother, but stopped myself. There was no reason why he couldn't tell Alice how to find Leisl. Indeed, there was no reason why she couldn't speak to Leisl at all. I hadn't suggested it before because I didn't want to cross him, and I'd hoped he would come to realize he was being obstinate. He had not so it was time to follow my conscience and not my heart.

"I know where to find her," I said.

Lincoln arched a brow at me.

"It's in the archives," I told him. "We can go this afternoon, if you like, Alice."

She beamed, turning her pretty face into one of classic beauty. "You will come with me?"

"Of course."

"So will I," Seth announced with a thrust of his square jaw in Lincoln's direction.

Lincoln didn't move. He didn't even blink. I suspected he was warring with himself over whether to forbid us or not. Forbidding me went against his principles nowadays, although it hadn't always been so. Those episodes had taught him that I rarely went along with such orders, and if I did, it never ended well between us.

"Thank you, Seth," Alice said. "But I'd rather we go tomorrow. Charlie will be needed this afternoon."

"Everything is organized for tonight," I told her.

"Little things will require your attention. My mother rarely held dinner parties, but when she did, something unexpected always came up and she was needed. You'll feel better if you're here to keep an eye on things."

"Tomorrow then," Lincoln said. "We'll go before lunch."

"You're coming with us?" I asked, unable to keep the smile out of my voice.

"Yes. And if you gloat, the engagement is off." The twitch of his lips turned his words into a tease.

9

"I would never gloat in public, Lincoln." I refrained from asking him why he'd changed his mind. Perhaps he was softening now that he was in love. I quite liked the notion and smiled at him.

He smiled back, if the brightening of his eyes could be considered smiling. "Seth, Gus, my office. We have work to discuss."

"Is this about the murder?" Seth asked.

"Murder?" several voices echoed.

"It's not so much the murder that caught my attention, although it was described in gruesome detail. It was the wolf sighting."

Alice clutched her throat. "Wolf!"

Seth picked up the newspaper and handed it to Lincoln. "A wolf-like creature was seen running away from the victim, whose body was found in Hyde Park. Two constables pursued it but couldn't find it."

"You're only giving this to me now?" Lincoln said, reading.

"I thought you'd already seen it. Besides, I've been busy."

"Doing what?"

"Er…" Seth cleared his throat and glanced at Alice.

"Does the article say anything else?" I asked.

"The constables found a man in bushes nearby and questioned him," Lincoln said, tossing the newspaper back onto the table. His eyes were hard, the good humor no longer in evidence. "He claimed not to have seen any wolves."

"But that's not the interesting thing about the witness," Seth prompted him.

"No," Lincoln agreed. "The interesting thing is that he was naked, and his clothing was nowhere to be found."

Oh God, not again.

Gus groaned and rubbed his jaw where the bruises obtained from the fight with the shape changers had only recently faded. "I hate them shifters. Lady Gilly excepted, of course."

"Does the article give a name for the witness?" I asked. The previous leader of the shifter pack was dead, and the new leader, Mr. Gawler, vowed to keep his creatures in check. Perhaps one of them had rejected his authority and left the pack.

Lincoln shook his head. "He was probably deemed unimportant by the reporter. The reporter did note something about the naked man, however. Something which doesn't quite make sense with what we know about Gawler's pack."

"What is it?"

"The witness is described as a gentleman."

Gawler's pack was made up of slum dwellers, except for Harriet, Lady Gillingham. "So there's a new shifter in London." My words dropped like stones in the silence. "And he's a murderer."

CHAPTER 2

I didn't see Lincoln, Seth and Gus for the rest of the day. They'd gone to speak with the newspaper reporter and Mr. Gawler, as well as the members of his pack. The tasks shouldn't cause them any problems, but I worried nevertheless. The pack members had no reason to like us after the fight that saw their previous leader captured and a friend killed.

Keeping busy calmed my nerves somewhat. Alice taught me a short piece on the piano, and Lady Vickers wanted to discuss seating arrangements for dinner again. Apparently Lady Harcourt shouldn't sit next to Seth, but she wouldn't tell me why. I suggested moving Seth to be next to Alice, but that wasn't acceptable, either.

"The problem is, there will be no eligible ladies, since Miss Overton came down with a sore throat," she said with a sigh. "You ought to have let me help you draw up the guest list, Charlie. I would have found someone to replace the Overton girl."

"Both Lady Harcourt and Alice are eligible," I pointed out.

"Neither of whom is suitable for my son."

"You'll get no argument from me on Lady Harcourt's account, but I do wish you wouldn't dismiss Alice."

She picked up a knife and made a great show of inspecting it for cleanliness. "Has she made a play for him?" she asked idly.

"Alice is not like that. She's very respectable." Unlike Seth, I might have added. The more I learned about his past, the more I realized he'd done a number of morally questionable activities to earn money to pay off his father's debts.

"That may be so, but she has nothing to offer him. They cannot be matched. You know that, Charlie. We've been through this."

I sighed. Like Lincoln, Lady Vickers had a stubborn streak as wide as the English Channel. "Leave Seth where he is," I said. "He's wise enough not to fall for Lady Harcourt's charms."

"I hope so. No doubt that woman's *charms* will be displayed to best advantage tonight."

I stifled a giggle as two maids entered, carrying vases of pink camellias. Mrs. Cotchin had ordered them from the Syon Park glasshouse, and they added a touch of color to the table centerpiece. Lady Vickers nodded in approval as the maids set the vases down between the two candelabras while a third brought in a tray of napkins folded into the shapes of rose buds.

"Very clever," I told her, inspecting the elaborate design.

Doyle entered and handed me a missive. "This just arrived for you, Miss Holloway."

I read the brief note from Lady Harcourt and passed it to Lady Vickers for her opinion. She read it then folded the thick paper in half and half again, running her thumbnail along the fold in a firm, precise motion.

She waited until the maids left before muttering, "That woman has a nerve. I always knew her to be vulgar, but this proves it." She handed the note back to Doyle.

The butler waited for instructions.

"We have to agree to it," I told the seething woman beside me.

She studied the set table, with its equal number of male and female guests; the perfect arrangement, as she called it. "Indeed. I recognize the name. I believe he's one of the Prince of Wales's friends. She left us no choice, Charlie. We must accommodate him."

"Doyle, please add another setting," I said to the butler. "The gentleman's name is Lord Underwood. Place him beside Lady Harcourt and move Seth to—"

"He can sit beside me on the end where the lack of a female between him and the head of the table isn't so obvious."

That put Seth between his mother and his employer. He would not thank me.

"This is what happens when foolish old men marry dancers," Lady Vickers said over her shoulder as she stepped out of the dining room in a rustle of stiff black skirts.

"They die and leave their widows free to invite an extra man to an already perfectly balanced dinner table?"

"There's no need for sarcasm, Charlie. You are correct, in essence. Their widows find themselves free to do as they please, and what they please to do is not what a woman of their station ought."

And that, coming from the woman who ran off with her second footman, was enough to have me biting back my smirk.

"You forgot to tell Doyle to alert the kitchen to the extra place," she told me as she swept into the drawing room. "You don't want them bringing up sixteen plates instead of seventeen."

"I haven't forgotten," I lied. "I just thought I'd tell Cook myself."

"Charlie," she chided, "let the servants do their job without your interference."

"I'm not interfering. I want to oversee matters down there."

"You won't be welcome. Cook will be far too busy to indulge you."

"He never indulges me."

She gave me an arched look.

I headed down the stairs then veered toward the back of the house. Delicious aromas of roasting meats, baking bread, and spices drifted out to me from the kitchen at the center of the service rooms. One of the temporary maids hurried along the corridor ahead, cloth and polish in hand. She spotted me, emitted a small gasp of either surprise or horror, bobbed a curtsy and looked uncertain what to do next.

"Continue with what you're doing," I told her in my best mistress-of-the-house voice.

She bobbed another curtsy and went on her way. I passed the empty butler's office and followed the sound of Cook's voice barking orders at his new staff. I dared to sneak a peek into the kitchen and was almost barreled over by the heat and a footman carrying an empty silver tureen.

"The larger one be around somewhere," Cook bellowed after the lad. "Ask Doyle. Charlie! What you be doing down here? You there," he said to a pink-cheeked maid rolling out pastry on the table where we had often dined when it was just five of us living at Lichfield. "I rest my head on a pillow thinner than that. Something you want, Charlie?"

The kitchen maids watched our exchange from beneath lowered lashes, no doubt wondering why the cook addressed the lady of the house by her first name. Cook wiped his hands down his apron then dabbed his shiny pate with it. He gave me a smile but his gaze darted between each of his staff and the boiling pots on the range.

"Is there enough food for one more?" I asked him. "Lady Harcourt's bringing a guest."

"Lady V. won't like that," he said.

"A few terse words passed her lips but the gentleman is a friend of the prince's."

If Cook had eyebrows they would have risen half way up his forehead. "What did Fitzroy say?"

"He doesn't know yet. So is there enough food?"

"We got enough to feed half of London."

"Anything leftover can be sent to Mrs. Sullivan and the orphans in the morning."

The maid standing by the range cleared her throat and tried to catch Cook's attention. I left him to his work and returned to the drawing room, only to realize it was time to dress for dinner.

Lincoln, Gus and Seth returned in time to change. We all met in the drawing room just before our guests were due to arrive.

"Well?" I asked Lincoln. He cut a dashing figure in his tail-coat and white silk waistcoat. He'd tied his hair back with a black ribbon, and had removed all trace of stubble from his chin. He looked like a gentleman pirate. "What did you learn?"

"That the newspaperman did not find out the witness's name, and that Gawler claims his pack members had nothing to do with the murder." His fingers touched my gloved ones. "You look beautiful, Charlie."

"Thank you. You look very handsome too. Something's troubling you, though. What is it?"

"Where's your imp?"

16

The necklace with the amber orb containing a supernatural creature had been a gift from my birth mother. The imp inside had saved my life, and I liked to keep it close. Unfortunately, amber didn't go with my evening gown of blue satin with white and silver beads and embroidery at the bust, sleeves and down the front panels. "I don't need it tonight," I told him, looping my arm through his. "You're here to protect me."

"Is that so? And how do you expect me to protect you when we're not seated together?"

"You'll find a way." I squeezed his arm. "You're very resourceful, Lincoln. Besides, there won't be any dangers tonight."

"Where have I heard that before?" he muttered under his breath. He cupped my jaw and stroked his thumb along my cheek. "You're beautiful."

"You already told me so. But thank you anyway."

"Mr. Fitzroy." Lady Vickers' picked out the consonants in his name with brisk precision. "No touching your fiancée before, during or after dinner."

"The guests aren't here yet," Seth told his mother. "Besides, it's his house and he can do as he wishes."

"Not if he wants to launch Charlie into society. He must follow the rules, just like everyone else, or she'll be an outcast forever."

Being an outcast didn't always strike me as a terrible thing where London's society was concerned. But I bit my tongue and nodded my agreement. I wanted to host a successful dinner party. I needed to, if only to know that I was capable.

"Most of the guests know all about Charlie," Seth went on.

Lady Vickers touched the earbobs at her ears. They were imitations, not real diamonds, but only those of us who knew she'd sold all her jewels would be aware. "Most know," she admitted, "but not all."

The first guests to arrive were Lord and Lady March-bank, the eldest committee member and his wife. She fell into easy conversation with Lady Vickers on the sofa while her husband asked Lincoln if he'd seen the papers. Other friends of Lady Vickers' soon arrived. They'd invited us to dine with them in previous weeks and so I had repaid their kindness with an invitation to Lichfield Towers. I enjoyed their company, despite the age difference, and appreciated the friendship they gave Lady Vickers.

Lord and Lady Gillingham arrived at a quarter past eight, and Lord Gillingham promptly turned his back on his young pretty wife. She didn't seem to notice, too intent was she in waiting for an opportune moment to draw Alice and me away from Lady Vickers and her friends. I could tell from her barely contained smile that Harriet had news for our ears only. She finally succeeded in getting us alone and steered us toward the window.

"Harriet, you're hurting me," Alice whispered when we were out of earshot.

Harriet's big hands released us. She clasped them at her breast and bounced on her toes. Her blonde ringlets bounced too and she broke into a grin. "I can't hold it any longer. I have to tell you my news. I'm with child."

I recovered from my shock rather rapidly, but Alice continued to stare. "Congratulations," I said before Harriet could notice Alice's reaction. "That's wonderful news."

"Isn't it the grandest news of all? You know how I've longed for a child, Charlie. Finally, I am to be a mother with a little one of my own. It's all I've ever wanted since my marriage to Gilly."

Marriage to such a snake must be both a disappointment and a trial, so it was hardly surprising that she wanted a baby to cherish, since cherishing her husband was out of the question. Yet she had hinted that he ended all marital intimacy when he discovered she could shift shape into a large, hairy wolf-like creature, and a baby seemed a dream never to be fulfilled. It begged the question—had Gillingham overcome his fear of his wife and lain with her, or had she sought intimacy elsewhere, perhaps with his blessing?

"Congratulations," Alice finally said. "How delightful." She looked away, clearly unsure how to ask the question we both wanted to know the answer to. Unfortunately her gaze fell on Lord Gillingham who happened to glance over at us.

He flushed to the roots of his receding ginger hairline and quickly turned back to Lord Marchbank.

"He doesn't want me to announce it yet," Harriet said, unconcerned that her husband had caught her doing just that.

"Why not?"

"He says it's too soon, but I disagree. I know the little one is strong. I can feel it already."

"You'd best be careful," I told her. "He might retaliate somehow if you go against his wishes." While it galled me that anyone should bow to that horrid man on any point, I didn't want Harriet to bear the brunt of his anger.

"No, he won't," she said with a tilt of her chin that was unique to persons of her class. "He wouldn't dare. He no longer tells me what to do. *I* tell *him*. After I reminded him that I am the strongest in our marriage, he has been more accommodating toward me. We get along quite well, now."

She had certainly changed since she began regularly running with Gawler's pack in her animal form. She was still silly and girlish at times, but the demure shyness was gone. I could well believe she now stood up to her husband, and he cowered before her.

"Oh," Alice said, staring at Gillingham's back. "I see."

"Good for you, Harriet." I took her hand in mine. "And good luck. If you need anything, just ask."

She squeezed my hand. "Thank you. You're a true friend." She looked past my shoulder and blinked rapidly. "You invited Lady Harcourt?" Harriet's lips twisted as if she'd tasted something sour. "She's so vulgar. I do hope you don't consider her a friend, Charlie. That sort can bring you low."

Didn't I know it, although I suspected her definition of being brought low was different to mine. I went to greet Lady Harcourt, Andrew Buchanan, and their friend, Lord Underwood. Underwood was about the same age as the Prince of Wales, Lincoln's father, with florid cheeks and a stomach that looked as if another hearty meal would be one too many for the buttons on his waistcoat.

Lady Harcourt made introductions with a smile firmly in place, despite the stares of the other guests. Now that her secret past as a dancer was out, she could not venture anywhere without extra attention. Sometimes I thought she despised it, but at others, she seemed to relish her new notoriety and perhaps even played it up by wearing even lower-cut gowns and cinching her corset even tighter. Her choice of gown tonight was rather daring. The jade green and black dress hugged her tiny waist and showed off her deep décolletage and the emerald pendant nestling there like the key to temptation.

"Julia tells me you're a friend of her late husband's," Underwood said to Lincoln. "I must say, I was expecting someone...older."

Buchanan smirked. "And not so handsome, I'd wager."

"Harcourt was a good man," Lincoln said.

"And you are still a friend to his widow," Underwood went on. "That's decent of you to act as her protector."

"I've found Julia is more than capable of taking care of herself."

"It's those of us caught in her web who need protecting," Buchanan muttered.

"Allow me to introduce you to the other guests, my lord," I said, taking his arm. I led him around the room and discovered that he already knew most. He was quite charming to everyone, particularly Alice after learning she was not spoken for.

On the other side of the room, Lady Harcourt kept an eye on them as they conversed. Her lips pinched once, as Alice laughed at something Underwood said, but otherwise she looked like a woman confident in her chosen man's affections.

"He's a fine fellow, isn't he?" Buchanan whispered in my ear. Despite the softness of his voice, I detected the sneer. "Very agreeable, just like his friend the prince."

"You sound as if you like him, yet I find that unfathomable considering what your stepmother means to you."

"Very astute, as usual, Charlotte. I didn't say I like him, but he is perfect for her."

"In what way?"

"Dear, innocent Charlotte. Didn't I explain it to you?" He huffed out a breath reeking of liquor. "Julia *will* marry again, and I am determined she will marry a man she can't possibly love. He must be like my father—old, rich, titled and either dull or ridiculous."

"And which is Underwood?"

"Both. Oh, he's charming enough, and can hold a conversation in this sort of setting, but there is little by the way of substance in his brain. Once polite topics are exhausted, he's at a loss. He can't abide politics, talk of money is too vulgar, and I doubt he's read a book since his school days. His wit is the obvious kind, and he hasn't a clue when someone is mocking him. Believe me, I've tested that on numerous occasions. Julia couldn't ever love him but she could marry him.

She prefers her lovers subtler, cleverer, and vastly more handsome."

I barked out a laugh. "Like you?"

"Like your fiancé," he bit off, all humor gone.

I refrained from stomping on his toe or elbowing him in the jaw like Lincoln had taught me to do when a man accosted me. While it might make me feel better, it would ruin the evening.

"But since the amazing Lincoln Fitzroy is happily engaged to you, she is once again giving me the attention I so deserve." He winked at me, and yet the bitterness in his voice grated.

I made my excuses and sought out Lincoln.

"Was Buchanan bothering you?" he asked.

"Yes, but that's not unusual." I glanced toward Lord Underwood, now engaged in conversation with Gillingham and Marchbank, Lady Harcourt's fingers wrapped around his arm. She listened as he spoke and laughed when he laughed, but there was no spark in her eyes. She glanced at Lincoln and me before quickly looking away again.

"You spoke to Harriet earlier," Lincoln said to me. If he'd noticed Lady Harcourt looking at us, he gave no indication. "Did you ask her about the pack and whether one of them could have murdered that fellow?"

"I forgot. Something more important came up."

"What could be more important?"

"She's with child."

He gave a business-like nod. "We must add the information to her file."

I laughed. "Is that all you can think about?"

"No, but I don't want to dwell on the manner in which she coerced Gillingham into lying with her."

The sound of the dinner gong saved me from thinking about it too. We entered the dining room in pairs, with Lady

Marchbank on Lincoln's arm since she was the highest ranked lady, and me on the arm of Lord Underwood, a marquess. Lady Harcourt had set her sights high with him.

Cook and I had spent a lot of time preparing the menu for the evening, along with Lady Vickers' input, and I was pleased to see that everyone seemed to enjoy the first three courses of soup, followed by fish, then quails with watercress. Cook would be thrilled. Conversation flowed as much as the wine. Inviting the two couples and another gentleman who were not part of the committee, or related to the committee members in any way, turned out to be a good idea. Talk remained genial through the meat and vegetable courses until the footmen brought out the ices and a four-tiered jelly surrounded by strawberries. The guests marveled at the out-of-season fruit and Lord Underwood mentioned eating peaches at a recent dinner hosted by his friend, the Prince of Wales.

"Was Sir Ignatius Swinburn there?" Buchanan asked with a wicked gleam in his eye. He'd been well behaved the entire evening, but now an uneasy feeling settled in the pit of my stomach. It grew when Lady Harcourt stiffened and shot him a flinty glare.

"He was," Underwood said, watching Doyle slice through the jelly. "You know Sir Ignatius?"

"We've met. It was very late in the evening and I wasn't at my best, if you know what I mean." Buchanan laughed, revealing teeth stained red from three glasses of claret. "It was only last week. Oh!" He covered his grin with his napkin. "I forgot. He asked me not to say anything about it." He set down a napkin and picked up his glass. "Pretend you heard nothing, and certainly not from me."

Underwood chuckled. "Don't fret. Swinburn spends an awful lot of time at his club so you're bound to run into him sooner or later."

"It wasn't at a club." Buchanan leaned forward, conspiratorial. "It was a private residence."

Lady Harcourt's fingers tightened around the stem of her wine glass. She did not look at her stepson. She did not look at anyone.

Buchanan winked at Underwood. "You'll get nothing more out of me. As I said, he ordered me to keep it a secret, and I'm not such a fool as to make an enemy of a rich and powerful fellow like Swinburn."

"He's not so frightening when you get to know him," Underwood went on. "Indeed, he's very agreeable. He has to be, or he wouldn't have His Royal Highness's ear."

"It's no wonder he's considered quite the catch for eligible women of all ages then. Money, power *and* charm are far more important than youth and good looks in the marriage market, much to my detriment. Isn't that right, Julia?"

She hesitated for a beat and finally turned to him. "Don't despair, Andrew. You'll find the perfect girl for you once you look properly. Indeed, there's a lovely girl here tonight." She nodded at Alice, seated near the other end of the table and not privy to our conversation. "What a shame you weren't seated next to her."

"I'm sure our hostess had her reasons." Buchanan lifted his glass and saluted me.

After pastries and lemon ices, the ladies retreated to the drawing room for coffee while the men played billiards. They joined us after a half hour, smelling of cigar smoke and brandy. Lincoln lifted an eyebrow in question, and I gave him a small nod. Everyone had got along, even with Lady Harcourt in our midst. The other women were far too well brought up to show their dislike of her to her face. Indeed, most of the discussion had centered on the Gillinghams' news. Harriet simply couldn't keep it in any longer and had announced it as soon as we'd settled.

Lord Gillingham was inundated with congratulatory handshakes upon his arrival in the drawing room. His face flamed again and he didn't say a word.

Lord Underwood wedged himself between Alice and Lady Marchbank on the sofa and engaged Alice in conversation until she shot me a pleading look. Before I could rescue her, however, Seth intercepted and drew Underwood into a conversation, freeing Alice to join me.

"I'll have to thank Seth later," Alice whispered. "Lord Underwood is pleasant enough, but people were beginning to talk."

"And you don't wish them to talk about you and a marquess in the same breath?" I teased.

"He's more than twice my age!"

"According to Buchanan, that's irrelevant, as far as women seeking a husband are concerned. You should have heard him at dinner, spouting such nonsense. It was definitely an allusion to Lady Harcourt's choice of men." I spotted Harriet coming toward us, her hand splayed over her flat waist. "Remind me to tell you later what he said about another fellow and his stepmother. Harriet! Just the person I wanted to speak to," I said as she joined us. "Come to the window where it's a little cooler. You look quite warm."

She patted her pink cheek and allowed me to lead her to the window. Alice peeled away and sat with Lady Vickers and her friends. Some of them made appearances of leaving.

"Did you read about the murder in today's newspapers?" I asked.

Harriet's face paled, and she covered her gasp with her hand. Perhaps I ought to have been a little subtler, but there wasn't time. "I don't read the newspapers," she said. "Do we have to speak about murders now? It's been a marvelous evening. Don't spoil it, Charlie."

"I must tell you something else." I told her about the gruesome death and the naked witness seen near the scene shortly afterward.

"A shifter," she whispered in horror. "My god. Who?"

"That's what I wanted to ask you. The reporter said he was a gentleman. None of Gawler's pack can be called that, and he doesn't believe any would commit murder. But what do *you* think? Would one of them go against Gawler's wishes and kill?"

"No! He's forbidden the taking of life, and we obey our leader in all things. That's pack law. Besides, despite the trouble stirred up by King, they're not bad people. A little rough, but they have good souls, and they're loyal to Gawler now that he is leader. Of course, if a stronger leader came along, they would switch allegiance—as would I—but no one has attempted to take it from him."

"Then who could the murdering shifter be?"

She surveyed the room then leaned closer. "I don't know, but I think there *is* another pack here in London."

"What?"

"I don't know who's in it or where to find its members. It could even be just a rumor. But soon after I joined the pack, one of my pack mates asked me why I hadn't joined the toff shifters, as he called them, since I was a countess. I told him I'd never been invited, and that was the end of the conversation. I haven't brought it up since." She lifted one shoulder. "I like my pack and have no interest in finding another. Running with the lower orders is rather thrilling, Charlie. Rather thrilling indeed. I don't think I'd have nearly as much fun with creatures of my own class."

I nodded and smiled, yet I couldn't help thinking about the fight with her pack that had given Lincoln, Seth and Gus terrible injuries. Gawler's pack was capable of inflicting great harm if an immoral leader took over. And Gawler wasn't a strong leader. King had beaten him and taken the group down a diabolical path, so why not another?

"You will report to us if a new shifter approaches you or anyone in your pack, won't you?" I asked.

Harriet took my hand in her big one and squeezed. "Come on. Let's rejoin the party."

CHAPTER 3

I reported Harriet's answers to Lincoln after our guests left. We lounged in the drawing room to deconstruct the evening along with Gus, Seth and Alice. Cook and Lady Vickers had already retired, as had the staff.

"I'll visit Gawler again," Lincoln announced with a disappointed shake of his head. "I hadn't detected his lie but a lie it must have been."

"Maybe he doesn't know about the toff pack," Gus said.

"If one of his pack told Harriet then he must know too. A leader knows everything that goes on in his organization."

"Not everything," Seth said into his glass of brandy.

"Everything," Lincoln repeated with firm finality.

Seth sank into the armchair and sipped.

Lincoln rose and took my hand. "Tonight was a success, Charlie. Well done." He kissed the back of my hand, a smile in his eyes as he looked at me through his thick lashes.

"Cook did a wonderful job," I said, "as did Doyle and Mrs. Cotchin."

"And me," Gus declared.

"What did you do?" Seth asked.

"Whatever was needed. Stirred pots, washed dishes, listened to gossip."

"What did the servants gossip about?" Alice asked.

"This and that, who they've worked for in the past, which toffs are good and which run their staff ragged. Apparently the Marchbanks pay generously, but Lord Underwood don't."

"He's not as wealthy as he makes out," Lincoln said.

"You know that?" Alice asked, half laughing. Her laughter faded away upon Lincoln's nod.

"I'd wager Julia doesn't know," Seth said with a shake of his head. "Or she wouldn't have insisted he come tonight."

"She might not be with him much longer anyways," Gus said, stretching out his legs. "One of the footmen reckons another toff visits her some nights."

"Buchanan alluded to it at dinner," I said. "He was subtler, and I don't think Underwood realized he was implying that Swinburn comes to *her* house late at night, but I'm quite sure that's what he meant."

"It seems she's dangling a carrot in front of both Underwood and Swinburn," Seth said. "That's a risky game, but she's playing for high stakes."

"I remember what you said about Swinburn after we saw him at the Hothfields' New Year's Eve ball."

"An upstart whose grandfather was a mere sailor?"

"That he's not the marrying kind," I reminded him, "and discards his lovers when he tires of them, which is often."

"Ah yes, it's all true, but I wouldn't put it as nicely as that. He's a revolting rakehell who takes advantage of desperate women."

"Lady H ain't desperate," Gus said.

"She's getting on in age, and she knows she's only got a few good years left before her looks fade. If she hasn't snared a rich husband by then, she'll never remarry. There's nothing else going for her."

For someone who counted Lady Harcourt among his past lovers, Seth sounded a little cruel. I could see from Alice's wrinkled nose that she thought he was being harsh, too.

Lincoln bade us goodnight then left to change and visit Gawler again. I almost asked him to take either Gus or Seth with him but stopped myself. He would be all right on his own, and I didn't want to tell him what to do, especially in front of the others.

"Maybe Underwood didn't notice Buchanan's remarks because he ain't all that interested in Lady H after all," Gus said when Lincoln was gone.

He had a good point, and I told him so. "He gave Alice far too much attention for someone supposedly smitten with another."

"Turd," Seth spat.

Alice gave him a sweet smile. "That reminds me. Thank you for rescuing me tonight, Seth. There's only so much talk of the prince's hunting parties one can endure."

Seth straightened, looking pleased with himself.

"Peacock," Gus muttered.

Seth shot him a glare, and Alice pressed her lips together to smother her smile. She didn't quite succeed.

"I'm going to bed," Seth announced with a sniff.

I followed him and caught up to him on the staircase. "Be yourself with her, Seth."

He took three more steps before he answered. "What if she doesn't like me?"

"Since when do you worry about women not liking you?"

"Since I met Alice and she doesn't seem to like me." He lowered his voice. "It matters, Charlie. It matters more than I care to admit."

It was a little disturbing seeing the confidence of this golden Adonis shaken to the core. I never thought it would happen, and yet here he was, uncertain about himself, and because of a woman, too.

"Then stop pretending you're perfect," I told him. "Be the man you are, not the man you think she wants. She's clever. She knows you're acting the role of respectable gentleman around her, and she doesn't like swindlers."

"I'm not trying to swindle her."

"When someone is pretending to be something they're not, that's how it seems. Remember, her family treated her badly. She can't trust them and she needs to be able to trust a man if she is to fall in love with him."

He paused at the top of the stairs and studied the carpet. "My past is…vivid. I didn't always do things I'm proud of. If I am to be myself then she'll have to learn about it."

"There's no need to launch into your entire history just yet. You could introduce it to her slowly, beginning with the least scandalous bit."

He considered that then nodded. "I'll try."

"And, for goodness' sake, find that sense of humor that women adore."

The return of his crooked smile was a welcome relief. It had been missing since Alice came to live with us. He leaned down and whispered in my ear. "I won't tell Fitzroy that you adore me."

I thumped his arm. "I said your sense of humor, not you. Now go, before he catches us and gets the wrong idea. I like your face the way it is."

It was a joke, and we both knew it. Lincoln wouldn't get jealous of Seth exchanging whispers with me.

"Thank you." He kissed my forehead. "Tonight was a triumph. They'll talk about you and your dinner party for years to come. Decades!"

"Go away before I feel compelled to advise Alice to avoid you at all costs."

* * *

I COULDN'T SLEEP, so I waited for Lincoln in the private sitting room adjoining his study. I stoked the fire to life and added more coal from the scuttle then stretched out on the sofa, a blanket covering me. I breathed deeply, drawing in the faint scents of smoke and Lincoln's cologne. I'd once lain in this room with a knife hidden beneath me. Lincoln had known I had it, of course, but he had let me believe I was in control of the situation until the moment I'd woken up without the knife. That night seemed so long ago.

The fire's warmth must have lulled me to sleep because I awoke to the sound of Lincoln's rumbling voice. "Charlie."

I opened my eyes to see him crouching before me. "What time is it?" I sat up and yawned.

"Two. Why are you in here?"

"I couldn't sleep."

"Your snoring implied otherwise."

"I do not snore!"

He sat at his desk and rested his elbows on the chair arms. "You should go before anyone realizes you're in here."

"Nobody's awake. And besides, I'm your fiancée." I got up, padding over to him and sitting on his lap. "Nobody minds if an engaged couple spends time with one another in private."

"The sort of people we had to dinner tonight mind." He rested his hands on my waist, but before he could push me off, I threw my arms around his neck.

I leaned in and brushed his lips with mine. He had no scent, as if the fresh air had blown away the smells of smoke, cologne water and brandy. "Then I don't wish to be their friend anymore. Your good opinion is the only one that matters," I murmured in a voice thick with desire.

He suddenly stood, dislodging me. He caught me before I

hit the floor like a sack of potatoes and held me until I regained my balance. "Then stop teasing me."

"I'm not teasing you," I said hotly. "I only want to kiss you. A proper kiss," I said when he reached for my hand. "On the mouth. Passionately."

He cleared his throat and settled his hands on my waist again. Light and shadow sharpened his cheekbones and emphasized the intensity in his gaze. A gaze that did not meet mine. He pressed his lips to mine and planted a chaste kiss.

I drew back. "That's a terrible kiss."

"Are you an expert?"

"I would not have thought so." I dug my hands through his loose hair and stood on my toes. I pressed my body against his, relishing the feel of the hard muscle beneath his clothing, and kissed him with abandon.

It took only two seconds for his arms to circle me. His lips and tongue tasted me and his heart skipped to an erratic rhythm. Well, that had been easier than I expected. And now I found I could not stop. I wanted to abandon all common sense and fall into bed with him. I wanted to drag his shirt off and remove my nightgown to feel skin against skin. I wanted to—

He suddenly pulled back and let me go. His chest rose and fell with his deep breaths and his hair had become tangled where my fingers played with it. He watched me with eyes as deep and black as two wells.

"Goodnight, Charlie."

"Goodnight, Lincoln." My voice sounded ragged, yet his had been quite normal. Damn him. "I hope your dreams will be sweet."

"I doubt they will be."

I left and it wasn't until I lay in my own bed that I realized I hadn't asked him what he'd learned from Gawler.

* * *

I REMEMBERED to ask him the following morning on our way to Leisl's house. He paid me very little attention as we drove to Enfield, preferring to stare out the window. Had our kiss disturbed him that much? Or was it because he really did fear for my virtue when I was alone in his room in the middle of the night? Perhaps I shouldn't feel so pleased about the effect I had on him, but I couldn't help it.

"Gawler claimed not to know anything about another pack," he said without taking his gaze off the dreary streetscape. "Apparently there was a rumor some time ago, but nothing came of it. He didn't tell me the first time I asked because he assumed it had been untrue. King never mentioned another pack to him."

"He still should have told you about the rumor," Alice said. It was just the three of us inside the carriage with our new coachman, Tucker, up front. Gus and Seth had been ordered to remain at the house, much to the annoyance of both.

A thought struck me. "Perhaps the toff pack financed King." While we'd never proved that someone had paid King to impersonate the queen's deceased husband, we strongly suspected it. He'd risen from the slums to Bloomsbury very quickly and splashed his money about. A great many people would have paid handsomely if they'd known about his talent for shifting into the shape of different people, not just a creature like the rest of the pack. But very few had known.

"King's dead," Alice said. "So you've foiled whatever plans he was involved in."

"Yes," Lincoln said simply.

But it left me feeling uneasy, not knowing where to find this new pack. They may not have been behind King's duplicity, but they had the potential to be very dangerous. One murder might not be enough to satiate their appetites.

Leisl's home wasn't at all what I expected. It was nothing like the gypsy camp we'd visited at Mitcham Common back in the autumn. For one thing, she lived in a cottage, not a caravan, with a neat garden out the front. Little flowers poked their white bell shaped heads through the earth along the path leading from the gate to the front steps. Budding trees and shrubs promised more color in the weeks to come.

Leisl opened the door herself and, after a gasp of surprise, ushered us inside. "You are most welcome. All of you. Very welcome. Come in, come in." Her face creased into an uncertain smile and her gaze darted often to Lincoln but never lingered. As always, when I saw her, I marveled at the similarity of their eyes and strong features. On Lincoln, the sharp cheekbones were handsome, but they gave Leisl a more weathered appearance, as if time had worn the skin smooth there.

She led us into a small sitting room packed with furniture and knick-knacks. It reminded me of Lela's crowded van in Mitcham Common with its multi-colored rug and tasseled cushions in vivid hues. Nothing looked faded or dusty, and the room had a cozy feel. The fire's warmth welcomed us as much as Leisl's smile.

"Sit, sit." Leisl ushered us to the chairs just as a young woman entered, an apron over her blue and white checked dress.

The woman's dark brows lifted in question. "Mama?" So this was Leisl's daughter. She looked to be in her early twenties and bore the same striking cheekbones and eyes as her mother and half-brother. Her hair was as glossy black and wavy as Lincoln's. She wore it in a simple style, high on her head, unlike her mother who wore her gray locks loose.

"Eva, come." Leisl beckoned her closer. "This is Miss Holloway and Miss Everheart. And this is Mr. Fitzroy."

Eva's brow arched ever so slightly before lowering again.

Her other features remained schooled, as did Lincoln's. "A pleasure to meet you, sir." She dipped into an unconvincing shallow curtsy.

"And you, Miss Cornell," he said stiffly.

"Call me Eva," she said, matching his tone. I couldn't tell if she intended to or if it was simply an inherited trait neither of them was aware of.

Lincoln nodded once. I resisted the urge to nudge him with my elbow and decided to rescue him instead.

"You must call us by our first names, too," I told her. "I'm Charlie, this is Alice, and he's Lincoln."

"It's an odd name," she said, not showing any surprise, however. It was likely she knew the explanation behind his name.

"I did not choose it," her mother said a little defensively. "Eva, bring tea and cakes."

Eva shot an appraising glance at Lincoln before leaving. She neither smiled nor frowned at him, merely taking in his appearance with clinical interest.

"Eva is a good girl," Leisl said. "She helps me keep house and is learning to be a nurse, too. She is busy and will become busier when she weds and has children."

"She's getting married?" I asked.

"She will after she meets him."

I almost choked on my laugh. I managed to turn it into a cough, although I doubted I convinced anyone. Leisl must have seen Eva's future husband in one of her visions.

"And is your son well?" I asked. "Your other son, I mean."

"David is a fine young man. I wish he was here for you to meet, but he is at the bank where he works. He is a clerk, but will rise higher." Again, the certainty. If only I could see the future like that.

"You have abandoned the gypsy life completely," Lincoln

said. I thought it rather a rude comment, but perhaps, as her son, he could be forgiven.

"That life was hard and the general gave me this house and money to live." She was matter of fact about the compensation paid to her for giving birth to Lincoln and being abandoned by the Prince of Wales after their one night together.

Alice, however, looked quite uncomfortable, even though she knew the details surrounding Lincoln's existence. Her middle class prudery ran deep. Mine had been abruptly cut off when I was thirteen. Very little made me feel uncomfortable now.

"My husband was English man, not gypsy," Leisl went on. "He worked hard in a factory but did not bring home much. The general's money give my children a good education so they do not need to work in a factory like their father. I am grateful."

It sounded like she did not regret giving Lincoln up. I couldn't fathom it. If I had a child, I would fight for him or her, and no amount of money could compensate for my loss. But perhaps Leisl had always known her fate was to be the mother of the first man to lead the Ministry of Curiosities in centuries and she had made peace with that even before she'd met the prince at the fair.

Lincoln sat like a statue, his hands resting lightly on his thighs, no outward appearance that this meeting played havoc with his nerves. But I knew it did. He wouldn't have avoided visiting for so long if it was easy for him. "We came to ask you what you know about Alice," he said. "You called her a door."

"To other worlds, yes." Leisl's gaze settled on Alice. "I have not known of one like you before."

"But you recognized me as a door when you saw me," Alice said.

Leisl nodded. "I have heard stories."

"What is my purpose? Why am I like this?"

Leisl lifted one shoulder. "Why am I a seer? Why can Charlie raise the dead? We do not know. If there is purpose, the gods keep it to themselves."

"Tell us what you do know about Alice," Lincoln said. "And about other realms."

Eva returned carrying a tray that she set on the table. She poured the tea and, when her mother didn't respond to Lincoln's request, urged her to go on. "I must know these things too, Mama. Sooner or later, I need to learn about supernaturals. I'm a seer too," she told us. "I inherited my mother's abilities."

"Thank you for telling us," Lincoln said. "Charlie will create a file about you in our ministry archives. It's important that we catalog all supernaturals. The information will remain confidential."

"Very well. I will allow it."

"It wasn't a request."

"Thank you, Eva," I said quickly. "Your details will not be shared with anyone outside the three of us." I did not tell her that Gus and Seth had access to the files too. I didn't want her changing her mind.

"Tell me what being a door to other realms entails," Alice pressed. "People haven't really come from other places to here, only figments of my imagination. They only exist in my dreams and disappear when I wake. So how am I an actual door?"

Leisl accepted the teacup from her daughter. "It is not a real door, but a spirit one. They are spirits traveling here using your dreams. Your dreams are like a...like a coach or train. They bring the spirits here, but they can only enter through you, the door."

"Does it work the other way?" Lincoln asked.

"Yes," Alice said before Leisl could answer. She blinked at

him over her teacup, her eyes huge. "I recall now. When I was very young, I had a dream about a strange land. I met some odd creatures, had some odd adventures, and then woke up. I haven't had that dream since, and I hadn't connected it to the strange goings on that have occurred recently. Until now."

Leisl nodded. "Your spirit went there, and now their spirits come here."

"If it's merely spirits, why are we able to touch them?" I asked. "And they us?" The weapons used by the Queen of Hearts's army against us at the School for Wayward Girls had caused some very real damage. They would have captured Alice's physical person if they could. And Gus would swear on his life that the talking rabbit felt real enough.

"I do not know," Leisl said with a shrug. "Perhaps I am wrong. Perhaps it is more than the spirit that travels between worlds. It may be that the spirit becomes real *because* of you. Perhaps that is the true secret of the door." She shrugged again. "My mother taught me this but she had never met a door before. You are special, Alice."

"I wish I weren't," she muttered into her teacup.

I laid a hand on her arm for reassurance. "You're not alone."

"If she is a door," Lincoln said, "then presumably the door can be opened or closed."

Alice's head snapped up and her bright eyes studied Lincoln and then Leisl. "Is it possible? Can I close the door and stop these dreams?"

"Doors do open and close," Leisl said. "Sometimes a key is needed."

"What my mother is trying to say, in her unique way," Eva said, shooting Leisl a warning look, "is that she doesn't know."

Leisl used her hands to gesture both agreement and apology. "I do not. This is for you to learn, Alice. Lincoln will help, no?"

"I want to get to the bottom of Alice's dreams as much as she does," he said.

"Perhaps not quite as much," Alice said. "You mentioned other *realms* before, in plural? Are there more than one?"

Leisl nodded. "I do not know the number. Perhaps no one does. It is not easy to move between realms and count."

"Only through people like me and my dreams."

"There are portals that are not human. Places that are special and open up to let demons from other—"

"Demons?" three female voices cried. Lincoln remained quiet.

"Creatures from other worlds are called demons," Leisl went on patiently. "You did not tell Alice this?" she asked Lincoln.

He hesitated then said, "I've heard only one other person call them demons. I didn't think it an adequate word, considering the negative connotations. Apparently not all demons should be feared or reviled."

My teacup began to rattle in the saucer. I put the set down, but could not shake the thought that had just occurred to me. But I couldn't question Lincoln about it here.

"So demons can come to our world through these portals," Eva said to her mother. "The real portals, not the spirit ones like Alice. Correct?"

Leisl nodded.

"Good lord," Alice said on a breath. "That's worrying."

"How do *those* portals open and close?" Eva asked. "Perhaps it can help us with Alice's problem." She was clever, like her half-brother. I could see in Lincoln's curious gaze that she intrigued him.

"I do not know," Leisl said.

"A complex spell is required to open and close it," Lincoln said, taking over the explanation.

"It?"

"I only know of one such portal."

Frakingham House. The portal *must* be there. It *had* to be linked to Jack Langley and his home. Langley was the only person Lincoln had questioned recently in relation to Alice's dreams. Why hadn't he told me? He'd let me believe he'd learned nothing of use.

"The guardians of the spell don't like anyone knowing about the spell or the portal," Lincoln said. "For obvious reasons."

"It could prove dangerous in the wrong hands," Eva agreed.

"You must tell me who these guardians are," Alice blurted out. Her color rose, and I thought she might leap across the space and shake Lincoln. "Perhaps the spell can be used to stop my dreams."

"It's doubtful," he said.

"Do you know for certain?"

"No. Nor do they."

"Then we must try."

"Speaking the spell could have untold consequences. I'm sorry, Alice, I can't allow it."

I took her hand in mine and squeezed hard, anchoring her to the sofa as much as offering comfort. At least now I understood why Lincoln hadn't wanted Alice to know about Frakingham. It was cruel to raise her hopes then dash them like this. He'd wanted to spare her the heartache. But why keep it from me?

"Is there anything else you can tell us?" Lincoln asked his mother.

She shook her head. "There is no need to rush off," she

said, even though he hadn't made any move to get up. "Have cake."

He shook his head and rose. "We're very busy."

"Organizing a wedding?" Eva said with a tilt of her lips. "Mama told me congratulations are in order." She took my hands as I stood. "I'm very pleased to have met you, Charlie. I may not know my new brother very well yet, but I am glad that he has found happiness." She leaned in and kissed my cheek. "And Mama is very glad too," she whispered.

There were so many things I'd like to tell her about Lincoln, so many questions I'd like to ask her and Leisl, but I simply smiled and thanked her. Lincoln stood by the door, hands behind his back, waiting.

Eva walked us out to the carriage, but Leisl remained in the cottage. She looked small and too thin, and very much like a gypsy with her long gray hair hanging loose around her shoulders. I waved and she waved back.

"Your mother requires a housemaid," Lincoln said to Eva without looking at her. His gaze roamed the street, up and down, as if he were searching for something. "I'll make sure she receives more funds if you wish to hire someone."

"*Our* mother will not thank you," Eva said with an emphasis on 'our' that wasn't lost on anyone. "She thinks only the lazy need a maid. Apparently I am enough."

"And what do you say?" I asked.

"That I appreciate the offer and will gladly accept some help, particularly with the cooking. I'm quite hopeless at it, and it takes up so much time. I need to study."

"For nursing," Alice said with a nod. "What a wonderful vocation."

Eva gave her a tight smile. Her gaze raked up and down Alice's length through eyes that missed nothing. She suddenly blinked then folded her arms, as if warding off the cold. She looked away, her jaw tight.

Had she seen something in Alice's future? Something to fear or worry her? I couldn't tell and I dared not ask. I didn't want to make Alice aware of it too.

Lincoln opened the carriage door and held his hand out to me. "Do you have your imp?" he asked.

"Yes." I studied his face. "Why? What's wrong?"

"Someone followed us here and is perhaps waiting for us to leave. I sense them but can't see anyone. Hold the orb and be ready to speak the spell to release the imp if necessary."

His words sent my heart racing. I pulled the orb pendant out from beneath my bodice and held it tightly. It did not throb, however. I checked the vicinity but saw only a dozen or so people strolling along the street, all women and none acting suspiciously. A carriage rolled past as Lincoln guided me up the coach steps followed by Alice. The passing vehicle rolled on without stopping. It was empty.

At least now I knew why Lincoln had been distracted on the journey to Enfield. He wasn't ignoring me because of our kiss.

We traveled home in silence, all of us alert for someone following. With our attentions on the street outside, no one brought up the discussion with Leisl. Perhaps Alice didn't want to dwell on the fact that we'd learned so little. Even so, she must be disappointed.

"Anything?" I asked Lincoln as we approached the iron gates to Lichfield Towers.

"I can't see anyone," he said. "But I can sense something."

Alice and I exchanged glances. I didn't ask Lincoln to elaborate. It was likely he couldn't explain it anyway.

His head suddenly jerked as a flash of red appeared between the gaps in a hedge. Before I could take up a better position by the window, he opened the door.

I didn't have time to catch his sleeve before he leapt out. "Drive on!" he called as he landed on his feet and took off at a sprint. Thank God he was all right. Anyone else would have fallen.

Sunlight glinted off the blade he held in his hand. He must have pulled it from beneath his sleeve, where he often kept one strapped. There would be another on his lower leg. I prayed he wouldn't need to use them.

The coach slowed but didn't stop as we turned and headed through the gates. I pulled the door shut before turning to look back through the window. I gasped.

Lincoln ran along the road, chasing a figure dressed in the distinctive red and gold of the royal livery.

"I don't understand," I said, shaking my head.

"I don't either," Alice said, also watching. "Why is the queen's man running away from Lincoln?"

"Why was the queen's man spying on us?"

CHAPTER 4

I pushed past Doyle when he opened the front door. "Gus! Seth!" My shout echoed around the broad entrance hall and spiraled up the stairwell.

They appeared moments later. "What is it?" Seth called down.

Cook approached from the rear of the house, a large carving knife in hand. "Charlie?"

"It's Lincoln," I said. "He's chasing someone along Hampstead Lane. We must help him."

"Pistols." Seth raced down the stairs and disappeared in the direction of the gun room.

A wide-eyed maid blinked after him until Doyle ordered her to hurry along. Seth returned moments later, loading a pistol, another tucked under his arm. He handed one to Gus, and they headed outside. Cook followed. He may not have a gun but he could throw a carving knife with precision.

I went to follow but stopped at the top of the steps. "Wait! There he is!"

Lincoln jogged along the drive at an easy pace. I let out a pent-up breath.

Alice looped her arm through mine, offering comfort without needing to say anything. Seth, Gus and Cook went to meet Lincoln, but I could see that he offered no answers to their questions.

"Well?" I asked when he reached me.

"Will I be met with this kind of welcoming party every time I return home?" he asked.

"Save your jokes for when I'm not so worried."

He clasped my hand and kissed it gently then led me inside. "My study," he said simply. "Immediately."

Whether he intended all of us to go wasn't clear. It would seem we all intended to hear what he had to say, however, including Cook. Seth and Gus handed their weapons to Doyle and asked him to disarm them before storing them safely, but Cook kept his knife with him. He rarely let anyone touch his knives. I was only allowed to handle them during throwing practice.

We filed into Lincoln's study and sitting room. Alice and I sat, but the men remained standing.

"Sorry to state the obvious, but you didn't catch him," Seth said from where he lounged against the door, arms crossed.

"I did not." Lincoln undid his tie and the top button of his shirt. He didn't look as if he'd sprinted down Hampstead Lane then jogged home. He looked as deliciously ruffled as always but not out of breath. "He had too much of a start on me."

"He wore red and gold livery," Alice told the others.

"What?" Seth exploded, pushing off from the door.

Gus rubbed his jaw. "One of the queen's men?"

"Or the prince's," Seth added, shaking his head. "Let's go to the palace and confront him now."

"You be mad," Cook said. "You can't just go in. You got to be invited."

"Then let's knock until we're invited in, shall we?"

"I agree with Seth," Gus said. "We have to confront him. Could you write and ask to be seen, Fitzroy?"

Lincoln held up his hand and the men quieted. "It was most likely not a royal footman."

"But Alice said—"

"Alice said he wore royal livery, not that he was from the royal household. If the queen or prince sent someone to spy on me, they would not have dressed them in such distinctive clothing."

"Oh!" I said, realization dawning. "You think someone dressed in royal livery to make it *look* like the royal family are spying on you."

Lincoln nodded.

"Someone's trying to blame the queen?" Alice asked. "But why?"

"It could be as simple as trying to throw suspicion onto anyone, and the royal angle was a convenient one, or it could be a more specific reason."

Cook grunted. "Don't seem too convenient to get hold of livery. Wager you can't buy it from the rag man."

"King could have stolen it from the livery room at the palace while impersonating a servant," Lincoln said. "It wouldn't have been difficult for him. Everyone would assume the servant was getting it repaired or cleaned."

"So he gave the uniform to someone else before he died," I said. "Then it's likely he wasn't working alone."

Lincoln nodded. "Perhaps he intended to use it himself. It's possible he did on one of his visits to the palace and we don't know it. It seems clear, however, that you're right, Charlie, and he passed the uniform on to someone else before his death."

"Whoever it was," I said, "I wonder why he was following us."

"Something to do with the murder?" Seth suggested. "Perhaps Lincoln interrogating Gawler has caught someone's attention."

I shivered. "By someone, you mean the killer."

Lincoln came to stand beside me and rested a hand on my shoulder. I touched it and smiled wanly up at him. He did not smile back.

"Seems likely," Gus said. "Are you going to visit Gawler again?"

"Perhaps." Lincoln's answers were far too evasive for my liking.

"If you do, you're taking someone with you," I told him.

"Aye," Gus chimed in. "We'll bring pistols."

"Perhaps you need a necromancer too. One who can call on the dead. if necessary."

"Steady on," Seth said. "No need to go in with explosives when guns will do."

"Speak for yourself," Gus shot back. "Explosives sound like a good idea to me."

Seth wagged a finger at Gus. "And you think this man a fitting father-figure to walk you down the aisle, Charlie."

"I'm going to request an audience with the queen," Lincoln announced. At our stares, he added, "She spoke to King alone before he died. If he didn't outright tell her what he wanted—or what his employer wanted—in that meeting, then he probably hinted at it."

"You going to interrogate the queen?" Cook smirked. "Don't get yourself hanged for treason."

"I'll be subtle."

Seth and Gus both snorted a laugh.

"Charlie will do most of the talking." Lincoln removed his hand from my shoulder and returned to his desk. "That's all, for now. I'll let you know what I decide to do when I've thought it through."

The others left; even Alice, who I thought might have

some questions for him about the information that had arisen from our meeting with Leisl. I overheard Seth asking her how it went as I shut the door on them.

"You always assume my dismissal doesn't mean you," Lincoln said, not looking at me. He pulled a piece of paper and the inkstand toward him. "Why am I not surprised?"

I rested my hands on his shoulders and massaged. The tension eased and he tipped his head back to peer up at me.

"Go on," he said. "Ask me your questions so we can get on with it."

"Get on with what?"

"Me enjoying your company. Perhaps a kiss."

I ran my fingers through his hair. "I thought you were worried about kissing me in private."

His eyelids fluttered closed. "I'm still undecided on that matter."

"Well, kisses will depend on your answers, so think carefully before speaking."

"I'm listening," he murmured.

I stopped touching him, and he opened his eyes. I sat on a chair, keeping my distance. For now. "Why didn't you tell me about the portal at Frakingham House before?"

"What makes you think it's there?"

"It wasn't difficult to work out. You said you wanted to speak to Jack Langley about Alice because you had an inkling. It wasn't an inkling though, was it? You already knew he had information."

He stretched out his long legs and crossed them at the ankles. It was a surprisingly relaxed position considering the pressure he was under to find not only the killer, but a solution to Alice's problem. "I guessed. I knew immediately upon arriving at Frakingham that something was different about it. I felt...a disturbance in some ruins on the grounds. The air felt different there. I questioned

49

Langley, and he gave me the answers which I mentioned today."

"About the spell to open the portal?"

He nodded. "He refused to tell me more. It wasn't enough to help Alice, and I didn't want to get her hopes up, or yours, by mentioning it."

"We gave you no choice," I said heavily. "I am sorry, but you should have told me, Lincoln."

"She's your friend, and I know you're worried about her. I didn't want to upset you."

I sighed. His heart was in the right place, but he still didn't quite understand. "You and I are partners in everything now, and that means I share your burdens. You no longer need to bear them alone. I am strong enough."

"I know. So now do I get a kiss?"

I fought back my smile and my impulse to take his hand. "Not yet. I have a question about Harriet. Is she a demon?"

His moment's hesitation was the only indication that he was surprised I'd reached that conclusion. "In my opinion, yes. From what information I could read, and the little I managed to extract from Langley, she certainly resembles one, as do King, Gawler and the others. Shape shifters are a type of demon, but there are other types too. They seem to be the most common form of demon here on our realm, however, which suggests to me that their realm is closest to ours."

"Why have they come here?"

"I don't know."

"How many are there?"

"I don't know that, either. I do think Langley has grossly underestimated their number, however. He didn't seem to think them a problem anymore, and he also seemed to think the only portal is on his property, where he can keep an eye on it. Hence his reluctance to share too much information with me."

"He deems it unnecessary," I finished for him.

He nodded. "Any more questions?"

"Just one."

He sighed. "It had better be a good kiss."

"You will have earned it if you answer this one honestly. I want to know how you feel after spending time with your mother today and meeting your sister."

He breathed deeply and let it out slowly. "I don't know what I feel."

"You looked tense. Were you tense?"

"I wasn't relaxed."

"What did you think of the house?"

"It was tidy with an outward appearance of Englishness, but once inside I could see Leisl's Romany influence."

"What did you think of Eva?" I asked.

"She seems intelligent, and she's good to her mother."

I didn't correct his use of "her" mother instead of "our." He wasn't ready for that. "She seems like someone I'd like to get to know better," I said. "Would you like that, too?"

He hesitated. "If it's what you want then it can be arranged."

I rolled my eyes but did not say anything. It had been enough that he'd gone to the house. Lincoln needed time to adjust to new people in his life. I knew that all too well.

I stood and approached him. He pulled his feet in and blinked up at me. The boyish look almost undid me. I cupped his jaw with one hand and leaned on the arm of his chair with the other. "Those were good answers," I murmured. "Now, for your reward."

His eyelids shuttered. "I feel manipulated."

I chuckled. "You might as well get used to it." I touched

my lips gently to his. They quivered with his restraint. They were so warm and impossibly soft for such a hard man.

I deepened the kiss, or perhaps he did, but not too much. Not beyond the point of no return. It wasn't a kiss filled with unbridled passion, but it connected us. It was filled with my love for him and his love for me, and with our respect and understanding. No ring on my finger could do more.

When I finally drew back and released him, my body felt both tingly with desire and languid with contentment. I watched him as his eyes slowly opened. I'd never seen such a look of peace on his face.

He stroked his thumb along my jaw. "You can manipulate me any time you like, Charlie."

* * *

LADY VICKERS WAS BUILDING up to something. I couldn't quite tell what, but I suspected it had something to do with Alice, because she requested Alice's presence as we ate a light luncheon together in the parlor overlooking the garden.

"Just we ladies," Lady Vickers said, nibbling on cold chicken left over from dinner. "We can discuss wedding arrangements. Tell us, Charlie, have you finalized your guest list?"

"Almost," I said.

"Will Lord Underwood be on it?"

"Underwood! I doubt it. I don't know if I even want Lady Harcourt there."

"Perhaps you ought to invite him here again, without her. You might find you like him."

I stared at her. Alice stared at her. One of us made an odd sound that Lady Vickers took as a request to go on.

"He's very well connected, not to mention he's a

marquess. Marquesses aren't like earls, you know. You can't find one on every corner. Unmarried ones are even rarer."

Ah. Now I understood the direction of her thoughts. I eyed Alice to see if she did too, but she was concentrating on buttering a slice of bread.

"It's perfectly acceptable for you to invite him and not Lady Harcourt," Lady Vickers went on. "Mr. Fitzroy should be present, but it's not entirely necessary. This is for Alice's sake, after all."

Alice's head snapped up. "Mine?"

"Yes, dear, of course." Lady Vickers looked at her as if she were a simpleton. "Surely you weren't blind to his interest in you. It was quite obvious to everyone else, including Julia. She was rather put out, wouldn't you say, Charlie?" A small smile touched her lips. "Quite put out."

If she'd been discussing anyone other than Lady Harcourt, I would have thought Lady Vickers cruel. But it was difficult to muster sympathy for the woman who'd tried to keep Lincoln and me apart.

"I...I'm not interested in Lord Underwood," Alice said.

Lady Vickers set down her fork and laid a hand on Alice's arm. "I know he's a lot older than you, but you ought to consider him."

"It's not just his age." Alice appealed to me, but I merely urged her with a nod. "He's rather vacuous."

Lady Vickers recoiled. "Nonsense. He's a marquess!"

"His conversation wasn't all that interesting. I found him a little irritating, to be honest."

"Goodness, child, if we dismissed men because we found them irritating, the pool of eligible ones would shrink dramatically. Surely you can overlook that and find *something* worthwhile in him." She searched Alice's face. "Can't you?"

"I don't think so."

Lady Vickers plucked up her fork and stabbed a large

piece of chicken. "You should be pleased that such an elevated man took notice of you. I certainly would have been flattered at your age."

"Then why don't *you* court him?" Alice threw her napkin on the table and stormed out of the room, her bustle bobbing with her purposeful strides.

Lady Vickers half-rose, but I caught her arm and she sat down again. She concentrated on shredding her chicken but did not eat it.

"Lady V, you offer me so much good advice," I said. "Will you allow me to offer you some?"

She sighed but did not tell me to go away.

"Don't interfere. The more you try to keep Alice and Seth apart, the more Seth will rebel. It only makes him want to win her over even more."

"He is rather contrary towards me." She sighed again. "He's such a fool when it comes to women. He falls in love too easily. He has fancied himself in love with half the women of London, of all different classes. Alice is merely his latest infatuation, and I don't want either of them to make a mistake then regret it. She's not the sort of girl he can discard like the others."

"It's kind of you to have her wellbeing at heart."

"And Seth must marry an heiress." She'd said it many times, but this time there was no vehemence in the statement. It was as if she were merely repeating the words out of habit.

I did not remind her that Seth had declared he would marry for love, not fortune. Unlike his mother, he didn't believe his family needed money to restore its good name. He'd worked hard to pay off his late father's debts when she'd run away with her new husband, but beyond that, he had no ambition. He was an honorable man. Perhaps the most honorable one I'd met.

* * *

We received a note from the palace the following day in reply to Lincoln's letter asking for an audience with the queen. Our presence was requested that afternoon.

Buckingham Palace awed me every time I saw it, inside and out. It wasn't simply the scale of it—although it was enormous—or the richly appointed rooms, but the busyness. Courtiers mingled in groups or strolled singly through the rooms. I couldn't discern why they were there at all. Were they friends of the queen's? Family? Were they awaiting an audience or did they live there? Dozens upon dozens of footmen stood around like statues, awaiting orders or hurrying silently past. And those were just the servants I saw. There would be many more working out of sight. No wonder it had been so easy for King to get in.

We were led to a different part of the palace than on our last visit. Open windows let in light and fresh air, and they offered beautiful views to the gardens. This wing wasn't like the queen's private rooms, where gloom and mustiness reigned. The further we walked, the more I realized we were again venturing into a private area. There were fewer people about and it was quieter. One of the queen's ladies usually escorted us to the monarch's rooms on previous visits, but this time it was a footman.

He paused in an open doorway and bowed. "Mr. Fitzroy and Miss Holloway," he announced to the Prince of Wales and another gentleman seated in what appeared to be a large office. The ornately carved desk took pride of place in the center of the room, with all the other furniture arranged to draw one's eye to it. The paintings on the walls depicted hunting scenes, and the burgundy and green color scheme of the furnishings unmistakably marked this as a gentleman's room.

I curtseyed and Lincoln gave a perfunctory bow. I could feel the uncertainty vibrating off him. He'd not expected to see his father again. "I was led to believe the queen requested my presence," Lincoln said carefully. "Is she here?"

"She's away." The Prince of Wales nodded at the footman, who exited and shut the door. "You're right, Fitzroy, I did lead you to believe that Her Majesty responded to your missive. I wasn't sure you would come if you knew you would be meeting me. I hope you're not disappointed, and perhaps I can help you anyway. May I introduce you to my brother, His Royal Highness Prince Alfred, the Duke of Edinburgh." It was smoothly done, not allowing Lincoln any cause to protest. There was nothing to do but greet both men cordially.

"Your Highness," Lincoln said stiffly to the gentleman who looked very much like his older brother. They both bore neatly trimmed greying beards, their slick hair parted severely down the middle. Deep-set eyes, so much like their mother's, were surrounded by puffy, loose skin, a sure sign of late nights and the excesses of a comfortable life.

I curtseyed again as the Prince of Wales informed his brother that I was Lincoln's fiancée.

"I read the announcement in the newspapers," the Prince of Wales said.

"Just like everyone else, eh?" The Duke of Edinburgh grunted in what I supposed was a laugh. He pushed himself out of the deep leather armchair and strolled up to us, hands behind his back. He ignored me and inspected Lincoln like he was a thoroughbred in a stable. "So this is he?"

My breath caught. He *knew*. His older brother must have told him that Lincoln was his illegitimate son. How many others knew? I watched Lincoln out of the corner of my eye, but he remained unmoved. He watched the duke and, when the duke looked up to study Lincoln's face again, he was startled. He backed away.

"Fine fellow, isn't he?" The Prince of Wales said with a puff of his chest. "Handsome, strong, clever too."

"Hmmm." The duke eased himself into his chair and reached for a silver cigar case. "Pity."

Pity that Lincoln was everything a man could want in a son and yet he could not be acknowledged? Perhaps. It was impossible to tell his meaning from that one word.

"Has he met your other children?" the duke asked his brother.

"Of course not," the Prince of Wales snapped. "Why would he?"

"If Mr. Fitzroy is an investigator, he could look into that Cleveland Street incident and find out what really happened." The duke gave a lazy shrug. "Just a thought."

The prince's face colored. "He's not that sort of investigator, and the Ministry of Curiosities is not that kind of department."

I recalled the Cleveland Street incident. It had been quite a scandal. Just after I settled in at Lichfield Towers, the newspapers had reported on a police raid at a house in Cleveland Street after an investigation revealed it to be a brothel catering for gentlemen wanting liaisons with other men. That had been shocking enough, but even worse, Seth had recently heard a rumor that the Prince of Wales's eldest son had been a customer at the brothel. As second in line to the throne, after his father, the rumor could damage the royal family's reputation.

The only reason I could think why the duke would bring up the subject in our presence was to rile the Prince of Wales and perhaps embarrass him in front of his very masculine yet illegitimate son—the son the Prince of Wales wished had been his legitimate one and his heir.

If Lincoln thought the same, he gave no indication. He hardly batted an eyelid. If he'd been stiff when he'd met Leisl and Eva then he was positively frozen now. I wished I could touch his hand to offer support, but he might not appreciate the gesture. He had, however, brought me here for one thing. To talk. That I could do.

"Sir," I said to the Prince of Wales, "may we speak freely?"

"You may," he said. "My brother knows everything about the break-in and that fellow King. It took some convincing but he believed me in the end. And, as you can probably tell, he knows everything about my private business, too. Her Majesty keeps me informed, and I keep my brother informed, as a matter of insurance, you see."

In case something happened to the reigning monarch, I supposed, although I failed to see why it was necessary for the Duke of Edinburgh to know that his brother's eldest child had been born on the wrong side of the blanket. Perhaps, like most people, royals needed someone to confide in too, and brothers naturally turned to one another.

"We requested an audience with the queen because she spoke to King in private that day he entered the palace under the guise of your father," I said. "We need to know what he said to her."

"Why?" the Prince of Wales asked.

"It's likely someone was paying him. We want to know who."

"There's been a murder linked to King," Lincoln added. "And someone dressed in royal livery is following us."

The Prince of Wales's mouth worked soundlessly before he managed to speak. "Good lord. Not again."

The duke pointed his unlit cigar at Lincoln. "Are you accusing our staff of spying on you? Or of my brother ordering you be followed?"

"That's not what he's suggesting," the prince chided.

"Isn't he?" The duke struck a match. "Sounds like it to me."

"That's because you're not *listening*, Affie."

His brother shook the match to extinguish it. "Someone dressed in royal livery can only mean one thing," he mumbled around the fat cigar.

Lincoln held up a hand for silence, a bold move considering whom he addressed. Both men quieted, but the duke seemed more startled at being silenced by a nobody than actually acquiescent.

"We don't think the spy received his orders from the palace," Lincoln clarified. "It's likely King stole the uniform and passed it on to someone else before his death. That's why we'd like to know whom he worked for, and to know that we must speak with Her Majesty. She's the only one who can shed light on what King wanted from her."

"She told me he said nothing of importance," the Prince of Wales said.

"I'd like to ask her again."

The duke unplugged the cigar from his mouth. "Are you calling your queen a liar?"

Lincoln let the question go unanswered. The silence thinned and stretched with the duke glaring at Lincoln and the prince looking decidedly uncomfortable.

"I'll write to her," the Prince of Wales said quickly. "I'll emphasize the importance of her being open with us for the sake of the realm. That ought to convince her."

"The realm always comes first," the duke muttered, returning the cigar to his mouth and inhaling deeply.

"Please inform me when you have her reply." Lincoln bowed and held his hand out to me, steadying me as I hurriedly curtsied. He was in a rush to get away.

This time, I couldn't blame him. While I didn't mind the Prince of Wales, I found the duke to be condescending and manipulative. If the brothers actually liked one another, it was impossible to tell from that meeting.

* * *

LINCOLN WOULD NOT BE DRAWN on his opinion of either of the royals, no matter how many times I asked on the journey home. I stopped asking when he narrowed his gaze at me on my fourth attempt. I spent most of the rest of the way thinking up subtler questions while he spent it looking out the window.

"Did anyone follow you?" Seth asked when we found him and Gus playing croquet with Alice on the lawn.

"Only to the palace," Lincoln said.

I gasped. "I didn't see anyone."

"He was there," was all Lincoln said.

With Gus and Seth's backs to her, Alice took the opportunity to nudge the croquet ball with her toe. She winked at me. I tried not to smile.

"Now what?" Gus asked.

Alice placed her foot on the ball and rolled it forward.

"Now we return to what we do know," Lincoln said.

Gus and Seth looked to me. I shrugged. "What do we know?" I asked.

"That there is a dead man lying in a mortuary, due to be buried soon. Everything else is supposition, including the witness being a shifter."

"Do we even know the victim's name?" I asked, watching Alice move the ball once again.

"The newspapers haven't reported it," he said. "It's likely it has been suppressed."

"Because it was someone of consequence," Seth muttered, nodding. "How terrible."

Gus swung his croquet mallet in an upward arc and

rested the handle on his shoulder. "Just as terrible if it was a factory hand, or hackney driver, or baker."

"I didn't mean that it wasn't," Seth said.

"You implied it."

Seth rolled his eyes. "Honestly, Charlie, if you choose him over me to walk on your left, what will people think?"

"That she got sense and good taste in her choice of friends." Gus turned back to Alice. He frowned at the ball, looked up at her, and the frown deepened.

She smiled sweetly, settled her stance, and swung the mallet. The ball rolled neatly through the hoop.

Seth applauded. "Well done. Good shot."

Gus thrust one hand on his hip. "But she—"

Seth slapped Gus's back, wrapping his hand around the base of Gus's neck. From Gus's wince, I suspected Seth was squeezing him hard. With a firm shake and an innocent smile for Alice, Seth let him go and took his shot. He missed.

"Ah well. I'm having a run of bad luck today." He trotted off in the direction of the ball.

Gus sighed. "I hate this game. Next time he complains about having nothing to do, I'm going to challenge him to a duel. Bit of blood sport'll liven up the day, and he'll get cut to ribbons if he don't play proper." He trudged after Seth.

"You did speak to Seth, didn't you?" Alice asked me. "About his behavior?"

I nodded. "There's been no change?"

"No. He's still sickeningly sweet and complicit. I can't bear it."

"Then I am at my wit's end," I said. "Nothing I do makes him want to be himself around you. I am sorry, Alice."

"Never mind." She put her hand up to shield her eyes from the sun as she watched the men pull the hoops out of the lawn. "It simply isn't meant to be between us."

I decided not to tell Seth that. He would be devastated.

Besides, I wasn't entirely sure it was hopeless. Once she got to know him, she would fall in love with him. She just needed to get to know him. The real him.

I set off after Lincoln, who'd headed back to the house. "Wait!" I called out, and he stopped near the terrace at the back of the house. He offered me his arm and I took it. "We didn't finish the discussion about the victim. You said we have to start there. Are you implying what I think you're implying?"

"Yes."

"You want me to raise his spirit?"

"After we find out his name. We'll go tonight."

If a spirit had crossed over to the otherworld for their afterlife, I needed their full name to summon them back. The newspaper hadn't reported it in the article about the murder, and there'd been no more articles since.

I groaned. "You're going to break into the police station, aren't you?" I didn't like the thought of Lincoln doing that, even though we'd both done it before.

"No. I'm going to bribe my contact at Scotland Yard. The breaking-in part will be at the mortuary tonight."

"You want to see the body? Why not just the spirit?"

"Because if the victim knows who killed him, we can confront the murderer straight away and end this. I expect a more dramatic and honest result if the murderer is accused by the man he killed."

"You have quite a unique way of getting results, Lincoln. Effective but unique."

"Will you be all right? I doubt it will be a pleasant sight, considering he was mauled."

"I've seen enough death to not let it affect me." It was a lie, but I didn't think he detected it. "We'll all go," I said. "Seth and Gus, too."

We climbed the stairs and entered the house through the

doors leading to the morning room. He made to continue on, but I caught his hand.

"You haven't spoken much since leaving the palace," I said.

"There's nothing to say."

"Are you surprised the prince told his brother about you?"

He considered this a moment and then nodded. "I thought it would be a secret he'd take to his grave. When he found out who I was, he seemed...shocked."

"But he also seemed to accept it quickly after the shock faded."

"He didn't tell the queen."

"Grown men probably don't confide in their mothers very much, even if she does rule the country."

His jaw relaxed a little. "I am surprised he told anyone at all."

"It just shows that he's not ashamed of you, Lincoln. Quite the opposite, I think."

"If it became public, the newspapers would be relentless," he went on.

"His brother is hardly likely to tattle. Imagine the things they must know about each other." I squared up to him and clasped his arms. "Besides, it seems to be common knowledge that your father isn't exactly honorable when it comes to his marriage vows, so a by-blow should surprise no one. That had better not be an inherited trait, by the way."

He pressed his forehead to mine and clasped my hands. "I can assure you, it's not."

"I know," I said gently, and I meant it.

* * *

LINCOLN'S CONTACT at Scotland Yard was a corrupt detective whose career depended upon Lincoln not divulging the man's connection to a smuggling ring operating from the docks. By ten o'clock, he sent Lincoln a message with a name on it: Roderick Oswald Protheroe.

We waited until midnight then drove to the Westminster mortuary with Seth and Gus sharing the coachman's seat. The insipid light from a streetlamp failed to penetrate the dense darkness outside the mortuary building, and with the coach's lamps covered, we could not easily be seen.

Lincoln shuttered his lantern before alighting. The horses shifted, their clanking bridles the only sound in the eerie quiet. Seth climbed down and soothed them with pats and whispers. Perhaps they could sense the death beyond the brick walls.

It unnerved me too.

I held the lantern, the shutter slightly ajar, as Lincoln used his tools to unlock the front door. Two clicks had it swinging open with a groan of hinges. The horses moved again and I glanced back. The coach had stopped in the darkest part of the street, and only its silhouette was visible.

Lincoln pushed open the door just as footsteps sounded on the pavement to the right. A constable emerged through the fog like an apparition, another figure behind him. Lincoln grabbed my hand and pushed me inside.

Too late. We were seen.

"Halt!" a voice barked. "Who goes there?"

"They went in," the other policeman said. "Come on. We got 'em cornered."

CHAPTER 5

*L*incoln signaled for me to flatten myself against the wall. He stood between me and the door, his arm touching mine. Tension coiled his muscles tight, ready to spring. He held no weapons, even though I knew him to be armed.

The larger constable edged through, inch by inch, truncheon raised. Lincoln struck a blow on the side of the man's head then kicked his legs out from under him.

The second constable turned and ran. Lincoln followed, his footsteps so light I couldn't hear them. The man on the floor groaned.

I searched the small reception room then headed into a corridor that led to an office and a windowless room containing a table but no chairs. A body-shaped object covered by a sheet lay on the table. I breathed deeply to steady my nerves and coughed as the tangy scent of carbolic soap cloyed at the back of my throat. The soap didn't quite banish the stench of death.

I lifted the corner of the sheet, but stopped as Lincoln entered, carrying the first constable over his shoulder like a sack. He dumped the body on the floor then disappeared. The constable wasn't groaning now. He made no sound and didn't move. Surely Lincoln hadn't...

He returned with the second constable and set him down beside the first. "They're alive," he answered my unasked question. "They passed out from lack of air."

"I remember when you did that to me," I said without thinking. "You seem to have had no problem silencing those two, but may I request you leave one to me next time?"

He joined me by the table. "I thought you'd be pleased." He sounded put out. "I didn't kill either of them."

"Yes, but I didn't have the chance to put my training into practice."

"A fair point." He picked up the lantern I'd set on the table near the head of the dead man and carried it to the nearby desk. He looked through the papers stacked there, scanning each page quickly until he found the information he wanted. "It was fortunate we came tonight," he said. "He'll be buried tomorrow."

"Has there already been an inquest?"

"The coroner decided it wasn't murder; 'Mauling by a crazed dog' is the official verdict. The police report is attached, and that was their conclusion, too." He returned to the table and held the lantern high. "Ready?"

"Ready."

I peeled back the sheet to reveal the dead man's face. It showed no signs of an attack, only the pallor of death. "He looks young," I said.

"Twenty-four."

"Too young to die." I pulled the sheet down further, revealing gashes to his throat and chest. Most of the blood had been cleaned away but some dried clumps matted his chest hair. The cuts looked very deep, from the way the flesh lay open, but I didn't inspect too closely. "Claws," I said simply.

"No wonder the police and coroner concluded it was a mauling," he said.

"Why haven't we read about it in the papers since that first article was printed? Shouldn't the police warn the public that a mad dog is on the loose in Hyde Park?"

"They don't want to alarm anyone. Not yet. Another attack will change that."

"Then let's hope there're no more attacks." I lifted the sheet back up to the victim's chin. "Roderick Oswald Protheroe, come to me," I intoned. "I call on the spirit of Roderick Oswald Protheroe."

The silvery mist seeped out of the wall and floated gently around the room before settling into the ghostly form resembling the young man lying dead on the table. He looked confused, and I quickly tried to reassure him.

"You're dead and in spirit form," I said, realizing too late that those probably weren't the most comforting words one would want to hear.

The man looked down at his ghostly body. "Yes," he said simply. "I remember. Is that...me?" He edged closer to the table and peered at the exposed face. He shimmered and went to pass a hand over his face but it went right through the mist. "Do my family know?" He had the cultured accent off the upper classes, and the bearing too.

"Yes," I said, assuming the police had informed them.

"And Leonora? Dear God, poor girl. My poor dear Leonora, all alone now."

"Who is she?"

"Leonora Ballantine, my intended. Well, not quite my intended, although we had an understanding. We are—were —in love. I suppose she can do as her father wishes now," he said bitterly. He went to run his hands through his hair, but once again his fingers passed through. "Who are you? Why am I here?"

"My name is Charlie Holloway and this is Lincoln Fitzroy. I'm a necromancer, and I summoned you here to ask your assistance in finding your killer."

He looked to me then to Lincoln and shook his head. "You're mistaken. I wasn't killed by a man. It was a…a wolf, I think. Bigger than a dog, at least." He indicated the size with his hands, as tall and broad as a man.

Damnation. He hadn't seen the wolf change into its human form. We were no closer to finding the killer shifter, and coming here to the mortuary had been a waste of time. I could have summoned him from home with just the name. There would be no confronting anyone tonight, with or without the dead Mr. Protheroe.

I repeated his answer for Lincoln's benefit. He simply nodded for me to go on with my questions.

"May I see the rest of me?" Protheroe asked.

I exposed a little of the body's throat but not too much. Protheroe's spirit recoiled, breaking up before coalescing into his shape again.

"It's possible you weren't attacked by a dog or wolf," I said.

"I was. I saw it. Big ugly thing. And no human did…" He waved at his body but turned his face away. "That."

"Despite the evidence, you were probably murdered, Mr. Protheroe."

"We think someone set their animal on you," Lincoln said. I supposed it wasn't far from the truth, and it was certainly an easier explanation than the real one.

"What the blazes! Who would do that?" Protheroe dared another look at his ruined body.

"That's what we'd like to find out," I said. "Did you have enemies?"

"None that I know of. I'm quite a likeable fellow. Everyone says so."

"Who gained from your death?"

"You mean financially? No one. I have an older sister, happily settled with a rich gentleman. Everything that was set to come to me upon the death of my father will probably go to her now, but she doesn't need it. Besides, we got along splendidly. None of my family would want me dead."

I repeated his answer for Lincoln then was about to ask more questions when one of the policemen groaned.

"Blimey," the ghost said, startled. He hadn't seen the men in the dark corner. "Why are there bobbies on the floor? Are you sure you're investigating my death, miss?"

"We are. The police don't think it's murder, but we do. We had to sneak in here after dark. They'll be fine."

"We must go," Lincoln announced. "There's no point staying here if the killer is unknown." He ushered me out. The ghost followed and Lincoln shut the door. He used his tools to lock the mortuary door then led the way back outside. The policemen would be found safe and well in the morning.

"Would you mind coming with us?" I asked the spirit. "We have more questions."

"Er…"

"Please," I said, not wanting to tell him that I could force him to come with me. "We want justice for you. Your family will appreciate it."

"Very well."

The spirit settled in the coach alongside me just as if he were alive. Fortunately Lincoln, who climbed into the cabin after the coach rolled on, did not sit on him.

"Where had you been that night?" I asked Protheroe. "Why were you in Hyde Park so late?"

"I was walking home after visiting Leonora. It was dashed

difficult getting into her room, not to mention expensive after bribing her servants, but I managed it. It was the first time I'd dared a nighttime liaison. And the last," he said, looking deflated.

I repeated this for Lincoln. "You say her father didn't like you," Lincoln said. "Could he have orchestrated your murder?"

"Good lord! No!" Protheroe shook his head over and over but it became less and less vehement. "Surely not." He blinked back at Lincoln. "I...I'm not entirely certain he'd have the bottle."

"He wouldn't have done it himself," I said, "but set dogs onto you."

"He didn't own dogs. Not here in the city, anyway. Perhaps on his estate in Bristol."

Again, I repeated this for Lincoln then asked a question of my own. "What about a rival for Leonora's affections?"

He stretched his neck, jutting out his chin. "Leonora's damnably pretty and terribly kind-hearted. A sweeter girl you would not meet. Her father is rich, titled and well connected, so she's quite a catch. But I'm eminently suitable. My father's a baronet, and I have twenty thousand a year."

"So why did Mr. Ballantine not want you marrying his daughter?"

"It's Lord Ballantine. He's a baron. Had his sights set higher than a baronet's son, that's the problem. The old fool thought he could get someone better," he bit off. "But Leonora believed in love, and she loved *me*."

"She refused the men her father tried to marry her to?"

He nodded. "She told him I was the only one for her, and she didn't care who the other fellow was."

I filled Lincoln in on the discussion thus far.

"Was he going to force her to marry someone else?" Lincoln asked.

"He tried, but the other fellow wouldn't commit. Apparently he wanted to but didn't think his family would approve, her being only a baron's daughter. Those are Leonora's words—*only* a baron's daughter." He shook his head sadly. "Her father encouraged him to pursue her, and she's a good girl. She didn't like other people to dislike her, particularly her own father, so she went along with it for a time, hoping the fellow would lose interest eventually. But she'd finally had enough of pretending, and she worried he would approach his family soon and successfully plead his case. That's why Leonora and I met that night, to plan our escape. We were going to run away together, in case she was betrothed to this bore without warning. My poor Leonora. She'll give in now, I know it."

"Do you know the man's name?" I asked after repeating his words for Lincoln's benefit.

"No," Protheroe said. "She refused to tell me. She said she didn't want to affect my opinion of him in case we ever met. So good of her to be selfless like that."

I told Lincoln his answer and asked him if he had any more questions for Protheroe.

"Not yet," Lincoln said.

"Then I release your—"

"Wait!" Protheroe's spirit rose off the seat. "Will you pass on a message to my dear sweet Leonora from me?"

I hesitated, not wanting to make a promise to a dead man that I couldn't keep. "I'll do my best."

"Tell her I loved her with my whole heart and knew she loved me just as much. Tell her I want her to live a full and happy life. Even if that means she must marry this other fellow." If ghosts could get teary, I had no doubt that the man whose spirit sat beside me would have done so. "You'll find the Ballantine house on Queen's Gate, South Kensington."

"I'll try to speak with her alone," I said. "Goodbye, Mr. Protheroe. You are released."

His spirit disintegrated and disappeared. "We have to speak to Leonora Ballantine," I told Lincoln. "She lives in South Kensington."

He nodded, watching me carefully.

"I think the girl's father killed him," I said. "Or the other suitor."

"Both are a possibility."

"We have no other suspects. If only we could find out the witness's name and interrogate him."

"According to my contact, he gave a false name to the police."

I tipped my head back and rested it against the wall behind me. "Poor Mr. Protheroe—and Miss Ballantine, of course. They were just a young couple in love and now her dreams are shattered and his life cut short. Part of me hopes we find another reason for the murder, something unrelated to her."

He switched seats to sit beside me and clasped my hand in his. "Perhaps there's another explanation. None of what Protheroe said had anything to do with King."

"You're right. There's most likely another reason. We just need to keep searching for it. Perhaps Leonora can help us." I yawned and rested my head on his shoulder.

"You don't need to convince me to visit her, Charlie. We'll go tomorrow."

"I'm coming with you."

"That was never in doubt."

He angled his body so that he could place his arm around me and I could rest against his chest. The steady rhythm of his heartbeat and the gentle rocking of the carriage lulled me. I fell asleep soon after he kissed the top of my head.

* * *

A FLURRY of messages arrived while we were still at breakfast. Lincoln read each one then folded them up and tucked
them under his plate. He continued to eat his eggs as if
receiving five messages in the space of thirty minutes was
not odd. Seth, Alice and Gus looked to me. I shrugged.

As soon as the new footman, Whistler, left with the empty
teapot, I spoke up. "Who are they from and what are the
contents?"

Lincoln set down his knife and fork and picked up the
letters. "The Bank of London," he said, indicating one. "Two
are from the General Register Office, one of which is from
their births department and the other from the census
department. This one is from the Land Registry," he said,
holding up a fourth letter. "And this is from an orphanage."

"Orphanage?" Alice asked.

Lincoln handed the letters around to us. "They were sent
to me because yesterday someone made inquiries at each of
those places about me or this address."

"Your triggers," I said, reading the one from the orphanage. It claimed that a gentleman had tried to discover if the
orphanage had adopted out a baby by the name of Lincoln
Fitzroy almost thirty years ago. "He has them set up at
various departments and organizations," I told Alice. "If
someone goes searching for information about Lincoln, a
note on his file says to inform him immediately. I believe it
costs a small fortune in bribes."

"A nominated committee member is also a point of
contact," Lincoln added. "One of them will receive these too,
depending on whose turn it is."

"But why?" Alice asked. "Do you stop the person who is
making the inquiries? There are no names on these notes so I
don't see how."

"There's a name on this one," Seth said, handing her the letter from the Register Office.

"That'll likely be false," Lincoln said. "No doubt it was the first place our anonymous inquirer went. I'd start by looking for my birth record too."

"It's where I began my search when I tried to learn more about him," I told Alice. "I learned nothing. He's not listed."

"They got nowhere at the bank," Gus said, reading the letter. "Told him customer records are confidential. Would bloody hope so."

"I see the pattern," I said. "Whoever it was went to the Register Office first. They tried both your name on the birth register and this address for the census. They came up blank on both counts."

"I wasn't living here at the time of the last census," Lincoln said, buttering his toast. "I was still at the general's house in eighty-one. I expect our anonymous inquirer will learn that, soon enough. He didn't ask for the general's address at the census office, but I expect him to return today, after he learned late yesterday that I now own the general's house."

"From the Land Registry," I said, picking up the letter from where Alice had put it down. "You would have both this property and that one listed under your name now."

Alice held her teacup to her lips but did not sip. "If you can set up triggers, why not have your files removed altogether?"

"Too suspicious," Lincoln said. "If someone learns I live here but there's no record of anyone owning Lichfield Towers it would set alarm bells ringing."

"The only thing that matters is keeping your birth parents a secret," I said. "And there are no records of your birth at the General Register Office. I suppose that's why he tried the orphanage."

He nodded. "I doubt they'll continue that line of inquiry.

74

There are too many orphanages. Most likely he'll give up and assume I was handed in to an orphanage and my name changed by my new family, or I wasn't born in England."

"So we have no need to worry that someone is trying to find out more about you?" Alice said carefully.

Lincoln drank the rest of his tea and stood. "There is some cause for mild concern, simply because someone is trying to learn more about me. The question is, why."

"And is it the same spy dressed in royal livery," I said.

"Ready, Charlie?"

I followed him out of the dining room. "You're more worried than you let on," I said, taking his arm.

"It's possible the inquirer is trying to find a link between me and Leisl after following us there. The most obvious link is the one that is actually true."

"Does it matter if they do know you're her son?"

"I'm not yet sure."

I squeezed his arm. "I think you're worried about her, but I also don't think you should be."

We walked slowly up the stairs, our steps in harmony. "I am not worried about her any more than I would be worried about a member of the public," he said. "With that being the case, why don't you think I should be worried?"

"Because if someone wanted to get to you, they would target me."

He grunted. "Thank you, Charlie, that doesn't help ease my mind."

I hugged his arm. Pointing out the obvious wouldn't change anything, since he already knew it, but it might ease his mind knowing that I was aware of the situation.

"I will remain vigilant at all times," I assured him. "And I have my imp with me."

* * *

BY THE TIME a well-dressed young woman stepped out from Lord Ballantine's South Kensington terrace on Queen's Gate, the clouds had closed in and the air turned chilly. Lincoln and I had waited for over three hours and not a single soul had come or gone before the dark haired beauty emerged. For that reason, we assumed she was a resident, not a visitor. She had only a maid with her, fortunately. Our plan would be easier to enact with just a maid rather than an overbearing parent.

We'd decided that I should speak to Leonora Ballantine alone, so as not to startle her. I waited until she and her maid were out of sight of the house before falling into step alongside them.

"Excuse me, are you Miss Leonora Ballantine?" I asked.

Her steps slowed as she studied me through eyes swollen from crying, but she held her head high and did not shy away. "Have we met?" she asked, not at all put out by my boldness.

"My name is Charlie Holloway, and I mean you no harm. Indeed, I have a message to pass on from a friend of yours."

She stopped and her maid too. A small frown creased her forehead. "Who?"

"I can only tell you in private," I said, eyeing the maid. At her hesitation, I added, "Perhaps your maid can stand over by the church gate, where she can still see you. The message is for your ears only."

"There is no one I wish to receive secret messages from," Leonora said. "You may tell me here or not at all."

Oh dear. Now I had to say the word, and in front of her maid too. I disliked this part. "I am a necromancer."

Leonora shivered, burying her hands deeper into the muff. She ought to don a cloak in this weather too, but a muff was better than nothing. My hands and feet felt like ice.

"What's a necromancer?" the maid asked, blinking at her mistress. "Miss, I don't like this."

"Stand by the gate," Leonora told her.

"But—"

"Go, Ryan."

The maid reluctantly moved away, her gaze never leaving her mistress.

"I'm sorry for the secrecy," I said to Leonora, "but, as you've probably guessed, the message is from Mr. Protheroe and is for your ears only."

She blinked huge brown eyes at me and nibbled on a full lower lip. She was as lovely as Protheroe described with a slender figure and childlike face. Her willingness to believe me and send her maid away hinted at a spirited nature, but her red-rimmed eyes held no spark. She looked utterly forlorn.

"A necromancer speaks to the dead, correct?" Leonora asked.

"Yes."

"How do I know I can trust you?"

"Mr. Protheroe's spirit told me of your plans to run away together."

She gasped and bit her lip again. Tears welled in her eyes. "Not even Ryan knew," she whispered.

I glanced toward the maid, who was watching us intently. "We must speak quickly, Miss Ballantine. What I'm about to tell you will shock you, but please hear me to the end. Mr. Protheroe believed he was murdered."

She gasped again but did not interrupt.

"He tasked me with learning the identity of his murderer," I said, launching into the story Lincoln and I had practiced while we waited. We'd decided to lie a little rather than tell her about the ministry and shape changers. The less she knew about supernatural creatures, the less hysteria may ensue. "He didn't see his attacker, and he believes the only reason to kill him is because he was about to run away with you."

Her face paled. "No," she whispered. "Surely that's not it. Wh-why doesn't he think it was a random attack?"

"That is a possibility, but we must rule out a deliberate one."

She shook her head slowly, her unseeing gaze staring straight ahead. She was thinking it through, weighing up the implications of my words, perhaps even wondering if she ought to believe me after all. "But if his death was because of our liaison...then the only person against us was my father." Her gaze suddenly focused on me. "Surely you don't think he would go to such great lengths to stop us!"

"It's not me who mentioned him," I said carefully.

The muscles in her face twitched, as if she were warring with her emotions, trying to hold herself together. She was succeeding, but only just.

"What of your other suitor?" I said. The one your father wanted you to marry? Perhaps it was he."

"He didn't know about Roderick." Her voice sounded thick with unshed tears. "Only my parents did. My mother was satisfied with Roderick as a husband, but my father wasn't. He had plans for me, you see." Her mouth twisted, her voice turned bitter. "Ambitious ones."

"Is your father capable of murder?" I asked. "Perhaps not committing the crime himself, but paying another?"

"I...I don't know. He has a temper, but he has never hurt me. He was extremely angry when I told him about Roderick, though. He railed at me for encouraging Roderick and forbade us to see one another. The entire household heard his shouting. Roderick and I met in secret after that, with Ryan's help. She's good to me, and she risked everything to help us meet without..." Her face crumpled and her lips trembled. "Without my parents' knowledge."

I fished out a handkerchief from my reticule but she shook her head. A moment later, she was once again composed. "You say the other suitor didn't know about Mr. Protheroe," I said. "But what if he found out and became jealous?"

She lifted one shoulder. "He's very nice and not at all violent in nature. Indeed, I like him. Not love, understand, just like."

"Men who aren't violent in nature may still pay someone who is."

She nodded weakly. She looked deflated, as if the little courage she'd clung to since learning of Protheroe's death had finally deserted her. I felt awful for being the one to rob her of it. It felt so cruel.

"What is his name, so I may investigate him?" I asked.

She shook her head. "I shan't tell you. Please, don't ask again. I cannot say. Father has forbidden me to speak his name to anyone. It needs to remain utterly secret until his family are informed. But I can assure you, Miss Holloway, he's not a killer, and nor would he pay anyone to kill on his behalf. I am certain of it. He's far too honorable."

I gave her a tight smile and nod that I hoped appeared genuine. As badly as I wanted to know the other man's name, I couldn't pressure her to go against her father's wishes. She was fragile enough. Besides, there were other ways to find out.

"Mr. Protheroe asked me to pass on a message to you," I said gently.

Her eyes glistened and a look of joy passed over her face. "He did?"

"He wants you to know that he loved you and that he knew you loved him deeply."

Her face crumpled again. "Oh, Roderick."

I moved closer and touched her elbow to steady her in case she felt weak. "He said he wants you to have a happy life and to not mourn him too long. He even suggested that you ought to consider the other fellow your father wishes you to marry."

"How can I?" she said through her sobs. "How can I ever love another?"

I had no answer for that. I doubted I could ever feel the same love for a man that I felt for Lincoln. I offered her my handkerchief again but she didn't take her hands out of the muff and shook her head.

The maid, Ryan, glared daggers at me from the church gate but did not approach.

"It is possible there is another reason for Mr. Protheroe's murder," I said. "Can you think of anything that may have slipped his mind?" I knew it was unlikely that she would know something the victim did not, but the question had to be asked.

She shook her head. "Nothing. Roderick's right. Our relationship was the only contentious issue in his life. His family adored him, his friends admired him, and I loved him. He was a gentleman in every sense of the word. Oh, Miss Holloway, how can I go on without him?"

She burst into tears again, and her maid rushed to her side, her glare almost sharp enough to slice through me. "There, there, Miss Ballantine. You'll feel better after a walk and some air."

I didn't think a walk in the cold could mend poor Leonora's broken heart.

The maid pulled a handkerchief from the cloth reticule dangling from her wrist. "Dry your eyes now, Miss, then let's be off. The further away we get, the better," she added, shooting me an accusatory look.

Leonora removed her hand from the fur muff and took the handkerchief. I swallowed the gasp that surged up my throat.

Her hand was extraordinarily large. A quick glance at her booted feet confirmed that they were also big for a woman of her size.

Leonora Ballantine was a shape changer.

CHAPTER 6

I watched Leonora and her maid walk off then returned to Lincoln standing at the end of the row of terrace houses on Queen's Gate. He leaned against a lamp-post, newspaper in hand, looking devilishly handsome and relaxed. A closer inspection revealed him to be focused on his surroundings, not the paper. I doubted anybody but me noticed.

"I have a question for you," I said to him before he could ask me what I'd learned. "Why does a woman not wear a warm cloak in this chilly weather yet carries a fur muff?"

His eyebrows shifted ever so slightly. "She's a shifter," he said with curiosity.

"I saw her hand and it was big. Her feet too. Lincoln," I said, hardly able to keep the excitement out of my voice, "this means Protheroe's murder is almost certainly tangled up with the shifter community. We just need to discover how."

"Just?"

"Perhaps it won't be as easy as that."

He offered me his arm, and we walked slowly to the other

end of the street where Tucker waited with the carriage. "Did you learn anything else from Miss Ballantine?"

"Very little. She doesn't think her father or the secret paramour would kill Protheroe, yet she couldn't think of another reason he would be murdered."

"And the other man's name?"

"She refused to tell me, but I know someone who might."

"The maid?"

I nodded. "She does seem loyal but maids are not paid well. She might tell us. If she does indeed know it."

"She will."

"You're very certain," I said as we reached the coach. "You won't threaten her, will you?"

"No, but I can't promise that she won't be frightened into telling us."

I wasn't sure how that was any different, and I was about to ask him when he suggested we dine early and perhaps see a theater show. "To fill in time until the maid retires for the evening," he said. "Her guard will be down when she's tired."

We had neither dined alone nor seen a show together. Ever. My surprise must have shown on my face because he smiled as he handed me into the carriage. "Kettner's in Soho," he told Tucker.

"Do you have a reservation?" I asked as he settled opposite me.

"No, but they won't be busy this early."

"What sort of restaurant is it? Am I dressed appropriately? Shouldn't I change into something more elegant?"

"You look elegant enough to me." At my arched look, he added, "You're dressed appropriately."

Even so, I didn't relax until we were seated at a table in a quiet corner of the little restaurant with wood panel walls and polished tables. There were few other couples, and I did not feel out of place in my blue and white day dress. The

French proprietor greeted us with a heavy accent and signaled for a waiter to serve us. Once our orders were taken, Lincoln asked how the wedding plans progressed. I'd expected him to ask for my thoughts on Leonora Ballantine. He was full of surprises tonight.

We talked of the wedding as dusk turned to evening and the restaurant filled with more happy couples. Couples like us. *We* were a happy couple. Happy and normal, in our own way.

We didn't bother with the theater after leaving the restaurant nearly four hours later. The restaurant staff had not hurried us so we'd spent the evening talking quietly—but not about the murder. We discussed everything *except* ministry business. It was refreshing. Lincoln laughed and smiled; several times, in fact. I'd enjoyed myself so much that I forgot about Protheroe, Leonora and shape changers. It was vital that we learn who killed him and why, yet in those few hours, the world felt safe and wonderful. There was no reason to rush off, so we didn't.

"Are you warm enough?" Lincoln asked, as he signaled to the nearest hackney cab waiting for patrons to leave the music halls, small theaters and French eateries that squeezed into the street. He'd sent Tucker home before we entered Kettner's.

"I am," I said. "We made the right decision, Lincoln."

"I thought you'd like Kettner's."

I laughed softly. "I meant deciding to marry."

"Yes," he said quietly. "It was the right decision."

The hack took us back to the South Kensington residence of Leonora Ballantine. Lincoln paid the driver to wait for us then we crossed the road and descended the steps to the service area. It took a few minutes and more knocking before a footman dressed in full livery of swallow-tail coat with silver buttons and a white tie finally answered.

"Yes?" he snapped.

"Is Miss Ryan in?" Lincoln asked.

"She's busy." The footman went to close the door, but Lincoln wedged himself into the gap and forced it back wide.

"Please tell her Miss Holloway wishes to speak to her."

"I beg your pardon? What are you doing? You can't come in!"

Lincoln barged past him. "Is there somewhere we can wait?"

I gave the footman an apologetic smile. "We are sorry for the intrusion at this hour, but it is important we speak to her."

"What is it about?"

"A private matter," Lincoln said.

The footman sniffed then led us through to a small office that must be used by the housekeeper, going by the sewing kit on the desk. Shortly after the footman departed, the housekeeper arrived and questioned us again. And again, Lincoln said it was a private matter.

"We'll require the use of this room," he said.

His commanding manner worked. She stuttered an agreement then left to fetch the maid.

I turned back into the office after she shut the door and my heart stopped. The ghostly apparition of a young girl sat in the housekeeper's chair behind the desk. I placed a hand over my heart to settle it and attempted a smile.

"Good evening," I said. "My name is Charlie. What's yours?"

"Lilith," she murmured, blinking at me. "You can see me?"

Lincoln followed my gaze but remained silent. He'd guessed what I'd seen.

The girl, who couldn't have been more than ten or eleven, approached me. She would have had dark hair in life, although it was impossible to tell how dark from the sketchy outline of her spirit. She'd been pretty, with large eyes and a face that reminded me of Leonora's. But what struck me were her large hands and feet.

"I can see ghosts," I said. "And you are a ghost."

"I know that. I've been dead a year."

Most ghosts weren't aware of time progressing. Even those who chose to remain on this realm seemed to grow muddled when asked how long ago they'd died. "How do you know it's been a year?"

"I saw Mama wish my sister a happy eighteenth birthday not long ago." Ghostly fingers twirled a lock of hair around her finger. "Leonora had just had her seventeenth birthday when I died of a fever. I was ten."

"I'm very sorry," I said, perching on the edge of the desk. "You haven't crossed to your afterlife, Lilith. Why? Is something the matter?"

The twirling became more vigorous. "Mama asked me not to leave her. When I lay dying, she begged me not to go. So I won't. I'll stay here until she can join me, and then we'll cross together."

Tears welled unbidden. I nodded and gave her a wobbly smile. "You're a good girl to think of her. I'm sure she'll be happy to see you when her time comes."

The door opened just as Lilith asked me why I wanted to speak to Ryan. I winked then turned to the maid standing by the door, eyeing me with defiance. It would not be easy to extract answers from her. Lincoln may have to employ his usual methods after all.

"Miss Ryan," I began, "this is Mr. Fitzroy, my fiancé. We need to ask you something about Miss Ballantine that—"

"No." The maid crossed her arms over her chest. "And don't try and bribe me. You can't pay me enough to tattle. I won't tell you nothing."

"Anything," the ghost girl corrected. "Honestly, she's quite stupid. Loyal, but stupid. Leonora always did like her, though. Mama never understood why, but she gave in and allowed Leonora to have her as her maid after I died."

I nodded my appreciation of her candor in the hope of encouraging her to continue. The answer I needed might come from Lilith rather than the maid. "I know your mistress is very upset by Mr. Protheroe's death," I said to Ryan. "But it's imperative I know the name of the other gentleman seeking her hand."

Ryan turned her face away. "If she didn't tell you then I won't." So she knew it.

"He may be responsible for Mr. Protheroe's death."

"Really?" Little Lilith came to stand beside Ryan, her features crumpled into a frown. "I wish I remembered it. I heard Leonora call him by his first name. I think it started with the letter E." She cupped her hands around her mouth and whispered. "Leonora let him touch her here." She indicated her chest. "I thought it was wrong but Father told her it was what all men did when they were in love. He said it shows how much regard the man had for her. He then urged her to allow the gentleman to do more in order to secure his affections."

"Well," I said, feeling a little overwhelmed by her tale and quite uncomfortable.

Ryan must have thought I was prompting her to answer my question. "We weren't introduced." The maid gave me a smug look, thinking she'd outwitted me. "If it's so important to find out his name then Miss Ballantine will tell you."

"I wish I could remember," Lilith said, inspecting the maid. She even touched her face. Ryan didn't so much as blink.

"It's quite all right," I said.

"Who're you talking to?" Ryan backed up and would have stepped on Lincoln's toes if he hadn't laid a hand on her

87

shoulder. He'd moved to block the door so she couldn't escape. She whimpered and her gaze darted around the room. "There's someone else in here, isn't there? Miss Lilith? Is it her ghost?"

"She's right in front of you," I said.

Ryan covered her mouth, smothering her small squeal. Her big eyes turned to me. "N-necromancer."

"You remembered," I said. "Did Leonora tell you what a necromancer does?"

She nodded quickly. Her face had gone as white as Lilith's. The girl looked as though she were enjoying the exchange, dancing around the room on bare ghostly toes.

"Then you'll know that Lilith is able to tell me all sorts of things about you," I said. "For example, I know you let Mr. Protheroe into the house via the service stairs."

"I—I didn't!"

"She did too!" Lilith cried. "She let him in and took him up to Leonora's room. They were going to run away together. Father would have been furious."

"Miss Ryan," I said, gently, "I do not want you to lose your position here, so please cooperate. If you do not, I'll be forced to inform Lord Ballantine of your disobedience."

"No! Please don't do that. I want to stay here. I like being Miss Ballantine's maid. She's so pretty and kind to me. She gives me little trinkets, sometimes."

"Very well," I said. "I won't inform Lord Ballantine, but you must tell me the name of Leonora's second suitor."

"Freddie," she blurted out.

Lilith shook her head. "No, that's not it." She twirled her hair around her finger. "It started with an E, not an F."

"Lilith informs me the man's name began with an E," I said. "Please don't lie to me again, Miss Ryan. Lilith will be furious."

"Good show, Charlie." Lilith attempted to clap her hands, but they passed through one another.

Ryan began to cry, her entire body shaking. I put my arm around her shoulders. Lincoln watched on silently. "I don't like doing this," I said to the maid. "It pains me to force you to go against your mistress's wishes. You must understand that Miss Ballantine wanted me to know, but her conscience wouldn't allow her to speak his name. If *you* speak it, then her conscience is clear. So you see, it's quite all right that you tell me."

Lincoln smirked and nodded his approval at my new tactic.

Lilith's ghostly fingers attempted to open my reticule but gave up. I opened it instead and pulled out my handkerchief. Ryan took it and dabbed at her eyes.

"Very well," she said, her voice shaking. "If you think it's what Miss Ballantine would want."

"I do."

"I didn't hear his last name or if he had a title," she said. "Lord and Lady Ballantine never used it when any servants were near. But I was in Miss Ballantine's dressing room when I heard her refer to him as Eddy when she talked to her mother one night."

"Eddy!" Lilith cried. "That's it. Yes. Eddy."

"And how did Miss Ballantine meet Eddy?" I asked.

"How should I know?" Ryan said. "How do any of that sort meet one another?"

"Is there anything else you can tell us about him? Something that may identify him?" Half of England was named Edward. Finding this particular one would be almost impossible.

"He was a gentleman," Ryan said. "Lord Ballantine bowed to him, so I think he was more important than his lordship. That's all I know."

"Thank you, Miss Ryan. You've been a good, loyal servant to Miss Ballantine. It's no wonder she likes you."

"You won't tell Lord Ballantine what I done to help my mistress see her love?"

"No. Your secret is safe."

"And the ghost?"

"What about her?"

"Will you tell her to go away? She gives everyone down here the jitters. We know she's haunting the house. We can *feel* her."

Lilith crossed her arms again and struck a pose of childish petulance. "I'm not going anywhere until Mama comes for me."

"I'm afraid that won't be possible," I told Ryan. "But rest assured, she's quite harmless. She won't disturb you or anyone else as long as you remain loyal to her sister."

"And Mama. Not Father, though." Lilith pulled a face. "I don't care about him."

"And Lady Ballantine, too," I added.

Lincoln stepped aside and opened the door for Ryan. She slipped through and glanced back, scanning the room for the ghost, perhaps, before Lincoln closed the door. I was glad he did. I needed a quick word with Lilith.

"I am sorry we don't know that man's full name," Lilith said. "I liked Mr. Protheroe, and I want you to find his killer."

"You did your best. Thank you for your help tonight." I smiled gently and hoped she would not be offended by my next remark. "One more thing before you go. I see that you're a shape changer."

Lilith's spirit swirled like dust caught in a whirly wind then reformed. "Shhh," she whispered, a finger to her lips. "No one must know. Mama says it's our secret."

"I won't tell anyone. I know Leonora is one too, but what about your parents?"

"Both Mama and Father change into animals."

"Are their other forms always the same?" I asked, recalling how King could change into anything.

She nodded. "We look like wolves, but we're not."

"What about your pack? Who is your leader?"

"What's a pack?"

"The other people like you. The creatures you run with."

She stared blankly back at me. "I don't—didn't—run with anyone. I was too young, so Mama said."

"Whom did your parents run with then? Or Leonora?"

The door opened and the housekeeper ordered us to leave. I appealed to Lilith's ghost, jerking my head to indicate she should follow us to the front door.

"Lilith?" I whispered.

The housekeeper's step faltered. She looked at me then up and down the corridor, her throat working with her rapid swallows.

"I don't know who Mama and Father ran with," Lilith told me. "Leonora wasn't allowed to join them, even though she wants to. I've heard her ask Mama, but Mama said she's not ready. We were only allowed to change in private, when the servants had their afternoon off."

The housekeeper opened the front door and stood guard by it until we left. "Please make an appointment next time you wish to speak to one of the maids, sir." She shut the door in our faces, but not before Lilith gave me a wave goodbye.

* * *

"The victim's lover is a shape changer," Lincoln told Gus and Seth after we informed them of our movements today. The four of us sat in his office, the men with a glass of brandy and me clutching a cup of chocolate. The rest of the household had gone to bed.

"Blimey," Gus muttered.

"According to her dead younger sister, Leonora is too young to run with other shape changers," I said. "It does seem as if the parents are part of a pack, however."

"Now that is interesting," Seth said. "What are the chances the secret lover is a member of that pack?" We had already told them about the man named Eddy and his rival suit for Leonora's hand.

"Very likely," Lincoln said.

"He's probably the murderer." Gus drained his glass and held it out for a refill.

Lincoln picked up the crystal decanter from the drinks table. "Or it may be Leonora's father, wanting to keep the bloodline pure."

Seth nodded slowly, mulling it over. "Or the pack leader, if Ballantine isn't."

"We got to find out who is," Gus said.

Seth grunted. "How clever you are."

Gus rolled his eyes. "He's been like this all day, Charlie, because Alice don't want to talk to him."

"She does." Seth sniffed. "She was simply busy today, playing the piano and chatting to my mother. I didn't want to interrupt."

"Wish you'd find yourself a merry widow," Gus muttered into his glass. "Been too long, that's your problem."

"Don't be so crass in front of Charlie. And it hasn't been too long." He counted on his fingers and looked surprised when he needed a second hand. "Bloody hell," he muttered and stopped counting.

"We are in agreement," Lincoln said. "We must find out who else is in Ballantine's pack and who leads them. It may well be Ballantine himself, but I want to know for certain."

"We can ask the committee members what they know about him," I said. "If he's an important man in his social circle then he could be the pack leader. We should speak to them tomorrow."

"After we speak to Gawler again. If the killer wants the bloodline to remain pure then the obvious choice for a mate is from Gawler's pack. A mate chosen from them keeps the shape shifting trait strong while avoiding issues that arise from breeding within the same pack."

"You think Gawler lied to you?" I asked. "You think he does know something about them?"

Lincoln nodded. "The city is too small for two packs not to cross paths." I did not like the fierce look in his eyes. He hated when people lied to him.

"You'll be needing us then," Seth said, rising. "I'd better get to bed and rest."

"You sound like an old man," Gus said, also rising. "Let's go out. You've been trapped in here too long. You need some entertainment."

"It's been entertaining here."

Gus looked as if he was about to comment, but I shook my head in warning. "Well? Want to visit a gambling house? A fight?"

"Not tonight. Tomorrow, perhaps. But I won't gamble."

"Aye, I know."

"And I won't participate in any fights," Seth said. "My face has endured enough bruises of late."

"You don't have to do anything that will make you look even uglier."

Seth clapped him on the shoulder as they left. "We both know you think I'm handsome. There's no need to pretend otherwise."

* * *

WE FOUND Gawler at the Jolly Joker, a tavern that couldn't be

C.J. ARCHER

more unlike its name. The narrow building was wedged between two taller tenements on an East End street that looked as if daylight and a broom hadn't touched it in years. It was even darker inside with only a single hissing lamp. Three men sitting on stools at the bar looked up as we entered. Gawler groaned and hunkered over his tankard, protecting it between his hands.

"What d'you want?" he growled.

I followed Lincoln in, Seth and Gus at my back. One of the men stood and looked down his florid nose at us. "I don't want no trouble."

"You'll get none," I said when Lincoln didn't answer. "As long as Mr. Gawler cooperates."

The man limped around to the other side of the counter, taking his tankard of ale with him. The third man stood and backed away, stopping when he stumbled into a stool.

"A word," Lincoln said to Gawler.

Gawler sighed and indicated a table away from the bar. He held a chair out for me and I sat, folding my hands on the table surface. It was sticky so I removed them again. Both Gawler and Lincoln sat too. Gus cracked his knuckles. Gawler swallowed heavily.

"Tell me what you know about the other shape shifter pack," Lincoln said. "And this time I want a truthful answer."

"I have been truthful!" Gawler tucked his hands between his legs. "Mr. Fitzroy, sir, please. I don't know nothing about them."

"You knew of their existence."

"Aye, but they keep to themselves and so do we. They want nothing to do with us. We ain't good enough for them."

"How do you know that if you've never spoken to them?"

Gawler paled as he realized his mistake. "I never *spoke* to them."

"You communicated in your other form?"

Gawler glanced toward the two other drinkers then leaned forward. "We talked once in our animal form. Well, it ain't talking. Not like this. It's grunts and sounds, mostly, with body movements and the like to show what we mean."

"And what did you discuss?"

He shrugged and clutched his tankard hard. "Nothing."

Lincoln's hand whipped out and grabbed Gawler's jacket lapel. Ale spilled over the tankard rim and splashed on the table. Lincoln twisted his fingers into the fabric, tightening the collar until Gawler's face turned red. "I don't have time for games," Lincoln said calmly. "Tell me what you discussed."

I took out several coins from my reticule and placed them on the table. "For your next drink." I checked how much I'd set down. "Or several."

Gawler managed a nod and choked out some incoherent words. Lincoln let him go and Gawler slumped into his chair, coughing spittle down his chin. He rubbed his throat and swallowed several times before managing to speak. "It were about territories. We decided to keep to the East End and they could have the better parts of the city. There was no fighting."

"Was King with you then?"

Gawler nodded and wrapped his big hand around his tankard. "He fought me for the leadership soon after."

And won, sending Gawler away to live and run alone.

"Did King meet them again?" Lincoln asked.

"I don't know."

"And you have no idea of the human identity of any of the pack members?" I asked.

He met my gaze and shook his head. "No, ma'am."

"We believe a gentleman by the name of Lord Ballantine is part of that pack," Lincoln said. "Does the name mean anything to you?"

Again, Gawler shook his head. He hunched over his

tankard, looking more miserable with every passing minute. "I don't know their names or what they look like in human form, and no one from my pack does either. All I know is there were six or seven of them. They came from nowhere one night. After that, they left us alone and we never saw 'em again."

Lincoln remained silent a moment then suddenly stood. Gawler slunk down, as if he expected Lincoln to strike him.

"Do not lie to me again," Lincoln said.

"It weren't a lie!" Gawler cried. "I never *spoke* to 'em before, it's God's truth."

"Barking is speaking," Seth told him. "It's just a dog's way of speaking."

"We ain't dogs."

Lincoln walked off and held the tavern door open for me. He seemed tense but that could have been because he was staying alert for trouble. If Gawler had been with other pack members, this conversation could have ended differently. It was possible they were not far away, although all *should* be at work in the middle of the day.

"Barking ain't speaking," Gus said to Seth as we climbed into the coach.

"It is if it's how dogs communicate," Seth shot back.

"But that ain't speaking."

Seth appealed to me. "You want that pedant walking on your left on your wedding day, Charlie?"

I held up my hands. "Leave me out of this."

Lincoln ordered Tucker to drive us on to Lord Gillingham's house. Thankfully Seth and Gus ceased their arguing and fell into a discussion about the two London packs and whether they would always live in the same city harmoniously. We all concluded that their truce seemed as sturdy as a boat built from straw.

Harriet and Lord Gillingham were at home. Harriet

patted the sofa beside her and beckoned me to sit while a footman fetched Lord Gillingham.

"What a pleasant surprise to see you, Charlie," Harriet said. "And Seth, too. Oh, and Mr. Fitzroy and...your man."

Seth smirked. Gus didn't look the least upset that Harriet had forgotten his name.

"We've just come from seeing Gawler," Lincoln said, launching into our reason for calling.

Harriet pouted, perhaps sorry not to exchange gossip first. "Let's wait for Gilly before we begin. He'll be down soon. Owen, bring tea for our guests, will you?"

"Tea would be lovely," I said with a glare for Lincoln.

He pressed his lips together but did not refuse the offer of tea.

"How are you feeling, Harriet?" I asked her as the butler departed.

"Very well," she said, touching her belly and smiling. "Very well indeed."

Gillingham joined us, walking perfectly fine despite not having a walking stick to lean on. He greeted Lincoln but merely nodded at Seth. He didn't acknowledge either Gus or me at all. "Harriet told me about the murdering shifter," he said. "You could have called a meeting if you have to make a report, Fitzroy."

"I'm not making a report," Lincoln said. "We're here to ask both you and Lady Gillingham some questions."

Gillingham looked at his wife then ordered the footman to close the door and not disturb us.

"But I've asked for tea," Harriet said.

"Forget tea."

She sighed. "Very well. But come and stand by me" She held out her hand. He hesitated. She beckoned him with a wave. "Come, my dear. I want you to stand by me. You look so small next to Mr. Fitzroy and Seth."

97

Gillingham stretched his neck out of his collar as a blush crept up it. He joined his wife and stood by the sofa but did not hold her hand. She lowered it to her lap, her face a picture of disappointment. Gillingham noticed and lifted a hand. After a hesitation, he finally settled it on her shoulder. She smiled coquettishly up at him.

"What do you know about Lord Ballantine?" Lincoln asked.

Gillingham shook his head. "Very little. He's rich and well connected. Comes and goes from London, but I can't recall where his seat is."

"Bristol region."

"Harriet?" I asked. "Have you met Lord or Lady Ballantine? Or their daughter?"

"Not that I recall." She frowned hard then shook her head. "What rank is he?"

"Baron."

"That explains it," she said, as if it did. "And Lady Ballantine's people?"

"We don't know anything about them. Both Lord and Lady Ballantine are shape shifters."

"Oh!" She placed a hand over her black ribbon choker. "How marvelous! Are they part of the other secret pack?"

"Possibly," Lincoln said.

Gillingham patted his wife's shoulder lightly as if he wasn't quite sure he could trust her not to bite off his hand. "It's best if you don't meet them, my dear. They must be involved in this murder or Fitzroy wouldn't be asking about them."

They both looked to Lincoln. He neither confirmed nor denied it.

"Best to lay low now, anyway," Gillingham told her. "Wouldn't want to harm the baby, would you?"

A dreamy smile crossed her lips. "You're right. You're very good to think of me and Wolfy, Gilly."

"Wolfy?" I asked, as Gillingham made an odd sort of choking-coughing sound.

"The pet name I gave the baby," Harriet said, beaming. "I thought it was appropriate, considering it will be half like me. Gilly doesn't want me to call it that in public, but you're not the public." She placed her hand over his, completely covering it with her larger one.

Gillingham tried to tug free but she did not let him go. "Stop fretting, Gilly. These are our friends."

"Do you know anyone who associates with Ballantine?" Lincoln asked.

"The Prince of Wales, of course," Gillingham said. "He's part of that set, along with Underwood."

Well, well. Now *that* was an interesting connection.

"Speak with Julia," Gillingham added. "She'll have met him."

"That woman." Harriet pulled a face. "Stay away from her, Seth. You know what she's like."

Seth blinked, startled. "Er, yes. I'll be on my guard."

"You should have called a meeting about this, Fitzroy," Gillingham said.

"I will when I have something to tell you," Lincoln said.

"If there's nothing else…?" Gillingham pulled free and strode quickly toward the door. He flung it open and beckoned his butler.

"You be on your guard too, Charlie," Harriet whispered as she walked out with me. "Julia may have Lord Underwood to amuse her now, but she's always looking for new lovers and Mr. Fitzroy is just a man, after all."

"Uh, yes. I will be alert."

"He does seem utterly devoted to you, however. Just like my Gilly is to me. *Now.*" She smiled at her husband.

He spun on his heel and walked quickly off, taking the main stairs two at a time. The walking stick he usually carried was certainly an affectation, then.

We drove on to Lady Harcourt's Mayfair house where she lived with her stepson, Andrew Buchanan. He was not at home, however, and I was glad. Conversation with him was a trial.

"Probably out drinking," Seth muttered to me as we entered the drawing room where Lady Harcourt sat in a jade green and cobalt blue gown to receive us.

She was the picture of civility and elegance, but a closer inspection revealed the deeper grooves around her mouth and lackluster eyes. Something troubled her.

"Are you all right, Julia?" Seth asked, ever the gentleman. "You look unwell."

"Perfectly all right, thank you." She tucked a letter she'd been reading into the folds of her skirt. "This is quite the force. Is something wrong at Lichfield?"

"We need to ask about a friend of Lord Underwood's," Lincoln said.

"Underwood!" bellowed Buchanan, swaggering through the door. "Not that blathering fool again. Julia is still seeing him, you know, despite his interest in your friend, Charlotte."

I sighed. This interview was going to take longer now he was here.

"Stop it, Andrew," Lady Harcourt hissed.

He cocked his head to the side, considering, then said, "No, I don't believe I want to stop." He loosened his tie and undid his waistcoat buttons then flopped into a chair. He belched and wiped his hand across his mouth. "Yes, I'm drunk," he said. "Hardly surprising, is it? I mean, who wouldn't want to be drunk all the time while living here? It's the only way to get through the day. The nights, however..."

His mouth twisted into a cruel smile. "Those are worth being sober for."

Lady Harcourt closed her eyes and went very still, as if holding herself together. Was this how she lived now? With Buchanan coming home drunk in the middle of the day and mercilessly berating her?

"Stop it, Buchanan," Seth snapped. "You're making a fool of yourself."

"Me? Ha! You ought to have seen her the night after your dinner party. She begged Underwood not to leave her unsatisfied. But he didn't come in, so she begged me—"

"*Andrew!*" Lady Harcourt cried. Her chest heaved with her gasping breaths and her face turned a vibrant shade of red. Very little ruffled her feathers, but her stepson seemed to know which points to press.

"Enough!" Lincoln growled. "We need to ask Julia questions relating to a murder reported in the newspaper."

Buchanan snorted. "Don't believe everything you read in the paper. Oh, wait. Perhaps you should, if the source is a reliable one." His wet chuckle ended in a snort. "A reliable witness could be someone who knows what happened, who was there, watching the entire thing play out like a bad dream."

Everyone except Lady Harcourt knew he was referring to the report in the newspapers that had exposed her past as a dancer at The Alhambra where she'd met her future husband, Buchanan's father. Andrew himself had been the source. But from the slowly dawning look on her face, the very clever Lady Harcourt was piecing it together now from his drunken rambling.

"Andrew," she murmured, staring at him. "Andrew, did *you*...?"

Realizing he'd underestimated her, he sniffed and flicked unseen dust from his trouser legs. "We're not talking about *that* newspaper article. Your vanity knows no bounds, Julia. Not everything is about you."

He protested too much, and he didn't look at her. He was a hopeless liar.

An eerie silence thickened the air. Lady Harcourt's bloodless lips moved but no words came out. She stared at him, her eyes filling with tears. Then her body twitched, as if something inside her snapped. Her eyes dried and her lips peeled back from her teeth.

She shot to her feet and flung herself at Buchanan. He did not see her until she wrapped long, slender fingers around his neck. "I'll kill you!" she screamed.

CHAPTER 7

The reactions of Lincoln, Seth and Gus were not ordinarily slow, but it took a few moments before they wrestled Lady Harcourt off Buchanan. By that time she'd managed to scratch his face and spit in his eye.

Buchanan cowered in the chair, legs raised to protect his nether regions, and he held his arms up to shield his head from further injuries and spittle. Lady Harcourt struggled to free herself from Lincoln's grip. She did not give up, nor did she halt the stream of vile words spewing from her mouth. There was nothing of the lady about her now. She was all teeth and red, blotchy cheeks as she called Buchanan names I hadn't heard in months.

Realizing he was safe, Buchanan unfurled himself and wiped his sleeve across his eyes. When his fingers came away bloody after touching his face, he paled. "You bitch! That'll leave scars!"

"I hate you!" she shouted back. "I hate the sight of you!"

"Julia," Seth warned, "calm down. The servants can hear you. The entire street can hear you."

"I don't care," she snarled at him. She wrenched free of Lincoln's grip. Or, more likely, he let her go.

Buchanan shrank into his chair again until he realized she wouldn't attack him a second time. He removed his handkerchief and dabbed at the three scratches on his cheek. It looked like claws had left them.

"How could you?" she railed at him. "How could you do this to me after everything we've meant to one another?"

The muscles in his face hardened. His eyes narrowed. He slowly stood and took two determined steps toward her until Lincoln put up his hand to halt him. "What did we mean to one another, Julia?" His vicious snarl matched hers for venom. "Answer me that! Did you ever like me? Did you ever enjoy my company the way I enjoyed yours? Or was I simply a stepping stone to get you where you wanted to go? As soon as my father appeared at The Al, you walked all over me to get to him, and you've been walking over me ever since." He choked out a bitter laugh. "Until your star fell from its lofty heights and you needed me to secure you invitations, that is."

"My star fell because *you* went to the newspapers!" She folded her arms, much of the fight leaving her, although I suspected a spark would ignite it again at any moment. "Anyway, I no longer need you for anything. I have Lord Underwood and his friends now. They appreciate me."

"For how long? Underwood is already losing interest. You saw how he treated that girl the night of the Lichfield dinner."

"Alice is not 'that girl,'" Seth snapped before I could. "And don't bring her into this. She's far too good for this sordid discussion."

"She's too good for you, then." Buchanan's chuckle came out strangled. "When it comes to sordid, you're the king of the heap."

Seth punched him. He must have pulled back, however,

or Buchanan would have lost some teeth. As it was, he stumbled to the floor, clutching his jaw. Nobody went to his aid.

"You ought to keep your dogs on a leash, Fitzroy," Buchanan said as he picked himself up.

"You're a glutton for punishment," Gus said with a shake of his head.

And therein lay the problem. Buchanan hated himself. He hated what he'd become, and he hated that he was in love with a woman he couldn't have and who didn't love him back. He hated his desperation and possibly the erosion of any good qualities he may have once possessed. But even more so, he hated that he didn't know how to—or didn't want to—change.

I'd met men like him when I lived on the streets. Society fretted about "fallen women" and yet, in my experience, there were more men than women falling from their perches. Men like Andrew Buchanan, who'd been given so much in life but failed to fulfill the expectations of others, as well as their own. Instead of picking themselves out of the gutter and taking steps to correct their failures, they'd chosen to wallow there and blame others for their misfortune. Some drank themselves to an early grave. Some froze to death in winter. Some took their hatred of themselves and the world out on others. Those were the ones I learned to avoid. Those men could be dangerous.

Andrew Buchanan fitted into that category.

"Want to swipe at me again, eh?" Buchanan goaded Seth. "Want to be the hero in front of the ladies?"

Seth let out a long, measured breath, and I relaxed. His temper had cooled and he wouldn't be tempted to hit Buchanan again.

Buchanan must have realized his goading wouldn't work anymore. "God, how I hate you, Vickers," he blurted out. "I should hate *him* for the hold he had over Julia for so long." He angled his bruised jaw at Lincoln. "But you...*you* are everything I loathe in a man."

Seth looked taken aback by the viciousness, but I wasn't. Buchanan saw Seth as the man he could have been, and he felt like a failure in comparison. Both men were handsome, from gentry stock, with the world and women at their feet. They had grown up with everything before both men had fallen low. Yet Seth had pulled himself out of the quagmire, while Buchanan remained there. Seth was the master of his own life again, whereas Buchanan was at the mercy of Lady Harcourt's whims. He wished he were Seth and yet he wasn't prepared to emulate his hard work.

"Get out!" Lady Harcourt screamed at Buchanan. "Get out of my house!"

"You can't throw me out," he said with a slick smile. "My father's will stipulated that I have a home here."

Her chest rose and fell with her deep breaths and her hands fisted at her sides. I worried that she might attack him again. Lincoln would stop her, though, perhaps after a hesitation in which she had enough time to inflict more damage.

"Leave us, Buchanan," Lincoln ordered. "We have ministry business with Julia."

"I should hear it," Buchanan said. "I am going to replace her, one day, after all."

"*If* you outlive her," Seth said. "That's not looking likely at this moment."

Buchanan snorted. "Is that a threat, Vickers?"

One corner of Seth's mouth flicked up into a wicked smile.

"Seth, Gus," Lincoln ordered. "Remove him."

"Gladly." Seth grasped Buchanan's arm and Gus took the other. They dragged him from the room and tossed him out.

Buchanan landed in a heap on the entrance hall tiles. Seth shut the door and dusted his hands.

"This will get out, Julia," he warned her. "Your servants will talk."

She inclined her head then sat regally on the sofa. If it weren't for the slight flush lingering on her cheeks, it would be impossible to reconcile this woman with the wildcat of earlier.

I went to sit too, but noticed a piece of paper on the floor. No, not paper, a card. It had fallen out of Lady Harcourt's pocket when she flew into a rage. I picked it up and, unable to control the compulsion to glance at it, read the names the anonymous writer called Lady Harcourt. It was difficult not to see the words "vile," "immoral" and "debauched" since they were underlined and written in a large hand. It would seem associating with Lord Underwood hadn't polished away the tarnish marring Lady Harcourt's reputation. Perhaps because Lord Underwood had no intention of marrying her.

I handed it to her and she scrunched it in her fist. "What do you want?" she said without the hint of a quiver in her voice.

"Do you know Lord Ballantine?" Lincoln asked.

She nodded. "He attends parties with Lord Underwood sometimes."

"As part of the Prince of Wales's set?"

"Yes. Has he done something wrong?"

"His daughter was the lover of a man mauled to death, most likely by a human in his other form of a wolf-like creature."

Her brows lifted. "You think Lord Ballantine is involved in the death?"

"He is also a shape shifter, as is his wife and the daughter."

She considered this a moment as if it were no more newsworthy than idle gossip. "I didn't realize."

"Why would you?" Seth said. "They would hardly go about telling people."

"Tell us what you know about him," Lincoln said. "And about Lady Ballantine."

"I've met them both." She touched her hair and tucked away a strand that had worked loose from the complex arrangement. "He is a sycophant. She seems a little unsophisticated and out of place among the prince's friends. I don't think she's used to such illustrious company."

"Do you think him capable of murder?"

Her gaze slid to the closed door. "Anyone is capable of murder if pushed too far."

"Do you think anyone else from that set is a shape shifter?" Lincoln asked.

"I didn't know Lord Ballantine was one until you told me."

"And what of a young gentleman by the name of Eddy? Does that name mean anything to you?"

She thought for a moment. "There is Edward De Greer, but he's over forty. Indeed, there are few young gentlemen at the prince's parties. He prefers more mature company. Who is Eddy?"

"A rival suitor for Lord Ballantine's daughter's hand."

"Ah." She nodded knowingly. "A love triangle. We all know how dangerous those can be."

Whether she meant the love triangle involving herself, Lincoln and me, or herself Buchanan and Lord Harcourt, I couldn't tell. Her glassy eyes and calm manner gave nothing away.

"If you find this Eddy fellow, you will find your killer, Lincoln," she said. "Do be careful. Lovesick puppies can be sinister." She glanced again at the closed door. So she was referring to *that* love triangle.

"Grown men are hardly puppies," I said. "Even lovesick ones."

She looked surprised that I'd spoken. Surprise turned to distain with a curl of her top lip.

Lincoln didn't fill the silence that followed so I filled it instead. "Thank you, Lady Harcourt." I was about to rise when I had an idea. "When will you see Lord Underwood and his friends again?"

"He's holding a...a dance tomorrow night."

"Can you secure Lincoln and I an invitation?"

Lincoln didn't move, so I suspected he approved of my suggestion.

"And me," Seth said.

Lady Harcourt shook her head. "That's impossible."

"Nothing is impossible," Lincoln said. "Secure us an invitation."

She bristled. "No."

"I have some sway with the Prince of Wales now," Lincoln told her. "I could put in a good word for you."

She twisted a large gold and sapphire ring on her finger and met his gaze. He didn't blink. After a moment of taut silence, she sighed. "Very well. I'll have an invitation for you and Seth by the end of the day. But not for Charlie."

It was my turn to bristle. "Why not?"

"You're too...pure."

I laughed. "You do remember where I spent five years of my life."

"Ah," Seth said with a nod. "One of *those* sorts of dances. She's right, Charlie. You shouldn't go."

"I am definitely going now," I told them both, and Lincoln too before he could agree with them. "It sounds intriguing."

Seth rolled his eyes to the ceiling. "I should have kept my mouth shut."

"Aye," Gus nodded darkly. "Charlie, if Seth thinks you shouldn't go, you shouldn't go."

"They will find her of great interest, Lincoln," Lady Harcourt warned with a silky smile. "She's young and pretty and not everyone knows you well enough to fear you."

"They will quickly learn if they try to touch her," he said simply.

"If the prince is there, I'm sure I'll be safe from any roving hands," I said. "He may like his women and wine, but he's still a gentleman. As is Lord Underwood."

She sighed, and I knew she couldn't argue my point. "Very well. Beyond securing the invitations, I will *not* be part of any interrogations. I cannot afford to upset anyone right now, particularly Lord Underwood and his friends."

Lincoln agreed with a nod.

We made to leave, but before he opened the door, Lincoln addressed Lady Harcourt. "Do you want me to have a word with Buchanan?"

"And threaten him? I doubt it will make a difference." She laid a hand on his arm, massaging with her thumb, and tipped her head back to peer up at him. "Thank you, Lincoln. Despite everything, you remain a true friend." She let him go, or perhaps he moved.

"You courted this, you know," Seth said with a nod at the door through which Buchanan had exited. "You threw fuel onto a fire then wondered why it burned fiercer."

"Do be quiet," she spat back, proving that her serenity was all for show. "*You* can hardly talk. The only reason you're not still being beaten up for sport or auctioning yourself off to the highest bidder is because Lincoln saved you." She made a shooing motion with her hands. "Go! All of you, leave me in peace. My head aches."

Seth opened the door to see Buchanan sitting on the floor, outstretched legs spread wide, a brandy tumbler in hand and another beside him. He lurched to his feet and picked up the glass. He sauntered across the floor on wobbly legs, a drunken smile in place, and held out the tumbler to Lady Harcourt.

"You look remarkably alluring all riled up like this." He

smiled and held the glass out further. "Thought you might need this."

She hesitated then took it. The liquid rippled with the trembling of her hands. She sniffed it, as if she suspected it might be poisoned, then sipped.

"There now," Buchanan said. "We're friends again."

"Where are the servants?" Lady Harcourt asked.

"Cowering downstairs, afraid to venture up. Ah, here's the indomitable Millard, come to see out our guests."

The butler had always seemed so fierce and proper, yet even he looked unsure how to treat his master and mistress now. They must have heard the row downstairs. All of London's servants would be made aware of it by the end of the week, and some would pass on the gossip to their employers. Lady Harcourt would be ruined even more. The only thing saving her was Lord Underwood's favor, and that thread was thinning.

"Good afternoon," Lady Harcourt said with a small, sad smile for Lincoln. "Millard will see you out."

She turned and headed up the staircase, the glass dangling from her fingertips. She moved smoothly, her hips swaying and loose strands of hair tumbling down her back.

Buchanan followed but stopped on the bottom step. "Off you go," he said to us. "There's no need to worry."

We all watched him follow his stepmother up the stairs, her steps slow and seductive, his quick and unsteady.

"Should we leave them alone together?" Gus asked.

Nobody answered. Millard opened the front door for us. His eyes had resumed their usual blankness, and his back was as straight as ever.

"You know where to find me," Lincoln told him as he exited.

The butler gave a single nod and shut the door.

Lincoln assisted me into the carriage, and I sat with a

deep sigh. "Sometimes I wish we'd left Buchanan in Bedlam," I said.

Seth settled opposite me. "Only sometimes?"

* * *

I EXPECTED Lincoln to try to talk me out of going to the party, but he did not. Not even when we went for an afternoon walk through the orchard. Spring blossoms covered the trees and carpeted the ground, and bees darted merrily between branches, spoiled for choice. The prettiness was a welcome antidote to the sordid visit to Lady Harcourt's house.

"Do you think they'll be all right?" I asked, unable to forget the topic.

"Julia and Buchanan?" he said, as if he'd already set thoughts of them aside. "Don't worry about them. They know what they're doing."

"But they're so destructive and cruel toward one another. Where will it end?"

He didn't answer that. I suspected he didn't have the answer. I, for one, couldn't see it ending until Lady Harcourt found herself a new husband and moved out of the house. It may have been left to her in Lord Harcourt's will, but she would never be free of Buchanan while he lived there.

"I wrote to Leisl," Lincoln announced.

I stopped and took his hands in mine. "That's wonderful. I knew you could express your feelings to her if you just tried."

"I told her that someone followed us to her house and to be careful of spies."

"Oh. That's…sensible. Is that why you brought me out here? To tell me?"

"No." He looked back at the house. Seeing if anyone

watched us? Was he finally going to do more than simply kiss me?

I reached up and wrapped both arms behind his head. "Go on, Lincoln," I said in a breathy voice.

His mouth twitched which I took to mean my seductive voice needed practice. "There are three reasons why I brought you out here." He circled his arms around my waist and drew me gently against his body. He kissed the skin beneath my earlobe. "First," he murmured, "where do you want to go on our honeymoon?"

I giggled as his lips tickled. "I don't know. Not Paris again. Why not surprise me?"

"I know a nice little place in the Orient where they teach an ancient fighting technique. We could train together."

I pulled back to study his face. He was smiling. I thumped him lightly on the arm. "Very amusing."

"A surprise it is," he said. "But the discussion about training leads me to my second point. It's actually a question. Do you think the servants will be shocked if we practice out here on the lawn?"

We used to train outside in the warmer weather but retreated indoors to the ballroom during winter. We'd kept the doors shut so the servants couldn't see, but I saw no reason why they couldn't watch. "They'll grow used to it. Besides, we can't hide from them forever. They're probably already curious about the sounds coming from the ballroom every day."

"Lady Vickers won't like it."

"Lady Vickers is our guest. If she doesn't like it, she can move out."

"Yes, ma'am."

I gave him a withering glare before he dared salute me. "Both of those things you could have asked me in the house. So what is the third thing?"

"Ah." His arms tightened and his hands splayed at my back. "My third point is that I wanted to kiss you in one of my favorites places."

I smiled. "Beneath the blossoms in the orchard? I didn't know this was a favorite place of yours. You only ever come out here with me."

His lips brushed mine in a delicate, teasing touch. "That's what makes it one of my favorite places."

My smile widened. "Lincoln Fitzroy, you are quite the romantic."

"Don't tell anyone. I have a reputation to uphold."

He kissed me thoroughly until the breath left my body and my knees turned weak.

* * *

GUS AND SETH didn't get out of bed until noon the next day. According to Cook, whom I questioned in the parlor mid-morning, they'd returned near dawn after spending all night out.

"They started at a gambling house but that ain't no fun when you got no spare ready," Cook said, linking his fingers over his bulging stomach. He sat on the sofa, his legs stretched out and his ankles crossed. He looked like the lord of the manor. His apron spoiled the effect somewhat. "Then they went to an alehouse and then another, and then on to the private residence of a fancy woman."

"A fancy woman?"

"Lady this or that." He waved his hand in dismissal. "Prob'ly a widow, knowing Seth."

"Seth went to a lady's house? But he's—" I was about to say sweet on Alice, but stopped myself. Alice had not encouraged him, and Seth was a free man. He could do as he pleased. Still, I felt some disappointment in him. He may not have betrayed her, yet it felt like a betrayal of his feelings for her.

"They came home when I be firing up the range this morning." He chuckled. "Got sore heads, the both of 'em. I got a mind to bang the pots outside their rooms."

"So do I."

Two hours later, Seth ventured down. After spying his mother sitting with Alice and me in the parlor, he veered off to the library instead. I found him sitting at the desk, his forehead resting on his folded forearms.

"Did you eat breakfast?" I asked.

He groaned.

"Are you ill?"

"Yes," he mumbled into the desk.

"Is it self-inflicted?"

"You need to ask?"

I leaned my hip against the edge of the desk and waited until he glanced up at me through bloodshot eyes. "You look wretched."

"I feel wretched," he mumbled.

"Cook told me what you did."

He groaned again and lowered his head back down on his arms. "Spare me the lecture, Charlie. You can't possibly berate me more than I've already berated myself."

Well, that was promising. Perhaps his feelings for Alice ran deeper than I thought. "You drank too much," I said. "And I know the situation between Buchanan and Lady H affected you more than you let on yesterday. It's understandable that you sought…entertainment and…release."

"Don't excuse it."

"I'm not, but I don't like seeing you berate yourself either. You are not promised to…to anyone. You can do as you please."

He sat upright again and pinched the bridge of his nose

between thumb and forefinger. Blond hair flopped into his eyes until he pushed it back. "I've changed my mind. Lecture me, Charlie. I deserve it."

"I planned on coming in here and doing just that, but you don't seem to need it. You feel guilty enough."

"Today, yes," he said quietly. "But last night, I...I didn't care." He lifted heavy lids to meet my gaze. "That's the problem, Charlie. Last night I didn't think about Alice. I should have. Thoughts of her should have stopped me from being with another woman. Shouldn't it?"

My heart tugged. Poor Seth. He looked so vulnerable. I wanted my cavalier, confident friend back, not this confused wreck. "You were drunk," was the only comfort I could give him.

"Fitzroy would never do it to you, even before you got engaged." He kicked the desk leg. "No matter how drunk he got, he would never forget his feelings for you."

"He doesn't get drunk."

"That's because he's perfect. It's nauseating."

I bit back my smile. "Join us in the parlor. You can help me untangle a skein of wool for the knitting I've been putting off."

"You knit?"

"Alice is teaching me. I'm quite bad at it, but it's either that, sewing or embroidery when there's no investigating to do."

"Sounds dull."

"You have no idea," I said on a sigh. "Come on." I held out my hand to him. "We could do with some male company, and being near Alice will help you remember why you like her so much."

"Why do I get the feeling that I am the entertainment?" he asked, but he followed me anyway.

He dutifully spent the half hour before luncheon helping

me untangle a skein of wool, doing his best to ignore his mother's lecture about drinking until all hours. After five minutes I caught her eye and gave a half-shake of my head. She stopped; rather reluctantly, if her severely pursed lips were an indication.

Alice's cool gaze quickly assessed Seth's state upon his entry then returned to her embroidery. She glanced up at him often, but only through her lashes. He, however, ignored her. If I hadn't known he was embarrassed about his actions, I would have thought him rude.

I explained as much to Alice after luncheon when we sat by ourselves in the music room. I did not tell her all the details of his evening, but let her think his excessive drinking was to blame for his guilt. She didn't question me, merely accepting the explanation with a nod.

"He's a grown man," she said with apparent indifference. "He can do as he pleases. If he chooses to get drunk and gamble, it's none of my affair."

"Not gambling," I said. "He's very much against it after his father's excesses ruined the family."

She fell silent, and I thought the conversation over, but then she set down her embroidery and stared out the window. "He was so quiet earlier as he helped you with the wool, Charlie."

"It was most unlike him," I agreed.

"Is it? You mean he talks a lot all the time? I thought it was just because I made him nervous."

"Do you mean to say you prefer him when he's not talking?"

"It gives me a chance to admire his handsome face." She winked and laughed.

I would have laughed too but a movement outside caught my attention. "We have visitors."

Alice followed my gaze as the hansom cab pulled to a stop

on the drive. "None of the committee members have ever arrived in a hansom."

I watched as a woman climbed down and held her hand out to assist the second passenger. "It's not a committee member. It's Leisl and Eva."

Alice's sharp intake of breath was at odds with her sudden stillness. "Perhaps they learned more about me and my dreams." She stood and made her way to the sofa where she sat demurely, her hands clasped in her lap, her anxious gaze on the door, waiting.

Outside, Leisl suddenly turned to the window. She smiled at me. Eva noticed and looked too. She did not smile. She looked uneasy, as if she didn't want to enter the house.

She tilted her head back and clutched her hat to her head to stop it falling off. I knew how awe-inspiring Lichfield Towers could be upon first seeing it. With its dominant central tower used to harbor the occasional captive, it was not a pretty house. It was commanding, austere, and in poor light it looked grim. Yet I loved it more than any house, castle or hovel I'd lived in.

I sat alongside Alice on the sofa then rose as Doyle announced our guests. I greeted them both and asked Doyle to fetch Lincoln.

"Bring the others too," Leisl said.

"Others?" I asked. "Do you mean Seth and Gus?"

Leisl nodded. Eva frowned at her mother but Leisl didn't notice.

"I saw the way you looked at the house," I said to Eva as we waited. "I don't blame you for feeling overwhelmed. I did too upon first seeing it."

"It's not the house," Eva said.

I waited for her to explain why she seemed uncomfortable, but she didn't go on. She looked very pretty in a bold coral and black dress. It had no embellishments or lace, whereas her mother's layered skirt was swathed in ribbons, rosettes and beading. Eva didn't need the fussiness of trimmings. Her striking cheekbones, glorious dark hair and blue eyes were an alluring combination.

"I know it must feel awkward meeting your brother again," I said. "And I know you're not yet used to him, but he is a good man."

She lifted her eyebrows ever so slightly.

"He's like this house," I went on. "There's more to him than his severe façade. You just need time to get to know him."

My words didn't seem to have much effect in calming her nerves. She couldn't sit still and her gaze darted to the door at every sound. Finally Lincoln strode in. He greeted his mother and half-sister cordially. I scowled at him when he looked my way and he paused.

"It's a pleasure to see you both again," he added. "Will you stay for tea?" He shot me a questioning look, and I nodded my approval.

"Yes, tea is nice," Leisl said.

Seth and Gus strolled in. Time had improved Seth's appearance and he no longer bore the signs of a late night and excessive drinking. I wasn't the only one to notice. Beside me, Alice's back straightened, a small sign that she wanted him to notice her. I smiled.

And then I saw Eva's reaction. She'd noticed the men enter but now stared down at the floor with fierce intensity.

"We were not introduced last time," Leisl said with a smile for them both.

"Leisl, Eva," Lincoln said, taking the hint, "this is Gus—Mr. Sullivan—and...Lord Vickers."

Eva's head snapped up. She blinked at the men, a look of utter stupefaction on her face. Her mother was caught unawares by Seth's title too, but she recovered first.

"It is a pleasure to meet you, my lord, Mr. Sullivan," she said.

"Call me Gus," said Gus. "Everyone does. And he's Seth. Don't mind the lord business. We don't stand on ceremony here, do we, Fitzroy?"

"Don't let Lady Vickers hear you say that," Lincoln said.

"Lady Vickers?" Leisl asked with a tilt of her head.

"My mother," Seth said. "She's out. She will be sorry to have missed you."

"Ah. And we her. You must call us Leisl and Eva, since we are like family, no?"

Lincoln sat heavily in an armchair with a similar startled expression to the one his half-sister wore. It would seem this meeting had overwhelmed them both.

"Lincoln told me he sent you a message about spies," I said to Leisl. "We were followed, and he was worried someone might try to speak to you about him."

"I have seen them," she said.

"You have?"

"In my mind's eye, I see them. Eva too."

"You're a seer too, Eva?" Seth asked.

She nodded.

"Fascinating. If I had a supernatural power, I'd like to see the future."

"It's not always like that," she said. "Sometimes we merely sense presences and have feelings about future events. We predict danger, or joy, or any other number of emotions. Only sometimes do we see actual scenes."

"Fascinating," Seth said again. He glanced at Alice. "What can you sense about me?"

"Seth," I scolded. "They're not here to see *your* future."

"Why are you here?" Lincoln asked.

I sighed. He may have come a long way in learning to accept his emotions, but he'd not yet grasped the art of subtlety. "Are you worried about the spies?" I asked, attempting to soften his words.

"No," Leisl said with a shrug through her entire body. "If they ask me questions about Lincoln, I answer that he is my son. Why should I not?"

Lincoln dragged his hand over his jaw but no one countered her. It didn't matter if anyone found out that she was his mother. His father, however, was a different matter.

"And if they ask who my father is?" Lincoln asked.

"I tell them I not remember. Too long ago. I am old and forget."

Lincoln nodded his approval, but I wasn't sure her answer would convince anyone. I hated to think of something happening to her because someone desperately wanted to find out more about Lincoln.

"I say I give you away when you are baby, and I never see you again until the ball." She shrugged again. "That is all true."

"The spies are not why we came today," Eva said. She seemed to have rediscovered her confidence and was keen to get to the point of their meeting. "We've come to warn you."

"About what?" Lincoln asked.

"To beware of the queen."

CHAPTER 8

" *T*he queen?" several voices echoed.

Doyle entered carrying a tray with tea things and food, giving us all a moment to digest Eva's words. I took over the pouring and dismissed Doyle. He shut the door behind him.

"The queen's just an old lady," Gus said, helping me by passing out the teacups. "How can she harm anyone?"

"Because she's the *queen*," Seth said as if Gus were a simpleton. "She might not be able to slit anyone's throat herself but she could order someone to do it."

Alice and Eva both stared at him, twin expressions of horror on their faces.

"Figure of speech," he muttered into his teacup.

"You saw the queen in your visions?" Lincoln asked Leisl.

"Not a true and clear vision," Eva said. "As I said before, sometimes we don't necessarily see things, we sense them. I sensed her presence. It was regal and powerful and...and threatening."

"Threatening to whom?"

"Us."

Us? "You're including yourself?" I asked.

She nodded. "I don't know why, but I felt personally threatened. Two of you were with me, a man and a woman, but I..." She shook her head. "I couldn't quite see who."

Lincoln and I exchanged glances. He rubbed his jaw again. "Do you know where the threat takes place?" he asked. "When?"

She shook her head. "I'm sorry my information isn't more helpful."

"You warned us," Lincoln said. "That is enough."

"He's right. Thank you." Seth picked up the tray of doughy balls and handed them to her. "Have one of these. I don't know what they are but Cook's an excellent chef. They'll make you feel better."

Eva laughed, seemingly despite herself, and took one. Her mother did too and sniffed it before nibbling. Then both women turned to each other and said, "*Galuški!*"

"This is Romany," Leisl said, her eyes bright. "So good. Try, try."

We all took one of the delicacies. It tasted spicy and delicious.

"You used to cook these, Mama," Eva said. "But you haven't for years."

"It's difficult to find the spices here. Your cook make these?" she asked Lincoln.

He nodded. "Gus, send for Cook. He should hear Leisl and Eva's compliments in person."

Gus snatched another *galuški* off the plate before leaving the room. He returned a few minutes later with a rosy-cheeked Cook. He screwed his hands into his apron and nodded at Leisl and Eva in turn as Lincoln introduced them.

"They want to know where you learned to cook *galuški.*" He said it with a perfect accent, which seemed to take Eva by surprise but not her mother.

"Country fairs," Cook said with a shy nod at Leisl. "Before I be cook here in London, I worked at fairs."

"At a pie stand?" Eva asked. "Mama took us to fairs sometimes when we were children, to show us how she lived before she met our father. Her people often worked at the fairs, you see. I loved the pie stands. The berry ones were my favorite."

"I had a pie stand," Cook said. "But I be a knife thrower before that."

"Knife thrower?" Alice echoed. "You mean you threw knives at targets as part of a show?"

Cook nodded. "My cousin stood against a wooden board and I threw knives around her, like an outline."

She blinked at him. "That's quite a trick."

"He's very good," I said. "Extraordinarily accurate, in fact. You should ask him for a demonstration in the courtyard."

"Was your cousin forced to stand there?" Gus asked.

Cook chuckled, making his double chins wobble. "She wanted to be part of my act."

"That takes a lot of courage," Alice said, impressed. "She must have had enormous faith in your ability."

"I only cut her once." Cook touched his earlobe. "Here. That be because she moved. After that, she never moved again during the act."

"And the *galuški*?" Eva asked, indicating the plate of doughy balls. "How does a knife thrower turned pie man learn such an obscure recipe?"

"Through the Romany folk who worked at the fair," Cook said. "They come and go, but there always be a family or two traveling with us. I never cooked it but I tasted dozens as a boy. I be practicing ever since Fitzroy says you be Romany, ma'am," he said to Leisl. "I ain't got no recipe to follow, only this." He tapped his shiny head. "This be the first batch that tasted right to me. Baked them just this morning. So," he said shyly, "you like them?"

Leisl smiled. "Just like a Romany makes."

Eva nodded. "I can't taste the difference between these and Mama's. I could eat a plateful."

Taking the hint, Seth picked up the plate and passed it to her. She hesitated then took one. He offered the plate to the rest of the women. We all accepted one except Alice. Gus pounced on the last before Seth could claim it.

"Which fairs did your family attend?" Leisl asked Cook. "I may be there too, telling fortunes to the *gadze*."

They fell into a discussion about the traveling fair folk. Eva watched them through narrowed eyes until I distracted her with talk of the wedding.

"Is Seth giving you away?" she asked.

"No," Gus said, as Seth said, "Yes."

"Why does everyone think *he* should do it?" Gus muttered.

"I am sorry." Eva winced. "Will it be both of you?"

"Yes," I told her. "They wouldn't stop bickering until I agreed. Now they're bickering over who will walk on my left."

She smiled. "Good luck."

When it was time to go, I took her hand and squeezed. "Thank you for coming," I said quietly. "It was very pleasant." I was beginning to wonder if the warning had merely been a ruse to visit Lincoln in his home and get to know us better. And yet they had been quite worried about Eva's vision, and I couldn't believe they'd make something like that up just to visit us. "Do come again," I said. "You're always welcome."

"I—I'm not sure," she hedged. "I'm very busy with my studies."

"To become a nurse, yes. What a noble profession."

She gave me a tight smile that she turned on Lincoln as he

joined us, only for it to freeze. He watched her intently, his direct gaze boring into her. She looked away.

"Lord Seth," Leisl said to Seth. "Walk me out."

He complied with a smile and an offer of his arm. It was good to see him back to his charming self, even if that charm wasn't turned on Alice.

I walked behind them, close enough to hear her whisper, "You have a lot to learn about woman."

"Which woman?" he asked.

"All of them, but the one who loves you in particular."

"Are you referring to my mother?"

"Mama?" Eva cut in, falling back to walk alongside them. "Are you stirring up trouble?"

Leisl put her hands in the air. "No, no."

She walked on with her daughter, leaving Seth to stare after them, his mouth slightly ajar. "I have an excellent understanding of women," he muttered to me. "Just ask any of them. Clearly she's barking." His gaze skittered to Lincoln up ahead. "Do you think he heard that?"

I patted his arm. "Probably." In a way, Leisl was correct—Seth did have much to learn about behaving around Alice. But he seemed a little fragile today so I didn't tell him so.

We waved them off and headed back inside when their hired cab drove away. "Cook and Leisl got on," Gus said, watching Cook retreat to the service areas at the back of the house.

"Like two peas in a pod," Seth said. "Perhaps he'll be your new stepfather, Fitzroy."

Lincoln huffed. "Very amusing."

"What do you make of Eva's vision?" Gus asked. "Should we worry?"

"We'll remain aware but not concerned. Some visions are open to interpretation, particularly when it is sensed rather than seen."

"She seemed very certain that it was the queen who threatened us," I said.

Lincoln looked troubled. Or as troubled as he could ever look. "Leisl was lying about something." The abrupt change of topic caught me unawares and I didn't answer immediately. "Do you agree?" he prompted. He wasn't certain, even with his own superior ability to detect lies?

"I wouldn't call it lying," I said. "Perhaps withholding of the truth, but nothing more sinister than that."

"And Eva," Alice added. "There was certainly something... odd about her behavior. I wouldn't have mentioned it if you didn't point it out yourself, Mr. Fitzroy."

"I detected nothing out of the ordinary," Seth said with a shrug. "I thought them both charming. Your sister surprised me, Fitzroy. I thought she would be more like you, but she was delightful."

"You don't find me delightful?" Lincoln asked.

"No, but I'd be happy for you to prove me wrong."

A wicked smile touched Lincoln's lips. "There's a few hours before you need to prepare for the party tonight. You can practice combat moves with me in the ballroom until then."

Seth's face fell. "How does that make you delightful?"

"To you? It doesn't. But to Gus it does."

Gus chuckled. "Ain't nothing more delightful than seeing you lose a fight, Seth."

Seth shot him a withering glare then stalked off. "Let's get it over with. And the face is off limits. I've got to look my best for the dance tonight."

Gus rolled his eyes. "I'll give you a quid to give him a black eye, Fitzroy."

"I could do it for less," Lincoln said idly.

* * *

LINCOLN DIDN'T GIVE Seth a black eye but he did insure they both worked hard. Gus didn't just observe, either. He and I joined in for a spell of practice with the *nunchaku* and other Oriental weapons. Thanks to my smaller size and quickness of foot, I'd become quite adept at avoiding being hit, but was still rather inept when it came to wielding them. I preferred knives.

"Does the gown you're wearing tonight have long sleeves?" Lincoln asked me as he put his *nunchaku* back into their box.

I passed him mine. "No. It's an off-the shoulder gown with sweet velvet swathes here." I indicated where the fabric would sit just below my shoulder. "The swathe effect continues along my décolletage, forming a natural but delicate edge on the bodice. It's very pretty. But you're not interested in how it looks, are you?"

"Only if it's suitable for hiding weapons."

"Not on my arms. My gloves are long but far too tight to hide even a small blade. I'll strap one to my leg."

He nodded his approval and accepted the *nunchaku* from Seth. "It's unlikely you'll need it but I feel better if you carry one."

"It's your virtue we must worry about with that set," Seth said, "not your life. Don't glare at me like that, Fitzroy. It's not my fault she'll be an object of interest to the old cads. You're the one allowing her to come along."

"You're exaggerating," Gus said. "Besides, Fitzroy will be there. No one will flirt with her with her fiancé near."

"A little bit of flirting has never harmed a girl," I told them all. "I am quite capable of taking care of myself. Now, if you don't mind, I need to dress."

"I'll help you," Alice said from the doorway. I hadn't noticed her arrival. She rarely watched us training; the violence made her uncomfortable. Sometimes I wondered if it was because she knew her presence distracted Seth and she was afraid of him getting hurt. It was very hard to gauge her feelings on the matter. Or on any matter regarding Seth. It was no wonder he felt somewhat at sea around her.

"How long have you been watching?" Seth asked, flicking his sweat dampened locks off his forehead.

"Too long." She handed me a lace-edged handkerchief embroidered with her initials and scented with lavender. "For your brow, Charlie. It shines."

I handed it straight back to her. "It's far too pretty. I wouldn't want to stain it."

"I cannot believe Lady Vickers approves of this," she said as we walked out of the ballroom together. Behind us, furniture scraped across the polished floor as the men put the room to rights.

"She doesn't," I said. "But she puts up with it. Does it upset you?"

"I don't like watching you try to hurt one another," she said carefully.

"We're not trying to hurt one another. We're trying to train ourselves so we don't get hurt in a real fight."

She wrinkled her nose. "I understand the reasons, but it's most unseemly for a lady. But I would hate to see you hurt for real, Charlie."

"Me in particular, or Seth too?"

Her mouth softened into a smile. "I wouldn't like to see his handsome features too damaged, but he does deserve to be knocked down a peg or two, on occasion. He can be far too charming for his own good. Not with me, you understand. His charms seem a little forced with me. But with Eva, for example. He did lay it on thickly today."

I laughed. "You think that was thick? Oh, Alice. You've not seen him at his best. Or perhaps it's his worst." I laughed again, but she didn't join in. She simply walked faster so I had to lengthen my stride to keep apace.

* * *

LADY HARCOURT always caused a sensation wherever she went, and her arrival at Lord Underwood's Mayfair house was no exception. It wasn't merely her low-cut gown, although it dipped so low it almost revealed her nipples, but rather the company she brought with her—us. Despite our official invitation from Underwood, it seemed the other guests hadn't been notified of our attendance. All heads swiveled toward us upon our entry to the ballroom. More than one gaze settled on me. Lincoln tensed beside me.

Lord Underwood broke away from a group and greeted us smoothly, as if we were old friends. He took my hand in his and kissed it. "You look lovely, Miss Holloway. A lovely peach, that's what you are! Isn't she a delight, Julia?" Before Lady Harcourt could respond, he ushered us further into the room. "Such a shame your sweet friend Miss Everheart couldn't come tonight. I did enjoy her company. Such a rare jewel, that girl. One wouldn't have guessed her humble trade origins from her bearing. She reminded me a little of you, Julia, in your younger days."

Lady Harcourt swallowed then put out her hand. Underwood kissed it, but his hot gaze fell on her bosom, rising and falling in a dramatic rhythm.

"Allow me to introduce you to my other friends," she said. "Seth, you will already know many guests from your more wayward days as a…a prize."

He grunted. "You'll have to try harder than that to hurt me, Julia. Your barbs hardly sting anymore."

She turned a sickly sweet smile on him. "Perhaps it would

sting more if the sweet Miss Everheart were here. And you're wrong, anyway. Why would I want to hurt you, dear Seth?"

He looked as if he wanted to snarl, but he bore her attention with gritted teeth.

She looped her arm through mine and led me into the room. It was smaller than the Lichfield Towers ballroom, but with so few guests, it didn't matter. The candles in the crystal chandelier dazzled and, along with the tall candelabras stationed around the room, picked out the gems in the ladies' jewelry. Tropical palms did not look out of place in front of a mural of an island scene painted on the wall, and the pineapples and coconuts decorating the refreshment table completed the theme. The room felt warm, too, the heat coming from the large fireplace. It was too hot to stand near. Most of the guests stood by the large arch windows and doors that overlooked the street. No one had yet retreated outside to the balconies for fresh air, but if the room grew any hotter, I might be the first. It was stifling. Or perhaps it was my nerves making me hot. Certainly my nerves weren't helped by my tightly laced corset or the stiff confines of my silk brocade gown. The elaborate crimson embroidery, cream fringing and beads weighed down the bodice. It was a new gown, purchased from the same dressmaker charged with creating my wedding dress.

"Lord Underwood has done an excellent job at decorating the room," I said, admiring a vase filled with red spear flowers and dark green leaves.

"It's marvelous what hot houses can do these days," Lady Harcourt said. "Particularly for a gentleman with a fortune at his disposal. Now, enough talk of vulgar things. You wanted to come tonight, so I must present you."

She turned on a bright smile and greeted three gentlemen. After introducing us, they each bowed in turn over my hand. It was all very pleasing until one of them kissed it with far more vigor than Lincoln liked.

"Miss Holloway is my fiancée," he growled.

The gentleman dropped my hand and lifted his brows at Lady Harcourt. "Then what is the point?"

Lincoln took my elbow and steered me toward the refreshment table. Seth joined us and Lady Harcourt caught up.

"If you're going to behave so proprietorially toward Charlotte then you should not have come, Lincoln." She may have been speaking to him, but she did not look at him, or indeed any of us. Her gaze scanned the room, flitting from face to face. There were mostly gentlemen present, and all the women seemed about my age. Lady Harcourt was by far the most senior lady present. If she felt awkward, she didn't show it. I'd wager none of the women were the wives of the men whose arms they clung to.

"He's not here," Lincoln said to her.

Her gaze snapped to him. It was bright and fierce, challenging. "You presume to know whom I seek?"

"The Prince of Wales."

She bristled and looked away.

"You're angling to be *his* next mistress?" Seth scoffed. "Good lord, Julia, that's ambitious, even for you."

"I am not angling to be anyone's mistress, Seth," she bit off.

"Ah, yes, it's marriage or nothing now, isn't it? Be careful, Julia." He shot a pointed gaze at the expanse of exposed décolletage. "Your desperation turns them away, you know."

She turned on her heel and stalked off.

"I don't think she's going to introduce us to anyone else tonight." Seth surveyed the table with its exotic fruits and flowers. "When do you think they'll bring out the food?"

"No one has large hands or feet," Lincoln said. "Ballantine isn't here yet."

"There are some new arrivals." I nodded toward the entrance where two middle-aged gentlemen arrived with a younger man and woman in tow. The younger man seemed out of place and unsure where to look. His gaze settled on us and he nodded. Perhaps he saw kindred spirits in people closer to his own age than his male companions.

Spotting the man's interest, Lord Underwood ushered the newcomers toward us. "Lord Vickers, Mr. Fitzroy and Miss Holloway may I introduce you to my dear friends, Lord Ballantine and Sir Ignatius Swinburn, and their young friends, Mr. Franklin and Miss Collingworth."

I dipped into a curtsy, managing to keep myself steady despite the thrill of excitement racing up my spine. I studied Lord Ballantine's hands through my lowered lashes and almost lost my balance. He wore white evening gloves, but clearly his hands were not overly large. They were entirely normal size. His two younger friends, however, sported thick fingers and broad palms like Harriet and Leonora Ballantine.

I rose and wanted to glance at Lincoln, to see if he'd noticed, but dared not.

"Are you friends of Underwood's?" Swinburn asked with a genial air. More genial than I expected, although Andrew Buchanan had admitted that Swinburn had swagger and a certain appeal to women, despite his tendency to use them then discard them.

"We met him through Lady Harcourt," Seth said, taking the role of charming conversationalist upon himself.

"Ah, yes, the delectable Julia. It's hardly a surprise to see her here, but this is the first time she's brought friends." Swinburn's gaze sought her out and, when she spotted him, he sketched a bow.

He was shorter than Lord Ballantine, with a thicker build

not usually associated with the upper classes. Even though I knew he'd come from working class stock, it was at least two generations ago, if my memory served. He may be rich thanks to the success of his shipping empire, but he'd climbed very high for a man in trade. Very high indeed. The prince must find him to be good company.

"We're quite well acquainted," Seth said simply.

"Even with your young companion?" Lord Ballantine smiled at me. "Miss Holloway doesn't seem like the sort of person Julia would want near her."

"She tolerates me," I said with a laugh. "As much as I tolerate her. But in truth, it's Lord Vickers she prefers to have near her. Mr. Fitzroy and I are merely people she must endure if she wishes to see our dear friend, Seth."

Lord Ballantine slapped Seth on the shoulder. Seth smiled amiably enough but I suspected he wanted to throttle me. "Can we expect a duel between you and Underwood tonight? Pistols at dawn perhaps? My money's on you, Vickers. You look as though you could beat Underwood at any game he chose."

"You forget, Ballantine," Swinburn said. "Underwood has given her up. So it would seem you have won, Vickers."

"I am fortunate," Seth said without an ounce of humor.

Both gentlemen guffawed.

"I assume you will enjoy a *dance* with several of the other ladies here tonight, Vickers," Ballantine said, openly admiring two women who'd come to the table to inspect the exotic fruit. "Perhaps Miss Holloway dances?"

Swinburn winced at his friend's crass implication that Seth and I would do more than dance together.

"Miss Holloway is engaged to me," Lincoln said. "She only dances with me."

"Quite rightly," Swinburn cut in before Ballantine could speak.

"I can spare a dance or two with other gentlemen," I said quickly. "Perhaps Mr. Franklin will oblige, or even you, my lord." If I was going to learn anything about Ballantine, I needed to speak to him. And Mr. Franklin, too. He would be the perfect age for Leonora's other admirer, Eddy, and he was a shape shifter, if his large hands and feet were an indication. He was the obvious candidate for Lord Ballantine to push on his daughter. But was the baron a shape shifter too?

The four-piece ensemble increased the volume and tempo of their playing with a waltz. Lord Underwood swept across the dance floor and asked Lady Harcourt to open the dancing with him, proving that he had not entirely given her up. Unlike a proper dance, we ladies had not been issued with cards and pencils to write the names of partners upon. There were no elderly chaperones to oversee young charges, no wallflowers among the women, and no eligible young men, aside from Mr. Franklin and Seth.

"Your first dance is mine," Lincoln said in that growling voice.

I took his hand and allowed him to lead me onto the dance floor where we joined the other couples engaged in the waltz. I was rather pleased it was a waltz first. I did so enjoy being held by Lincoln. We were so close I could feel the heat coming off him, and the rigidity in his shoulder.

"I have to dance with them," I said as we twirled to the far side of the dance floor. "You know why."

"I haven't forbidden you."

"Oh. Good. Did you notice Lord Ballantine's hands?"

He nodded. "It would indicate he's not a shape shifter after all."

"Lilith claimed he is. Why would she lie?"

"I can't think of a reason."

We discussed the possibility of Mr. Franklin being Eddy, and agreed that my dancing and flirting with him was the best way to learn his name without raising anyone's suspicions. I expected Lincoln to watch us closely.

With the waltz completed, Lincoln led me back to the refreshment table where Mr. Franklin stood with Sir Ignatius Swinburn. The lazy eyes of the younger man followed us before drifting off. Unlike Swinburn, Franklin was tall and lean, his fair hair already thinning on top and his whiskers struggling to find purchase on his chin. He seemed a little in awe of the man standing beside him, but it was perhaps not surprising, considering Swinburn's extraordinary wealth and purported influence. I wondered how the two of them were acquainted. Swinburn did not have overly-large hands. Then again, neither did Ballantine.

Lord Ballantine had joined another group of guests. A woman clutched his arm and smiled up at him as if he said something vastly interesting. He hardly seemed to know she was there.

Seth rejoined us, Miss Collingworth at his side, blushing like a woman who'd exerted herself too much, or perhaps flirted too much. She was quite pretty, albeit not extraordinary, with fair hair and freckles across her nose. Seth let go of her hand and bowed deeply. She giggled until she caught Swinburn frowning at her. Mr. Franklin paid her no mind. So *he* had no interest in her, but perhaps Swinburn did.

"You're an excellent dancer," Seth told her. "Do you think we can have another?"

"No," Swinburn cut in. "She's much too tired. It wouldn't be healthful."

Miss Collingworth bit the inside of her lower lip. "Sir Ignatius is so kind to worry about me. He's right. I wouldn't want to exert myself before the Prince of Wales even gets here."

Swinburn nodded in approval, as if he'd schooled her in what to say to such requests.

"His Highness is coming tonight?" Lincoln asked.

"We do hope so," Miss Collingworth said, silently clapping her gloved hands.

"He's a friend of Sir Ignatius's and Lord Ballantine's," Mr. Franklin said, as if in answer to an unspoken question.

Lord Underwood approached, genial smile in place. "Is everyone enjoying themselves? Why are you young people not dancing? Mr. Franklin, Lord Vickers, you ought to be asking the ladies. Perhaps Mr. Fitzroy can spare Miss Holloway just this once?"

"I would love to dance," I said.

Silence. I suspected Seth knew I was attempting to force Mr. Franklin to ask me and didn't want to cut in. Mr. Franklin, however, simply cleared his throat, which only made the silence feel more profound.

"I'll dance with you later, Charlie," Seth said, coming to my rescue. "After a rest."

"You're not dancing, Mr. Franklin?" Lord Underwood asked. "Why ever not?"

"I am a terrible dancer," he said, his cheeks coloring. "I came here to talk and…and meet new people. Speaking of which, is the Prince of Wales coming?"

"Please say he is," Miss Collingworth said in a breathy voice. Did she want to become the prince's mistress? Good lord, but she was so young.

"Alas not." Lord Underwood looked devastated. "He had another engagement. His presence will be missed."

Mr. Franklin sighed and eyed the door.

Lord Ballantine rejoined us, without the woman on his arm. "When is His Highness due?" he asked Underwood.

"He's not coming." Miss Collingworth pouted. "What a disappointment."

Lord Ballantine clicked his tongue and he too eyed the door, as if he wished to make his exit.

Lord Underwood glanced between them, blinking hard. "Can we not have our pleasure without him? My dears, there is much joy still to be had. Look around you." He indicated the other guests. "There are lords aplenty, and several pretty young ladies who are not engaged. Go, Mr. Franklin. Ask one to dance."

"I'm not a very good dancer," Mr. Franklin said again, more irritably.

Lord Underwood fell silent, displeasure pinching his features. And then he spied Lady Harcourt coming toward us, all swaying hips and creamy skin. "Ask Julia! She's an excellent teacher. Indeed, she's just what you need. An older, accomplished instructress for an eager young gentleman."

Lady Harcourt stopped short. Her smile froze. We all fell silent and I wondered how long it would take Seth to rescue her. The gallant knight couldn't possibly stand to see a woman disparaged, even one he disliked.

It was Swinburn who moved first, however. He held his hands out to Lady Harcourt and kissed her cheeks. "You look well, Julia," he said. "Always a flower among thorns."

"Quite, quite," Lord Underwood muttered. His cheeks pinked, and I suspected he regretted his slight about her age in the face of Swinburn's friendship.

"I am sorry to hear that His Highness won't be attending tonight's dance after all," she said to Underwood. "Pity. So many here were looking forward to seeing him."

Underwood sniffed. "Yes. Well. It was too late to cancel after I learned of his inability to attend."

"Never mind. You have told us now. I do hope no one leaves early because of it."

Underwood glanced around the room at his guests.

"Everyone seems happy enough. And you, Julia? Are you happy?"

"I count my good fortune every day," she said, which we all knew was not an answer to the question.

Swinburn paused then offered her his arm. She accepted and he led her onto the dance floor. Her dancing was superb and her skill almost hid the fact her partner was something of a clod. At least he tried. Mr. Franklin still did not ask me, or anyone else, to dance. I would have to change tactic.

An opportunity presented itself when Lincoln melted away and Seth asked Miss Collingworth to dance again. Without the stern Swinburn there to order her not to, she happily allowed Seth to lead her out. They danced far away from Swinburn and Lady Harcourt.

Lincoln retreated to the window, but I felt his gaze on us. Hopefully Mr. Franklin did not.

"Your fiancé doesn't say much," Franklin said.

"He does once he gets to know people better." I nodded at Lord Underwood, flitting among his guests like a butterfly unable to decide which flower to settle on. "Speaking of which, how do you know these gentlemen?"

He clasped his hands behind his back, as if suddenly conscious of their size. "I've known Lord Ballantine all my life. He and Lady Ballantine are good friends of my parents. Sir Ignatius is a friend of his."

"And Lord Underwood?"

"Is a friend of Lord Ballantine's too. When I came of age, they included me in their circle. They've been very good to me. Very good indeed. And you, Miss Holloway? How did you meet Mr. Fitzroy and Lord Vickers?"

"Call me Charlie."

I waited, hoping my silence would prompt him to tell me his name, but he was too busy watching Seth and Miss Collingworth. Indeed, I doubted he even heard my response.

He frowned as Miss Collingworth laughed at something Seth said.

"Do you and Miss Collingworth have an understanding?" I asked boldly.

"Of course not. I just don't want her to develop a *tendre* for Lord Vickers."

"Why not?"

He turned away from the dancers to study the trays of sweets and jellies being carried out by the footmen. "There's an understanding that she'll marry someone else."

"She's betrothed?"

He glanced past me and quickly shook his head. "Lady Harcourt, come and try a jelly," he said as she and Swinburn returned from their dance. "This one is in the shape of a leaf. Miss Holloway and I were just admiring them."

Lady Harcourt refused a jelly.

"A bonbon then," he said.

"I'm afraid there's nothing on this table that can tempt me." She spied a footman bringing in glasses of champagne. "Ah, now that certainly can."

"Mr. Franklin, fetch Lady Harcourt and Miss Holloway some champagne," Swinburn said.

A woman approached and curled her long fingers around Swinburn's arm. Her hand lightly skimmed his jaw. "Come dance with me, Sir Ignatius." She leaned into him, her breasts pillowed against his shoulder. "You know how much I *adore* dancing." She giggled and her eyes sparkled unnaturally brightly. Perhaps she'd already consumed some champagne.

"Sir Ignatius has promised me another dance," Lady Harcourt told the woman.

The woman whispered something in Swinburn's ear. He laughed and shook his head.

"A little later, my dear," he said. "Dance with my young friend Mr. Franklin for now."

Mr. Franklin handed a glass to me and another to Lady Harcourt. She took it and arched a brow at the other woman. The woman took Mr. Franklin's hand. I watched as my opportunity to find out his first name slipped away. It would seem he was capable of dancing after all, just not with me. Or perhaps only when ordered by his superiors.

Another woman approached, this one younger and prettier than the first. She stroked Swinburn's arm with bare fingers and batted her lashes at him. Swinburn's eyes turned smoky. He invited her onto the dance floor.

"You promised me another dance, Sir Ignatius," Lady Harcourt protested.

"Later," he said, bowing to her.

The young woman shot Lady Harcourt a triumphant smile behind Swinburn's back. She might have poked her tongue out if he hadn't turned at that moment to lead her onto the dance floor.

"Little whore," Lady Harcourt muttered into her glass. She sipped, spying me over the rim. "Don't look so shocked, Charlotte. She is a whore." She huffed and her lips thinned. The tight smile was more self-deprecating than cruel. "As am I. Not by choice, you understand. Whores never throw themselves at men because they want to. Needs must, you see. Particularly now."

She drained her glass and signaled the footman for another. He exchanged her empty glass for a full one. The silence between us stretched, and I expected her to move away, since she could barely stand my presence. But she did not.

"Seth's right," she went on. "I am desperate. There. Another shocking admission. Pay attention, Charlotte, because I'm going to explain how life works. Or rather, my life. You see, the annuity my husband left me is no longer enough. I must marry again, and marry well, or I will become destitute. I can take in boarders, but once I do I'll be cast out by the friends I have left. No one wants to associate with a woman forced to become a pathetic landlady. My value is already hanging by a thread. That will cut the thread off, and I am not like Lady Vickers. I could never come back after being cast out. She was born into this, you see. These are her people, and they will take her back into the fold eventually. I don't hold as much currency." She shuddered and drank deeply. "Sir Ignatius is rich and available, so of course I hoped to catch his attention tonight," she went on. "What woman doesn't want him?"

She nodded at the couple clasping one another on the dance floor. Swinburn's hand sank low on the girl's back and his torso pressed against her. "He also has no children, and that is quite an attractive trait in a man, in my opinion." Her brittle laugh made the hairs on the back of my neck stand up. "You, Seth, Lincoln, even Andrew...you all judge me. Even those of you who ought to know better." Her eyes flashed in Seth's direction before looking away, somewhat sadly. "You think I've made some wrong choices. You all think you would do things differently. Well, perhaps *you* would, Charlotte, you self-righteous little bitch. But rest assured, without Lincoln you would still be in the gutter or dead. Am I so evil that I want a different fate for myself?"

I didn't bother to answer her. She didn't want to hear me tell her that I would never hurt people to secure my future. And, in truth, I didn't care enough to remind her. I wanted nothing to do with her.

I walked off and joined Lincoln as he strode toward me. "What did she say?" he asked, placing his hand on my back.

"Nothing of importance."

His gaze narrowed, and I suspected he knew there was more, but he didn't press me.

"This is quite the party," I said, watching as a gentleman

and a woman with painted lips disappeared into an adjoining room guarded by a footman. "Now I see why the refreshments are being served out here and not in there. It would seem it has another purpose."

"Are you shocked?"

"I was warned. Is this the sort of place you found Seth at?"

He leaned closer, a small smile touching his lips. "You know you have to ask Seth that, not me."

"I'll take that as a yes. Thank you for clarifying."

He frowned. "That's not fair."

"I don't always play fair."

He grunted. "Did you discover Franklin's name?"

"Not yet. I'll try to get him alone again soon."

"Not alone."

"Why not?"

He paused before saying, "My methods may be more effective in this instance."

I didn't ask how he expected to extract information from anyone using his usual methods in a ballroom with dozens of onlookers.

"Did he seem like a killer?" he asked.

"No, but what does a killer seem like, anyway? I wouldn't have picked General Eastbrooke as a violent man, and yet look how he turned out."

His hand squeezed mine. "A fair point."

I watched as the dance ended, and Swinburn led his partner back to the refreshment table then moved off to intercept Seth and Miss Collingworth. She nodded demurely, a pained look on her face, and allowed him to steer her toward Mr. Franklin and Lord Ballantine. The two older gentlemen spoke sternly to their younger friends, who seemed to take the chastisement with contrition. More than one reproachful glance was cast Seth's way.

"You seem to have caused a stir by dancing with Miss Collingworth," I told him as he joined us.

"She's a lively girl." He glanced at the party of four as it broke apart. "What's so awful about dancing with me, I wonder?"

"She's intended for another man," I said. "So Franklin told me."

"Intended for whom?"

"He didn't say. I assume her parents arranged it."

"Or Ballantine and Swinburn," Lincoln said. "As leaders of their pack."

Watching them together, it was easy to see the two older men as leaders, but I wasn't convinced they belonged to a pack. For one thing, we weren't even sure if they were shape shifters. They bore no evidence of it.

Lord Ballantine joined a group of whiskered gentlemen who stood aloofly separate from the women and other men, while Swinburn took the hand of Lady Harcourt's young rival and kissed her daringly on the neck. She tipped her head back to reveal more white flesh and smiled dreamily.

Lady Harcourt watched them too, her knuckles white around the stem of her glass. Then, with a sudden spin on her heel, she marched off toward Lord Underwood with a look of fierce determination.

"They're leaving," Lincoln said.

It took me a moment to realize he meant Miss Collingworth and Mr. Franklin. No one seemed to notice them exit together except us.

"Damn," Seth muttered. "Want me to follow them?"

"We both will, in case they separate," said Lincoln. "You too, Charlie. I'm not leaving you here."

"What about Swinburn and Ballantine?" I asked.

"We're more likely to get answers from their friends."

I set my glass down and hurried out alongside them. We

reached the door, however, and stopped as Prince Alfred, the Duke of Edinburgh and the Prince of Wales's brother, entered, a heavily rouged woman clinging to each arm. Whispers quickly spread around the ballroom as the guests recognized him. Lord Underwood glided across the floor to greet the new arrival, forcing his way past us. He bowed deeply.

"Your Royal Highness, this is a pleasure," he said with slippery smoothness. "I'm so glad you came."

The duke gave a regal nod before looking past Underwood to Lincoln. "Mr. Fitzroy, this is an unexpected encounter." He disengaged himself from the two women and held a hand out to Lincoln. "Come. Join me for a drink and conversation."

Bloody hell. It would seem we weren't going to chase Miss Collingworth and Mr. Franklin after all.

CHAPTER 9

"*My* apologies, Your Highness, but we were just leaving," Lincoln said, moving past the duke as he spoke.

The duke's two female companions looked horrified at Lincoln's audacious response. The duke himself stiffened. I worried he would demand Lincoln stay, but I worried more that Lincoln would refuse him again.

"Don't mind him, Your Highness," Lord Underwood said, bowing again. "He's nobody."

"It's not Mr. Fitzroy's wish to leave yet," I assured the duke in a loud voice for those nearby to hear. "He's only thinking of me, you see. I feel quite faint." I touched my forehead and fluttered my lashes. "Mr. Fitzroy is concerned enough to take me home."

The duke's gaze slid to Lincoln, waiting for me just beyond the door, then to Underwood. "It is rather hot in here." With that declaration, he signaled to his two companions to walk with him across the room.

Underwood followed a step behind and signaled wildly to a footman. "I'll have the doors to the balconies opened immediately, Your Highness."

Lincoln and I rushed down the stairs to the entrance hall. We grabbed hats and coats from the footman and joined Seth outside.

"They went that way on foot," he said, nodding to the north. "We won't be fast enough to follow if they change into their animal shape."

"Then we must hope they don't decide to go for a run tonight," I said, lifting my skirts and trotting down the front steps. "It would be difficult in their evening finery, anyway. They'd have to find somewhere to undress and store their clothing to retrieve it later. Take it from me, dressing into and undressing out of evening gowns are an ordeal best left for the home where skilled maids can assist."

We walked quickly up the street, passing well-lit terraced houses, some with footmen standing by the door. Music and laughter spilled from open windows above. Lord Underwood wasn't the only one hosting a party tonight.

I huddled into my coat as a gust swept down the street. I didn't bemoan the breeze as it kept our scents away from the two people we followed. Our brisk pace warmed me soon enough. Despite my tight corset and heavy clothing, I kept up with Lincoln and Seth. Our two shape changers maintained a steady pace too. We were still in Mayfair but would soon cross into Soho.

Miss Collingworth and Mr. Franklin stopped in front of a house. Lincoln hissed a command to retreat into the dark shadows just as our suspects glanced around. Mr. Franklin appeared to sniff the air and stepped in our direction.

I dared not breathe. Dared not move. His superior senses would easily detect us. He might already be able to smell us, despite the breeze.

He stepped off the pavement in our direction, but Miss Collingworth caught his arm. She said something and shook her head. A moment later, they both approached the front door to the house. Mr. Franklin knocked and they were let in by a man who greeted them with smiles and a friendly handshake for Mr. Franklin, a kiss on the cheek for Miss Collingworth. He wasn't a servant then. What grandiose Mayfair mansion kept no staff to greet visitors?

I let out a breath. Seth removed his hat and dragged his hand through his hair, causing it to flop over his forehead. "Now what?" he asked.

"We wait," both Lincoln and I said together.

"If either of them leave the house alone, we intercept them," Lincoln said.

Seth tugged on his white bow tie, stretching his neck out of his collar. "I feel conspicuous out here in my tailcoat and top hat. The damned streetlamp is too bright. Ha! Never thought I'd say that about a miserable London light."

Lincoln handed me his hat and coat then shimmied up the lamppost.

"I wasn't expecting him to do that," Seth said, watching.

With one arm wrapped around the post for support, Lincoln opened the glass case and moved the lever to turn down the gas then slid down again. While we weren't invisible, we weren't easy to spot in the dark either. Not that many people passed us by. The occasional carriage drove past or stopped to let out passengers, but the houses nearest us were closed up and silent, and it was much too late and cold for a stroll.

When it became clear the wait would be long, Seth sat on the pavement, his back to the wall. Lincoln laid his coat on the ground beside Seth and indicated I should sit.

"It's a little awkward in my gown," I said.

He put out his hand and I used it to steady myself as I sank to the pavement in the most ladylike fashion I could manage. Lincoln remained standing, even when I rested my head on Seth's shoulder. He noticed, but didn't say a word.

Seth tipped his head back against the wall. "Wake me when something happens."

I must have drifted off to sleep because Seth's jerking movement startled me. I sat up. "What's wrong?" I asked, squinting into the darkness.

"He kicked me," Seth whispered. "Something happening, Fitzroy?"

"Don't move," Lincoln whispered back.

The front door to the house was still closed and the building shrouded in shadows. I couldn't see what Lincoln had seen—or sensed. Nothing seemed to be happening at all.

Then something rose out of the service area below street level. The silhouette was animal, not human. It walked on all fours and its body looked muscular even from a distance. Its giant head sported pointed ears. I'd seen enough shape shifters to know what their other form looked like from afar.

It emerged cautiously, hunkering low to the ground. I couldn't see but I imagined it sniffing and watching, trying to detect if anyone was nearby.

I held myself still and thanked God the breeze had all but vanished so my skirt didn't rustle. Both Seth and Lincoln froze too.

Another creature joined the first and they moved off, with two more following. They slunk along the street like prowling cats. Then, when they reached the corner, the first sped up to a run. The other three followed. There was no way we could keep up.

Seth let out a breath. "More waiting?" he asked.

"Take Charlie home," Lincoln said. "It's late."

I shook my head. "You need Seth here."

Seth groaned. "If this becomes another fight, we're not going to fare well. There are four of them and two of us."

I cleared my throat.

"No offence, Charlie."

I stamped my hand on my hip.

He sighed. "Three of us."

"The plan hasn't changed," Lincoln said. "We're still going to wait for Collingworth or Franklin to leave in human form."

"What if they live here?" Seth asked.

"They can't remain in the house forever."

"We can't remain out here forever!"

"Have Lord Ballantine or Sir Ignatius come?" I asked.

Lincoln shook his head. "No one else arrived or left after you fell asleep."

"I didn't sleep. I merely closed my eyes."

"Me too," Seth said around a yawn. "That's why I'm so tired now. I definitely haven't slept a wink."

We continued our wait. My coat was no longer enough to keep me warm but I didn't dare tell Lincoln. He would make me leave, taking Seth, and that could render him vulnerable. My legs felt somewhat numb too, curled up beneath me and to the side in a manner that allowed me to sit on the ground. I got up to stretch them and yawned.

"What time is it?"

"Four-thirty," Lincoln said, without checking his watch.

Dawn was more than an hour away. I hoped the pack returned before then. Despite what Lincoln said, we couldn't continue to watch the house during daylight hours. We were too conspicuous.

A mere ten minutes later, the hulking wolf-like creatures returned. They hugged the walls and padded silently but swiftly toward the service stairs. They did not pause to sniff the air or listen for movement, and were soon gone from sight. We three did not speak as we waited and watched, and waited some more.

I started to think no one would emerge from the house at all in human form, but finally the front door opened, and Miss Collingworth stepped out along with another man and woman. With jaunty steps, they headed up the street. A few minutes later, Franklin emerged. He locked the door behind him and pocketed the key, then walked in the opposite direction to his friends.

We followed at a distance, keeping him in sight until he turned a corner. I thought we'd lost him when we turned the same corner, but then I spotted him disappearing into the shadows of a laneway.

"An ambush," Seth murmured.

Lincoln nodded and picked up his pace. "I'll be the bait. Come in after me. Hurry or he'll have time to change form. Charlie, stay out of sight. If anything happens to us, alert Gus."

Bait. I didn't like the sound of that.

I let them go on ahead then hiked up my skirt. I retrieved the knife strapped to my lower leg and gripped it hard. A pistol would have been better but the knife would have to do. Cook had taught me to throw it with accuracy from several feet away, but I wasn't used to a moving target, particularly one fighting my friends.

With my heart in my throat, I flattened myself, as much as my gown would allow, against the wall near the entrance of the lane. I didn't dare loosen my grip on the blade handle despite my aching fingers.

"Franklin!" Lincoln called softly into the lane. "I only want to talk. Come out."

Deep, dense silence closed around me. I couldn't even hear the hissing of the nearest streetlamp. Perhaps we'd been mistaken and Franklin had continued on. If that were the case, we'd lost him.

"Franklin," Lincoln said again. "I know you're in there. I can sense you as well as you can sense me."

The light *tap tap* of shoes on cobbles was music to my ears, because they were not rushed as if he were running to attack. "Sense me?" came Mr. Franklin's voice. "Do you mean to say you...you are...?"

"I'm not like you, no. I'm a seer, not a shape changer."

"Oh." Mr. Franklin cleared his throat. "I don't know what you're talking about. Shape changer?" He snorted an unconvincing laugh.

"I know you and Miss Collingworth are both shape changers. Your other form resembles a wolf. You went for a run just now with your pack."

Someone—Franklin, I assumed—sucked air between his teeth.

"You have no reason to fear me," Lincoln said. "I am merely curious about your pack. I want to study you, understand you."

The footsteps came closer again. He must be very near Lincoln now, at the mouth of the lane. Then the footsteps stopped suddenly. "I can also sense your man," Mr. Franklin said, a note of anxiety edging his words. "Make him come out so I can see you both."

Lincoln hesitated, then said, "Do as he says, Seth."

Seth moved out of my line of sight and toward Lincoln.

Mr. Franklin gasped. "Lord Vickers! Forgive me for calling you his man..." He trailed off, no doubt realizing the strangeness of the situation he found himself in.

"It's a mistake often made," Seth said with a dismissive wave of his head.

I bit my lip and hoped Mr. Franklin couldn't sense me too. I released my lip before my teeth drew blood. *That* he would smell easily.

"Well?" Lincoln prompted. "Will you answer some questions?"

"That depends on the questions."

"Let's start with an easy one. What's your first name?"

Mr. Franklin scoffed. "Nigel."

Not Eddy. I couldn't quite believe we'd gone to all this effort for nothing. He wasn't Leonora's second suitor. That didn't mean he couldn't have killed Protheroe but it did place him further down our list of suspects.

"Is Lord Ballantine like you?" Lincoln asked. "Is he a shape changer?"

"You'll have to ask him."

"How well do you know his daughter?"

"Leonora? Well enough. Why?"

"Are you going to marry her?"

He barked out a laugh. "What sort of question is that?"

"Just answer it."

"She's a capital girl, but I'm not good enough for her. So no, I won't be marrying her."

"And Swinburn? Underwood? Are they shape changers too?"

Mr. Franklin clicked his tongue in irritation. "Those are questions for the gentlemen themselves to answer."

"How do you know them?"

"As I told Miss Holloway at the dance," he said with strained patience, "I've known Lord Ballantine my entire life. He's a friend to my parents. He introduced me to both Sir Ignatius and Lord Underwood in more recent times. Now, since I don't see what these questions have to do with anything, I'll be on my way."

Footsteps shuffled, but I couldn't determine how many sets or in what direction. "Just one more question," Lincoln said. "Did you kill Roderick Protheroe?"

"I beg your pardon!"

"Did you kill Roderick Protheroe?"

A hesitation, then, "Who?"

"A gentleman by the name of Roderick Protheroe was attacked and killed by wild dogs in the city."

"And you suspect me?" Mr. Franklin's voice rose to a high pitch. "Are you from Scotland Yard?"

"He was Leonora Ballantine's fiancé," Seth told him.

"No, he wasn't. I would know if she were engaged. Look here, I did not kill anyone in either this form or my other one, and I resent the accusation that I did."

"We're not accusing you, Mr. Franklin," Lincoln said. "The fact is, a wild dog killed Protheroe and a naked man was found near the scene. To those of us who are aware of the existence of shape changers, that man is the likely suspect. If it wasn't you, do you know who did it?"

"Of course not."

"Who is your leader?"

The question must have taken Mr. Franklin by surprise because he took a few moments to answer. "We have no leader."

"I find that hard to believe, considering what I know about pack behavior."

"You're an expert, are you?"

"Somewhat."

Mr. Franklin snorted. The footsteps receded, and I sagged against the wall in relief.

But the footsteps stopped and I tensed again. "I've had a revelation," Mr. Franklin said from a short distance away. "If you're looking for a shape changer capable of killing, try Mr. Gawler of Old Nichol. Some of the members in his pack are dodgers, lurkers and cutpurses. Just look for the filthiest, most miserable tenement and you'll find him." The sneer in his voice told me what he thought of Gawler and his pack.

"Thank you, Mr. Franklin," Seth said when Lincoln didn't respond. "We'll speak to him."

The footsteps receded and disappeared into the foggy darkness. The men joined me and we walked off in a different direction, not speaking until we were well away from the lane.

"Perhaps he's right," Seth said. "Perhaps we shouldn't have dismissed Gawler's pack so easily. It could have been one of them."

"True," I said. "Could you sense if he was telling the truth, Lincoln?"

"Sometimes, but at others, I couldn't be certain." Lincoln put his arm around me, holding me close. He was wonderfully warm. "There *is* a leader," he went on. "He lied about that."

"You should have beaten the answer out of him," Seth said.

"And risked getting hurt?" I shook my head. "That would have been foolish."

"It would have also made him close up," Lincoln said. "Right now, he's wary of us, but not afraid. He knows we're curious about the murder, but he's not aware of the lengths we'll go to in order to uncover the killer."

"He'll tell Ballantine and Swinburn about this encounter," Seth said.

"I'm counting on it."

* * *

"How was Lady Harcourt?" Alice asked me as we sat with Lady Vickers in the music room. She had just finished playing a lovely soft piece, perfect for the afternoon after a late night. Seth and I had both slept in, and when I arose, I discovered Lincoln had already gone out. He hadn't told anyone where.

"As horrid as can be expected," I said. "Worse, in fact. It's as if her polite façade has been stripped away and she showed me her true self."

"You had seen the worst in her before last night," Alice said. "Perhaps she no longer felt the need to keep up the pretense."

"I think I preferred the pretense."

Lady Vickers peered at us over the letter she was reading. "That woman is her own worst enemy. It's difficult enough coming back from scandal, but she's making it almost impossible with her outrageous flirtations. She's so *desperate*, and to what purpose? No one can take away her home or her annuity. She won't be a pauper."

"She claims it's not enough," I said. "She wants more. She wants status and..." I trailed off, not entirely sure what Lady Harcourt wanted.

Alice's playing changed to a grander, more robust tune. "She already has status, thanks to her marriage. Perhaps it's love she's after."

Lady Vickers *humphed*. "She won't find it among the Prince of Wales's set. And I disagree that she wants love."

As did I. She could have had Andrew Buchanan's love, but she threw him away. And even though she'd loved Lincoln, she never wanted to marry him because he wasn't a lord. "Respect?" I offered. "From the people she considers her peers?"

"She may consider them her peers," Lady Vickers said, lowering her letter to her lap, "but they will not consider her theirs while she cavorts with *their* menfolk."

Alice stopped playing. "You're referring to the women, but the men might accept her more readily thanks to her flirting. Perhaps it's their respect she wants."

"There are two faults in that assumption, Alice," Lady Vickers said with the crisp authority of a schoolmistress.

"Firstly, it's the women who decide if another woman is deserving of respect. Men make the same decisions about other men, using different criteria. That's certainly true of elite society, but I cannot speak for the lower orders. And secondly, men do not respect a woman who throws herself at them. A mild flirtation is fine, but anything more overt is vulgar."

Alice returned to her playing. "You do like using that word," she muttered quietly, so that only I could hear.

Lady Vickers was too intent on imparting her wisdom on the topic to listen to anyone else. "While her behavior harms the ladies in her own circle, she will find herself forced out."

"How does it harm them?" I asked. "Neither Sir Ignatius Swinburn nor Lord Underwood are married. They seem to be her only two choices. She's after a husband, not a lover, so she told me."

"Both of those men are extremely eligible. While there are widows and daughters hunting for a suitable husband, she will be considered a rival. Her behavior gives them an excuse not to invite her to dinners and balls, thereby keeping her out of the way. Or so they think. I'm sure none are aware of the sort of parties Lord Underwood holds—or that she attends them."

"On that, we agree."

Seth wandered in looking handsome and fresh despite the late night. He stood by the piano and watched Alice's fingers dancing along the keyboard. She played for a few more minutes then stopped suddenly.

"Excellent," Seth said, clapping. "That was perfection, Alice."

"Thank you. How did you find the party last night?"

He looked at me but I gave nothing away. Alice was fishing and I wanted to see how he answered her. "Interminably dull," he said. "I was glad when we left early."

"Oh? Charlie told me you enjoyed dancing with one young lady in particular."

I'd done no such thing but I held my tongue. Seth shot me an accusatory glare.

His mother sat forward. "Who was she?"

"No one worth mentioning," he said. "Charlie's teasing you both. I only danced because Fitzroy ordered it. The girl is a suspect in the murder."

Lady Vickers slumped back in her chair and flapped the letter in front of her face. "Can you not attend normal parties and meet normal girls like a regular gentleman?"

"She was quite normal," he said lightly. "When in her human form."

His mother whimpered.

Alice smothered a laugh with her hand, making Seth smile.

"Ladies, may I interest you in a game of croquet on the lawn? Or tennis, if you're in need of some exercise?" he asked.

"You can't," Lady Vickers said. "I have a call to make this afternoon and you're going to accompany me."

"Er...I can't. Fitzroy asked me to help him upon his return. Which will be soon." He looked longingly at the doorway. "Very soon."

"Stop making excuses. You haven't even heard who we will be calling upon."

"It won't matter. You know what Fitzroy's like. He can be demanding and...and he needs me, particularly today."

"Oh?" I asked. "What does he need you to do?"

"To pay calls on suspects." He said it so quickly that I wondered if it were true. Then he ruined it by looking far too satisfied with himself.

"I'll ask him to spare you," Lady Vickers said. "I'm sure he can take Gus instead."

"Take Gus where?" Lincoln asked, entering the music room.

"To call on suspects," Seth said before anyone else spoke. "But you can't take him. Only I will do. Isn't that so?"

Lincoln looked to Lady Vickers, Alice and then Seth. "I only require Charlie. I am not an excuse you can use to avoid your obligations."

"Thank you, Mr. Fitzroy," Lady Vickers said with a nod. "We leave in half an hour, Seth."

Seth's mouth opened and closed until he finally muttered, "We can't leave Alice here on her own. She'll be bored."

"Don't mind me," Alice said. "I'll have Gus for company. Perhaps we'll play croquet together. I do fancy a game."

"I am defeated." Seth sighed, but it was more good humored than harried. "Very well, Mother, I'll come with you. Who are we visiting?"

"Lady Mallam and her daughter. You'll remember the girl. She was a plump little thing as a child."

"I do. Our nannies used meet in the park at the same time every day so Hettie and I could play together."

Lady Vickers folded her letter and removed her spectacles. "That is not why the nannies went to the park every day. They each had a young admirer and would take it in turns to meet with him in the park while the other nanny took care of both children. I dismissed yours when I found out."

"You let her go?" Alice said. "That's a little unfair, isn't it?"

"I gave her a reference. Most wouldn't. It's the way things are done, Alice. A nanny must be above reproach. There cannot be even a hint of scandal attached to her name. You'd best remember that if you apply for a position as a nanny or governess. Speaking of which, I'm happy to write a reference for you."

"But you don't have young children. How would a reference from you be worth anything?"

Lady Vickers's lips flattened and her eyes tightened at the corners. "Because it would have my name on it, that's why."

"Come, Mother, let's go now." Seth took his mother's elbow and helped her to stand, while at the same time appealing to me over his shoulder.

"Really, Alice, you have a lot to learn about the world," Lady Vickers said.

"Only your world, ma'am," Alice muttered, and returned to her playing.

I left with Lincoln, Seth and Lady Vickers to the pounding rhythm of a tune I'd never heard before.

"It's getting rather fierce between those two at times," I said to Lincoln as we headed up the stairs together.

"That exchange is considered fierce?" He smirked. "I have a different interpretation of the word than you."

"I do wish Seth would resolve the situation, one way or another."

"How?"

"By telling Alice how he feels then telling his mother she must accept her or lose him."

"Perhaps he isn't ready. Perhaps he's not sure if he loves Alice."

"Of course he does. You've seen him when he's with her. He's besotted."

"That means he's in love? Did I act like that near you?"

I laughed. "Quite the opposite."

"Then perhaps he's not in love."

"He must be," I said with a shrug. "She's perfect for him."

He caught me around my waist and pulled me to a stop. He kissed me lightly on the lips. "Men are blind," he murmured. "They're fools." He kissed me again, an achingly sweet nip of his lips that promised more.

I smiled against his mouth. "You forgot stubborn."

He laughed softly then offered only another little kiss.

"And frustrating beyond all measure." I clasped his head in my hands and held him there so I could kiss him properly.

* * *

LINCOLN and I visited Leonora Ballantine late in the afternoon. His earlier outing had been to the Ballantine residence in disguise. He'd paid one of the maids to deliver a note to Leonora, asking her to meet me alone in a street around the corner from her house at five. He'd mentioned only my name to allay any fears she may have of meeting a man she hardly knew.

I wasn't sure it would work. It was difficult for a young woman to sneak out of the house alone, and I suspected Lord Ballantine would be extra vigilant now that he knew we had an interest in his daughter's beau's death. Both Lincoln and I were quite sure Mr. Franklin would have told Lord Ballantine about our encounter by now. It remained to be seen how much it upset his lordship. His response would be telling.

The shadows grew long and the air cooler as we waited. And waited.

"She's not coming," I finally said as dusk rolled in. The lamplighter would pass by soon, before darkness took over completely. "It's likely she can't get away."

"Or doesn't want to," Lincoln said.

"She seemed keen to find Protheroe's killer last time we spoke."

"Yet she would not give us the name of the second suitor."

"True." I folded my arms, rubbing them to ward off the chill. "What shall we do now?"

"If she won't come to us, we'll go to her."

"How?"

He paused. "I'm not sure yet. Hopefully a plan will come to me before we get to the house."

161

"You weren't going to admit you didn't have a plan, were you?"

"If it were anyone else but you, I wouldn't let on."

I hooked my arm through his and we headed back down the street. "How many times have you made it up as you went along?"

"Too many times to count." He suddenly stopped as a hooded figure turned the corner at a brisk walk, her cloak flapping with each purposeful stride.

Leonora glanced over her shoulder then pushed back her hood. "I'm sorry I'm late. It was so hard to get away. Father is watching me keenly."

"We thought it must have been difficult for you," I told her. "Thank you for coming. This is Mr. Fitzroy, my fiancé."

She nodded a greeting. "We must be quick. What is it you wanted to tell me? Has Roderick communicated with you again, Miss Holloway?"

Oh dear. She thought I had a message from her deceased beau. I wondered if Lincoln had suggested it in his note or if she'd merely assumed. I wouldn't put it past him to deliberately mislead her to ensure she met with us.

"We have a few questions for you, Miss Ballantine," Lincoln said.

"Oh." She fiddled with the cloak's clasp at her throat. "About Roderick's killer?"

Lincoln nodded. "We know you're a shape changer."

Her face blanched. She stared unblinkingly at him.

"Your secret is safe with us," I assured her. "The ghost of your sister told me."

"Lilith?" she whispered. "You've seen her too?"

"She said your father is also a shifter, yet his hands show no signs of it." I touched her fingers. She had left the house without gloves and somehow that made her hands seem even larger.

"I don't know why his aren't big like mine, but he is a shape changer. So is Mama. Are you one too, Mr. Fitzroy? Is that how you know about our...condition?"

"No. A shape changer killed Protheroe."

Leonora stumbled back a step, her hand to her chest. "My god. *No.* Not Father. I...I don't think he's capable of such a thing."

"What of the others in your pack?"

"I don't know." Tears filled her eyes and she suddenly seemed much younger than me, even though the age difference wasn't great. "I'm not allowed to run with them yet, so I don't know all of them well, just those who are also part of our social circle."

"Like Mr. Franklin and Sir Ignatius Swinburn."

"It wouldn't be them. They're kindhearted and loyal."

"Loyal men kill for their leaders," Lincoln said.

She swallowed heavily. "Perhaps it wasn't someone from our pack. Perhaps it was the other pack." The notion enthused her and she blinked hopefully back at us.

"You know about them?" I asked.

"I overheard Father telling Mama about the East End pack a few weeks ago. He said they were causing problems. He mentioned the leader's name but I can't recall it now."

"Gawler?"

She shook her head.

"King?"

"That's it."

"King is dead. Gawler is leader now."

"Whoever it is, you ought to look there for someone to blame. Father told Mama they covet us."

"Covet?"

"Oh yes. Very jealous of our position in society compared to their pack's lowly one. Father even suggested they might try to marry one of us." She pulled a face. "Can you imagine? What audacity!"

"It would keep the shifter bloodlines strong," Lincoln said carefully. "A pack can only inter-breed for so long."

"It would certainly keep the shifter blood pure, which is probably why they killed my poor Roderick—to keep me available for one of their own." She shivered and looked behind her again. "Please don't tell my parents—or anyone— that I spoke freely about the pack to you. I shouldn't have, but I feel as though I can trust you, Miss Holloway, since you're also not normal."

I almost retorted that I was normal but bit my tongue. If she confided in us because she thought me a kindred spirit, I could be as odd as she liked.

"I ought to get back," she said.

"We'll walk with you until you're safe," Lincoln said.

She looked relieved and set off at a steady pace between us.

"Have you ever felt as though you were being followed or spied upon?" I asked her.

She shook her head and once again glanced around her.

"Has your father told you when you will run with your own pack?"

"No. He says I'm not old enough yet, but…" She sighed. "I think that's just an excuse to keep me away from them."

"Why would he do that?"

"To keep me safe."

"From what?"

She lifted one shoulder. "I don't know."

We walked on in silence for a few minutes until I heard her sniff. "What is it, Miss Ballantine?" I asked gently.

"I miss Roderick so much." She accepted the handkerchief Lincoln passed to her and dabbed her eyes. "I miss Lilith, too. Mama has not been the same since her death, and I feel I can no longer talk to her as we used to. I don't want to upset her, but I feel so isolated now."

"Perhaps you should tell your father," I said. "Tell him you need to speak with others like yourself. Perhaps he'll let you run with the pack then."

She nodded. "That would make me feel a little better. But it won't bring my Roderick back." She lowered her head and sobbed into her hand.

I glanced at Lincoln. He looked somewhat uncomfortable.

"Leonora!" bellowed a deep masculine voice ahead of us. "What are you doing with those people?"

Lord Ballantine! He stood several feet away, his stance wide, his thick bushy brows crashing low over his eyes. He lifted his hand and that's when I saw the pistol.

He aimed it at Lincoln.

CHAPTER 10

I swallowed my scream but Leonora did not.

"No!" she cried. "Don't! Please, Father, I am not harmed. I came willingly."

"Come here!" Lord Ballantine ordered with a wag of the pistol. "Now!"

Head bowed, she rushed to his side.

"What do you want with my daughter?" Ballantine snapped.

"We're trying to discover who killed Roderick Protheroe," Lincoln said calmly.

"That name means nothing to us."

Leonora began to cry again, her shoulders shaking. Ballantine offered her no comfort.

"That's odd," Lincoln said. I groaned silently. He was going to poke the wolf to extract answers. "We have it on good authority that your daughter and Protheroe had an understanding."

He glared down at Leonora. Her shoulders hunched as she shrank away from him.

"We didn't hear it from Miss Ballantine herself, you

understand," I said quickly. "Those were Protheroe's own words, and he may have overstated her commitment. Lincoln," I added in a whisper, "you'll get her into trouble."

Ballantine lifted the pistol again. "If I see you near my family again, Fitzroy, I *will* use this." He grabbed Leonora's arm and marched her back down the street and around the corner.

I blew out a breath and pressed a hand to my rapidly beating heart.

Lincoln touched the back of my neck, his thumb making small circling motions. He seemed utterly untroubled. "He wouldn't have used it," he assured me. "It's far too much of a risk. He's not above the law."

"Perhaps not, but he can make your death look like an accident or a wild dog attack."

"He would have to catch me first."

I thumped him lightly in the shoulder then threw my arms around him. He held me tightly. "Please stop being so cocky," I murmured into his chest. "It'll get you into trouble."

We walked in the opposite direction to the Ballantines toward a cab-stand. I clutched Lincoln's arm but glanced over my shoulder several times. "That man is horrible," I said. "Imagine treating his own daughter like that. He doesn't care about her feelings at all. The poor girl is in mourning for Protheroe, but no one understands the depth of her feeling."

"He probably thinks he has her best interests at heart."

"And what are those?"

"Marriage to someone better than Protheroe."

"If we had a daughter, would you want her to marry someone of good breeding? Someone others would consider better?"

He *humphed* softly. "Charlie, if I wanted my loved ones to marry someone better, I would have walked away from you."

It took me a moment to realize *I* was his loved one and he

considered himself beneath me. I grasped his hand and held on tightly. "I'm glad you didn't."

"So am I."

We reached the cab-stand, and Lincoln spoke to the driver before assisting me into the hansom. He settled beside me and closed the waist-height door.

"I hope Lord Ballantine doesn't punish Leonora for speaking to us," I said as we drove off.

He watched me from beneath lowered lashes, but made no comment.

"What is it?" I asked.

"Have you always thought me cocky?" he said.

"I refuse to answer that on the grounds I may incriminate myself."

* * *

"How was your visit to Lady Mallam and her daughter?" I asked Seth as we sat in the library after supper.

We'd retreated to the library along with Lincoln and Gus to discuss our meeting with Leonora and her father's reaction. After the discussion ended, Lincoln got up to stoke the fire. Gus appeared to be mulling something over and not listening to us.

Lady Vickers ate in her room, and Alice could be heard playing the piano. She and Gus had played neither tennis nor croquet but instead paid a visit to Gus's great-aunt and her orphan charges. They now resided at the late General Eastbrooke's house and, by all accounts, the children were thriving under Mrs. Sullivan's care. A teacher had also been appointed and lessons had begun in earnest, although some of the children weren't too keen on sitting in a classroom. It sounded like Gus and Alice had enjoyed a full afternoon.

"Interesting," Seth said, stretching out his long legs and

crossing them at the ankles. "My mother clearly has Hettie in mind for me, although I think Lady Mallam will take some convincing. Apparently a ne'er do well is not all that attractive in a potential son-in-law."

"You're not a ne'er do well," I said.

Gus snorted, proving he was listening.

"Not anymore," I added.

Gus snorted again.

Seth glared at his friend. "The interesting thing is that I enjoyed Hettie's company. She's clever and quick witted. She made me laugh." His lips curved up at the corners. "She is also no longer a plump little thing."

"How would you describe her now?" I asked.

"Shapely." His eyes brightened. "Pretty."

"Just the sort to interest you."

"They *all* interest him," Gus said.

Seth rose and peered down his nose at Gus. "Not anymore. Now, if you'll excuse me, I must see if Alice needs me."

"Why would she need you?"

"For my good company, of course."

Gus rolled his eyes. After Seth had gone, he said, "Just once, I want a woman to say no to him."

"Alice is saying no."

"He ain't tried everything with her yet. He's still got more tricks up his sleeve. You watch, Charlie. When he turns on the charm, she won't be able to resist."

"Perhaps that's why he hasn't turned on the charm yet," I said, remembering what Lincoln suggested. "Perhaps he secretly doesn't want to win her. He prefers dalliances, not commitment."

"Aye. True." He absently stroked his scar where it tugged down the corner of his eye and watched Lincoln, now perusing the bookshelves.

Lincoln pulled out a deep green volume and flipped open the pages.

"What are you looking for?" Gus asked.

"I want to re-read the information on wolves and pack behavior," Lincoln said. "I'm curious about both Ballantine and Swinburn being leaders. I didn't think it possible to have two but I'm not sure."

"Perhaps one is the leader and the other second in command."

"These packs may not follow regular animal behavior," I said. "Their habits could be quite different."

Lincoln nodded. "True."

He sat and read. I joined him, perching on the chair arm, and read over his shoulder.

Gus remained quiet for a long time, and I thought he'd fallen asleep, but then he shifted in the chair. "I've been thinking about Eva's warning, Fitzroy," he said. "About the queen threatening some of us."

Lincoln closed the book and gave him his full attention. "Go on."

"Eva says she didn't see the queen, just sensed her." Gus rested his elbows on the chair arms and leaned forward. It wasn't a small chair but his hulking frame filled it.

"What if what she sensed was *royalty?* It might not have been the queen, specific, but a prince or duke. You said yourself your uncle the duke don't like you."

"I'm not sure that he doesn't like me," Lincoln said.

"You did snub him last night at Underwood's party," I reminded him.

"That's hardly deserving of a threat."

"And I think you unsettle him. His brother is already fond of you, even proud of you. Perhaps the duke is worried that the future king will make you powerful. Or that he'll let slip your relationship at an inopportune moment and the newspapers will get wind of it."

"The Prince of Wales is not likely to forget his place and let something like that out, especially in public."

"I do think Gus has a good point, though. Eva may not have realized she sensed royalty. We should have asked if the threat came from a woman."

"I'll write to her," Lincoln said, taking my hand. "It's a very good point."

Gus beamed and pushed out of the chair. "Right-o. I'm to bed. If you don't need me tomorrow, I'm going to help my aunt out for the day. The house needs some repair work done."

"I can provide the funds for a builder," Lincoln said.

"No need. It'll keep me out of trouble." He bade us goodnight and closed the door behind him.

"What about us?" I asked Lincoln. "What are we going to do tomorrow? I can't see a way forward. Perhaps we can speak to Gawler again. Leonora suggested his pack wants to breed with hers so he could have killed Protheroe to remove him and free her. But I'm not so sure. For one thing, it's rather an extreme measure to stop her marrying Protheroe. And for another, I remember Gawler saying he thought it a good idea to breed out the shape changing trait altogether. Do you think he could have simply said that in a fit of pique after King ousted him as leader? Lincoln? Why are you looking at me like that?"

"Because I like watching your mouth move when you talk."

I smiled.

"And especially when you smile."

"So what do you think? Should we speak to Gawler again tomorrow?"

"If you want to." He lifted a hand and traced my top lip

171

with his thumb then my lower lip. "But right now," he murmured, "I want you to bring that mouth down here and kiss me."

He tugged me off the chair arm and onto his lap where he kissed me tenderly. I soon forgot all about shape changers and murderers. And Lincoln had certainly forgotten his rule of keeping his distance from me.

* * *

WE DECIDED NOT to visit Gawler again. Lincoln felt as though we'd extracted as much information from him as we could. That put us precisely nowhere with our investigation. Lincoln decided to adopt a wait-and-see approach. After Gus and Seth returned from Mrs. Sullivan's orphanage, Lincoln sent them to follow Lord Ballantine about the city. Hopefully he would meet with his fellow pack members to warn them not to talk to us. If he did, we would have more names. Of course, there was the very distinct possibility that he would simply send messages instead.

We had not expected Seth and Gus to return a mere two hours after they departed. I spotted them through the window, lingering near a poplar tree on the front lawn. They'd arrived behind Lord Ballantine's coach, which now waited in front of the Lichfield steps.

"Lord Ballantine," Doyle announced, showing his lordship through to where Lincoln and I sat in the drawing room. We'd seen the coach arrive and braced ourselves for another fiery encounter.

Lincoln left it to me to play the hostess and invite Ballantine to sit. Lincoln neither extended his hand for his lordship to shake nor welcomed him. I thought it a reasonable response considering the man had pointed a pistol at him the day before.

Ballantine did not sit. He didn't acknowledge my presence at all. The force of his glare focused on Lincoln. Lincoln glared right back.

"Close the door, please, Doyle," Lincoln said. "His lordship won't be staying for tea and we are not to be disturbed."

Doyle's eyes momentarily flared at Lincoln's brusqueness toward a peer of the realm, but he showed no other emotion and bowed out. My apprehension couldn't be as easily schooled. I swallowed heavily and watched Ballantine closely. If he was armed, we were in trouble.

Perhaps I ought to sneak out of the room and fetch a weapon.

"Stay away from my family," Lord Ballantine growled.

"Your daughter was happy to talk to us," Lincoln said.

"You tricked her! Leonora told me *she* pretended to have a message from Protheroe's ghost." He stabbed a finger in my direction.

I stilled, as if he'd pinned me to the spot with it.

"You don't deny knowing Protheroe then."

Lincoln's statement caught Ballantine by surprise. His jowls momentarily shook in confused indignation but he quickly recovered. "You even dragged my Lilith into this. That's low, Fitzroy."

"I did speak to Lilith," I said. "And Mr. Protheroe."

"Charlie," Lincoln warned with a shake of his head.

"I can communicate with spirits." Hopefully Leonora hadn't used the word necromancer to describe me to her father. Lincoln was right; the fewer people who knew about it the better. But it wasn't such a ghastly thing to be a medium.

Ballantine looked me up and down then turned away, dismissing me. Clearly he did not see me as interesting or threatening. I edged toward the door.

"What do you want, Fitzroy?" Ballantine spat. "Leonora said you're blaming me for Protheroe's death."

"I'm keeping an open mind," Lincoln said. "But he *was* murdered."

"I know nothing of his death. The man's family only let it be known he died suddenly. It couldn't have been murder. A murder would be reported in the newspapers and I read *The Times* daily."

I inched across the floor, skirting the room. I was very close to the large vase by the door.

"It was reported, but his name was not given," Lincoln said. "It was only reported as a dog attack, not a murder."

"There you have it. Not a murder."

"The police are wrong. It was murder and the killer was a shape shifter."

The whiskers above his top lip twitched. "Ah. There it is. Leonora mentioned you accused her of being some sort of animal."

"There's no point denying it, Ballantine," Lincoln said. "You have two forms, this one and a wolf-like one. Your wife is a shape changer too, and both your daughters."

Ballantine snarled then charged toward Lincoln. Lincoln did not move.

"Don't!" I cried.

Ballantine stopped as if he suddenly recollected his humanity. He paced the carpet in front of Lincoln, a prowling animal if ever I saw one. He had not pushed aside the wolf within completely. "You've got a nerve," he growled.

"Not only did Leonora admit it to us, but Lilith's ghost told Miss Holloway," Lincoln said far too calmly. I knew that calmness. He was prepared to fight if he had to.

Ballantine may be older, and didn't look capable of moving fast, but he was a shape changer. He was strong, even in his human form.

"Did Mr. Franklin tell you we spoke to him too?" Lincoln went on. "Did he tell you he confirmed our suspicions that he is a shape changer?"

"Franklin can say what he likes." Ballantine stopped pacing and squared up to Lincoln. "It's nothing to do with me."

"Isn't it?"

Ballantine bristled. "You're mad. You both are." He swung around and stormed toward the door, and me. "I don't have to listen to this. Out of my way, Miss Holloway."

I skipped to the side and he pushed open the door. It crashed back, startling Doyle standing in the entrance hall. He held onto Ballantine's hat only to have it snatched out of his grip.

"You will not speak with my family again." Ballantine shook the hat at Lincoln. "I've sent my wife and daughter away so you can't accost either of them anymore."

Away! Oh no. It was all our fault. Poor Leonora. I hoped she'd gone somewhere peaceful where she could start to mend her broken heart.

Doyle caught the front door before Ballantine slammed it shut. I did not wait to see the carriage drive away but walked quickly to the drawing room and peered out the window. I couldn't see either Gus or Seth and hoped they'd managed to reach the gate before Ballantine saw them. From there, they should be able to follow him in a hack.

"She's better off away from her father," Lincoln said from behind me.

"Leonora? Yes. Yes, she is." I sighed and sank onto the seat by the window. "That was quite an encounter."

He took my hand and rubbed his thumb over my knuckles. "How are your nerves?"

"Fine. Yours?"

"I'll recover."

175

I didn't laugh. His face was so straight that I wasn't sure if he meant it as a joke.

"I'm going out," he said. "I doubt Ballantine will return but I'll give Doyle instructions not to let him in. Or Swinburn or Franklin."

"Where are you going?"

"To find out where Leonora Ballantine has been banished to."

* * *

WE ASSUMED Leonora had been banished to the family estate near Bristol, but we were wrong.

"She's gone to the Isle of Wight," Lincoln announced upon his return. He'd found me in the attic, updating the ministry's archival records with all we'd learned in recent days.

"The Isle of Wight!" I looked up from the document laid out before me on the desk. "Do they have a house there?"

"They're visiting friends. That was all I could learn from the footman."

"How long will they be gone?"

"He didn't know."

"I should have gone with you and spoken to Lilith's ghost. She might have overheard more." I sighed. "Poor little Lilith. She only stayed for her mother and now her mother has gone. She must feel very much alone."

"Perhaps she'll move on to her afterlife now." He rested a hand on my shoulder and kissed the top of my head.

I spent another hour in the attic while he retreated to the library. After recording the Ballantine family's details, I searched the records for anyone who might have shape changing qualities. While we knew what to call them, previous catalogers from centuries past might refer to them as something else. But I found nothing of interest.

I was about to leave when Whistler, the footman, appeared. His gazed darted quickly around the room he was not allowed into unless asked, then settled on me. "Mr. Fitzroy requests your presence in the drawing room, miss. Lady Harcourt and Lords Marchbank and Gillingham have arrived and are staying for tea."

I groaned. What did the committee want now? "Thank you, Whistler, I'll be down in a moment."

I slid the filing cabinet drawer closed and locked it. I pocketed the key and followed Whistler down the stairs to where Lincoln stood in strained silence while the three other committee members sat. Lord Marchbank greeted me but the other two did not acknowledge me in any way. Lord Gillingham tapped his finger on the head of his walking stick while Lady Harcourt stared out the window.

"Finally!" Lord Gillingham declared, his finger stilling. "*Now* can we get on with it, Fitzroy?"

Lincoln waited for Doyle to set down the tea tray and leave, closing the door behind him. I poured and passed a cup to Lady Harcourt. She did not take it, preferring to stare into the distance.

"Julia!" Gillingham snapped before I could speak. "Take the bloody teacup so we can start this damned meeting. I don't have time for delays this morning. I've got to be at my club in half an hour."

"Your club can wait," Marchbank said. "This is more important."

Lady Harcourt turned slowly and held my gaze with her own. An icy chill skittered down my spine. The skin beneath her eyes was a little swollen, but that was the only sign she'd been crying. Her eyes drilled into me as brutally as ever. I got the feeling if we were alone, she'd wrap her fingers around my throat and squeeze as hard as she could.

She accepted the teacup. It trembled in the saucer until she plucked it off.

"Your time has been wasted coming here," Lincoln began. "I've kept you informed at every stage of the investigation."

"Have you?" Gillingham shot back.

"Yes."

"I'm with Gilly on this," Marchbank said. "There appears to be very little progress. We need an update, Fitzroy."

"There's little to report since my last message," Lincoln said. "Ballantine has sent his daughter away, just this morning, so now we can't question her as easily. He refuses to speak with us at all."

"Keep pressing Swinburn," Gillingham said.

"Why?" Lady Harcourt suddenly blurted out. "I don't see how he's involved at all."

Gillingham shook his head as if he were disappointed in her. "He is involved, Julia. He must be. The man's a filthy upstart."

"Because he's in trade?" She scoffed. "The only thing he's guilty of is being rich and influential without having peerage."

"He doesn't just lack a peerage, he lacks breeding altogether! The man's grandfather was a sailor, for God's sake. A sailor!" He snorted a laugh. "Not a captain. Not even a navy man, serving his country. He worked on some kind of fishing boat, I believe. It's ridiculously absurd."

"That's enough," Marchbank chided.

"Sir Ignatius has risen through his own hard work and perhaps a little good fortune." The spark of battle lit up Lady Harcourt's eyes and flushed her cheeks. It was as if her elegant façade had cracked beyond repair and she'd decided to shed it altogether. I braced myself for the carnage that lay ahead. "What have *you* done, Gilly?" she pressed, all gritted teeth and curled lip. "*You* inherited your money and position, and if it weren't for that, you would be destitute. You're too stupid to employ, too arrogant to learn, and too proud to listen."

"Julia, don't," Marchbank tried. "Let's leave it there before anyone regrets their words."

But neither Lady Harcourt nor Lord Gillingham seemed to hear him. "At least I didn't lie on my back and spread my legs for an old man with money and a title."

Lady Harcourt's breath left her in a gasp and her head jerked to the side as if he'd slapped her. Then, whip-fast, she threw her teacup at him. "How dare you!"

CHAPTER 11

*T*he cup missed its target, instead landing on the rug. Tea splashed over Gillingham's chest and arm, and a spot caught his chin.

He shot to his feet and brandished his walking stick at her. Lincoln stepped in front of him and caught it. Gillingham tried to wrestle it from him but, realizing the futility, gave up. He snarled obscenities at Lady Harcourt instead.

"You're vile, Julia. As vile as anything that crawled out of the gutter." Spittle formed in the corner of his mouth and landed on his chin, joining the tea he had not wiped away. "You and Swinburn belong together, that much is obvious now."

"Enough," Lincoln growled, but he was almost drowned out by Marchbank's palm slapping down on the table.

"Stop it, Gilly," Marchbank ordered. "The committee is bound together, whether you like it or not, and I expect civility from every member. Keep your opinions of one another to yourselves."

Gillingham tried pulling his walking stick free of

Lincoln's grip again, and appeared to be losing the battle until Lincoln released it. Gillingham fell backward into the chair with such momentum that it rocked on its back legs and looked in danger of tipping over.

Lady Harcourt turned to the window and appeared to drift away with her thoughts. I kept a wary eye on her, however, expecting her to flare up again at any moment.

"Lord Ballantine doesn't think the same as you when it comes to Swinburn," Lincoln said to Gillingham. I held my breath as I waited for another tirade to spew from his lordship's mouth.

But he simply removed his handkerchief from his jacket pocket and dabbed his sleeve where the tea had splashed. "Perhaps Swinburn has something over him," he said. "Perhaps he owes Swinburn money."

"Or Swinburn knows he had something to do with Protheroe's death," Lord Marchbank added.

"Ballantine's not involved," Gillingham said. "You know that, March. Stop stirring the pot."

"I know nothing of the sort. He seems to have the strongest motive."

"What about the second lover?" Gillingham said. "That Eddy fellow did it. That's my theory."

"Why are you discounting Ballantine without further evidence?" I asked.

Gillingham peered down his nose at me. "It's *Lord* Ballantine to you, Charlotte. As to why I don't think he's guilty? He's a peer from an upstanding family. That's why."

"He's a shape shifter," I shot back. "The entire family are shape shifters, and a shape shifter killed Protheroe."

"Swinburn may be a shifter too. Many people are."

"Who else?" Lord Marchbank asked, frowning.

Gillingham resumed patting down his damp clothing with his handkerchief, a pink tinge to his cheeks.

Marchbank looked to Lincoln. Lincoln gave a slight shake of his head. Marchbank wouldn't be so easily put off, and the frown did not disappear from his brow.

"My men are watching Ballantine," Lincoln said. "I will also watch Swinburn, but it's more likely that Ballantine is the pack leader, given his peerage. Eddy is still the key to solving this. Once we find out who he is, we'll have another person to question. Even if he's not involved, he might know why Protheroe was killed."

"That seems to be all we can do for now." Marchbank pushed up from the chair. "At least there have been no more deaths."

"Which confirms that this wasn't random but targeted," Lincoln said. "Protheroe was meant to die."

Marchbank shook Lincoln's hand and bowed to me. "Come, Gilly, Julia. Let's leave these two alone to plan their wedding."

"He's got more important things to do," Gillingham muttered.

The two men were met by Doyle, who led them to the front door. Lady Harcourt remained behind. I sighed. It would seem she had something to say.

"May I have a word, Lincoln?" she asked.

"Of course."

She gave me a flinty glare. "I suppose she's staying."

"If Charlie wants to."

I hesitated a moment, but my curiosity outweighed my displeasure at being in the same room as Lady Harcourt.

Lincoln closed the door behind the gentlemen and invited her to sit. She refused with a lift of her chin.

"I do not want you to treat Sir Ignatius like a suspect in the murder," she said.

"He is a suspect," Lincoln said.

She clicked her tongue, her irritation flaring again. "Can you not be more discreet with your questions?"

"No."

"Stop being so obstinate, Lincoln. Of course you can tread more carefully." She seemed to be waiting for a response, but when he gave none, she added, "There is no point in going in with guns blazing like a character from a penny dreadful. It only makes him defensive and less likely to cooperate."

"You think he'll cooperate if I tread carefully?"

"He might."

"I disagree. And anyway, I've had little to say to Swinburn. Most of my encounters have been with Ballantine, his daughter, or his young friend, Mr. Franklin."

"You don't understand," she hissed. "He knows I am connected to you. I invited you to Lord Underwood's party. He knows you're sniffing around him and Ballantine. Honestly, Lincoln, I hadn't expected you to be so obvious about it."

"Has he threatened you, Julia?"

She hesitated before saying, "No."

"Did he imply that he'll not be your...friend if we continued our questioning?" I asked.

She smirked. "Yes, Charlotte, he did imply that."

I suppose that was as good as a threat in her eyes.

"Let me be clear," Lincoln said. "This investigation is more important than your friendship with Swinburn or anyone else."

"Do be reasonable, Lincoln. I only asked you to tread carefully, be discreet. Surely even you can manage that."

Lincoln went quite still. I recognized the anger banking in his eyes, but it would seem Lady Harcourt did not.

"It would seem I wasn't clear enough," he said tightly. "I will not be changing the way I extract information from anyone, and that includes Swinburn."

"For goodness' sake, Lincoln!" she spat back. "I'm simply asking you to go about your business in a way that doesn't make it seem as if he, or his friends, are suspects. Why are you being so difficult about it?"

"This is not open for discussion. Your relationship with Swinburn is not to interfere with this investigation," he told her. "Is that understood?"

Her spine straightened. The muscles in her jaw worked. I held my breath, half expecting her to throw something at him. But Lincoln wasn't Gillingham, and she must know she wouldn't get away with the petulant act.

"There is no relationship between myself and Sir Ignatius," she said haughtily.

"Your behavior at the party would suggest that you wish there was. If your efforts are successful, you may have to give up your position on the committee."

"You think I would share ministry secrets with him?" she gasped out.

"If you believe it would win him, yes." His bluntness had me worried for the crockery in the vicinity of Lady Harcourt.

Her lips pressed together so hard they went white. She stepped up to him and swung her hand at his face. He caught it easily. She did not struggle but stepped even closer, her skirt crushed between them. Her top lip peeled back in a vicious smile and Lincoln let her go. He opened the door.

The color rose to her cheeks, but her lips remained bloodless, a white gash within her pink face. She had never looked so beautiful or so dangerous. Her gaze once again focused on me as if I was the root of all her problems and her life would be better if she could rip me out of the ground, out of Lichfield, and toss me away.

Part of me wished she'd try, just so I could test my fighting skills. But she did not. She stalked past me, her head high, her skirts snapping at her ankles with each stride. Doyle opened the front door for her and she left.

I breathed out heavily and sank into a chair. "That was eventful."

"And useful," he said, sitting on the chair arm. He stroked the back of my neck, but his mind didn't seem to be on the task.

"In what way?" I asked.

"She just confirmed that Swinburn is involved in Protheroe's murder. He may not be directly involved, but he knows something, thanks to his friendship with Ballantine, or he wouldn't have put pressure on her to speak to me."

I nodded slowly. "Do you think she meant to confirm it?"

He took his time answering, and I suspected it wasn't something he had considered. "I don't know. I do know we should find out how deeply their acquaintance goes."

"How?"

"By investigating the business dealings of both men."

* * *

LINCOLN SPENT the rest of the day and most of the next looking through financial records. I saw very little of him, or of Gus and Seth, who continued to follow Lord Ballantine about the city. Seth reported in after luncheon, when Lincoln was also home, and gave an account of Ballantine's movements. His lordship seemed to spend a lot of time at his club. While Seth could enter the club as a gentleman member, he'd decided against it. Ballantine already knew him, and his sudden appearance there would draw attention. It would be easier to follow him if he wasn't aware he was being watched.

Seth was about to leave and rejoin Gus outside Ballantine's house when Eva Cornell arrived. Leisl was not with her. Doyle showed her into the drawing room, where I sat with Lady Vickers and Alice. Seth joined us while Whistler went to fetch Lincoln.

"I thought I heard a new arrival," Seth said, smiling. "Good morning, Miss Cornell. What a pleasant surprise this is."

She eyed him with suspicion. "Good morning, my lord."

"Call me Seth. I hate the 'lord' bit. It makes me think of fat old men. If you call me 'my lord' I'll worry that I've put on weight or have gray hairs sprouting from my ears."

Eva laughed, only to stop abruptly. She bit her lip, apparently embarrassed to have found him amusing.

Lady Vickers clicked her tongue and lowered the shirt she was mending for him. "Honestly, Seth, how do you expect to get on if people don't use your title?"

"Not now, Mother," he said through a strained smile. "Are you here to speak with your brother, Miss Cornell?"

"Eva," she corrected, speaking carefully. "My brother... Yes. It's still odd thinking of him like that. We don't really know one another."

"That will change, now, won't it, Charlie?"

"If that's what Lincoln, Eva and her family want," I said. "Perhaps after this investigation is over they can all dine here."

Seth looked pleased with the suggestion. "You will come, won't you, Eva? And convince your mother and brother too."

"It would be our pleasure to dine at Lichfield Towers," she said. "Thank you, Charlie." Eva gave me a genuine smile that faded when she caught Seth smiling broadly too. Why was she so wary of him? He wasn't even being overly effusive in his charm. I'd seen him be bolder. Besides, he wasn't trying to charm her. Not with Alice present.

Alice watched the exchange quietly, her face unreadable. Her gaze tracked Seth's path toward where she sat on the sofa.

He cleared his throat. "May I sit here, Alice?"

"Of course." She moved to give him room.

He hiked up his trouser legs and sat. "Pleasant weather we're having."

Alice looked from him to Eva then back again. "Yes."

"May I be so bold as to say that you look very, er, pretty today."

"Thank you."

He smiled gently. She attempted to smile back, but it seemed a little forced.

"Why are you sitting down?" Lady Vickers glared at her son. "Doesn't Mr. Fitzroy have work for you to do? You can't sit here chatting to Alice all day. Go on. Off you go."

Lincoln entered before Seth could respond. He must have overheard Lady Vickers because he simply arched his brows at Seth.

Seth sighed and rose. "I'm going." He sketched a formal bow for Alice but smiled at Eva. "The sooner I can get back to work, the sooner we can catch our killer and end this investigation. And then we'll have the family dinner to look forward to. Until then, Eva."

"Goodbye, Seth." Eva caught Lady Vickers' glare and added, "My lord."

Seth pulled a face and patted his stomach with mock self-consciousness. "Charlie, will you check my ears? Can you see any gray hairs in there?"

"Go away, Seth," I said, laughing.

He grinned and winked at Eva. She looked away, her face pink. Alice watched him go, a confused frown drawing her brows together. She wasn't the only one confused by his behavior. I didn't understand his manner toward Alice at all.

"To what do we owe this visit?" Lincoln asked Eva.

"Will you stay for tea?" I asked before she could respond.

"No, thank you," she said. "I must get back. I have a class in an hour."

"There are nursing classes?" Alice asked. "I didn't realize. Are they like university lectures?"

"The hospital conducts them with a more experienced nurse. We attend her rounds with her. They're not classes, really, more first-hand experience."

"That sounds far more interesting than a dry lecture."

"It is. I believe I learn so much more this way." She spoke of her chosen vocation with enthusiasm and warmth. She would make an excellent nurse. "I do study with books, too, and read medical journals, but it's not the same as seeing a real patient."

"Book study isn't required to qualify as a nurse," Lincoln said.

Eva bristled. She stared at him and he stared back, challenging. What was the matter with him?

"It's a fine thing to further one's knowledge," I said to cover the awkward silence.

Not that Eva seemed worried or upset by Lincoln's challenge. It was as if *she* were challenging *him* to speak his mind, or accuse her of whatever he wanted to accuse her of. The similarity between their severely drawn brows and firm jaws only drove home the family resemblance. She was a female version of Lincoln in behavior as well as looks. I wondered if Leisl noticed.

"I decided to respond to your message in person, Lincoln," Eva said curtly. "Yes, a note would have sufficed," she added, as if responding to his unspoken words. "But I thought you might have further questions for me, and this way we can get them over with all at once."

"A good idea," he said simply. "So did you sense the queen, or merely royalty?"

"It was certainly queenly. The threat came from a female presence that was not merely royalty but *ruled*. It did not come from a princess, that much was clear to me." She shrugged. "Who else could it be but our queen, Victoria?"

Lincoln merely nodded. "Thank you for clarifying."

"At least we know she's no immediate threat to us," I said. "She's currently away. I wonder where she is and when she'll return."

"Osborn House," Lady Vickers said without looking up from her mending. "That's where she goes at this time of year. She stays until her birthday in May."

Lincoln turned sharply to me. "Osborn House," he repeated. "It's on the Isle of Wight."

Leonora had gone to the Isle of White. Was it merely coincidence?

If not, she'd been sent there by Lord Ballantine for a reason. What if that reason was to murder the queen?

"It is on the Isle of Wight," Lady Vickers went on, inspecting a stitch. "Magnificent estate, I believe, although I haven't been myself. My friend, Lady Curuthers, was invited to a shooting party at Osborn House once with her husband, many years ago. I believe they shot pheasant." She put down her embroidery. "Or was it partridge? Whatever it was, she told me they had a marvelous time. That was when the prince consort was still alive, of course. There are no shooting parties there now, not when Her Majesty is in residence. She takes such a sad air with her wherever she goes. Honestly, we've all lost someone dear to us but we manage to battle through it. I'm not unsympathetic, you understand, but it's different for her. She ought to have rallied by now. Speaking of which, I doubt the threats that Miss Cornell speaks of will amount to anything, Mr. Fitzroy. Her Majesty doesn't wield a great deal of power and the only people who suffer from her fierce temper and iron-will are her children and grandchildren. Now *they* have reason to feel threatened if they went against her wishes."

"Even so," Alice said, "Eva is certain the threat to herself, Lincoln and Charlie came from the queen."

"Not us specifically," Lincoln told her.

"You are correct," Eva said. "I cannot be certain it is you two with me, but I do think people associated with you are the object of her threats. Do you have any more questions for me? Only I must be getting on."

Lincoln and I had nothing more to say, and we walked with her to the carriage. Lincoln paid the waiting driver to take her wherever she wished to go. Eva protested and refused to accept his money, but the coachman had no such qualms and she had to acquiesce when he took it.

"Why were you being so difficult about her nursing?" I asked him as we watched the coach drive off.

"I wasn't," he said.

"You were. It was as if you were accusing her of lying."

"She is. Nursing doesn't require much study or reading before qualifying. It's learned through employment, by being mentored by senior nurses. Eva even admitted as much."

"Perhaps she wants to further her education and have a more thorough knowledge of medical theories. What's wrong with that?"

"Nothing. So why lie about it?"

"Are you certain she lied?" I asked, some of the wind knocked out of my sails.

He nodded. "I sensed it. Not about the study, but about her reason for studying."

"Why would she lie about that? And what is her reason for studying? Oh!" I nodded, seeing what he could see, finally. "You think she wishes to become a doctor, not a nurse. That would require study."

"It's likely."

"I still don't see the point in lying about it. Not to us."

He touched my fingers. "Not everyone is as open as you.

She may feel she can't confide in us. I'm sure she has met with resistance in her campaign to become a doctor."

"It's a perfectly legitimate profession for a woman nowadays. There is even the School of Medicine for Women in Hunter Street. Perhaps that's where Eva studies."

"It may be a legitimate profession but it's hardly acceptable." He held up his hands in defense when I glared at him. "In the eyes of other people. Perhaps Leisl is against it and Eva doesn't want us to tell her."

It seemed the only explanation for Eva not admitting the truth. Or perhaps she didn't want to seem less feminine in front of the very feminine and pretty Alice. I wondered how much Seth's opinion mattered, if at all. Eva seemed cautious where he was concerned, as if she expected him to do something unexpected and unwanted at any moment.

"What do you think of Eva's insistence that the threat came from the queen?" I asked as we walked slowly to the main staircase.

"That's not what interests me at the moment," he said. "I want to know why Leonora has gone to visit the queen at the Isle of Wight."

"*If* she is there to visit the queen. Perhaps it's just a coincidence."

"I don't believe in coincidences." He looked past my shoulder, and I turned to see Alice standing at the entrance to the drawing room, waiting for us to finish our discussion. "Meet me back here in fifteen minutes," Lincoln said to me. "We're going to find out what the Prince of Wales knows about the Ballantines."

He headed up the stairs and I joined Alice. "Is something wrong?" I asked her. "You look troubled."

"Not troubled. Not exactly." She glanced over her shoulder at the drawing room. "Can we talk somewhere privately?"

"Come and help me choose a hat to go with this outfit. One suitable for the palace."

She smiled and climbed the stairs alongside me. "Did you ever think when we were suffering through one of Mrs. Denk's lectures at the School for Wayward Girls that you would one day be hobnobbing with princes at Buckingham Palace?"

I laughed. "Never. I sometimes wonder what she'd say if she knew."

"I'll ask the girls next time I write. I already mentioned your first visit to the palace."

"You did not! Alice Everheart, you sly thing."

She giggled. "I told them that you attend parties with princes, princesses, ladies, lords and that your fiancé is as brooding as any hero from a sensation novel."

"Alice!"

"Speaking of lords," she said, her voice lower, "what do you think Seth is up to?"

I pushed open my bedroom door and invited her to enter ahead of me. "What do you mean?"

"You know what I mean. You thought his behavior odd too. It was written all over your face."

I opened my wardrobe door and pulled out the little stool at the bottom. The hat boxes were stored up high and I was too short to reach them. Alice, however, was not. She took down one while I retrieved the other two.

"You should speak to Seth, not me," I said, setting the boxes down on the bed.

"I can't," she wailed. "He's so…closed."

"Seth? Hardly."

"He is with me. That's the problem, Charlie. He was so easy with Eva, as if they were well acquainted." She flopped down on the bed and lay back against the pillows. "I can understand why he talks to you. You're like a sister to him.

192

But Eva is a stranger, and yet he's charming with her. With me, he's just...stiff."

I pulled out a green and black pillbox hat and fiddled with the froth of tulle on the front brim. Fortunately Alice didn't seem to notice that I was avoiding answering her.

"Why does he treat her so differently to me?" she said, a pout in her voice but not on her lips. "Why does he treat me differently to how he treats everyone else?"

I set the hat aside and sat on the bed too. "He's on his best behavior with you, Alice. We've been through this. You make him nervous."

"I wish I didn't. I only want to get to know him better."

"Then there's only one thing for it."

"What?"

"Flirt with him. Let him know you're interested. Be overt."

She frowned. "I'm not sure I know how to be overt." Her frown deepened. "I'm not sure if I *am* interested."

"Then why are we discussing him at all?"

"Because...because... Oh, I don't know!" She sat up and picked up the velvet bowler with feathers and ribbons. "This one goes with that outfit. The pillbox is too green and the bonnet is not elegant enough."

"Thank you." I gave her a hug. "Stop worrying about Seth. What will be, will be."

She sighed. "I'll try, but in all honesty, Charlie, I can't help myself. There's so little for me to do here that my mind keeps wandering back to him. I'm afraid I'm inventing intrigues where there are none and thinking through every encounter at least a thousand times."

"Plus you've become prone to exaggeration."

She laughed. "Come on. Let's pin this hat so you can meet your future father-in-law."

I giggled then sobered. Oh God. I was marrying into the

royal family, in a way. How daunting. How exciting. Should we invite the Prince of Wales to the wedding?

* * *

TO OUR GREAT RELIEF, the Prince of Wales was at home in Buckingham Palace. Less fortunate was the presence of his brother, the Duke of Edinburgh. He sprawled in an office chair with spindly legs and bright yellow upholstery.

The Prince of Wales greeted us cordially, if somewhat cautiously. I couldn't blame him for that. We only ever visited when something was afoot.

"Would you like us to open a window, Miss Holloway?" the duke drawled, a smirk tilting his lips. "Wouldn't want you to faint now."

"What are you talking about, Affie?" the Prince of Wales demanded.

"He's referring to the evening we met at Lord Underwood's party," Lincoln said. "We had to leave to follow a suspect but couldn't say as much in front of the other guests, some of whom are also suspects. Miss Holloway came up with the excuse that she wasn't well. I apologize for any offense, Your Highness. None was intended."

"A suspect, eh?" The duke nodded, thoughtful. Perhaps he was trying to recall who had been present. "What's the investigation? Are you allowed to tell me now?"

"Of course. You are both aware of the ministry. I see no reason not to inform you, especially since it seems to involve your family, in a way."

Both men sat up straight. "You'd better sit down," the Prince of Wales said quietly. "Affie, pour us all a scotch, will you? A sherry for you, Miss Holloway?"

I nodded, although I didn't feel like drinking with these men. I wanted to state our business and leave. Being in the palace made me feel a little uncomfortable, like I was out of place. The Duke of Edinburgh's presence added a healthy dose of anxiety to my nerves.

He handed me a glass of sherry but did not let go. He studied me in the brief moment he held onto the glass, as if he were trying to determine something about me. He did the same to Lincoln a moment later.

"Tell us about this investigation," the Prince of Wales went on. "Then I'll tell you what the queen said about King's visits."

I'd almost forgotten that we'd asked him to write to his mother about King in the hopes of discovering who might be following us. Since Lincoln hadn't mentioned anyone following us of late, I'd thought nothing more of it.

The duke sat with an audible exhale of breath. "How does your investigation affect us?" he asked Lincoln. "Come on, out with it, man."

"A young gentleman by the name of Roderick Protheroe was mauled to death in Hyde Park last week. The police think he was attacked by a dog, but evidence suggests it was a shape changer."

The Prince of Wales groaned. "Not another."

"This one is different to King. King was the only one we know of that could change into any shape. The others only have one alternate form, that of an animal. Not all shape changers are dangerous," Lincoln assured him. "But at least one is and has killed Protheroe. We don't know why."

"Why has it got anything to do with us?" the duke asked.

"He's getting to it," his brother chided. "Be patient."

"We've discovered a pack of shape changers among the elite of society," Lincoln said. "Some are your friends."

The prince expelled a breath and sat back. He drank deeply.

"Don't be ridiculous," the duke spat. "Our friends are above suspicion."

"No, they are not." Lincoln fixed his gaze on his uncle, and he held it until the duke looked away. "No one is above suspicion. Not even you, Your Highness."

"I beg your pardon!"

"Calm down, Affie!" The Prince of Wales flapped his hand at his brother. "*We* know our friends are above suspicion, but Mr. Fitzroy does not. He is simply doing his job."

The duke grunted. "You *would* defend him."

The prince rolled his eyes. "Who are these shape changers in our set?"

"Mr. Franklin is one."

"Who?" the duke asked.

"Mr. Franklin and Miss Collingworth. They're young friends of Lord Ballantine."

"Ballantine! Yes, him I know. Good chap."

"He's also one. Somewhat less certain is Sir Ignatius Swinburn," Lincoln added.

"Swinburn!" The Prince of Wales shook his head. "I doubt he's involved unless the fellow's death makes him richer. Money's all he cares about."

"Bloody hell," the duke muttered into his glass. Unlike his older brother, he seemed less certain of Swinburn's innocence. Perhaps he knew Swinburn better. Or perhaps he knew something *about* Swinburn that the Prince of Wales did not.

"Affie, mind your language in front of Miss Holloway."

The duke grunted an apology. At least, I think that's what it was. "I doubt Swinburn is involved, even if he is a shape changer," he said. "He's a good man. He wouldn't kill anyone, even if it somehow made him richer. He already has a fortune with no one to give it to. He's generous with it, too, so I can't see him going to any great lengths to get more. What makes you think this so-called pack is involved in the murder, anyway? Couldn't it be someone of King's ilk?

Someone to whom death and crime is an everyday occurrence?"

"The victim had a secret arrangement with Lord Ballantine's daughter," Lincoln went on. "They were going to run away together and marry against her parents' wishes. The link to Ballantine is too strong to ignore."

"You think Ballantine found out and killed the fellow?" the prince said.

"Or had him killed."

The duke shook his head. "Why go to such an extreme? Why not just lock the girl away or swiftly marry her to someone more suitable?"

"That was Ballantine's plan, and still is, but the suitor in question has not secured the approval of his family yet."

"The suitor is jealous," the duke declared. "He must be. That's why he killed the rival. Have you questioned this man?"

"Leonora Ballantine won't tell us his name."

"Apply more pressure." The duke cast a critical eye over Lincoln. "You look like a fellow who knows how to do that."

"It's not quite as simple as that," I said. "Leonora has been sent away to the Isle of Wight. That's why we've come here. We recently learned that the queen is at Osborn House, hence our concern that Leonora has been sent there for a reason. Does your mother know the Ballantine family?"

"The *queen*," the Prince of Wales said, "has numerous friends. I don't think Lady Ballantine numbers among them, but I may be mistaken. I doubt Her Majesty invited anyone to Osborn House, however. She rarely has visitors for extended stays nowadays. They irk her."

"Everyone irks her," the duke muttered into his glass.

The prince rose from his chair and pressed his knuckles on the desk. "Do you think the queen is in danger? Is that what you're implying?"

"We don't know," Lincoln said. "But it's—"

"My god, we have to warn her!" The prince pulled a piece of paper with royal letterhead off a stack and reached for the silver inkstand.

"While he writes," the duke said, "I might as well tell you what Her Majesty said in her letter. Apparently the fellow named King did speak to her about shifters such as himself. He claimed they are harmless."

"What did she think of that?" Lincoln asked.

"She did not say."

"Did they discuss anything else?"

"Nothing in particular." His gaze connected with his brother's as the prince paused in his writing.

"Tell him," the Prince of Wales said. "I trust the information will not leave this room."

"You have my word," Lincoln said.

"King spoke to her about my nephew, Bertie's eldest." He nodded at his brother, now blotting the ink.

"What did they discuss?"

"A recent scandal that his name was linked to."

"The Cleveland Street affair," Lincoln said, nodding. "Go on."

The duke glanced at me and his cheeks pinked.

"I am aware of the scandal too," I told him. "I know what went on at the Cleveland Street house." At least, I knew what the newspapers implied—that gentlemen went there to have secret liaisons with boys and men.

"While he wasn't mentioned in the papers, my nephew's name was bandied about," the duke went on. "The queen got wind of it. She was furious, of course, and believed every word. In the guise of our late father, King apparently assured Her Majesty that my nephew was not involved, and that he is very much interested in women."

King had done the family a service. How intriguing—and

somewhat unexpected. "Why would he do that?" I asked, more to Lincoln than the two princes. "What could have been his purpose?"

"That's a good question," the Prince of Wales said, setting his letter aside. "If King had suggested the opposite, and claimed the reports were true, then I would believe he was implying that my son was not fit to rule after me."

I agreed. "He could have been attempting to influence the succession in some way."

"To what aim?" the duke asked.

"It's irrelevant," Lincoln said. "King told her the reports cannot be believed, so he hasn't influenced the succession at all."

The prince got up and tugged the bell pull. "King is dead so we can't ask him what his intentions were."

"Thank you, I am well aware of that." The duke rolled his eyes. "Perhaps now that he is dead, the queen will stop believing everything he told her."

The prince stopped and frowned at his brother. "What are you implying? That Eddy *was* involved in the Cleveland Street business? Affie! How could you?"

"Eddy?" both Lincoln and I said together. I stared at him. He stared back.

We'd found our elusive second suitor—and he was a prince.

CHAPTER 12

*T*he Prince of Wales instructed a footman to send the letter to Osborn House immediately. I watched him leave the office, my mind awhirl. Leonora's second suitor was a *prince*.

"Eddy is your son?" Lincoln asked the Prince of Wales after the footman bowed out.

"My eldest," the prince said.

"Eldest legitimate son," the duke added with a smug smile for his brother.

"But he's Prince Albert Victor," Lincoln said. "Not Edward."

"Everyone calls him Eddy. Far too many Alberts in this family. If we didn't use monikers we'd all get confused." The duke chuckled.

"The name Eddy means something to you?" the prince asked.

"Is he visiting the queen at Osborn House?" Lincoln pressed.

"The Prince of Wales asked you a question, sir," the duke bit off. "Kindly answer it."

"Eddy's there for another week or so," the prince said, ignoring his brother. "Why? What has he got to do with any of this?"

"He's Leonora Ballantine's secret suitor." Lincoln's words dropped like stones into the room.

The prince slumped back in his chair with an audible expulsion of breath.

The duke barked a laugh. "You jest."

"I don't make jokes."

I could have told him, and them, that it wasn't true, but I didn't think it was the right time. "We only know him as Eddy," I said. "But it does seem likely that it is one and the same person. We do know that Leonora's second suitor had a higher rank than Lord Ballantine. A prince would be a sought-after son-in-law."

"But it's utterly ridiculous!" the duke declared. His brother merely sat in his chair and stared at the desk, as if he could not quite believe his son was tangled up in this. "Eddy will marry a foreign princess," the duke said. "Alix of Hesse and Margaret of Prussia are both candidates." He snorted. "Not Ballantine's daughter. He's just a baron, isn't he? Practically a nobody. The nerve of him, to think he could force a union behind your back, Bertie." Another snort. "The sheer stupidity that he thinks love matters when it comes to the marriage of the future king of England. Good grief. What's the world coming to? Bertie? Are you listening?"

"I...I am somewhat overwhelmed by this news," the Prince of Wales said. "It's one thing for Ballantine to aspire to have my son as his son-in-law, but it's quite another for Eddy to encourage this girl. He knows how things are."

"He has not mentioned being in love?" I asked gently. I felt a little sorry for the prince. He may be the future king, but he was also a father whose grown son didn't confide in him.

"No. He did not. And now he has caused all manner of havoc. Why would he encourage her?"

I did not mention love again. Neither the duke nor the prince seemed to think it a good reason to meet Leonora in secret.

"One thing we know for certain," the duke said. "Eddy is not your murderer. He's not some shape shifting creature."

That threw cold water on our theory that Ballantine wanted to keep the pack's blood pure.

I looked to Lincoln. He lifted a finger in a small gesture, telling me to leave my questions for later. He stood and held his hand out to me. "Miss Holloway and I are going to the Isle of Wight at the earliest opportunity to keep an eye on Lady Ballantine and her daughter. I suggest you summon your son home, Your Highness. There is a small possibility that we're wrong and his life is in danger after all."

The Prince of Wales nodded numbly. "Yes. Of course. I'll go in person. This is too important to be left to a letter."

* * *

"It's possible Prince Eddy, or whatever his proper name is, is a shape changer," I said as we drove away from the palace.

"It's not impossible," Lincoln agreed. "But I doubt he is. That doesn't mean he wasn't jealous of Protheroe. He could have had him killed by a shape changer. He could have enlisted one of Ballantine's pack; Ballantine wouldn't have refused him."

"That theory would not go down very well with his father and uncle. We're fortunate we didn't mention it. I quite like your head attached to your shoulders."

He tapped his finger against the window sill as he studied the park outside. We'd slowed down thanks to traffic ahead.

"It's likely Ballantine orchestrated the killing simply so Leonora could marry the future king of England."

"He's mad."

"Ambitious."

"They are often one and the same, in my experience."

He nodded absently. "The thing is, he must know he'll have a difficult time convincing the royal family to go along with it. He might have had more luck with the younger brother, Prince George. Prince Albert Victor will be king, and his uncle the duke is correct—nothing less than a foreign princess will do."

"Which perhaps explains why Eddy did not inform his family. He knows it's hopeless. Poor Leonora. He's simply toying with her, giving her false hope of a marriage."

"Not Leonora," Lincoln said. "She's not in love with him. Ballantine is the one being led. He thinks his plan could work; there's historical precedent." At my raised brow he added, "Anne Boleyn was the daughter of a minor nobleman who married the king."

"And didn't that end well. Poor Leonora. She's being used as a pawn, ordered to give the prince whatever favors he demands. What sort of father does that? He's despicable, and Prince Eddy is no better. He ought not take advantage of her if he sees no future for them."

Lincoln finally looked away from the window. "We're being followed again."

I touched the orb necklace nestled beneath my dress. It lay dormant, and I wondered if the imp inside was still alive. I hadn't felt its life force in some time. The notion that it might be dead saddened and worried me.

Lincoln leaned forward and rested one elbow on his knee. His other hand took mine. "I don't think we're in any danger," he said. "Whoever is following is merely gathering information."

"That doesn't worry you?"

He considered this a moment. "A little." I was about to ask him to elaborate but he sat back again and said, "I have another theory about Protheroe's death."

"You do?"

"It's a matter of the succession."

"Intriguing," I said. "Go on."

"Do you recall the Duke of Edinburgh also mentioned his nephew, Eddy, that first time we met him at the palace?"

"I do. He talked about the Cleveland Street scandal and Eddy's supposed involvement. The subject has been raised twice now."

"Why would he do that in front of us? It made me think that Eddy was on his mind for a reason, and that the rumors of Eddy's connection to the brothel were begun by none other than the duke himself."

"Good lord. You're serious!"

He nodded. "Perhaps the duke is trying to manipulate the succession by attaching scandal to Eddy, the second in line to the throne. Perhaps he would prefer the younger brother, Prince George, for a reason we have not yet uncovered. Or perhaps he plans to remove Prince George too, in favor of himself."

"Through a scandal? Surely Princes Eddy and George are above grubby gossip. The Cleveland Street event has all but blown over anyway."

"Has it? If the public found out, they would demand Eddy not become king. That sort of scandal would ruin him. He is not infallible. None of them are."

It was quite a thing to consider, and I wasn't entirely convinced he was right. Surely there were other ways to insure Eddy didn't become king.

On the other hand, short of death, I could think of nothing better than a scandal on the scale of the Cleveland

Street one. The public was not yet aware of Eddy's involvement—it was merely rumor among the upper class—but if he were linked to it in the newspapers, the people would be shocked. Perhaps even shocked enough that they would not want him as their king, forcing the queen to remove him from the line of succession.

The question remained, why would Eddy make a terrible king in the Duke of Edinburgh's eyes? Or perhaps a better question—what could he gain?

The coach picked up pace as we left the heart of the city behind, and I was rocked out of my thoughts. "What has the succession got to do with Protheroe or his death?" I asked.

"Perhaps Protheroe overheard a discussion within the Ballantine household. The duke is a friend to Ballantine and Swinburn, so he may have confided his plan to them. Or perhaps the plan originated with Ballantine or Swinburn and they enlisted the help of the duke. Either way, it's likely Protheroe overheard something while he was secretly courting Leonora. Or Leonora herself knew about it and confided in Protheroe."

"Then why did his ghost not mention it to me?"

"Perhaps he wasn't aware of the importance of what he overheard. Or perhaps Ballantine only *thinks* Protheroe overheard something and decided to kill him just in case."

"Just in case?" I echoed. "Good lord, Lincoln, your mind works in diabolical ways."

"It helps me understand people like Ballantine and Swinburn."

"And the Duke of Edinburgh," I added quietly. My stomach churned at the prospect. We were dealing with the royal family as suspects now. We had to tread very carefully.

* * *

DOYLE HANDED Lincoln a letter when we returned home. Lincoln opened it in the entrance hall and quickly read the contents before passing it to me.

"It's from a lawyer I engaged to look through the financial records of both Ballantine and Swinburn," he said.

The lawyer's first paragraph stated that he'd found no link between the two men specifically, although they occasionally invested in the same stock, but that was not unusual. However, the lawyer had learned that both men were from Bristol, where their families had lived for hundreds of years. Acting on a hunch, the lawyer looked for a link between the previous generations. He discovered that Swinburn's father had used a large amount of capital to start his shipping business when he was in his mid-twenties. It had been impossible to tell where the money came from, but again, acting on the theory that there was a link between the two families, the lawyer worked backwards into the records of companies in which Ballantine had stock and discovered that the previous Lord Ballantine had sold off his share in five different investments. The amount he earned from the sale equaled the amount Swinburn paid for his first steamship.

"We have it," I said, hardly able to contain my excitement. "We have the link between the two men. Only a relative or very good friend would lend such an enormous amount to someone."

Lincoln nodded. "Or a pack leader."

* * *

IT TOOK some convincing for Lady Vickers to allow me to travel to the Isle of Wight without a chaperone, despite having traveled with Lincoln before without one. In the end, I told her it had been arranged. Lincoln avoided her entirely.

He'd given instructions to Seth and Gus to continue

following Lord Ballantine in our absence. So far, they'd reported that Ballantine met with Franklin, Miss Collingworth and Swinburn every day, along with another man and woman. They had not changed their form, however, so we couldn't be sure if they too were shape shifters.

We had a compartment to ourselves for much of the railway leg of the journey, allowing us to discuss the murder before moving on to other topics. Topics like whether Lincoln wanted his family to attend our wedding.

"I knew you would bring it up," he said.

"Well?" I prompted. "Do you want Leisl there?"

"If Leisl is invited then etiquette states Eva and David must be invited too. We haven't met him."

"Meaning you don't want him to come?"

"Meaning it would be awkward."

"You're capable of feeling awkwardness?" I teased. "Lincoln, I learn something new about you every day."

"I like to keep you on your toes."

In all seriousness, I agreed with him. I didn't want someone I'd never met at our wedding. There was only one way to solve the issue. "I have already unofficially invited them to dine with us, but I think we ought to send proper invitations. That way we can meet him over dinner before the wedding."

"And if we don't like him?"

"We won't invite him to the wedding. But not everyone reveals their true nature on first acquaintance. David could be cool at first but thoroughly nice underneath a frosty exterior."

His gaze narrowed. "Was that a comment on how long it took you to get to know me?"

"Not at all. I knew you were the strong silent type the moment we met, and I *suspected* you were kind because you kept trying to feed me."

"Cook fed you."

"At your insistence."

"You were scrawny. If you didn't eat you were in danger of being blown away in a stiff breeze. I made you eat to keep you firmly on the ground. At Lichfield."

"And now?" I asked in my best throaty voice.

His eyes became smoky and his lips twitched at the corners. "And now you're...tempting."

"I find you tempting too, Lincoln. I have from the moment I laid eyes on you in your room. Thank God you thought I was a boy or I would never have the memory of your bare chest to keep me warm at night. You're far too proper to undress in front of a woman."

"You're forgetting that night in Paris."

"Oh, I remember that night very well." Indeed I did. It had been quite an education seeing him in all his naked glory. "But I walked in on you. You didn't undress in front of me."

His gaze slid to the door. "That's enough of that talk before we're married."

I swapped seats to sit beside him. I took his hand in mine and held it in my lap. "Perhaps we can pretend to be newly-weds and share a room at the hotel."

"No!" He untangled our fingers and swapped seats so that we were once again facing each other.

"You're such a prude," I said.

"Me?"

"Yes, you. Even your cheeks have gone pink."

"I do not blush."

I smirked. "We will be married in a few weeks' time, and I will get to see all of you then, and you me. So why wait?"

"It's not the proper way, Charlie, and I am only doing things the proper way where you are concerned. From now on," he added, as if he knew I would bring up our pasts again.

"This matter is closed. Gentlemen do not discuss such things with their fiancées."

I rolled my eyes.

"Rolling your eyes at me will not change my mind."

I stood and planted both hands against the wall behind his head. He blinked up at me with an innocence in contradiction to his defiant brows. I kissed him thoroughly on the lips, a more brazen move than I intended in a railway compartment. But he'd driven me to it. Indeed, the man drove me to madness sometimes, and I couldn't *not* kiss him. He'd foiled my plan of spending the night with him. I'd been looking forward to it ever since he'd announced we were both going to the Isle of Wight and the idea had taken root.

The kiss was as fierce as they always were between us, filled with our pent-up desire for one another and a longing stoked from months of living together. My hands dug into his hair, loosening it from the leather strip, and his hands pressed into my back, holding me in place.

Then he suddenly grasped me by the waist and forced me to sit down again.

"Kissing me won't make me change my mind either," he said. Despite his insistence, I knew the kiss had an impact. His breathing turned ragged and his eyes became even smokier. He smoothed his hair back, as if he needed the moment to gather himself and regain calmness.

My blood thudded along my veins to the beat of the train's rhythm. My skin felt hot, tight, and I suspected my cheeks were aflame. No amount of hair-smoothing would calm *my* nerves.

"If we need to travel again before the wedding," he said, "Lady Vickers is coming along."

"To stop me from visiting you in the night?"

"To stop *me* from visiting *you*. Contrary to popular belief, I am not a machine. Particularly after a kiss like that."

My lips curled into a smile. "I know. You could fool anyone else, but I see the signs, Lincoln."

He grunted. "You've always been able to see me. It's part of the reason why I love you."

My heart skipped merrily at his words, and I found I could not tease him any more. He loved me. That's all that mattered. The rest would come later, on our wedding night. I must dredge up some willpower and find some patience until then.

* * *

THE STEAM FERRY ride across the Solent was long enough to turn Lincoln pale from seasickness but not long enough to bring up his lunch. He didn't want my sympathy so I spent the journey admiring the dark blue-gray water against the retreating green of the mainland and the golden sands of the island. As we drew closer to Cowes, I spotted the towers of Osborn House peeking through the trees to the east.

Lincoln recovered soon enough once his feet were firmly on land again. His singular weakness was not mentioned. We found accommodation at the Fountain Inn, where the respectable innkeeper eyed us dubiously until we requested separate rooms.

"Do you know where Lady Ballantine is staying?" I asked as he handed Lincoln a key. "I heard on the ferry that she is here, and her daughter Leonora is a dear friend from school. I thought I might visit them tomorrow."

We'd decided it would be best if I made inquiries rather than Lincoln, and our presumption was rewarded. The innkeeper gave us instructions on how to find Beaulieu House, the residence of Mr. and Mrs. Franklin.

"The kin of our Mr. Franklin from London," I said to

Lincoln as we headed up the stairs to our rooms. "How interesting."

After an early dinner in the dining room, we said good-night to one another. Neither of us retired immediately to bed, however. Lincoln took advantage of the cover of darkness to investigate not only the village but Beaulieu House and possibly Osborn House. I made friendly approaches to one of the maids who delivered supper around nine.

My inquiries revealed that the Franklins had bought the old Beaulieu residence less than a year ago without viewing it first. It was near Osborn House, and the chatty maid assumed that had been its selling point, since the Franklins only came to the island when a member of the royal family was in residence. Mr. Franklin had joined the yacht club where he competed against the princes when they visited. Mrs. Franklin was reportedly a friend to Princess Beatrice, the queen's youngest daughter who, along with her husband, traveled everywhere with Her Majesty.

I reported all of this to Lincoln in the morning over a breakfast of sausages, mushrooms and eggs in the inn's dining room. It didn't taste as good as Cook's cooking.

"And how did your investigations go?" I asked him.

"Uneventfully," he said. "His Royal Highness arrived after us by private yacht and is now at Osborn House. Lady Ballantine and Leonora are staying with the Franklins but have not visited the queen. Two nights ago, Leonora met in secret with a stranger wearing a hood."

"Did her maid, Ryan, tell you that?" I asked skeptically. Ryan had been adamant she would never talk to us again, and I worried that Lincoln may have been heavy-handed with her.

"A groom was forthcoming with the information," he said. "Particularly after I planted some money in his palm. So forthcoming, in fact, that he showed me the secluded clearing in the garden where he'd taken Leonora every night to meet her lover. I waited in a nearby tree and was rewarded with a view of Leonora at around midnight."

"Did she meet anyone?"

"No. She left after an hour." He paused while the innkeeper's wife poured coffee into our cups. Once she'd taken her leave again, he resumed the story. "The Prince of Wales must have warned his son to stay away from her."

"Very likely. Did she seem upset?"

"I couldn't see her face."

"Then we ought to find out."

"Agreed."

We set out in the direction of Beaulieu House after breakfast. The air hadn't shed its nighttime crispness yet, and dew still glistened on leaves. The sun threatened to burn it off soon and the promise of a fine day buoyed my step. I was visiting a beautiful seaside village frequented by holiday makers with my fiancé at my side. What could be better?

Since it was early in spring, the island wasn't yet overrun by visitors. Lincoln and I fitted right in with the other couples strolling along the high street and admiring the view beyond the harbor. I clung to his arm and he shortened his step for me, but it wasn't until he almost steered me into a bollard that I looked from the view to him. He had not been looking out to sea, but at me.

"What is it?" I asked, smiling.

"Are you cold?"

"I'm fine, thank you." While the sea air was fresh, it wasn't windy, and we walked at a steady pace that kept the chill at bay.

Even so, he adjusted my shawl at my throat so that it covered the bare skin there. "Don't catch cold," he said simply, and walked on.

"Is this the vision you had once?" I asked. "Us walking along the beach together, happy and at peace?"

"No."

"What's different about it?"

"You carried a child on your hip."

His pronouncement took my breath away, and I couldn't think of a single thing to say. He must have realized because he squeezed my hand and said, "Are you all right, Charlie?"

"I will be. I'm just a little...overwhelmed." I smiled up at him. "And yet you once again seem so calm."

"Not calm. Happy." He kissed my forehead and then the skin near my ear. "Very happy."

We reached Beaulieu House and enquired after Leonora. The housekeeper claimed she wasn't in, but I wasn't sure if she spoke the truth.

"Do you feel her presence?" I asked Lincoln as we walked away. "Or did you detect a lie?"

"No on both counts." He looked back at the white stucco house with the bay windows commanding a view of the Solent. "That may mean nothing. My instincts aren't strong."

We decided to try Osborn House next and headed back down the drive to the gate. Lincoln's hand stilled on the latch. His chin snapped up and he tilted his head to the side. He seemed to be listening or perhaps stretching his seer's senses into the surrounding area. I could neither see nor hear anything except the garden, the house, and the sea. Everything felt as it should.

Lincoln let go of the latch and placed his hand at the small of my back.

"What is it?" I don't know why I whispered but it seemed necessary all of a sudden.

"I thought I sensed something."

I glanced around. "'Something?'"

"A presence."

I touched my imp's orb and did not ask him what kind of presence. If he'd sensed a person, he would have worded it differently.

We walked to Osborn House just a short distance away. We kept to the busy road and followed a delivery cart through the tradesman's entrance rather than the grander main gate. The house was far more impressive than Lichfield, all creamy yellow elegance against the bright green of the lawn and deep blue of the sky. I was so used to London's grayness and dense air that the sights and smells were overwhelming at first. But as we waited for the footman to inform the Prince of Wales of our arrival, I drew in deep breaths. The spring blossoms mingled sweetly with the sea's saltiness, the resulting scent one of pristine purity. It wasn't a scent I wanted to forget.

The Prince of Wales agreed to see us, and we were led through reception rooms of varying sizes to a sitting room. Fewer staff bustled about Osborn House compared to Buckingham Palace, and the softer colors and larger windows made the rooms bright and airy. This was a holiday home rather than a place of business like the palace. I liked it immensely, and I could see why the queen preferred to spend time here.

We were shown into a sitting room where the Prince of Wales waited for us. A younger man stood with him. His slightly receding hairline and heavy, deep-set eyes were so like the Prince of Wales's that I knew immediately he must be Eddy.

So this was Lincoln's half-brother. They looked nothing alike. Lincoln was dark, his features sharp and strong, whereas Eddy was fair and soft around the jaw. His frame was impressive enough, but Lincoln was taller, broader and had an effortlessly commanding nature about him. Eddy might be more senior in rank to Lincoln, but I would not want to take orders from him in a crisis. Lincoln had certainly inherited his looks from his mother's side.

"This is my son, Prince Albert Victor. Eddy, this is Miss Holloway and Mr. Fitzroy." The Prince of Wales introduced us as if we were no more important to him than passing acquaintances. It was a disappointment, and yet what did I truly expect? It was one thing to tell his brother about his relationship to Lincoln, but quite another to tell his legitimate son that he had an older, illegitimate half-brother whose mother was a gypsy. "I have informed my son of your investigation into Protheroe's death but not the manner of his death. The fewer people who know *that* the better."

I suspected that meant he hadn't told Eddy about shape shifters at all. That would limit the number of questions we could ask.

"You are free to speak to him," the Prince of Wales went on. "He will answer truthfully."

"I didn't do it!" Eddy blurted out. "I swear to you, sir, I am innocent." His eagerness to convince us confirmed two things—he was worried, and he didn't know Lincoln was his older half-brother. If his father had told him, he would have been far more curious about Lincoln. The declaration of innocence was directed entirely to his father.

"There," the Prince of Wales said to Lincoln. "You heard him. He's innocent."

I feared Lincoln would disagree, but he merely regarded Eddy with a bland expression. Perhaps he was wondering how he could be related to such a weak man. To be fair, the younger prince looked very tired. He must not have slept well after being spoken to by his father last night. Both men looked as though they needed to take to their beds.

"Now that we have settled my son's innocence, you can look elsewhere." The Prince of Wales tried to usher us out, but neither Lincoln nor I moved.

"What do you know about the victim, Roderick Protheroe?" Lincoln asked Eddy.

"Nothing!" The young prince swallowed. "My father told me last night that Protheroe was in love with Leonora, and that they had an understanding, but I don't believe that. I cannot believe it. She was in love with *me*. She told me so. If I can only speak to her, she will confirm it."

"You will not speak to her again!" his father roared. "Not only have you led the girl to believe that she had a future with you, but she is involved in this terrible crime up to her neck! You will not go near her or any of the Ballantine family. Have I made myself clear?"

Eddy blinked owlishly. "But I adore her. How can I give up such an angel? If only you could meet her. She's wonderful, kind and agreeable. We're so alike. We have the same interests, like the same poets and books."

"That's because she's been groomed to attract you," the Prince of Wales said. "She's bait, and you're the fish."

"No! It wasn't like that."

"Are you not listening?" the Prince of Wales exploded. "She had an understanding with Protheroe, *not* you." He stalked across the carpet and back again, his face a dangerous shade of red. "You fool, Eddy. You silly fool. This is why you must listen to the queen and myself when it comes to choosing a wife."

Eddy groaned and lowered his head to his hands. "She was so convincing. So utterly convincing."

"Who introduced you to Leonora?" Lincoln asked.

Eddy blew out a shaky breath. "A mutual friend by the name of Nigel Franklin. I met him here, at the yacht club. His parents have a house nearby."

I was not surprised, considering what we'd learned about the Franklin family and their presence on the Isle of Wight.

"Did you ever meet Lord Ballantine?" Lincoln asked.

"Several times, at their London house. I only ever saw Leonora under his supervision. He wasn't always in the room with us, but he certainly sanctioned our rendezvous."

"What about Sir Ignatius Swinburn?"

"I've never met him."

"I told you before, Fitzroy," the Prince of Wales snapped. "Swinburn is not involved in this. He's a good fellow and has nothing to gain from Protheroe's death."

"That has not been proven one way or another," Lincoln said.

The Prince of Wales clicked his tongue but didn't have a chance to speak before his son did.

"I cannot believe any of this," Eddy muttered into his hands. "She can't have been in love with anyone else. I would have known."

"Perhaps there was some regard on her part," I assured him. "But she is young and may not know her own heart yet. She may have been considering you both."

Lincoln frowned at me.

"Thank you, Miss Holloway." Eddy gave me a sad smile. "I don't profess to know how women think, but I...I felt as if I knew Leonora's heart." He lowered his head and shook it. "I cannot believe I was so wrong."

The Prince of Wales snorted. "I cannot believe you fell for Ballantine's trickery. The nerve of the man. I'll have to cast him out, now. He was an agreeable sort, too."

"It's probably for the best," I said. "And safer. Swinburn too."

"Not Swinburn," he said absently. "I don't mind that you led the girl to believe you had a future together, Eddy. The family's duplicity needed to be brought into the open, and you managed to do that, in your own bumbling way."

I didn't think it possible, but Eddy's head lowered further.

The Prince of Wales's eyes brightened and he wagged a

finger. "I've had a thought. What if the mutual friend, Franklin, is the killer? Perhaps he's in love with the girl too and got wind of Protheroe's claim on her. There. You ought to investigate *him*, Fitzroy."

"We are investigating everyone," Lincoln said simply. "For now, we have no further questions of you, Your Highness."

"For now?" Eddy echoed. He appealed to his father.

The Prince of Wales puffed out his chest and lifted his chin. "My son's part in this investigation is complete. Good day, Mr. Fitzroy, Miss Holloway. I wish you well in finding Protheroe's killer."

"When is His Highness returning to London?" Lincoln asked with a nod at Prince Eddy.

"Within two hours," the Prince of Wales said. "The sooner he is removed from the little trollop's sphere the better."

"She's not a trollop," Eddy said, but he spoke without much conviction.

Lincoln and I followed a footman back through the house but paused upon seeing the queen ahead, walking slowly with a younger woman at her side. The footman bowed and directed us to show deference to Her Majesty.

"Miss Holloway!" the queen said as I curtseyed. "And your fiancé too. What are you doing here?"

"We had business with His Royal Highness," I said.

"Spiritual business?"

I felt the hard gaze of the companion on me but I kept my attention on the queen. "Of sorts," I said.

"Will you join my daughter, Princess Beatrice, and I on a walk, Miss Holloway? Your fiancé can find something to do, I'm sure. You can try to reach the ghost of my husband. Albert loved Osborn House. He found solace in the garden and the sea."

Princess Beatrice looked horrified at the prospect. She

eyed her mother with alarm and me with disgust. "Is this her?" she asked. "The medium?"

The queen nodded. "It's a little cool to walk down to the shore, but the garden will suffice. Come, Miss Holloway. Walk with us."

I didn't want to refuse her, but I didn't want to walk with her—or communicate with the dead prince consort—either. I hoped Lincoln had no such qualms about offering up excuses, but he remained silent, damn him.

It was Princess Beatrice who came to my aid. "Miss Holloway looks very busy. Perhaps another time."

"Indeed I am," I said. "We are about to catch a ferry back to the mainland."

"What a disappointment." The queen's jowls sagged. "When I am in London again, perhaps."

We bowed then followed the footman through the house and out the front door. "Thank goodness we got out of that," I said, glancing over my shoulder. "No thanks to you, Lincoln."

"I was prepared for you to go for a walk with her. It would have allowed me to investigate alone."

"Investigate? Lincoln, you're mad. There are so many servants wandering about, you would have been caught.

"I would not." He tucked my hand into the crook of his arm. "*You* are young, Charlie," he said quietly.

"What has that got to do with anything?"

"You blamed Leonora's indecisiveness on her youth and not knowing her heart yet. She's your age."

"But I am wise beyond my years." I stroked his face until he looked at me. "Never forget that, Lincoln. I know my heart as well as anyone can, because it was my only companion for five years."

"That explains why I know mine. Now."

I hugged his arm. "Do you believe Prince Eddy had nothing to do with Protheroe's death?"

"I do."

"Because your instincts tell you so?"

"No, because he lacks the spine to kill. And his hands are normal sized."

"So are Ballantine's, and yet we know he's a shape shifter. Besides, Prince Eddy could have paid Franklin to kill for him. I'm not sure that a man needs a spine to employ another to murder on his behalf. I'm not willing to rule him out yet."

We walked beneath the gated arch and out of the estate. I lifted my face to the morning sunshine and smiled up at the cloudless sky. Seagulls drifted aimlessly, floating on the breeze without a care in the world.

And then they squawked and scattered.

Lincoln froze and pushed me behind him. I lost my balance but he didn't reach for me as he usually would. A knife appeared in each of his hands, pulled from hiding places in the moment of my distraction. He set his feet apart; a fighting stance.

The bushes rustled and my thudding heart plunged. Three huge creatures emerged, walking on all fours. They resembled wolves, and yet they were not. Their muscular bodies were covered in brown fur and their pointed teeth dripped with saliva. They growled. The deep, primal sound vibrated through me, settling in the pit of my churning stomach.

"Run, Charlie!" Lincoln ordered. "Get away!"

I did not. I couldn't leave him and there was no point. He would be dead before I could fetch help. I reached for my knife, strapped to my leg, without looking away from two of the creatures, now prowling toward us. Their giant paws padded across the gravel, the only sound in the dense silence. No birds chirped, no insects chirruped, and even the leaves had stopped rustling. We were utterly alone with three violent beasts.

I pulled the amber pendant from beneath my bodice and clasped it in my trembling fingers. It did not throb with my touch or grow warm. It could be dead. I felt sick at the prospect. Without the imp, we had no chance of survival against much stronger shape changers.

The two beasts advanced, the third hanging back near the bushes. Heavy heads hung low to the ground, ears pricked up, alert. They were fierce, wild, yet human intelligence shone in their eyes. That made them so much more frightening.

"I release you," I said to the orb around my neck.

Nothing happened.

I lifted the orb to my lips with shaking hands and said louder, "Imp, come out. I release you."

No light announced its arrival. No cat-like creature appeared. My words only managed to achieve the attention of one of the shape changers. It turned away from Lincoln and advanced on me.

CHAPTER 13

"*C*harlie, *go!*" Lincoln shouted.

I stumbled back but did not leave. Perhaps I could draw the second creature away from Lincoln to give him a better chance. The third wolf still kept its distance, swaying a little from side to side, watching.

The second wolf eyed my knife but did not stop prowling toward me. The lipless mouth stretched wide, a gruesome grin that revealed the jagged teeth, the lolling tongue and globs of saliva. I opened my mouth to try to summon the imp again when the first wolf attacked.

Lincoln stabbed upward and his knife struck the beast's shoulder. It yelped and slowed, but did not stop. Lincoln dove to the side and rolled on the ground before springing to his feet. Blood smeared the gravel and his torn clothes. He'd been hit. Oh God.

The second wolf growled at me.

I clutched the knife handle, blade pointed at the wolf, and screamed at my orb. "For God's sake! Come out before it's too late. I release you!"

The beast sprang. I somehow managed to keep my eyes

open, giving me the perfect view of the matted fur of its belly, the enormous pads of its paws, the yellow of its eyes… descending, descending. All I could do was hold the blade tight and pray it was enough.

A flash of light forced my eyes closed. An inhuman squeal ripped through the air. I opened my eyes to see Lincoln easily dodging the swipe of a distracted shape changer. Its focus was not on him but on the hairless, long-eared feline creature larger than a bull with sharp claws slashing at the wolf that had leapt at me.

My otherworldly imp had come to my rescue, finally.

Lincoln scrambled to his feet and came to my side. We watched as the imp hissed at the wolves and lashed out again, the razor-sharp claws just missing the face of the second shape changer. The wolf stumbled backward, bumping into the first one. The third whimpered and ran off into the bushes.

The other two tried to get past my imp to attack us, but it darted between them, slashing one and then the other, hissing and growling like a giant wild cat. The two creatures gave up and followed their pack mate into the thicket.

The imp sat on its haunches and watched the place where the beasts had vanished. It panted as if it had run miles then sank to the ground, resting its head on its front paws. After a moment, it shrank to the size of a house cat and mewled.

"Return now," I told it. "The danger is over." I hoped.

Another flash of light forced my eyes to close. When I reopened them, all was quiet, the bushes were still, and my orb once again felt warm to touch. The imp was safely inside —and alive. Thank God.

"Lincoln," I managed, my voice trembling. "You're hurt."

"A scratch. You?"

"Those are not mere scratches." I tried to see his wounds

on his arm but he moved toward the bushes where the wolves had disappeared.

"Come back from there," I said with less command than I wanted, thanks to my shaking voice.

"They're gone," he announced. Even so, he only returned one knife to its hiding place up his sleeve. He adjusted his grip on the other, picked up his hat, and returned to me. The sharp planes of his cheeks and jaw were rigid, his eyes as black as a moonless night. His gaze swept up and down my length, then, apparently satisfied that I was unharmed, he took my hand and led me along the road.

My heart lurched at the rumble of wheels up ahead but it was only a cart pulled by an ancient horse and driven by an equally ancient man. He touched the brim of his straw hat in greeting. I managed a "Good morning," in return, but Lincoln did not.

We did not speak until we reached the nearest village of East Cowes where he found a coach to take us back to the inn at Cowes. The driver nodded at Lincoln's arm. The sleeve of his jacket and shirt were torn, the fabrics drenched with blood.

"Need a doctor?" the driver asked.

"I'll see one in Cowes." Lincoln assisted me into the carriage. His grip was firm, his balance steady. If the injury affected him, he did an excellent job of hiding it.

"Will you see a doctor?" I asked him as the coach rolled forward.

"No."

I drew in a deep breath, my first proper one since the attack. I drew in another for good measure and brought Lincoln's hand to my lips. He had not let me go on the walk into the village and still did not try to extricate himself.

"That was close," I said.

"Yes." He slipped his knife back into his boot then cupped

my face. He stared into my eyes a moment, then moved his hand from my cheek to the back of my neck. His firm grip pulled me forward. I thought he was going to kiss me but he didn't close the gap between us. "When I order you to leave, you leave. Is that understood, Charlie?"

I sat back slowly, forcing him to remove his hand. I did not release his other but clasped it tightly in my lap. "Your anger is better directed at the shape changers, not me."

"I'm not angry. I'm..." He lifted one shoulder and shook his head, as if he couldn't put his emotions into words.

"You *are* angry with me. I defied you and you don't like it."

"No. I do not like it."

"That's unfortunate, Lincoln, because I will defy you if you order me to leave you again. Whether you're ordering me away from Lichfield to keep me safe, or because you think it's better for me, or ordering me to flee when you are being attacked, I *will* defy you. Every time. Is that clear?"

His gaze bored into mine. His nostrils flared. I prepared for a battle.

"If I think I can be of use," I went on, "then I will stay and fight. If I believe my presence is a hindrance, then—and only then—will I go. You can rant and rave all you want, but I won't change my mind."

He withdrew his hand from mine, tipped his head back against the wall, and muttered something in a language that I couldn't understand.

"Cursing me in a foreign tongue won't make me change my mind either." I glanced out the window. We were already half way between villages. "Why won't you see a doctor?"

"I can't risk the questions." He separated the shredded pieces of his sleeve and inspected the cuts on his right arm. "You can stitch them."

"Me?"

"You've done it before."

"Yes, but I disliked you then. I didn't care if I hurt you. It's different now. Let's find a doctor."

"And risk infection with poorly prepared instruments? Not all medics understand the importance of a sterilized environment. Besides, we don't want awkward questions being asked. You can do it, Charlie. I brought a medical kit with me."

I groaned. "You won't let me get out of it, will you?"

"No, but when have you obeyed any of my orders?"

"I obey the reasonable ones."

* * *

I WAS ACUTELY AWARE THAT, aside from the hand holding, we'd hardly touched since the attack. Simmering anger still vibrated from Lincoln, although he did not mention my defiance again. I suspected he knew it was a battle he could not win.

A maid brought up a jug of boiling water upon my request and left it beside the bowl in Lincoln's room. If she thought it scandalous that we were alone together, she made no comment. I tipped water into the bowl and dropped the needle into it. Lincoln removed his jacket and waistcoat then carefully peeled off his shirt.

"It would have been less painful if you'd just let me see your nakedness last night," I said. "But I'll take this, blood and all."

He eyed me with a flinty glare. So he was still angry.

"I'll try not to ravish you in your delicate state," I went on as if he'd found his sense of humor. "But I can't make any promises."

He turned to the side, presenting me with his shoulder. The gashes on his upper arm weren't too deep or long, but they needed proper treatment. Lincoln had taught me a little about wound care and sterilization. I took care to wash my hands and clean the area around the cuts with the carbolic acid from his medical kit. He made no sound, although it must have stung. Despite my quips, I wasn't feeling at all confident about stitching him up.

I drew a deep breath and threaded the needle. I would have told him to be still or to prepare himself, but no one could ever be more prepared for pain than Lincoln. Even so, I winced each time the needle bit into his flesh, and I stitched as fast as I could to get it over with sooner. He only flinched on the first stitch.

"There," I said, tying a knot in the end of the thread and snipping off the excess with the scissors. "Done. Are you all right?"

He nodded and inspected the stitches. "A fine job."

I packed away the medical kit, concentrating hard on every instrument and not on the semi-naked, wounded man whose presence made my heart thud louder and who could have died today if not for my imp.

I failed. Tears blurred my vision and clogged my throat. If he thought I would ever leave him to face something like that alone, to die alone, he was sorely mistaken and he didn't know me at all.

"It was Leonora, and probably her mother and Mrs. Franklin." He sounded close behind me. "The one that didn't attack was Leonora. I'm sure of it. And as far as we know, the only pack members on the island are Lady Ballantine and Mrs. Franklin. Mr. Franklin could be here but those creatures were female. It must be them."

I heard rustling. Perhaps he was putting on a clean shirt. But then he spoke again, and this time he was at my back. I could *feel* him even though we weren't touching. "Do you agree?" he asked softly.

I nodded, but couldn't speak with the tears trickling

down my cheeks. I didn't want him to know I was crying. I wanted to be strong. I wanted to be someone he could rely on in a dangerous situation.

"Charlie?"

I nodded, hoping that was enough of an answer.

It was not. He touched my shoulder. "Charlie," he murmured.

He gently turned me around and lowered his spare shirt to the chair. He brushed my cheek with his knuckles and pressed his other hand to the small of my back.

"I'm not angry with you," he said.

"I know."

"Then why the tears?"

"Because you got hurt. It could have been worse."

"It wasn't."

"But it could have been, if I hadn't been there and if my imp hadn't come out..."

He said nothing and simply kissed me on the lips. The tenderness of it brought on a fresh bout of tears. I tried so hard to stop them but couldn't. His lips moved from my mouth to my cheek then to each eyelid, and I finally stopped crying.

He wrapped his arms around me and I pressed my cheek against his chest. His skin felt warm, the scattering of tiny black hairs soft, but it was the reassuring beat of his heart I loved most. Its strong, steady rhythm reinforced my fragile one until I felt better.

Yet I did not pull away. I enjoyed the closeness too much to want it to end. I splayed my hands at his back and stroked the smooth skin stretched over straps of muscle. I closed my eyes and breathed him in, not just into my lungs but into my soul. Being with him like this felt so right. *We* were right. I had never been more certain.

"You should go," he said, his voice vibrating from his chest through my body. Yet he did not move away or set me at arm's length.

"When I can be sure you won't faint from your injuries."

I felt rather than heard his laugh. "At least we know your imp is still alive."

"Thank goodness it was merely in a very deep sleep."

"We can't always rely on it."

"No," I said, not wanting to explore what could have happened if I had not worn the necklace.

He finally did set me aside then and I sighed inwardly. I sighed again when he put on his clean shirt, covering up his athletic frame. His mouth twitched in amusement, I was pleased to see. It meant his injuries didn't pain him much. It also meant he was no longer angry with me for defying his order to leave the scene of the attack. He might not like that I stayed, but he had accepted it.

"Should we be concerned about three shape-shifters roaming the island?" I asked.

He shook his head. "They were only after us. They must have seen us at Beaulieu House, or heard about our visit, and realized why we'd come."

"What did they hope to achieve in attacking us? If they'd succeeded, it would have caused chaos. Imagine the upset when the newspapers reported a wild dog attack near Osborn House while the queen and the next two heirs to the throne were in residence."

He lowered the waistcoat he'd been about to put on. "Perhaps they did not intend to kill us, only to frighten us away."

"That's certainly not how it seemed at the time." I placed the cloth I'd used to clean Lincoln's wounds into the bowl of bloody water.

"It's likely they panicked after learning we were here," he said. "Their attack could have been a spur of the moment decision."

"Leonora hung back. She didn't want to harm us. That could work in our favor."

He nodded slowly as he put on his waistcoat. "That's why I intend to visit her in secret."

I set the bowl of water down again. "By secret you mean without her mother or Mrs. Franklin knowing."

He nodded.

"And you also intend to take me with you," I said with a questioning arch of my brow.

He picked up his tie and did it up without looking in the mirror, or at me. I straightened it after he'd finished then gave it a fierce tug. He finally met my gaze.

"I'm coming with you, Lincoln. Leonora trusts me."

He gave a small nod. "We'll leave immediately. Until Prince Eddy has left the island, I want to know where Leonora and the other shape shifters are."

"You think his life is in danger?"

"Not his life, his heart. He's still in love with her. And she must not be allowed near him to compromise him in any way."

"By compromise you mean trick him into an illicit liaison. You think her that cunning?"

"Not her, but those advising her. And the young prince is both gullible and in love. If his father lets him out of his sight, Leonora could easily lure him into the bushes and have her way with him before he departs. If there were witnesses then it would be extremely difficult for the royal family to sweep it under the carpet. Public exposure might be just what Ballantine wants to force the issue."

"Then we'd better go now. He's due to leave soon."

* * *

FROM MY VANTAGE POINT, behind the hedge bordering one

side of Beaulieu House, I peered up at the second window on the top floor and willed Leonora to come down. She sat in the window, staring at the sky, her head resting against the pane of glass. She looked miserable.

But at least we knew she was there. Both Mrs. Franklin and Lady Ballantine were inside too. We'd seen them through the ground floor windows, their heads bent over needlework. The peaceful domestic scene was in stark contrast to their attack on the road from Osborn House.

"I hope the prince got away safely," I said. More than two hours had passed since the Prince of Wales told us Eddy was due to depart.

Lincoln didn't answer. He crouched beside me, gloved fingers pressed to the earth for balance. I shifted my weight, attempting to get more comfortable. Crouching in heeled boots, a bustle dress and two petticoats was not at all comfortable. I'd not yet taken to wearing corsets, although I suspected the day was coming when I must don the restrictive garment. I'd gotten away with it when I was thinner, and then under heavy coats and jackets as my body shape changed with more regular meals. Now that warmer weather and lighter clothes were on the horizon, I must wear some kind of under garment.

"We'll go," Lincoln announced. "It's lunch time."

"You're abandoning the task in favor of your stomach? I never thought I'd see the day."

He directed his cool gaze to me. "I see no point in waiting here, watching her do nothing. Prince Eddy will have gone, so her plan is foiled."

"But we should speak to her."

"Without the others present."

"Then we should wait here until they go out."

He edged away from the hedge, keeping low and out of sight of the house. He stopped when he realized I wasn't following. "I'll come back tonight," he said. "The climb up to her room shouldn't be too arduous."

I lifted my skirts off the ground and joined him. "I'm coming back with you."

We were far enough away that we could both now stand without being seen from the house. "Your presence isn't necessary, Charlie."

"I beg to differ. Leonora will scream the house down if a man climbs through her window. If she sees me, she'll remain calm." When he made no comment, I added, "Luckily I brought my boys' clothing with me. Dresses are not ideal for climbing."

I thought I heard him sigh but it may have just been the breeze. "We'll return after dark."

* * *

IT WASN'T SO LONG AGO that I climbed up to another shape changer's bedroom with Lincoln behind me. That time it had been to see Harriet. I wasn't sure if Leonora's reception would be as civil. The climb was easy enough, thanks to the addition of modern plumbing at Beaulieu House and the external pipes that went with it. With one foot and one hand on the pipe, I reached out and tapped on Leonora's window. The sash flew up, startling me. My foot slipped off the clamp holding the pipe to the wall. My fingers clung on tighter but I was stopped from falling by Lincoln. He held onto my foot and guided it back to the clamp. He showed no ill effects from his injury.

"What the devil— Miss Holloway!" Leonora whispered loudly. "What are you doing?"

"Visiting you without your mother knowing," I whispered back. "May we come in?"

She peered past me, squinting into the darkness below, and sniffed the air. "Is that Mr. Fitzroy?"

"It is. We have questions."

She groaned. "I can't. I'll be in enormous trouble if someone sees you."

"Please, Miss Ballantine. You owe us after that ambush earlier."

She gasped. "How do you know it was me?"

"Please, let us in. We only want to talk to you about Eddy." When she hesitated, I added, "We know he's a prince."

She nibbled her bottom lip then opened the window fully. She helped me through, her unnatural strength a blessing as she lifted me over the sill. Lincoln needed no assistance. He swung through the window and landed silently on both feet. I would never be that graceful, no matter how many times I practiced.

He closed the window and guarded it with his arms crossed. "Did you intend to kill us today?" he whispered.

Leonora plopped down on the bed and drew the covers over her nightdress to her chin. Her unbound hair flowed over her shoulders in silky waves and her big eyes blinked back at me. She looked demure and childlike, yet this woman had kissed the prince, and perhaps done more, to lure him into marriage. She was no innocent. "I didn't want you to get hurt," she insisted. "I didn't want to participate at all."

"You were forced to," I said. "We understand."

I felt Lincoln's glare piercing my back. But while we needed answers, I would be kind to Leonora. Besides, she was a victim too. She'd lost her lover and been manipulated by her parents. She hadn't asked to be born a shape changer, nor did she want to participate in her father's scheme, but she had no choice. Like so many young women of her station, she was a pawn in the game of power.

I sat on the bed near her feet. "We have some more questions for you," I said. "And you must answer them truthfully."

She sniffed. "I've been warned not to speak to you again."

"By your father?"

She leaned forward and lowered her voice. "He'll be so angry if he finds out you were in here."

"He won't learn about it from us, but Miss Ballantine, you must understand that you are involved in a treasonous plot now."

"Treason!"

"Your father's scheme is either designed to cause scandal, thereby forcing the queen to remove Eddy from the line of succession, or end in marriage. Trapping a prince into marriage is a treasonable offense." I had no idea if that were the case but it seemed like it could be. Ballantine wanted power through his daughter's marriage to the heir to the throne. Why else would he want that power if not to manipulate it to his own ends?

"Not scandal," she muttered. "We don't want Eddy cut off. But you're right. The aim was for him to marry me. As to why, I don't know. You'd have to ask my father."

"Was it he who encouraged you to make a play for Eddy?"

She drew up her knees under the covers and wrapped her arms around them. "And Sir Ignatius."

I resisted glancing back at Lincoln. This was the first time we'd heard Swinburn's name directly connected to the scheme.

"Who is the leader of your pack?" Lincoln asked.

"Sir Ignatius."

I sucked in a breath. I hadn't expected that answer. Swinburn was the lesser ranked of the two men, his beginnings far humbler, and yet he'd risen to pack leader, perhaps on the basis of superior strength alone. A pack's makeup appeared to be founded on the baser qualities of the animal kingdom rather than those of nineteenth century human society.

"Did Swinburn introduce you to Eddy?" I asked.

"Nigel Franklin did. It was probably at Sir Ignatius's instruction, however." She sniffed again. "He controls everything the pack does. That's not entirely a bad thing," she added quickly. "He only has our best interests at heart. He's a good man."

"Then why did he order your lover be killed?" Lincoln said.

Leonora's jaw went slack and she stared at him. She shook her head. "No he didn't."

"Are you sure?"

"Of course. Why would you say such a thing?"

"Because your marriage to Roderick Protheroe would have ruined Swinburn's plans for you to marry royalty."

"But murder!" She settled her chin on her knees. "Impossible. And anyway, I didn't tell him about Roderick. How would he have found out we were running away together?"

"Your maid, other servants, your mother, Protheroe himself. There are numerous ways if one has access to your household, as he does."

She considered this then shook her head. "Sir Ignatius is not as greedy for power as you make out. He's a wonderful, generous man. My father, however, now *he* might have done it," she bit off. "Not in person, mind. He's not that blood-thirsty."

"You think he ordered Franklin or one of the other pack members to do it?" I asked.

She pressed her forehead to her knees and hugged them tighter. "It's possible," she mumbled. "Nigel is obsequious enough that he'd do whatever Father ordered. He thinks being agreeable to Father and Sir Ignatius makes him indispensable and liked. It only makes him ridiculous and dull."

"You lived near Bristol before you came to London," Lincoln said. "Did your family mix with Swinburn's there? And what of the other pack members? Are they from the same area?"

"Our family has lived there for centuries, along with others from the pack. I don't know the history very well, but I think they moved to be near us after word got out about a powerful leader who wanted to expand his pack."

"Swinburn's ancestor?" I asked.

"No. Mine. Swinburn is the current leader, but before him, members of my family led the pack for, well, forever."

I wondered what Lord Ballantine thought of a sailor's grandson taking over the leadership after centuries of rule by the rich and powerful Ballantines.

"Swinburn's father was given money by your grandfather to start his own business," Lincoln told her. "Do you know why?"

"Of course I don't. Ladies do not concern themselves with vulgar matters."

I somehow refrained from rolling my eyes. She would not think that way if she'd ever had to worry about money.

"What was Swinburn's father like?" Lincoln asked.

"I never met him, but I heard he was strong in his other form, like Sir Ignatius. He was very clever too. He wouldn't have done so well in business if he was not."

Nor would he have done so well without an injection of money from an investor. "Was it Swinburn's idea to come to London?" I asked.

She nodded. "He decided to move his company headquarters to the city, although he still has an office in Bristol. He thought London would be a good place for the pack to live, so we all moved with him, although we return home from time to time."

"Just like that?" I said. "You make it sound like such a move was easy."

She lifted one shoulder. "Where our pack leader goes, we all go."

But if that pack leader had his business interests at heart rather than the pack's wellbeing, would any of the pack members realize? Or care? "Does Swinburn's success mean success for you all?" I asked.

"You mean financially? Not directly. But if he rises, we all rise because he helps us. We help one another. That's how packs work." She shoved off the covers with sudden vehemence and climbed off the bed. "I shouldn't be talking to you. It's a betrayal of my leader's direct orders. I could be excluded from the pack if anyone found out."

"Your parents wouldn't exclude you," I said.

The clock on the mantel chimed. She glanced at it and gasped. "It's ten already! You have to go *now*." She pushed me toward the window.

"What happens at ten?"

"My mother and Mrs. Franklin bring up a cup of milk for me. They're very punctual. Please go before you're caught. I'll be in enormous trouble and they'll see you as a threat."

Meaning they would attack. I did not need to be told twice.

Lincoln pulled up the window sash just as voices sounded outside the door. My heart skid to a halt in my chest. We had mere seconds. Lincoln assisted me out and I scrabbled to find purchase on the pipe. He was half out of the window before I had secure footing but I had to make room for him. My hand wrapped around the pipe but the bloody clamp where my foot should go eluded me.

Above me, Lincoln hung from the sill by his fingertips, his toes pressed against the wall beneath. He could not hold on for long. With the window open, the shape changers would be able to smell his scent too. Leonora could not close it with his fingers in the way.

She settled in the window embrasure and stared dreamily out at the sky. A pale sliver of moonlight struck her throat. She swallowed heavily but continued to stare into the distance. The bedroom door opened with an ominous creak.

"Leonora!" a crisp voice snapped. "What are you doing? Why is the window open?"

Oh God. If I did not move, Lincoln would be seen. But without a secure foothold, I would fall.

So I jumped.

CHAPTER 14

*J*umped to the side. My hand slipped down the pipe but I managed to partially grip it with the soles of my shoes, stopping me from sliding too far. I used my thighs and knees to clamp myself to the pipe and shimmy down. The cold metal stung my bare hands but it was not yet slippery from dew or rain and I managed to maintain my grip.

No sound came from above me. I glanced up and breathed a sigh of relief when I spotted Lincoln following me down the pipe. He must have secured his position with stealthy silence. I felt like an elephant in comparison.

"What are you doing by the window?" the shrill voice demanded. "Who's out there?"

"No one, Mrs. Franklin," Leonora said with a convincing sigh. "I'm just thinking of my poor Roderick."

"Forget him. He's gone."

"My darling child," came another, softer voice.

A figure blocked the light from the room. I held my breath and glanced up to see a woman's back as she brought her arm around Leonora. Her hand was bandaged. Leonora closed the window without looking down at us.

I shimmied the final few feet to the soft earth. Lincoln landed beside me, took my hand and we slunk off into the night.

I didn't take a full breath until we reached the beach at East Cowes. "That was close," I said, speaking for the first time.

"They would not have attacked," he said. "I'd wager they don't want us associating them with their shape changing form."

"But they already know that we know they're shape changers."

"Leonora does, and her father, but I'd wager he didn't share the information with his wife. Otherwise they wouldn't have attacked us earlier. They were counting on us blaming wild dogs if we managed to escape."

I checked behind me to make sure we weren't followed. No one did, yet I felt uneasy. "So Swinburn is pack leader," I said, "and he wants to get his pack member into the royal family through marriage."

"Not just one pack member. Do you recall his behavior toward Miss Collingworth at the dance? He did not want her flirting with Seth."

"I remember Franklin saying she was intended for another."

"Prince Eddy's younger brother, George, perhaps."

He put his arm around my shoulders and I felt the tension leach away. In fact, I began to enjoy the moonlight walk. The waves lapped gently at the shore, a soothing balm for my frayed nerves. The air was cool but not cold, particularly with Lincoln's arm around me and my body tucked against his. The man always managed to feel warm, no matter the weather.

I breathed in the salty air and looked up at the sky. It was the same sky as London's, and yet different. There were more stars, away from the city's miasmic haze, and even the crescent moon offered enough light to see by. Beyond its enchanting reflection on the water, endless darkness yawned, the lights from the mainland too far away to see.

"We should come back here again," I said, snuggling into Lincoln's side. "It's beautiful."

"If you wish." The softness of his voice had me looking at him.

"*You* don't wish to come back?"

"I only want to be where you are, Charlie."

I smiled and rested my head against his shoulder. His grip tightened and he kissed the top of my head. "You must be able to appreciate this place for its own merits," I said. "You don't find it beautiful?"

"I appreciate beautiful scenery," he said. "But beautiful scenery is not why I choose to visit a place."

"That's because you never take holidays. You only leave London if it's ministry business."

"If you want to leave London for a holiday, then I have no objection."

He didn't understand what I was saying at all, but it didn't matter. He wanted to be with me, and *that's* what mattered. "What if I want to sail around the world?"

He fell silent, and I worried I'd offended him by teasing him about his seasickness. "Will you tend to me in my weakened state?"

"Of course."

"Then I have no objection."

"I hear New Zealand is lovely."

* * *

WE ARRIVED BACK at Lichfield late the following day to a rather frosty household. Seth and Lady Vickers were not on speaking terms after she took Alice with her on her afternoon calls. I thought it sweet of her and told Seth so, only to be informed that there'd been gentlemen present on both occasions. Young, eligible gentlemen, and they'd taken an interest in Alice.

So much so that one had sent her a letter and the sister of the other had asked if she'd like to join her on a walk around Hyde Park the following day.

"Hyde Park!" he declared. "And with the sister no less."

We sat alone in the library with the doors closed. Lincoln and Gus had departed in haste after we'd exchanged ministry news. I think they'd seen the troubled expression on Seth's face and decided they'd rather be anywhere else but listening to his lovesick moaning. I was beginning to wish I'd gone with them.

"What's wrong with Hyde Park and sisters?" I asked.

"It allows Alice and the fellow to meet without raising suspicions. Everyone wanders through Hyde Park at some stage, so it wouldn't be suspicious if one stumbled upon an acquaintance there. And the sister is merely the one issuing the invitation for propriety's sake. That's the benefit of sisters. They can act as co-conspirators."

"Diabolical."

"Don't mock me, Charlie. I am bruised enough."

"And what does Alice say about these two gentlemen?"

"How would I know?"

"By asking her."

He pulled a face. "I can't ask her *that*. She'll think me desperate."

"She'll think you're jealous, which you are."

"Yes, but I don't want her to know."

"You do if you want to secure her affections. A jealous

man is quite attractive, as long as it doesn't become an obses-sion. A little jealousy shows her you're interested in her."

"She knows I'm interested."

I sighed. He and Lincoln had more in common than either realized—women were attracted to them and yet they were both inept when it came to genuine courtship.

"You need to speak to her, not me," I told him.

"I can't."

"Just try."

"No, I mean I can't because she hasn't come out of her room since the mail arrived."

"After receiving the gentleman's letter?"

"She received that and another, from her parents, so Doyle said."

"You asked Doyle to tell you who sent her mail? Seth, that's underhanded."

He slumped further into the chair. "Fitzroy would have done it."

True, and it wasn't fair for me to judge Seth harshly when I wouldn't have judged Lincoln. The thing was, I expected Lincoln to be underhanded. For some reason, I put Seth above Lincoln on the honesty scale, and that wasn't fair to either man.

"I'm going to freshen up," I said, rising. "It's been a long day and last night's sleep was broken."

"A good night, eh?" His lips didn't move but his eyebrow quirked, telling me exactly what he thought Lincoln and I had got up to on our last night at the Fountain Inn.

"Because we were speaking to Leonora," I said, hand on hip, "not because of...*that*."

"I didn't say a word!"

"Your eyebrow said it for you."

He pressed his fingers to his brow. "It has a mind of its own. I'd never suggest such a thing to a lady. Or to you. I mean *you* are a lady, now." He cleared his throat. "Don't tell Fitzroy I disparaged your virtue. He'll kill me."

"He won't kill you. Hurt you, yes, but not kill you. He's grown rather fond of you."

"He has an odd way of showing fondness. I swear he growled at me just now."

"That wasn't a growl, it was a groan. He groaned because he didn't want to hear about your woes with Alice. Nor do I. I want to hear how you've wooed her and won her over with your charm."

"I'm beginning to think it hopeless." He sighed and pushed out of the chair. "My charm has deserted me."

"Nonsense. You charmed Eva the other day."

"That's because I like Eva."

"You don't like Alice?"

He made a sound in the back of his throat as if he were frustrated. At my misunderstanding or his inability to express himself? "She's not intimidating like Alice. She reminded me of you. Like a sister, but not really."

I hooked my arm through his and hugged it. "Thank you, Seth."

"For what?"

"For being my big brother."

"I said *like* a sister, and then I added 'not really'. Typical sibling. They never listen."

We both grinned as we exited the library.

Seth headed to the kitchen to avoid seeing his mother, and I went in search of Alice. She was indeed in her room and invited me in with an unconvincing smile.

"I'm so glad you're back, Charlie," she said, hugging me far too tightly considering the short length of our separation.

I clasped her arms and met her gaze with mine. She looked away and returned to her dressing table. Unlike my dressing table, with its sparse contents, hers was covered with enamel combs, a brush, hand mirror, two bottles of perfume, a pair of gloves, a fan, reticule, and some pots of varying sizes containing creams. The letter perched on the side seemed out of place among the feminine things. It wasn't until I drew closer that I saw another letter crumpled on the floor in the corner where she'd tossed it.

"Was your journey to the Isle of Wight productive?" she asked.

"In a way." I sat on the end of the bed. "How have things been here?"

"Fine."

"Then why do you look so unhappy?"

She blinked at me in the mirror's reflection until her eyes filled with tears.

"Is it Seth?" I pressed. "Has he been..." I didn't know how to finish. I couldn't imagine Seth causing her this much sorrow. He was just too amiable.

"No, not Seth."

"The calls you've made with Lady Vickers then? Did one of the gentlemen offend you in his letter?" I nodded at the piece of paper on the floor.

"This is from the gentleman I met yesterday," she said, tapping the letter on the dressing table. She carefully folded it and placed it at the back of the dressing table. She did not want me to see it and she did not elaborate on its contents. That didn't bode well for Seth's cause.

"Then what upset you?" I asked.

She frowned at the crumpled wad of paper, as if she could make it catch fire with a single fierce look. I picked it up instead and handed it to her.

She did not take it. "It's from my parents. Read it."

"Are you sure?"

She nodded.

I sat again and smoothed out the paper, slowly, deliberately. The last missive she'd received from her parents had implied she was living in a house of ill repute and suggested that Lincoln was taking advantage of her. He and Alice had both written back and assured them that wasn't the case, but the Everhearts' lack of response was telling. They likely did not believe their own daughter.

The letter was written in a scratchy scrawl that I guessed was a man's, but was signed with an impersonal 'your faithful parents'. It consisted of one densely packed paragraph and began without preamble or an exchange of news.

Alice,

We have employed the services of an investigator to look into the affairs of Mr. Fitzroy and other members of the Lichfield Towers household. After receiving his report, we felt compelled to write to you and urge you to return home AT ONCE. We are sickened by what he discovered, and heartily concerned for your reputation at this crucial time. You may not be aware that you are living with men of ill-repute including a gypsy, a pugilist, and an East End thug. The females are just as morally bankrupt, both having liaisons with men who are not their husbands. In the case of your so-called friend, Miss Holloway, she is cavorting with Mr. Fitzroy right under your very nose! If you do not return home, we will come to London and remove you from that vile, perverted Hell.

I stared at the letter and shook my head, over and over. What harsh, cruel words to say to their own daughter. It was impossible to believe that they could be so righteous after banishing Alice from the family home when her nightmares became real, and then refuse to take her back when Mrs. Denk threw her out of the School for Wayward Girls.

"They are the vile ones," I said and crumpled the paper up

again. "They twist the truth to suit their own views." I immediately regretted my outburst, however. They were Alice's parents, after all, and she must harbor some love for them still.

She took the paper from me and threw it into the fireplace where it blackened, curled, and finally ignited. "That's what nonsense deserves," she spat.

I was glad to see her fieriness win over her sorrow. It meant she neither believed them nor would give in. "Do you think they'll come?" I asked. "Or are they all bluster and no action?"

She stared at the flames. "They will come. The part about my reputation 'at this crucial time' is telling. I think it means they have a husband in mind for me. Someone eminently suitable, no doubt, and terribly dull."

"You don't have to go," I said. "You don't have to leave Lichfield if you don't want to."

She threw herself onto the bed beside me with a low moan. "You've been so good to me, Charlie, but I will not bring my troubles down on your head too. You should be looking forward to your wedding and a life with Mr. Fitzroy, not worrying about me."

I lay on my back too and stared up at the ceiling. "You can't go before my wedding. I want you to be my maid of honor."

She flipped onto her side. "Truly? Me?"

"Yes, of course."

She embraced me fiercely, sending her unbound hair tumbling over my face. "Then I won't leave yet."

I pushed her hair aside. "You won't leave at all if you don't want to. Promise?"

"Promise."

We talked some more about the wedding, the Isle of Wight, and her gentlemen admirers. The topic of her parents didn't arise again. I couldn't stop thinking about their letter, however, and went directly to Lincoln's chambers to inform him.

We sat in his sitting room, both of us on chairs at opposite ends of the room. It would seem neither of us could trust ourselves in close proximity to the other after our wonderful sojourn. It may not have been a holiday, but it felt like one.

"She believes they'll come for her," I said.

He nodded, somewhat absently.

"Lincoln? Is something the matter?" The news seemed to trouble him more than it did me, and that meant I'd missed something.

"I was thinking about the investigator they sent," he said. "It's possible it was his presence I felt following us."

"But you saw someone in royal livery. It's unlikely the Everhearts' investigator changed clothes to follow us about, let alone changed into clothes that are difficult to come by."

He nodded slowly. "Then we had two sets of people following us. Someone sent by the Everhearts and someone with access to royal livery."

"The Ballantines, from their association with King."

"Or Swinburn. As pack leader, he's the more likely suspect."

* * *

I AWOKE to the sound of a door slamming and sprang out of bed, fully alert, heart pounding.

"Charlie!" It was too dark to see more than her silhouette, but I knew Alice's voice. It did not usually sound so panicked.

"Alice, what is it? What's wrong?"

Someone pounded on the door. "Open up! You have to come with me, Miss Alice." I recognized that voice too, and groaned. The white rabbit from her dreams was back.

Yet Alice was awake.

I blinked at her but she must not have seen in the dark. She was too busy pushing against the door to keep the rabbit from entering.

The creature hammered on it again. "We're going to be late!" He sounded as panicky as Alice. "Please, Miss Alice, if you don't come, I'll be in—" He choked on the final words and all went silent.

"Come away," I said to Alice.

"But he's still there!" She pressed her ear to the door. "He sounds as if he's being strangled."

I pushed her aside and flung open the door. Lincoln had the rabbit's head in a choke hold, its long white ears brushing Lincoln's chin. The rabbit's paws scrabbled at his bare arm, but it was too dark to see if he drew blood.

"Don't kill him!" I hissed. No one else was about so I assumed—hoped—none had woken from the noise.

I was wrong. Seth and Gus emerged out of the dark corridor, throwing on shirts as they ran softly toward us. They stopped short when they spotted the rabbit in Lincoln's grip.

"Bring him in here," I whispered. "We need to interrogate him."

"Him?" Seth asked. "You sure it's a male?"

"It's wearing trousers, you dolt," Gus whispered back.

"Huh. So it is."

Lincoln grabbed the rabbit by the arms—or forelegs—and shoved him in the back.

"Ow!" the rabbit protested.

"Shhh," I hissed. "You'll wake up the household."

Alice lit the lamp on the table by the door as the men piled into my room. Lincoln pushed the rabbit onto my bed. The creature landed on his large back paws and hopped off the other side.

Lincoln didn't chase him but stood with his arms crossed over his chest. The rabbit swallowed and adjusted his tie, his nose twitching madly. He was better dressed than Lincoln. While the rabbit wore a blue waistcoat and trousers, Lincoln wore only his loose exercise trousers and nothing to cover his chest. The white bandage on his upper arm stood out against his skin. His other arm sported scratches where the rabbit had dug in his claws.

"What the bloody hell do you want with Alice?" Seth demanded from where he and Gus guarded the door.

"I've been tasked with bringing her back to Wonderland," the rabbit said with as much snootiness as Lady Vickers. "Hand her over."

"No."

Alice shot Seth a wan smile of thanks. He looked pleased, even though he pretended not to notice.

"What is Wonderland?" I asked.

"Another realm," the rabbit said.

"And why do you need to take her there?" Lincoln demanded.

"To face trial for treason."

Alice gasped. "Trial!"

"Treason!" I said. "How can she have committed treason when she's never been to your Wonderland realm?"

The rabbit sniffed. "You're stupid. Everyone in this realm is stupid. I don't know how you can bear it, Miss Alice."

"I...I..." Alice clutched her throat and appealed to me.

I simply shrugged. This entire situation was not only absurd, it was confusing. "Why are you still here when Alice is awake?" I asked the rabbit. "Her dreams should vanish when she wakes up. They have in the past."

"Things are progressing," the rabbit said.

"What things?" Alice pressed.

"Matters in Wonderland." The twitching of the rabbit's

nose became more vigorous and his eyes darted between Lincoln and his quarry. "You're wanted, Miss Alice. You must face your trial so the realm can move on. Come back with me. Please. It's urgent now."

Alice shook her head, over and over, her eyes huge. "You're talking gibberish. I don't understand any of this. Wonderland...trial...treason...why does it involve me?"

The rabbit clicked his tongue. "I don't have time to explain now. I'll tell you when we get there." He reached out his front paw. "Come now, Miss Alice. Come back with me."

"Back?" she echoed. "Do you mean to say I've been there before?"

The rabbit stretched out his paw again, pleading. The scene was utterly ridiculous, and yet no one laughed. A thousand questions churned through my head but I asked none of them. For one thing, Alice needed to ask the questions important to her, and for another, I doubted the rabbit would answer me. Indeed, all of us except Alice seemed unimportant to him. We were merely in the way of him completing the task he'd been charged with.

"I know you don't remember," the rabbit said gently. "But you will. I'll explain when we get there and it will all become clear again." He beckoned with his outstretched paw. "Come with me, Miss Alice. You know you must."

She chewed her bottom lip and for one heart-stopping moment, I thought she would take his paw. Then she looked to me, her heart in her eyes, and clasped my hand. "No," she told the rabbit. "I'm staying here."

The rabbit huffed out a breath and lowered his paw. "You silly, silly girl. She'll be furious. Her ranting will be heard clear across the realms." He gulped. "And I must be the one to tell her you won't come."

The rabbit's paw touched his waistcoat pocket and

Lincoln leapt onto and over the bed then pinned him to the wall.

"I just wanted to check the time!" the rabbit protested, paws in the air. "My watch, sir. May I?"

Lincoln eased back enough so the creature could tug on his watch chain. He flipped open the case and pressed the button on the top. The watch chimed once and the rabbit disappeared into thin air.

Lincoln fell forward, his forearm smacking into the wall where the rabbit had been a moment ago. He swore.

"Where did it go?" Gus asked, looking around the room.

Seth opened the door and checked outside. He returned, shaking his head. Gus checked under the bed, in the wardrobe, and also shook his head. We all looked to Alice.

She lowered herself onto the chair at the dressing table, her mouth ajar. She reached out a shaking a hand toward me and I took it. "This is…so odd," she whispered.

Seth placed my wrap around her shoulders and crouched before her. "You're safe now."

"But I…I am awake," she said in a small voice. "And he remained. How can that be?"

"Events in Wonderland are escalating," I said, rather stupidly. Like Alice, I couldn't make head nor tail of what had just happened. "That's what he told us." I looked to Lincoln, hoping he had some answers, but he merely shook his head.

Seth took her hand in both of his. "We'll get to the bottom of this, Alice. Don't worry. You're among friends who'll protect you."

She attempted a smile. "Thank you, Seth. And Gus and Mr. Fitzroy too," she added. "I appreciate your assistance more than I can ever express. I only wish I knew what it all meant and what it has to do with me."

"As do I," Lincoln said, none too gently.

I scowled at him but he did not look repentant.

Alice's gaze met Lincoln's and something passed between them, something that worried me. He made no verbal acknowledgment, but I got the feeling they'd exchanged an understanding. He strode out of my bedroom, the muscles across his broad back and shoulders tense and his hands fisted at his sides.

I did not go after him. "Shall we go to the kitchen for hot chocolate?" I asked Alice.

She began to shake her head but changed her mind. "I'd like that."

"I'll make it for you," Seth said, rising.

"No. Please, just Charlie and me. Thank you, Seth. I do appreciate it."

He gave her a tight smile and left with Gus. I fetched another wrap and some slippers and we headed down the stairs together, stepping lightly so as not to wake the staff or Lady Vickers. We worked together to heat the milk and shave the chocolate into the saucepan, watching as it melted. Neither of us spoke until we sat down at the table, our backs to the warm stove and cups in hand.

"Tell me what happened," I said.

She drew in a breath and let it out slowly. "I dreamed the rabbit watched me as I slept, talking to me, begging me to go with him. He was desperate, telling me he would be in awful trouble if I didn't go with him. Then he did something and said some words in a language I couldn't understand, and I woke up."

"Do you think it was a spell?"

She nodded.

Perhaps it was the same one spoken to open the Frakingham House portal. The key, Leisl called it.

"He looked pleased with himself, too," Alice went on. "As if he wasn't sure the spell would work."

"And then what?" I asked.

"I was utterly terrified. I got out of bed, pretending that I would go with him, but when he tried to take my hand, I ran out the door. He was on the other side of the bed so I managed to get a head start on him. I ran straight to your room. I'm sorry, Charlie, I shouldn't have, but your room is closest to mine and..." She choked back a sob.

"It's all right." I tucked her hair behind her ear and smiled gently. "I'm glad you came to me. Imagine if you'd gone to Seth. He would have taken it entirely the wrong way."

She managed a watery smile. "Mr. Fitzroy is furious with me."

"Don't mind him. I'll give him a stern talking to in the morning."

She shook her head. "No, don't. He's simply worried about you being hurt and...and so am I."

I sat back hard and the wooden slats on the chair dug into my spine. "You're not leaving, Alice."

"I'll stay until the wedding."

"You're *not* leaving. Where will you go?"

"Perhaps I'll have employment by then. As a governess or shop girl. Lady Vickers is helping me by asking her friends and supplying me with references."

"Don't get your hopes up. Her old friends may be inviting her back into the fold again, but they're still wary of her. Her reputation was shattered to pieces when she ran off with her footman, and it'll take some time to repair completely. I'm not sure they'll trust her opinion about a woman she hardly knows."

Alice sighed. "Then I'll find employment on my own. Whatever happens," she said, cutting off my argument, "I will stay for the wedding. I'll leave after that. I can't stay here forever, though. I can't bring danger to you any more than I already have."

"You can't take your rabbit and army with you elsewhere

either! At the least, your dreams will frighten people, and at the most, they'll endanger the lives of others."

She cradled her cup of chocolate to her chest and stared down at the table surface. "I will stay for your wedding, Charlie."

I sighed. It would take more than my pleading to convince her that she was safest here with us. I'd have to enlist Seth's help, and perhaps even that of his mother. The real problem, however, was Lincoln.

I tried convincing him to talk to her the following morning, but he would not. "She can't stay," he said.

"I know you're worried about me, Lincoln, but I can take care of a rabbit. He may be quick but he's not violent."

"And an army?" He looked up from the letter he was reading at his desk.

"They haven't appeared here. Perhaps they've given up."

"Or perhaps they're waiting for the rabbit to fail." He set the letter down. "And anyway, it's not just you I'm afraid for. It's everyone in this house. You can defend yourself, but can Lady Vickers? And what of the staff? Doyle is aware of the goings on here, but the others aren't. Can you imagine the uproar if the rabbit goes into their rooms by accident one night?"

I perched on the edge of his desk and crossed my arms. He had a valid point, but I wasn't going to admit it. "If she leaves, where will she go? We can protect her here, and those who live and work at Lichfield. But if she goes elsewhere, we cannot."

He frowned but did not offer a counter-argument. Yet I didn't feel as though I had won. He picked up the letter that had arrived over breakfast and changed the subject. "This is from the Prince of Wales. I wrote to him yesterday, apprising him of what we'd learned, including Leonora Ballantine's statement that Swinburn is the pack leader."

"He's still refusing to believe it," I said, scanning the letter. "He wants proof of a connection between Franklin and Swinburn. Why Franklin?"

"Because like me, he suspects Franklin is Protheroe's killer. He fits the description of the naked witness who was near the scene, according to my Scotland Yard sources."

"But he did not act alone," I finished for him. "Are you sure about that?"

"Almost. I've seen no evidence that he's in love with Leonora and acted out of jealousy. If he were in love with her, he should have killed Eddy, too."

I agreed. I'd also seen no evidence in Leonora's manner that Franklin meant anything more to her than a friend. "So we think he was directed by Swinburn but the Prince of Wales doesn't believe his friend capable of murder."

"Nor can he believe that his friend is a shape changer." He pointed to a line near the end of the page. "He thinks the Ballantines and others are setting him up."

"He gives no reason for believing that."

"No."

"We need to know for certain." I handed back the letter. "So how do we get proof of a connection between Franklin and Swinburn?"

"We force a confession from Franklin."

"Force?" I asked, carefully.

"Perhaps I should have said scare a confession out of him."

"Scare?" It still sounded as if violence would be involved. "How will you do that?"

"Not me, you. You're going to summon the dead and bring all manner of hell down on him."

CHAPTER 15

J used to find Highgate Cemetery frightening at any time of day or night, but I now found it peaceful, even in the dark. I felt at home among the exposed roots of the oak trees, the leaning headstones and grand statues. Some of the graves contained the bones of spirits I'd summoned, like Gordon Thackeray and Estelle Pearson, and others I simply felt as though I knew personally, I'd passed their graves so many times. I did not visit my mother's grave anymore, however. Not after Anselm Holloway, her husband and the man who adopted me as a baby, was now buried beside her. I visited her only in my memories now.

Lincoln had found Roderick Protheroe's grave earlier that day and led the way. We both wore dark clothing, me in my boy's attire and a warm coat, Lincoln in drab working man's trousers and jacket but no overcoat. He didn't wear gloves either, preferring bare hands in case he needed to grip something. I wore gloves, but they did little to stop the cold. Wintry weather had returned tonight, with the biting wind threatening to blow my cap off and expose my long hair. At least it didn't rain.

Protheroe's grave smelled of freshly turned earth. A posy of daffodils announced the recent visit of a loved one. Not Leonora. She wouldn't be allowed.

I set down my lantern and glanced up at the trees surrounding us. The branches thrashed and leaves shook as another gust swept through the cemetery. If I were an anxious person, it was just the sort of night to terrify. It lacked only thunder and lightning.

"When you're ready, Charlie," Lincoln said, his voice deeply reverent.

I gathered my nerves with a steadying breath. I didn't like disturbing the dead. It felt wrong to bring back those who'd chosen to cross, but I told myself Protheroe wouldn't mind helping us catch his killer.

"Roderick Oswald Protheroe," I began. "I summon your spirit to me, Roderick Oswald Protheroe."

The swirling mist plunged from the tree, as if it had been lurking up there, waiting. But I knew it had not, that the tree had merely been in its path. The form of Leonora's beau coalesced in front of me. He frowned at me then down at his headstone.

"My resting place," he said heavily. He crouched to read what was written on the stone, then stood. Whether he approved of what was inscribed or not, he did not say. "Has my killer been found, Miss Holloway?"

"No, but we have a suspicion," I told him. "We need your help extracting a confession from him."

"How?"

"By frightening him with your animated corpse."

"Ah. Necromancy. Yes, I almost forgot you are more than a medium. How diabolical."

"Quite."

"My apologies, Miss Holloway. Please forgive me. I find it hard to reconcile the pretty young woman before me with a person who can raise the dead. It doesn't seem possible, somehow. You ought to be an old crone with a wart on your nose."

I laughed, despite my nerves, and he smiled back. Not for the first time, I could understand why Leonora had fallen in love with this charming man. "Do you mind if we use your corpse in this way?" I told him what the process involved, and how his spirit would move his limbs but I would continue to control him if I chose to.

He did not hesitate in agreeing. "I want to catch my killer, and if this is the only possible way then I'll do it."

"We need to know for certain," I said. "If we can frighten him sufficiently then we may extract an answer not only about his guilt, but also about who directed him."

"An equally important goal," he said with a nod and a glance at Lincoln, who had not yet spoken. "Very well. Let's begin." He settled his ghostly feet on the earth and squared his shoulders. "What do I do?"

"Descend into your coffin and then your body. Your spirit can control its movements. Your limbs will feel awkward from ill-use but you'll be incredibly strong. Use that strength to break through the coffin and dig your way out. It's a messy affair, and an arduous task, but I know you can do it."

"You've seen others succeed." It was not a question.

"I have."

His spirit rose and slipped through the ground, disappearing from sight. The seconds ticked by, or perhaps it was minutes, until finally the earth near our feet erupted and a fist punched through. Lincoln assisted him out, much to Protheroe's surprise. Dark, empty eyes stared back at us without really seeing. It never failed to unnerve me that the risen saw with their spirit sight.

"Thank you," Protheroe said in a brittle, frail voice. He touched his throat and repeated himself, a little stronger this time. "There is no vibration," he said with wonder. "Interesting."

"Come with us," Lincoln said, his words edged with impatience. "We'll return you here when the deed is done."

I picked up my lantern and walked beside Protheroe. It took several steps before he was able to smooth out his jerky gait, and even then it wasn't a gentleman's way of walking, but somewhat self-conscious and awkward. Lincoln followed, no doubt to keep the dead man in his sights for precaution. Lincoln was not in the habit of trusting strangers, even if they were friendly and helpful—and dead.

"You're remarkably calm, Miss Holloway, considering I must look gruesome," Protheroe said.

"I'm used to it," I told him. "And you don't look too awful. Your burial suit hides the wounds and your face is unmarked. Besides, you haven't been dead long."

I didn't tell him that my lantern's light picked out the deathly white pallor beneath fresh dirt on his face, and the dry, bloodless lips. He'd only been in the ground less than a week, so he'd not begun to disintegrate. However, I'd wager if I touched him, his skin would flake.

We exited the graveyard through the main gate and climbed into the waiting carriage. Seth and Gus sat on the driver's perch. They both doffed their caps and Protheroe nodded in return.

"How is Leonora?" he asked when we settled onto the red leather seats.

"She's strong," I said. "But she misses you terribly."

He fell silent as he turned his head to the window and watched the darkened streets slip by. I suspected he saw nothing, however, his thoughts on Leonora. I did not disturb him on the journey to the Mayfair house where we'd seen Miss Collingworth and Mr. Franklin the night of Lord Underwood's dance. Lincoln had discovered the house belonged to Franklin's father, a second generation industrialist who'd risen from humble beginnings, much like Sir Ignatius Swinburn's family.

As the coach slowed, Protheroe glanced up at the mansion. "So we're going to confront the Eddy fellow? Is he my killer?"

"No," Lincoln said. "He had nothing to do with your death. Your killer is Nigel Franklin."

"I remember him. *He* killed me?" He swore then apologized to me. "I am overwhelmed by the news, Miss Holloway. Please forgive my coarseness."

"There is nothing to forgive," I said. "You have every right to be angry with him."

"Why did he kill me? I hardly know him."

"That's what we want to find out," Lincoln said. "The thing is, Mr. Protheroe, Franklin is not entirely human. He's a supernatural that can change shape into a wolf."

"Blimey!"

"His claws inflicted the fatal wounds on your chest."

He pressed a hand to his chest where his heart once beat. "I see."

"He took your life away," Lincoln added. "And he took away Miss Ballantine's future."

Protheroe's face performed an odd contorted movement, as if he were trying to frown but could not get all the muscles to work. "He did, didn't he?"

I knew Lincoln was attempting to rile the rather placid man to a more passionate response in order to frighten Franklin. Politeness wasn't going to extract answers. We needed fury. Indignation would do at a pinch.

"Knock on the door," I directed Protheroe. "They keep no staff here so he ought to answer it himself."

I hoped Franklin was present and alone. Gus, Seth and Lincoln had all been out earlier to ascertain the evening movements of other pack members to insure they weren't running together. They discovered that all the male pack members had plans. Miss Collingworth's and the other young woman's movements were unknown. Lady Ballantine, Leonora and Mrs. Franklin had not returned from the Isle of Wight.

Mr. Franklin did indeed answer the knock, although it took several minutes, and he was dressed in a robe, carrying a candlestick. He stood in the doorway and held up his candle to better see the man who'd come calling in the middle of the night. The flickering flame illuminated the horror on his face perfectly.

He dropped the candle and backed away. He tried to shove the door closed, but Protheroe muscled his way in, Lincoln at his heels. I followed with Gus while Seth, who'd chosen the short straw, had to stay with the carriage.

I picked up the candlestick but the flame had gone out. If nothing else, the solid brass stick was a good weapon. I stepped over the threshold and tried to make sense of the dark shapes. A square of light from a doorway to our left fell across the carpeted floor but failed to illuminate more than that. We would have to use our instincts, something that Lincoln excelled at. Protheroe would not find it difficult with his spirit sight. Gus and I would struggle, however. I hung back with him as he shut the front door.

"Wh-what...?" Franklin mumbled. "Who are you?"

"You know who I am." The harsh, guttural voice was not at all like Protheroe's gentle ghostly one. "My name is Roderick Protheroe, and you killed me."

"I...I..." Franklin's audible swallow filled the silence and his silhouette stood taller. "You're not he! This is absurd. I should have known you were behind this, Fitzroy. What do you want?"

Lincoln moved into the adjoining room and returned with a lamp. He held it up to Protheroe's face.

Franklin gasped and he stumbled backward, bumping into a table and knocking off the onyx statue that stood there. It fell with a thud on the floor but did not break. "Bloody hell!" He steadied himself with a hand on the table. "What in God's name is going on? You...you can't be him. You can't be!"

"Why?" Protheroe spat. "Because you saw me die?"

Another audible swallow from Franklin. He did not deny the accusation.

"I am dead." Protheroe attempted to undo the buttons on his jacket but his stiff fingers couldn't manage it.

I stepped forward to help him and we soon had his jacket and shirt undone. I'd seen the injuries in the mortuary soon after death. Now, days later, rot had set in and they looked ghastly. The deep gashes exposed bone, muscle and organs. Innards spilled out, and the skin surrounding the wounds had turned black. I covered my nose and mouth as I caught the unmistakable smell of putrid meat.

Franklin showed no signs of repulsion. He merely stared closer at Protheroe's face as if trying to place him.

"Look at my wounds!" Protheroe shouted. "Look at your work, *Ripper*."

I shivered. The reminder of that terrible time when Jack the Ripper terrorized the city was still fresh in my memory.

"What do you want?" Franklin snapped.

"Answers," Lincoln said.

"You'll get nothing from me." He flapped his hand at Protheroe. "Your actor is unconvincing."

"Actor!" Protheroe strode up to Franklin and pointed at his damaged chest. "You think this fakery? These are very real. You did this. You *murdered* me."

The accusation hardly made an impression. Franklin

seemed to think we were putting on a show, and he no
longer looked afraid. "Then how can you be here? Do you
take me for a fool?"

I stepped forward and removed my cap and unpinned my
hair. It fell past my shoulders. "He's here because I brought
him here."

"Miss Holloway?" Franklin gathered the edges of his robe
together where it gaped at his chest. "I see now. Lord Ballantine told me you're a medium. So have you summoned
Protheroe's spirit thinking that would frighten me? What a
joke. I'm not scared of an apparition." He reached out to push
a hand through what he thought was a ghost, but hit solid
corpse. He recoiled and scampered away until he smacked
into the wall. His chest rose and fell with his rapid breaths.
"That's... You're... *No*. Impossible."

"I'm not a medium," I told him. "I'm a necromancer. Do
you know what a necromancer does?"

Franklin nodded quickly but did not take his eyes off
Protheroe.

"Mr. Protheroe wanted to meet you," I said.

"Me?" Franklin's voice pitched high. "Why?"

"You know why."

"Because of this." Protheroe grabbed Franklin's hand and
pressed it to his ruined chest.

Franklin tried to pull away but couldn't. That seemed to
frighten him more than being touched by a corpse. He
suddenly realized the dead have unnatural strength. Franklin
was used to being stronger than a human, but now he found
himself at a disadvantage.

"Because you murdered me," Protheroe went on. "And I
want to know why."

Franklin tried twisting his hand free, but Protheroe did
not let go. "No!" he cried. "It wasn't me."

Protheroe smashed his free hand into Franklin's jaw.

Franklin fell to his knees but was saved from collapsing by Protheroe.

"It was you," Protheroe snarled.

Franklin cowered on his knees. Protheroe leaned over him. He wasn't a big man, but he seemed to enjoy the power he now held. His lips stretched into a malicious grin.

Franklin stared up into Protheroe's dead eyes. "Go away. Leave me alone. Miss Holloway, I beg you, make him go away. His death is not my fault. I swear to you! Not my fault."

"But you did it," Protheroe said. "On another's orders, perhaps, but *you* killed me."

Franklin winced and turned his face away. Protheroe squeezed Franklin's wrist.

Bone cracked. Franklin screamed. He doubled over in pain and tried to wrench free, but could not.

"Talk," Protheroe snarled. "Or I break the other one and your ankles too. Try and run then, *wolf*." He'd realized something I had not. Franklin could function in his human form with a broken wrist, but his freedom in his other form was now curtailed. Indeed, he could not run until his bones healed.

"Yes," Franklin gasped out. "I did it."

Protheroe's face distorted in rage, and I thought he would hurt his murderer more but he restrained himself.

"What now?" Franklin appealed to Lincoln. "You can't take this confession to the police. They won't believe you. All evidence points to a dog, not a human. So what was the point of all this?"

"Who ordered the killing?" Lincoln asked.

Franklin swiped his good hand across his nose, wiping away the snot. "I can't tell you that."

Protheroe kicked him in the stomach, sending Franklin careening into the wall. The plaster cracked and the entire house shook. The crystals hanging from the chandelier above us tinkled. Franklin groaned.

"No more," I said to Protheroe. "Give him a chance to speak."

"Well?" Protheroe snapped. "Who ordered you to kill me?"

Franklin sniveled and wiped his nose again. His robe had fallen open to his waist but he didn't bother to fix it as he staggered to his feet. "You can beat me until I'm unconscious, but I will not reveal anything to you. If I did, I might as well be dead."

Protheroe took a giant stride forward and smashed his fist into Franklin's nose. Blood sprayed. Bone crunched. Franklin fell back against the wall again, clutching his face. Protheroe stepped up to him and swung his fist, but this time Franklin ducked out of the way. He caught Protheroe around the legs and tackled him to the ground.

Protheroe struck the floor. His head thudded and something cracked. He got to his knees and a tooth fell out of his mouth. He laughed.

"Fool," he said. "I feel no pain. You can hit me as many times as you like but I will keep getting up." He lurched to his feet, his cruel grin at odds with the gentlemanly spirit I'd grown to like. He beckoned Franklin to come at him again. "Let's see how strong you are. Can you keep me down, wolf?"

Franklin didn't rise to the bait. He collapsed against the wall and slid down it until he sat, legs outstretched, breathing hard. Blood streamed from his nose and sweat dampened his hair. Both his lips and one of his eyes had begun to swell. "You win," he choked out. "You may as well kill me because I won't give you the answer you seek." He closed his eyes and cradled his broken wrist to his chest. "Go on. End it."

Protheroe's lips drew back, revealing loose teeth. "Damn you! Damn you!" He pulled his fist back to swing another punch. Franklin opened his eyes and watched. He just sat there, ready to take whatever Protheroe served.

Protheroe growled and grabbed Franklin by his robe and swung his fist at Franklin's cheek.

"Stop, Mr. Protheroe!" I cried.

Protheroe halted, his fist a whisker from Franklin's face. He jerked his head to me and growled again. "Let me kill him. He deserves it. He deserves to die for what he did to me, to Leonora. My beloved..." He shook his head and his shoulders sagged. "Please, Miss Holloway, let me do this to avenge my death."

"I cannot. I'm sorry. Go now, Mr. Protheroe. I release your spirit. Rest in peace."

"No! Not yet!" The corpse's mouth stopped moving half way through his protest, but his spirit finished it. The others would not have heard all the words, but I did. "Miss Holloway, I beg you. Let me do this. Let me send him to hell."

I watched as the ghostly mist broke apart and *whooshed* up to the chandelier. Then he was gone.

I looked down at the corpse now lying in a crumpled heap on the floor. Franklin kicked it then drew back his legs as if he expected it to hit back. When the corpse didn't move, he tipped his head back and laughed. It was a half-crazed sound mixed with a splutter. He wasn't laughing, he was crying.

"Get yourself to a doctor," Lincoln told him. He signaled to Gus to remove the corpse.

I opened the door and Gus passed me, the body flung over his shoulder. I waited for Lincoln but he still stood near Franklin. I worried that he was too close to the strong shape changer, but I need not be. Franklin was too broken to attack. He still bled profusely from his nose and his eye had swollen shut. His hand hung limp from the wrist.

"We will find out who ordered you," Lincoln said. "You

won't get away with this."

"On the contrary," Franklin said. "We already have. Scotland Yard will not arrest people like us. We're too powerful and no evidence points to us."

"There are other forms of justice that don't involve the police." Lincoln turned his back and strode to me.

He followed me outside and into the carriage where we sat opposite the body of Roderick Protheroe. Gus had propped him up in the corner as if he were alive. It didn't remain upright for long as Seth drove at speed through the streets, back to the cemetery where we re-buried the body.

I leaned the daffodils against the headstone and silently apologized to Protheroe for disturbing his rest. He would not hear me if I'd spoken aloud anyway, but I needed to tell him in my own way. I felt as if we'd failed not only him but Leonora too. We were no closer to learning who ordered the murder, and Franklin had been correct—we couldn't do a thing with the knowledge. The police wouldn't arrest anyone for the crime.

I watched Lincoln as I sat across from him in the coach for the short drive back to Lichfield. His dark eyes were like fathomless pits that sucked everything into their depths—the air, sound, me. The silence in the cabin thickened, pressing down on me, yet I didn't know how to break it. Lincoln didn't want to talk to me. I didn't need to see his face clearly to know, I just did. He was rattled. He'd not come away with the outcome he expected, and he wasn't sure what to do next. He didn't want comforting, he wanted a plan of action. I could offer none so I went to bed with only a "Goodnight," spoken between us.

I lay under the covers, thinking of how I'd disturbed Roderick Protheroe's peace, of how he'd become a violent man in death, and how Nigel Franklin was prepared to die to keep his secret. I knew one thing for certain—he had been ordered by someone to kill Protheroe, and that someone had enormous power over him. He was willing to die to protect them. If it were me, I'd only be prepared to die for Lincoln, someone I loved very much. We'd not learned of Franklin being in love, although he might be prepared to protect his parents.

But the more I lay there, staring up at the bed canopy, the more I felt certain he was protecting his pack leader. Swinburn.

* * *

THE ARRIVAL of Eva early in the morning interrupted our meeting. Lincoln had told Gus, Seth and me that he wasn't going to tell the committee about our nocturnal visit to Franklin, chiefly because I'd used my necromancy and we knew how that would rile some of them—namely Gillingham. We were about to discuss what to do next when Whistler came to fetch us. He said Miss Cornell waited in the drawing room with a gentleman. He failed to tell us the gentleman was her brother, David.

"I'm so pleased to finally meet you," I said when Eva introduced him. "I'm Charlie, Lincoln's fiancée."

He smiled unconvincingly and glanced past me to Lincoln. Introductions were not necessary for him to recognize his half-brother. He seemed to know that the man who looked remarkably like himself was his mother's eldest child. The resemblance was striking. Both men sported sharp cheekbones and the dark complexion of the gypsy. They were both tall, although Lincoln's shape was more of a V with his broader shoulders. Most striking of all was their eyes, the color of pitch, which now regarded one another with an equally cool measure.

I cleared my throat and glared at Lincoln. He finally

looked at me and realized he had to introduce himself to our guest. He reached out a hand. After a telling hesitation, his brother took it.

"Cornell," Lincoln said.

"Fitzroy," David said.

Oh dear. So it was going to be like that. I wished Seth and Gus had joined us, or even Alice and Lady Vickers. More people meant more conversation and less chance for the ice to set.

"May we speak about something in private?" Eva asked with a glance at Doyle. The butler left and closed the door behind him. Eva wrung her hands in her lap and did not meet anyone's gaze.

"Is something the matter?" I asked. "You look upset."

"That's because she is." David pointed a finger at Lincoln. "And it's your fault."

"David," his sister chastised. "We don't know that for certain."

"We do know. Everything was fine until Mama met him. Ever since New Year's Eve, things have started happening."

"What things?" Lincoln asked.

"Nothing too terrible," Eva said.

"Don't play it down," David told her. "At first, we didn't think much of it," he said to us. "Mama felt she was being violated. It was just a feeling, and nothing came of it."

Lincoln stilled. "Violated?"

"Like her affairs were being investigated," Eva said. "You understand, Lincoln."

He nodded.

"I don't," I said. "What affairs?"

"A feeling that someone is trying to find out more about her," David told me. "She felt as though her personal records had been searched. Births, marriages, property rights, et cetera. Publicly available records, that sort of thing."

"But not like an actual trigger," I said, more for Lincoln's benefit.

He shook his head. "Her seer's senses felt the violations."

"She's strong enough to do that?"

"Yes," all three said.

David plucked at the cord edging the chair arm and shifted his feet. Where Lincoln was always so still, his half-brother was fidgety. "And more recently," he went on, "people have been following her. Then this morning, someone confronted her in the street outside our home."

I gasped. "Confronted her!"

Lincoln's lips flattened, a sure sign that this news troubled him. I wasn't sure if the others would notice the small movement, however. Most wouldn't. "Who?"

"How do we bloody know?" David shouted.

"Shhh," his sister said. "Getting upset will achieve nothing."

"Except conveying how upset we are."

"What did the person who confronted her look like?" I asked.

"Male, average size, average looking," David said. "She was shaken, and I'm not sure she took much in. I doubt she could pick him out again. She's frail. Her character may be strong, but this sort of thing troubles her nerves."

"As it would any woman," I said. "What did this man say specifically?"

"He wanted to know who your father was, Fitzroy."

Hell. At least we knew it wasn't someone connected to the Prince of Wales, since he already knew. It could be Alice's parents, although it seemed such an odd thing for them to care about. More likely it was Swinburn.

"And how did Leisl answer?" Lincoln asked.

"She refused to tell him," Eva said. "A neighbor walked by

and she took the opportunity to invite her inside for tea to get away from the stranger."

"Thank goodness for that," I muttered.

"Then she wasn't threatened," Lincoln said.

David frowned. "Pardon?"

"He did not tell her that ill would befall her if she didn't tell him the name of the man who sired me. So she was not threatened, as you claimed just now."

David threw his hands in the air. "Semantics."

"David," his sister hissed. "Stop it."

"Eva, he's not giving this the due concern it deserves."

"On the contrary," Lincoln shot back. "I am concerned."

"Bloody odd way of showing it."

"David," Eva snapped again. "That's enough."

"Lincoln is taking the matter very seriously," I assured him. I cast a glare at Lincoln but he wasn't looking at me. "This is a nasty business, and poor Leisl must be frightened."

"She won't admit it, but she is." Eva rubbed her forehead, smoothing her wrinkled brow. "We hoped you might know who it was and warn them away."

"Or just tell them who your father is," David said to Lincoln. "What does it matter who knows, anyway?"

Lincoln didn't reply and that only seemed to rile David more. He plucked the chair arm with vigor, all the while his intense gaze on Lincoln. Lincoln met it with an equally intense one.

Eva caught my attention and mouthed "Help."

"It's my fault," I told David. "Not Lincoln's. I was the one who insisted we visit Leisl and get to know her better. Someone followed us and worked out the connection. I think."

David stiffened and his fingers stilled. "*You* didn't wish to get to know your own mother better, Fitzroy? It took your fiancée to convince you?"

"I have no need of a mother," Lincoln said, matter of fact.

A small crease appeared between David's eyes. "No man *needs* his mother, but I can't imagine anyone not wanting to know her."

"That's because you don't know me."

This meeting was going from bad to worse.

"David," his sister warned, as if she knew what he would say next.

He tossed her a tight smile. "You're worrying for nothing, Eva. I wasn't going to say anything more to our *brother*, except that he must fix this mess. Our mother doesn't deserve to be subjected to that sort of treatment at her time of life. She made one mistake, thirty years ago, and has led an exemplary life since. Yet that mistake haunts her."

My heart dove to my stomach. I wanted to take Lincoln's hand and assure him that he was not a mistake, that his birth was foretold and that Leisl probably lay with the Prince of Wales because she knew it had to be. But I could say none of that in front of Leisl's legitimate children, particularly David. He would only hate me for saying it about his mother, and I didn't want to alienate Lincoln's family, no matter how much some of its members didn't like him.

Eva's breath hitched. She shook her head in reproach at David. A flicker of regret passed across his eyes, but he did not apologize. He got to his feet and held out his hand to his sister.

She cast me a sad look then took his hand. "We ought to go," she said. "We don't want to leave Mama alone for long in case the man comes back."

"If he does threaten her," Lincoln said, also rising, "notify me immediately."

"And you'll do what?" David snapped.

"Insure it doesn't happen again."

"How?"

"You don't wish to know the answer to that," I cut in quickly. I slipped my hands around Lincoln's arm, but it did nothing to ease the tension rippling through him.

"I do," David said, squaring his shoulders.

"No," I said, more firmly. "You do not."

David's frown deepened as Eva ushered him toward the door. "Thank you for seeing us without notice," she said to me.

"Not at all. You're welcome to call on us at any time. That reminds me. I'll send an invitation to dine with us as soon as things settle down here. We're rather pre-occupied at the moment. I hope you can all attend."

"We will all be happy to come, Charlie. Thank you."

David said nothing until she pinched his arm. "Thank you. It was a pleasure to meet you, Miss Holloway. I can see you have your hands full. I wish you luck."

"Er, thank you. And please call me Charlie since we are almost family."

"Come along, David," Eva said when he opened his mouth to speak.

Lincoln opened the door and allowed our guests to walk ahead. Gus and Seth hovered in the entrance hall and greeted Eva. I suspected they wanted to know what David looked like and find out how he and Lincoln got on. Gus couldn't stop staring at him. Seth, however, showed more interest in Eva. He smiled and gave her a shallow bow. She turned to David, presenting Seth with her shoulder.

"This is Gus and Lord Vickers," Eva told her brother. "Friends of Lincoln and Charlie's."

"What's with the 'my lord' business?" Seth smiled crookedly. "It's Seth, remember."

"I prefer we use titles," she told him.

"Why?"

"It's more appropriate."

He blinked at her. "Oh. Very well. If that's what you prefer, Miss Cornell, then I'll oblige. But I can't guarantee I'll answer to Vickers, although you do make it sound more important than I deserve." He winked at her.

She blushed and hurried after her brother.

Once they were gone, Gus gave a gruff laugh and shook his head. "Blimey, you're like your brother, sir."

Lincoln strode off. "We're nothing alike."

I sighed and asked Gus and Seth to join me in the drawing room where I told them what had transpired. "David is furious. He thinks it's Lincoln's fault that his mother was accosted."

"It is, in a way," Seth said, stretching out his legs. "Their lives were peaceful before the New Year's Eve ball."

"Leisl chose to come to the ball, and she knew Lincoln would be there," I said hotly. "Lincoln had no choice in the matter. None of this is his fault. You should have heard David. He was not very nice at all."

"Jealous," Gus said. "He looks like Fitzroy and yet he ain't got a house like this or lots of money."

"Nor does he have a fiery little fiancée like Charlie," Seth said with a crooked smile. "I agree. He's jealous. Pay him no mind, Charlie."

I sighed. "I suppose he must see it as unfair. Lincoln is the illegitimate one and yet he has so much at his disposal, whereas David and his sister must work hard for meager wages. I only wish he knew that money isn't everything, and Lincoln has had a cold and hard life without a mother's love. I'm sure if he knew, he wouldn't be jealous."

"But you're not going to tell him, are you?" Seth said carefully. "Fitzroy wouldn't like it."

I sighed again. "I'd better go and see him. He looked upset."

"He did?" Seth looked to Gus. Gus shrugged. "He looked

the same as he always does to me."

I was waylaid by Lady Vickers on the staircase. She asked me to pay calls on her friends today if I was free. Alice had declined and she wanted company. I agreed, as long as Lincoln could spare me.

I found him in his rooms at his desk. The desk surface in front of him was bare and he did not greet me. I laid a hand on his shoulder and kissed the top of his head.

"What are you thinking?" I asked.

"Nothing."

I circled both arms around him and whispered in his ear. "What are you thinking, Lincoln?"

I felt him sigh, even though he made no sound. "I'm wondering who cares enough about my parentage to question Leisl."

"Not the Everhearts," I answered for him.

"Doubtful."

"The palace already know."

"Yes."

"That leaves Swinburn and his pack."

"It does." He'd clearly reached that conclusion before I entered the room.

"So the question is," I said, "who told Swinburn that your father is someone who matters? He seems to think it knowledge worth having."

"Keep going." He was encouraging me to follow the line of thought, not because he hadn't already followed it, but because he wanted me to reach it on my own.

"Er, how long will it be before Swinburn hurts Leisl to get answers?" I suggested. "Is that what's on your mind?"

He placed his arms over mine, holding me against him. He tipped his head back to look at me. Earlier, his eyes had been as hard as stones. Now they swirled like smoke in the night. "What if he decides to target you instead?"

I frowned. "Why would he do that? He must know I'm well protected here."

"Well protected because I care about you. If he wants to get to me, he'll target you."

"You're jumping to conclusions, Lincoln. He only wants answers."

"For now."

I moved so that I could see him better and caught his face in my hands. I smoothed my thumbs over his cheeks until I felt him relax a little. "Lincoln, you're making a mountain out of a mole hill. No one has been threatened. Even if Swinburn is willing to hurt someone to get his answers, he'll choose Leisl, not me. She's a far easier target, and there's always a chance you haven't informed me of your father's identity. He's not going to target me, Lincoln, particularly after Franklin informs him that I can call the dead to my aid." I caressed his cheek with my thumb. "Plus he will have heard about the imp, too. Stop worrying about me."

He plucked my hands off and turned away. "Easier said than done."

"I think this *is* about Leisl," I said as a thought struck me. "You are worried about her, but you don't want to admit it. You want to pretend that I'm the only one you care about because you can't even admit to yourself that your heart is capable of loving more than one person."

His brow crashed down and he pushed up from the chair. "You're wrong." He strode to the door and jerked it open.

"You're throwing me out?"

"Encouraging you to leave."

"Why?"

"Because I'm busy and you're a distraction."

"Ha!" I stood there and tried to glare hard enough to dig the answer out of him.

It didn't work. He placed his hands on my hips, picked me up, and lifted me over the threshold. He set me down gently.

"What are you going to do, Lincoln?"

He hesitated then said, "There's only one thing I want to do." He pulled me against him and kissed me with more passion than most people thought he possessed. Then he let me go and closed the door in my face.

* * *

I couldn't concentrate when we visited Lady Vickers' friend. I was too worried about Lincoln to sit still and contribute to the conversation. When she asked if I wanted to return home instead of calling on her next friend, I eagerly told her I would. She decided to remain at Lichfield too, postponing her calls for another day.

"Stay here," I ordered Tucker after I assisted Lady Vickers down from the cabin. "I may have need of you."

I raced up Lichfield's front steps, a sense of foreboding settling over me. "Is Mr. Fitzroy at home?" I asked Doyle as he opened the door.

"No, miss. He went out an hour ago."

An hour. Damnation. "Did he take Seth and Gus with him?"

"Yes, and Lord Vickers asked me to give you this." He handed me a note that had been folded in half. It simply read "Swinburn."

I released my breath. Thank God I'd asked Seth to leave me a message if they went out. Not that it was difficult to guess their destination. I picked up my skirts and passed Lady Vickers on her way inside.

"Where are you going, Charlie?" she asked.

"To stop Lincoln from putting himself in danger." I only hoped I wasn't too late.

CHAPTER 16

Sir Ignatius Swinburn lived next door to Lord and Lady Ballantine on Queen's Gate, Kensington. He was not at home, according to his butler, and I could not see Lincoln, Seth or Gus lurking in recessed doorways either. The butler wouldn't tell me where his master had gone, but an enterprising errand boy who overheard me trying to bribe the butler told me Swinburn hadn't been at home since the previous afternoon. I paid him a shilling for the information and directed Tucker to take me to Franklin's house. I opened the coach door and paused, one foot on the step.

Lincoln sat inside. He held out his hand and assisted me in.

"What are you doing here?" I asked, settling on the seat. "And how did you sneak in without me seeing you?"

"I'm waiting for Swinburn. The answer to your second question is stealth. Why are *you* here, Charlie?" His voice sounded casual, disinterested, but I could see by the way he watched me that he was very interested in my answer.

"To make sure you didn't do anything foolish."

"I never do anything foolish."

"Anything dangerous, then."

He leaned his elbow on the window sill and rubbed the side of his finger across his lips.

"You left while I was out," I went on. "On purpose, I might add, to avoid divulging your plans to me. Your secrecy tells me one thing, Lincoln—that I won't approve."

"You knew where to find me," he said. "That's hardly being secretive."

"Only because Seth left me a note."

"Thank you for confirming my suspicion."

"Don't you dare punish him for following my orders."

"Since when do you give orders to my men?" He looked to the ceiling with a shake of his head. "Since when did they follow your orders at the risk of angering me?"

"Since they realized you won't get angry with them for using their good judgment."

He sighed. "Go home, Charlie. I'll face Swinburn without you."

I sat forward and peered out the window. We were heading out of Kensington. "You gave Tucker instructions to return to Lichfield, didn't you?"

He thumped on the roof and the coach slowed to a stop. Lincoln pecked my cheek and got out. "Go home, Charlie." He gave Tucker a nod then closed the door.

I sat back and crossed my arms. I shouldn't be angry with Lincoln; he was worried about me. And in truth, I wasn't angry, I was frustrated. He wasn't the only person in our relationship with a right to worry.

There would be no convincing Tucker to return to Swinburn's house now. He knew who paid his wages, and it wasn't me. So I sat with my mounting frustration for company while we drove to Highgate. The sun broke through the clouds as the coach slowed to turn through the Lichfield gates. It promised to be another lovely day. Perfect for walking out of the estate and finding a hack to take me back to Mayfair.

The sudden, violent stop threw me onto the other side of the cabin. I landed on the opposite seat with a thud in an unladylike position. The horses whinnied and shied, jerking the cabin to the left. Tucker tried to soothe them but his voice was not at all soothing and only seemed to agitate them more.

I pulled down the window. "Is everything—" I gasped as the figure standing there, pistol pointed at me.

"Don't move, Miss Holloway," Sir Ignatius growled. "You," he said to the driver while keeping his gaze on me. "Drive us away from here. It doesn't matter where. I won't harm your mistress unless she tries something foolish or you attempt to return here. I only wish to talk to her, but I will pull this trigger if either of you try to trick me. Understood?"

"Yes, sir," Tucker said quickly.

Swinburn climbed into the cabin. He sat opposite me and did not lower the pistol. I slowly raised my hand to touch my necklace, but he shook his head.

"Don't reach for your...device," he said. "You attempt to release whatever lives in it and I will shoot before you finish the order."

My heart ground to a halt. Without my imp, my only weapon was the knife tucked up my sleeve, and I doubted I could easily retrieve it. He did not take his gaze off me.

"What do you want, Sir Ingatius?" I asked, far more boldly than I felt. "Capturing me will achieve nothing."

"On the contrary. It will send a message to Fitzroy that I will not stand idly by while he terrorizes my people." His nose twitched, like an animal scenting its prey.

I licked dry lips and willed my fiercely beating heart to calm. It made it difficult to think, and I needed to think. Needed to disarm this man and free myself. Lincoln couldn't save me. My imp couldn't save me. I had only my wits and a small knife. The odds were not in my favor.

"Mr. Franklin murdered Mr. Protheroe," I said. "Protheroe wanted justice. He only terrorized Mr. Franklin, not your other friends."

"An eye for an eye," Swinburn said. "That would be fair, except that Protheroe was brought back by you, Miss Holloway, and was encouraged to violence by Fitzroy."

"He needed no encouragement. Mr. Protheroe was upset, and rightly so. He simply fell in love with the wrong woman, and for that he was killed, quite horribly too."

He smiled but it barely lifted the edges of his mustache. "Perhaps a less violent solution could have been found, but not one that would have been so...final. Protheroe was about to ruin my plans."

"What plans are those?"

He grunted. "Abandoned ones. For now." He stroked his thumb and forefinger along his mustache, a slow and calculated move that set me even more on edge. "I should kill you for what Fitzroy did to Nigel Franklin. That might be a message he'd understand."

"Mr. Franklin is not dead." I stretched out my arm, exposing the flesh at my wrist. "Go ahead, sir. Break it. An eye for an eye, isn't that what you said?"

He stared at the inch of bare flesh between my glove and cuff. "I'm not such a fool as to think I would get away with harming a hair on your head, Miss Holloway. Fitzroy would kill me."

"You have every reason to fear him." Yet I didn't believe he was afraid of Lincoln. He was much too cocky, too self-assured. I suspected he didn't know what Lincoln was capable of. Yet. "What do you want with me, Sir Ingatius? You told my driver you wanted to talk, so talk."

"I want you to tell Fitzroy to leave my people alone."

"By people you mean your pack." I checked his hands again. They were small, like Lord Ballantine's, and very human. Everything about him seemed human, yet Leonora told us that both Ballantine and Swinburn were shape changers and that Swinburn was the leader. Perhaps they were merely more advanced changers and able to hide features like large hands and feet.

"He'll listen to you, Miss Holloway," he said. "If you tell him to leave my people alone, he will do it."

"You think so?" I lifted a finger to halt his protest. "I will try, on one condition. You leave Leisl Cornell and her family alone, and everyone at Lichfield too."

"You're proposing a truce?" He twisted his mouth to the side, thinking through the merits of my offer, and perhaps considering how it would fit in with his plans, whatever they were. "Will your fiancé agree to it?"

"He will, but there can be no more killings."

"There won't be." He sounded sincere but I'd been fooled before. "I can only agree to the truce if you tell me one thing."

"And that is?" I asked.

"Who is Fitzroy's father?"

"I don't know," I said, not missing a beat or lowering my gaze. If I was to cut off his line of questioning, I had to sound convincing.

"Liar." His nose twitched and panic rose in me. What if he could smell my lie? "I ask again, who is his father?"

"It's the truth." I could do this. I'd lied for five years about being a boy, and even Lincoln hadn't guessed. "I don't know his name. No one does, not even Leisl Cornell. I'm sure by now you know she's Lincoln's mother." The best lies were couched in truth. It never hurt to direct the conversation away from the lie, either.

"She *must* know who the father is," he said. "She's not a loose woman, by all accounts."

"You have done some thorough research. You're right, she's a very upstanding woman, and was then, too, so I've been told. But Leisl knew her duty was to couple with the stranger who flirted with her at the fair where she told fortunes. She's a seer, Sir Ignatius, and she had a vision about her role in Lincoln's birth well before his conception. She knew from the vision that the stranger would be the father of her first child and that child had an important role to fill in his adult life. So she did her duty by whatever forces led her to have that vision and lie with the man. She never saw him again, and nine months later, she bore his son."

He studied me carefully, watching for signs that I misled him. He shook his head and lines appeared across his fore-head. My heart sank. I felt sick. "What rot," he spat. "What are you talking about? What duty?"

I clasped my hands in my lap and squeezed hard. "I see you're not fully aware of Lincoln's importance. His birth was foretold centuries ago by a seer, perhaps an ancestor of Leisl's. He was heralded as the next great leader of an organi-zation that is now known as the Ministry of Curiosities. The ministry keeps the peace between the human realm and the supernatural." I lowered my gaze to my hands. "Please don't ask me any more questions. He won't like me telling you any of this. The ministry is not well known, you see, and we prefer it that way considering the nature of our business."

I hazarded a glance at him to see if my demure plea had an effect. To my surprise, he no longer looked like he wanted to break my bones, but instead he looked intrigued. It was impossible to tell whether he'd heard of the ministry before, but it didn't matter. I'd told him nothing of importance and several supernaturals in London already knew about us anyway.

"So do we have our truce, Sir Ignatius? Your pack stops its killings, you leave us alone, and we leave you alone." I extended my hand.

He hesitated then shook it. "We have a truce, Miss Holloway." He thumped the roof of the coach. "Instruct the coachman to drive to my house so we can inform Fitzroy."

"You know he's there?" I asked as the coach slowed.

His smile did not reach his eyes. "I wouldn't come to Lichfield and abduct you without knowing he was far away."

I pulled down the window and gave Tucker instructions. We were not far from Kensington, since Tucker had taken it upon himself to return there, perhaps hoping to alert Lincoln somehow. Swinburn undid his jacket and tucked his gun beneath the flap.

"This will remain pointed at you until I have Fitzroy's assurance that he agrees to the truce," he said. "It will be up to you to convince him of my intent to fire if I feel threatened."

We traveled the rest of the way in silence. I stared unseeing out the window but felt his gaze drilling into me. When we finally reached our destination, he ordered me to open the door.

Lincoln was already making his way to the coach, no doubt ready to reproach both Tucker and me for returning. Gus and Seth emerged from their hiding places behind him. They looked curious, not worried. They hadn't seen Swinburn, hanging back in the cabin.

I stepped down to the pavement and put up a hand to halt Lincoln's progress. The hard barrel of the gun dug into my back.

Lincoln stopped dead.

"Bloody hell!" Gus exploded. "Charlie!"

Lincoln's chest rose and fell once then stilled. His jaw stiffened. His gaze quickly scanned over me, then flicked to Swinburn before returning to me.

"I'm all right," I assured him. "We've been talking."

"Let her go, Swinburn," Seth growled. "You hurt her and he'll kill you and your entire pack too."

"I won't shoot," Swinburn said. "Unless someone does something foolish. You won't do anything foolish, will you, Fitzroy?"

Lincoln's fists curled at his sides. "What do you want, Swinburn?"

"I want to tell you about our truce. Miss Holloway and I have had a productive drive together. She has convinced me to leave you and your family alone, Fitzroy, but only so long as you agree to leave my pack alone."

A carriage approached and let a lady out a few doors away. No one spoke until she entered the house and the carriage left the street altogether. Despite the lack of conversation, Lincoln managed to seem threatening thanks to the fury rippling off him. He looked as if he wanted to kill Swinburn there on the street, regardless of who watched on.

I ached to go to him, but I didn't dare move.

"Well?" Swinburn prompted.

"I won't agree to anything until you let her go," Lincoln said.

"It's all right," I told him.

"It's not all right!" He rarely shouted at me, at anyone, because his orders were always followed without question. He got angry, yes, but usually his anger was controlled. This explosion was borne out of frustration and helplessness.

"Let me go to him," I said quietly to Swinburn over my shoulder. "Let me assure him you won't harm me."

"How can you be sure that I won't?"

I turned to see him better. I wished I hadn't. His eyes

were cold and devoid of compassion. He was as angry as Lincoln, and I suddenly realized that he loved his pack as much as Lincoln loved me. He would do anything to protect them and he hated that we'd hurt Franklin. But I had to trust that he would honor our truce and not make us pay for that pain.

"Because you're afraid for your pack," I said. "Because you know that Lincoln will kill every last one, starting with you, if you hurt me."

"You forget that I hold the gun and therefore the upper hand."

"Just because you can't see his gun doesn't mean he doesn't have one. Gus and Seth, too. In the time it takes you to pull the trigger, all three will draw their weapons." I turned back to Lincoln and took a small step forward.

Lincoln stepped forward too but halted. His gaze flicked to mine then past my shoulder to Swinburn. He swallowed.

"Say you agree to the truce," Swinburn said.

I took another step forward. Lincoln did not move this time, but Seth put up his hand to stop me.

"Stay there, Charlie," Gus said.

"Say you agree to the truce, Fitzroy," Swinburn said, louder. "Or I shoot her dead."

I closed my eyes then opened them again. "Lincoln," I warned.

His nostrils flared. The pulse in his throat jumped.

I stepped forward again and Lincoln paled. Behind me, the gun cocked, the *click* as loud to my ears as any gunshot.

"I agree," Lincoln said on a rush of breath. "I agree to the truce."

I went to him and he enclosed me in his arms. He drew in a shuddery breath and pressed me against his body. I looked back to see Swinburn lower his weapon, his eyes bright and a curious little smile on his lips.

He nodded then climbed the steps to his front door. His gun was nowhere in sight.

I took Lincoln's hand and led him to the carriage. We got in, Seth and Gus too, without an exchange of words. Lincoln was still angry, but something underlay it, and I could only guess that it was worry.

"I had to make the truce with him," I said. "He has promised not to kill anyone, or interrogate your family anymore. I think I satisfied him with my answer anyway, of sorts. I didn't tell him about your father, Lincoln, only that no one knew who he was, not even Leisl."

"You managed to do that?" Seth nodded his approval. "Good work, Charlie."

"Aye," Gus said, patting my hand. "Gave me a bloody fright seeing him step out behind you. But you got it all in hand on your own."

I did. So why wasn't Lincoln pleased?

"The truce won't hinder us," I told him. "We've promised not to harm his pack, but we can still investigate them and keep our eye on them."

His lashes flickered and he nodded. "Good work."

I wanted to ask him why he was still upset but not in front of the others. He wouldn't answer me. Besides, it was likely he was still recovering from the shock of the confrontation. My nerves continued to jangle and my heart had not resumed its regular, steady pattern.

I got my chance to speak to him alone when we alighted from the coach at the front of Lichfield. Lincoln took my hand and walked with me to the apple orchard. His strides were so long that I had to take two steps to his one to keep up.

He stopped under cover of the blossoms and branches where we couldn't be seen from the house, drive or outhouses. He pressed me hard up against a tree trunk and I opened my mouth to tell him to calm down, but his kiss stole my words. It wasn't a sweet kiss yet it wasn't brutal either. It was filled with the darker kind of passions within him that he rarely unleashed. The sort of passions he kept locked away because he thought they scared me.

But this man didn't scare me. He never could. I knew him, the good and the bad, and I knew those dark passions would never overrule him to the point where he'd hurt me. Others, perhaps, but never me.

Yet sometimes I suspected he scared himself by releasing them. Like now.

I kissed him back just as fiercely, to prove that I didn't fear him, and just because I wanted to. I cradled his head, stood on my toes, and arched into him. I welcomed his passion, wishing I could absorb the darkness but knowing I could not. It throbbed through me as it throbbed through him, wild and strong. Mad. Perhaps that's what it was, a kind of madness that we both felt on occasion. It was certainly difficult to think clearly with my blood racing and my mind reeling and his lips claiming me.

Finally the kiss gentled and he pulled away, the darkness once again safely locked up. A remnant of it swirled in his eyes and in his fingers, massaging my waist so hard he was in danger of putting a hole in me.

I touched his cheek and smiled up at him. "Say something," I said.

He shook his head. Because he had nothing to say or because he was afraid his voice would tremble? He backed away and lowered his head. Strands of black hair fell across his face, hiding his eyes.

"Swinburn will keep his end of the bargain," I assured him. "He's just as afraid of your wrath as you are of him harming your family."

He looked at me through his hair. His mouth opened then

he shut it again. He turned and strode away. "I'm proud of you, Charlie. The truce was a good idea."

I picked up my skirts and trotted after him. When I fell into step alongside him, I took his hand. He squeezed and his thumb stroked mine. He was proud of me, of that I was certain, and he did think the truce was a good idea. Yet he was troubled. He'd been afraid for me and he hated that. He saw it as a weakness.

Last time he'd been afraid for me, he'd sent me away for safekeeping at the school. Back then, he hadn't recognized his fear or his love. Now, I only hoped he'd progressed enough to curb the instinct to send me away from the danger. From him.

* * *

THE INEVITABLE MEETING with the committee occurred the following morning in the library. Lincoln had delayed it as long as possible, hoping to hear back from the Prince of Wales first. He sent a letter to him the evening before, apprising him of events, theories and the truce. The prince's response had not arrived by the time the committee meeting began.

"Sir Ignatius Swinburn is *not* involved," Lady Harcourt spat. "This is absurd. Slanderous!"

"Sit down, Julia," Lord Marchbank bellowed. "Hear them out."

Lady Harcourt did not sit down. She paced the carpet, showing off her fine figure and full bosom to best effect with her heaving breaths. I suspected that was the reason why she paced past Lincoln and Seth most of all. They happened to be standing next to one another, having both stood when Lady Harcourt shot to her feet. They were nothing if not gentlemanly, preferring not to sit when a lady in their presence did not.

"I'm leaving," she suddenly announced.

"Gus," Lincoln said.

Gus moved in front of the door, blocking her exit.

"How dare you!" she railed at him.

Gus settled his feet apart. "Sorry, ma'am."

She whirled around and threw herself onto a chair. Her skirts puffed up and her bustle was crushed behind her, but she didn't seem to care.

"Bloody women and their hysteria," Gillingham muttered. "Shouldn't be allowed in these meetings."

Lady Harcourt's glare would have pierced him if it were made of steel.

"If you'll listen to the evidence," Seth said to her, "you'll come to agree with our conclusions."

She sniffed and turned her face away.

Lincoln allowed Seth to report on everything we'd learned since our Isle of Wight expedition. He left nothing out, and made a good account of our conclusions. He finished with details of the truce.

"A truce!" Gillingham threw his hands in the air. Since he still held the walking stick, it was fortunate he didn't knock over the vase of flowers on the table nearest him. "Fitzroy, have you gone mad?"

"It was the best outcome," Lincoln said.

"Not mad, soft." Gillingham eyed me, as if he knew the truce was something I brokered. "You should have killed Swinburn."

"He would have shot Charlie before I could draw or attack," Lincoln said.

Gillingham smirked, as if that was hardly something worth worrying about.

"I would have killed him," Lincoln went on. "But his pack

would have killed me and my men. They're stronger than us and outnumber us. The truce was the only way out and the only way forward."

"Agreed," Marchbank said. "Are you sure you can trust Swinburn to keep it?"

"We have to."

Marchbank's lips flattened in thought.

"He'll come here and kill you all in your beds," Gillingham said. "Mark my words."

Lady Harcourt whimpered. "Stop it. Stop this talk at once. The man you're describing is not the man I know. He's ambitious, yes, but he's attentive and generous."

"Do be quiet, Julia," Gillingham said. "Stay out of this until you come to your senses and see that Swinburn is a danger."

"He's not a danger!"

"How do you know? Because he prefers to fornicate with you rather than kill you? You do know you're not the only woman warming his bed."

Her nostrils flared and her top lip peeled back from her teeth.

"Don't talk to a lady like that in my house," Lincoln said, his rich voice rumbling through the library.

Gillingham huffed out a humorless laugh and crossed one leg over the other.

"Fitzroy's right," Marchbank said. "That was uncalled for. Your behavior to the other members of this committee has been appalling these last few months, Gilly. As senior member, I'm ordering you to be civil from now on. You're not so important that you can't be thrown out."

Gillingham spluttered a protest but quieted with a single sharp glare from Lincoln. Lincoln was still angry, and Gillingham must have realized that he would only bring that anger down on himself if he continued.

"What of the relationship between the young Prince

Albert Victor and Leonora Ballantine?" Lord Marchbank asked, thankfully returning the meeting to its original agenda.

"The Prince of Wales has put a stop to them seeing one another," Lincoln said. "There'll be no more contact between her and Prince Eddy."

"How can you be sure? If the man's in love with her, nothing will keep him away."

"He knows that she was in love with another the entire time," I said. "He realizes he was duped and that she had a part in duping him. That dampened his ardor considerably."

"I don't doubt it."

"That's women for you," Gillingham said, rubbing his palm over the head of his walking stick.

Lady Harcourt turned ice-cold eyes onto him. "Just because your wife tricked you into her bed doesn't mean all women are devious. Oh, wait." Her lips curved into a seductive, beautiful, and utterly cruel smile. "Or did she use her wolf strength to ravish you?"

Gillingham shot to his feet, his face crimson. He raised his walking stick but Lincoln caught Gillingham's wrist before he could strike her.

"What?" Marchbank frowned at Lady Harcourt then Gillingham. "What's this about wolf strength?"

"Julia!" Seth warned. "Don't."

It wasn't so much that she was alluding to Harriet being a shape changer that interested me. It was that she was in possession of the knowledge in the first place. Had Swinburn told her? Why would the subject have come up between them?

"Seth will see you out now," Lincoln said to Gillingham.

Seth grabbed Gillingham's arm and marched him to the door. Gus stepped aside and let them pass. Gillingham didn't appear too fazed to be thrown out.

"Thank you, Lincoln," Lady Harcourt said breathily. She touched her temples and swayed in the chair. "I feel quite faint from the excitement. I cannot believe Gilly would be so violent. Would you mind escorting me home? I'm afraid for my safety."

"You'll be fine," Lincoln said, turning his back on her. "He wouldn't dare strike you." He poured a brandy at the sideboard and handed her the tumbler.

She accepted it but not before blinking pathetically at him. She had quite a nerve, flirting with him in my presence. Or perhaps she knew she had nothing to lose since I already despised her and she me.

Seth returned, dusting off his hands as if he'd just thrown out the rubbish.

Lord Marchbank thanked him. "Gilly's temper is getting worse."

"Because he has no control at home anymore." Lady Harcourt threw back the contents of her glass. "So he tries to take control elsewhere, like here. Especially here."

"It seems I'm the only who doesn't know what you're alluding to," Marchbank said darkly. "Go on, out with it."

"Julia," Seth warned again. "It's not our business."

"Harriet is a shape changer," she said.

Marchbank sank into his chair and rubbed his scarred jaw. "Well. That explains a few things about Gillingham's behavior of late, toward the ladies in particular. Why wasn't I told, Fitzroy?"

"It wasn't necessary." Lincoln addressed Marchbank but kept his gaze on Lady Harcourt. She shifted her weight and toyed with the lace collar of her dress. "How do you know about it?" he asked her.

"That is none of your affair," she said with a sniff.

"It is."

"You gave up the right to ask questions about my personal life when you walked out of it."

"This is not personal, it's ministry business."

"Oh?" she said with sickening sweetness. "Then why wasn't the entire committee made aware of Harriet's condition? You can't have it both ways, Lincoln."

He slammed his hand down on the table near her. We all jumped. Lady Harcourt paled. "How did you find out about it?" he ground out.

She sat straight, her shoulders back, her eyes flashing. "You know very well that I have my own sources of information separate from the ministry ones. You'll have to torture me if you want more than that. Now," she said crisply. "The reason I haven't walked out yet is that I need to inform the committee of my intentions to change my will."

"Your last will and testament has nothing to do with us," Marchbank said.

"The part about the heir who will take over my position on the committee does."

"It won't be Buchanan?"

"No. I've thrown him out of the house and I wish to cut him out of my life altogether. That's what one does with tumors."

"Didn't your husband's will stipulate he could stay there as long as he wanted?" Seth asked.

"It does, which is why I expect him to return, unfortunately. In the meantime he has gone to live with Donald and Marguerite at Emberly Park."

"Bloody hell," Seth said with a shake of his head. "Is that a good idea, considering Marguerite's delicate mind? Not to mention her affection for Andrew and the fact the Buchanan brothers hate each other."

She lifted one shoulder. "They can kill one another, for all I care. Perhaps that will solve all my problems."

"Who will you nominate to replace you on the committee if you should die?" Lord Marchbank asked.

"Seth."

Seth blinked.

The clock on the mantel chimed and she gathered up her reticule. "I must go, but one last warning, Lincoln. Do not accuse Sir Ignatius of anything. He's innocent."

Lincoln strode to the door, opened it, and waited for her to leave.

Seth, however, rose to the bait. "You're biased, Julia. Your self-interest in this matter is clear to everyone in this room."

"You're just jealous, Seth dear. You always have been jealous of my other lovers."

"Not for a long time, Julia. Seeing you for the person you really are has been a liberating experience. It's as if a noose has been removed from around my neck."

She headed for the door, her stiff skirts snapping at her ankles with her purposeful strides.

"Swinburn is pack leader," Seth said to her back. "He is as guilty of Protheroe's murder as Franklin, and you'd better remember that or you might find yourself in danger."

"I'm in no danger from him. He adores me."

"He hides it well. The last time I saw you two together, he showed no more interest in you than any other woman. Perhaps because you're not a shape changer."

She rounded on him, her nostrils flaring like a raging bull's. "How dare you!" she screeched. If he'd been any closer, she would have slapped him.

"How dare *you*, Julia." Seth stabbed a finger in her direction and bared his teeth. I'd never seen him so angry. She'd pushed him over the edge this time. "As a committee member, you ought to have the ministry's best interests at heart, instead of your own. Lately you seem to have forgotten that. If we find out that you told Swinburn about

Leisl or anything else related to Fitzroy and the ministry, you will be removed from the committee."

Her lips flattened, a severe red streak across pale skin. "You get ahead of yourself, Seth dear. Until, and indeed *if*, you inherit the committee position from me, you're just Lincoln's lackey. You can't threaten me with anything."

"But I can," Lincoln said. "Seth is correct. If you reveal anything to Swinburn, being removed from the committee will be the least of your concerns."

Her throat worked with her swallows, and she folded her arms as if warding off a chill. "Empty threats, Lincoln," she said, rallying. "That's all you've got now, just threats we all know you won't follow through on. Not now that *she* has filed down your edges. Edges that made you the powerful man you once were. Now you're just an ordinary man with an ordinary life. How dull you've become."

Her gaze slid to me beneath lowered lashes. I stiffened but didn't shy away. She didn't frighten me.

"That's enough, Julia," Marchbank barked. He grabbed her arm and marched her out of the library into the entrance hall where Doyle handed out coats and hats as if nothing were amiss.

"Do be careful, Lincoln," she tossed over her shoulder. "Sir Ignatius is not someone you can accuse without repercussions." She shook off Lord Marchbank's grip and let herself out the front door.

"The gall of her," Seth bit off. "She can't be allowed to get away with helping Swinburn under our very noses."

"We can't be certain she is the one who gave him the information," I said. "I think she's overplaying his regard for her, for one thing."

"Which is exactly why we must be careful. She's desperate enough to win his attention that she'll give him whatever information he wants."

"She wouldn't betray us," I said. For one thing, I still believed she cared too much about Lincoln to want any real harm to befall him.

Lord Marchbank stood by the door and flipped up his coat collar. "Vickers is correct. She is desperate, and desperate people do things a normal person would not. I believe her capable of anything, right now. Be careful, Fitzroy. Keep an eye on her."

CHAPTER 17

*L*incoln gathered the entire household together over an informal luncheon in the dining room, including Doyle and Cook but excluding the other servants, and informed them all that Lady Harcourt could no longer be trusted. "Anything you hear within these walls cannot be repeated to her," he said.

Lady Vickers patted the corner of her mouth with her napkin. "I always knew she would be the agent of her own downfall. Horrid woman."

"Indeed," Alice said. "To think that she would care so much about money and position to betray her friends."

"We are in agreement for once, Alice," Lady Vickers said. "She ought to know better at her age."

"She has no friends here, and I doubt she ever did," Seth said quietly.

Gus snorted. "You've changed your tune from a few months back."

Seth gave a desperate half shake of his head. Fortunately Alice seemed not to notice but his mother did.

"Oh, *Seth*," she muttered, pulling a face.

Seth shot me a pleading look, but I didn't have the heart to help him out of his sticky situation. It was time Alice learned of his past anyway, even if it was painful to hear. He couldn't hide it from her forever, not if he wanted a future with her.

She lifted her brows but did not ask for more information. I suspected that would come later.

"Lady Harcourt ain't going to get no more nice cakes from me," Cook said, picking apart his sandwich and removing the ham. "Ain't too many on the committee I want to feed no more, only you and Marchbank, sir."

"We won't invite them to dine," I assured him. "Only Lord and Lady Marchbank, from time to time, but not on ministry business."

Doyle had refused to sit or eat and he now asked if he could be excused to oversee the staff. Lincoln let him go.

Lincoln seemed to have calmed down somewhat since the meeting, but I could still detect anger simmering beneath the surface, and probably worry, too.

Doyle returned with a letter for Lincoln. It bore the royal seal. We all leaned forward as he opened it and scanned the contents.

"It's from the Prince of Wales," he announced, passing it to me. "In response to my letter informing him of our investigation."

"He still refuses to believe that Swinburn is involved," I said, shaking my head. "How can he be so blind in the face of the latest evidence?"

"How can Swinburn be so convincing?" Gus said. "He's got a hold on His Majesty, that's for sure."

"His Highness," Seth corrected. "Majesty is for kings and queens, highness is for princes and princesses."

"Who bloody cares? None of 'em are here so it don't matter. I can call him His Nibs if I want."

"You can *not*," Lady Vickers bit back.

Gus muttered an apology.

"I wonder if it's more the Duke of Edinburgh's influence," I said, re-reading part of the letter. "It says here that the duke thinks the ministry is pointless and we're merely stirring up trouble. How can he think that?"

"As long as the Prince of Wales doesn't think it, it doesn't matter," Seth said. "He's more superior."

"But the duke has a lot of influence too," Lincoln said. "We can't ignore him or his opinions. He seems to have some sway with the Prince of Wales."

"Do the palace have the authority to shut down the ministry?" Alice asked.

"A good question, Alice," Seth said. "A very good question. They don't, as it happens. The ministry is above politics and royal decrees."

"Their displeasure would only force us to go under-ground," I told her. "The ministry has been in hiding before, and we can do it again if necessary. But we will always exist."

I waited for Lincoln to chime in with an assurance, but he did not. "The letter blames Ballantine for the murder, in conjunction with Franklin," he said. "His Highness calls Ballantine a social climber who tried to trap his son into an unfavorable marriage."

"That's quite true," Lady Vickers said, reaching for another sandwich on the platter near her. "I don't blame the royal family for being upset. Surely he's not going to let Ballantine get away with it."

"He's not," I said. "He's having Ballantine sent to India as a special envoy."

"India!" several voices exclaimed.

"The pack will be split up," Seth said. "Swinburn won't like that."

"Swinburn may yet wield enough influence with both the

prince and duke to stop it," Lincoln said. "The position won't be finalized for some weeks, giving him plenty of time to convince his royal friends not to go through with it."

"I don't think he'll win," I said. "The prince was furious with the Ballantines for manipulating his son."

"He was just as furious with Prince Eddy," Lincoln reminded me. "He is not without blame."

We ate in silence for a few minutes, with a heavy air enveloping us. Every now and again I felt Lincoln's gaze on me, but whenever I looked up, he was concentrating on his food. I sighed and tried to swallow my sandwich but I'd lost my appetite. With the pack going unpunished for their crime, it felt like our business wasn't finished.

"This ain't right," Gus finally announced, pushing his empty plate away. "Charlie's getting married in a few weeks. We should be happy."

"So true," Alice piped up. "Let's discuss something to do with the wedding. Not the dress," she said with a smile. "Mr. Fitzroy mustn't know anything about it until the big day."

"How 'bout we talk about the food," Cook suggested. "I want your opinion on what to serve for dessert."

"Jelly." Gus sat back and licked his lips. "And custard."

"Not for the most prominent London wedding of the season," Seth said. "The food must be grand."

"I can make jelly grand," Cook told him.

"See!" Gus patted his stomach. "Love me a big wobbly jelly drowned in custard."

Seth rolled his eyes. "We can do better than that."

"It ought to be French," Lady Vickers announced. "Everything *a la mode* is from France nowadays, and I know Cook has the culinary skills to pull it off."

Cook's whole head blushed.

Seth frowned first at his mother then at Cook. "God help me," he muttered under his breath.

"Speaking of the wedding," Gus said, "I've decided you can walk on Charlie's left, Seth."

Seth's gaze narrowed. "What do you expect in return?"

"Can't a fellow be generous to his friend without expecting something back?"

Seth's gaze narrowed further. "You're up to something."

"I ain't! I just think you're more like a brother to her than me. I'm like a friend."

"I suppose."

"So that leaves me to be best man for Fitzroy."

"Ah. Right. Forgot he needed a best man." Seth reached across the table and shook Gus's hand. "That sounds fair. You be best man and I'll walk Charlie down the aisle. You in accord, Fitzroy?"

"Do I have a choice?" Lincoln asked.

Gus smiled. "Right-o. It's settled. You walk with Charlie and I'll stand with Fitzroy. It will be my pleasure to sit beside Miss Everheart at the wedding breakfast."

Seth's smile froze.

Lady Vickers lifted her glass of lemon water. "It's settled."

"And without bloodshed too," Cook said, chuckling.

"To Charlie and Lincoln. June can't come fast enough for either of them, I'm sure."

Lincoln joined in the toast, and I swear one side of his mouth lifted in a small smile. It was a good sign that he wasn't as tense as I thought. Unfortunately, the smile and his good mood didn't last. His gruffness returned and, even worse, so did his silence. He avoided me most of the day but I managed to corner him in the evening. He hadn't dined with us, preferring to eat at his desk as he worked.

"You can't avoid me forever," I told him as I let myself into his rooms.

He looked up from his paperwork. "I'm not avoiding you.

303

If I wanted to avoid you I would have locked the door, or left the house altogether."

I leaned back against the door, uncertain if he wanted me to approach. Keeping our distance seemed to be the safer option of late, particularly when we were alone and our kisses became heated. With his arms crossed and his eyes shadowed, I guessed he preferred having the vast space of his study and sitting room between us. But it wasn't easy to stay away. He looked roguishly dashing with his hair loose, wearing no tie or waistcoat, just a shirt with the top button undone.

"Why the smile?" he asked.

"I'm smiling because I can't believe you're mine."

"I see. And is that why you came? To look at me?"

"Is that not a good reason?"

"It's valid enough. I admit to seeking you out on numerous occasions to do just that. And yet I suspect there's something more to this visit."

I crossed my arms too. He knew me well, but that's one of the things I loved about him. "Can't I simply want to see you without an ulterior motive?" I said.

He considered this a moment. "Come here then." He met me half way and folded me into his arms. He smelled of the nutmeg and cloves in Cook's pudding and that unique scent that was his alone. His small sigh ruffled my hair. "But on this occasion you have an ulterior motive." He lifted my chin to look at me properly. "Go on. Out with it."

I suddenly found I couldn't be frank with him. He hated reminders of the time he'd sent me away, and he always cut me off whenever I brought the topic up. The memory of the man he'd been then was painful for him, but I disagreed with his opinion that it shouldn't be discussed. He may have come a long way, but I wasn't so blindly in love with him to think he'd changed and thoughts of sending me away never occurred to him now.

"It may be nothing," I hedged. "I could be seeing a problem where there is none."

He settled his arms around me, linking his hands at my back. "But?"

I blew out a breath. "If you try to send me away again, I won't go."

I felt the shock ripple through him, saw the disbelief in his eyes. Disbelief that I could think he'd do such a thing? He released me and returned to his desk. He perched on it and gripped the edge with both hands. "Why do you think I'm going to send you away?"

I lifted one shoulder. "Because you're worried about my safety with Swinburn and his pack going unpunished."

He winced as if my accusation had hurt him physically. Or perhaps hit its mark. "I promised never to send you away again, and I intend to keep that promise."

"Yes, you're right." I threw my arms around his neck. "I'm sorry, Lincoln," I whispered in his ear. "Truly, I am."

I tried to move away but he pinned me against him. He buried a hand in my hair and pressed his forehead to mine. I suspected he wanted to say something so I didn't try to break apart, but it was an awfully long time before he finally spoke. "Your concern is not entirely unfounded," he finally said.

I jerked back to see his face better. "You can't say that and then leave it there for me to fill in the blanks. You know I'll fill them in with the worst possible scenario."

He raked his fingers through his hair and peered back at me through lowered lashes. "There are so many things that are out of my control now. Things that can go wrong. Badly wrong. Swinburn's pack is still roaming freely, and he ostensibly has the protection of the palace. He's more powerful than I realized.

Indeed, he's untouchable. Even more of a concern is that Swinburn knows all about the ministry, my origins, and the people who live here. He knows that you're my weakness, Charlie."

"Not just me," I said. "Your mother too. Don't deny it, Lincoln. You care enough about them to want to keep them safe."

"As safe as I want to keep any member of the public. And pointing that out doesn't help."

I touched his jaw. "Sorry."

"I'm worried he'll use you to get to me, to weaken me."

I folded him into my arms, as he'd done me, and held him. I stroked his hair back and kissed the top of his head. "There is that concern. There will always be that concern, even after we diminish Swinburn's power. It's something you have to come to terms with. We both do."

He nodded and pulled back. "There's more. Eva's vision about a threat from the queen is troubling, and Alice's problem has the potential to become *our* problem. A rabbit is one thing, but an army is entirely another."

"I know."

"Do you? Do you know what it's like for me to feel powerless to keep you safe? It's not a feeling I'm used to, Charlie, and not one I like."

I stroked his face then cupped his cheek. "I know," I said again. "But this is what it means to be in love and to care about someone. It means there is the possibility we'll lose one another. I'm afraid too, Lincoln. You're the one who is always putting himself in dangerous situations. If anything is going to happen to one of us, it will likely happen to you. But I love you and I want to be with you, and that means watching you put your life at risk and praying you come back to me in one piece."

"At least *you* can communicate with me after I am dead."

"Lincoln!"

He gave an apologetic shrug.

I hugged him again, and he circled his arms around me. We were of a height, with him sitting on the desk and me standing, and I was able to speak to him face to face. "While it would be safer if we never had to confront shape changers or mad scientists, life would be too quiet without the ministry in it. I don't want to hide away here, and I don't think you want to, either."

He searched my face, a small frown line connecting his brows. "I would step away from the ministry if it meant keeping you safe, Charlie. You're more important to me than anything. Do not forget that."

I toyed with a lock of hair skimming my shoulder, running it through my fingers, twisting the end. "I do know it. We'll simply take one day at a time, face one problem at a time, and we'll do it together. That's how we'll get through."

He met my gaze with his and nodded. It was all I needed. It was enough.

Then his lips twitched. "My fierce little warrior."

I laughed and thumped his arm. "Try saying that without smirking next time."

He grinned and pulled me closer for a heart-stopping, heat-inducing, very inappropriate kiss.

THE END

*A*UTHOR'S NOTE:
Many of you already know that Jack Langley of Frakingham House (mentioned earlier in this book) is a character from my Freak House series. If you haven't yet read the Freak House books, now is a good time to start.

LOOK OUT FOR

VOW OF DECEPTION

The 9th Ministry of Curiosities Novel
by C.J. Archer

When Swinburn's pack breaks the uneasy truce, the ministry's very existence is threatened. Charlie and Lincoln must risk everything to save one another and have their happily ever after.

A MESSAGE FROM THE AUTHOR

I hope you enjoyed reading VEILED IN MOONLIGHT as much as I enjoyed writing it. As an independent author, getting the word out about my book is vital to its success, so if you liked this book please consider telling your friends and writing a review at the store where you purchased it. If you would like to be contacted when I release a new book, subscribe to my newsletter at http://cjarcher.com/contact-cj/newsletter/. You will only be contacted when I have a new book out.

GET A FREE SHORT STORY

I wrote a short story featuring Lincoln Fitzroy that is set before THE LAST NECROMANCER. Titled STRANGE HORIZONS, it reveals how he learned where to look for Charlie during a visit to Paris. While the story can be read as a standalone, it contains spoilers from The 1st Freak House Trilogy, so I advise you to read that series first. The best part is, the short story is FREE, but only to my newsletter subscribers. So subscribe now via my website AT WWW.CJARCHER.COM if you haven't already.

ALSO BY C.J. ARCHER

SERIES WITH 2 OR MORE BOOKS

Glass and Steele

The Emily Chambers Spirit Medium Trilogy

The 1st Freak House Trilogy

The 2nd Freak House Trilogy

The 3rd Freak House Trilogy

The Ministry of Curiosities Series

The Assassins Guild Series

Lord Hawkesbury's Players Series

The Witchblade Chronicles

SINGLE TITLES NOT IN A SERIES

Courting His Countess

Surrender

Redemption

The Mercenary's Price

ABOUT THE AUTHOR

C.J. Archer has loved history and books for as long as she can remember and feels fortunate that she found a way to combine the two. She spent her early childhood in the dramatic beauty of outback Queensland, Australia, but now lives in suburban Melbourne with her husband, two children and a mischievous black & white cat named Coco.

Subscribe to C.J.'s newsletter through her website to be notified when she releases a new book, as well as get access to exclusive content. She loves to hear from readers. You can contact her in one of these ways:

Website: www.cjarcher.com
Email: cjarcher.writes@gmail.com
Facebook: www.facebook.com/CJArcherAuthorPage
Twitter: @cj_archer